PENGUIN BOOKS
NIGHT OF THE KRAIT

Shashi Warrier turned to writing after careers in consulting, journalism and computing. He is the author of several books: *Hangman's Journal*, *Sniper*, *The Orphan*, *The Homecoming*, *Sally and the Warlocks and Other Stories* and *The Marblewood Forest*. He is a member of the adjunct faculty of BITS, Pilani, from where he completed his master's in economics in 1981.

In between bursts of writing and lecturing, he likes to listen to music, mostly Hindustani, and to ride motorcycles.

He lives in Mangalore with his wife, Prita, and their two dachshunds.

NIGHT OF THE KRAIT

Shashi Warrier

PENGUIN BOOKS

PENGUIN BOOKS
Published by the Penguin Group
Penguin Books India Pvt. Ltd, 11 Community Centre, Panchsheel Park,
New Delhi 110017, India
Penguin Group (USA) Inc., 375 Hudson Street, New York, New York 10014,
USA
Penguin Group (Canada), 90 Eglinton Avenue East, Suite 700, Toronto,
Ontario, M4P 2Y3, Canada (a division of Pearson Penguin Canada Inc.)
Penguin Books Ltd, 80 Strand, London WC2R 0RL, England
Penguin Ireland, 25 St Stephen's Green, Dublin 2, Ireland (a division of
Penguin Books Ltd)
Penguin Group (Australia), 250 Camberwell Road, Camberwell, Victoria
3124, Australia (a division of Pearson Australia Group Pty Ltd)
Penguin Group (NZ), 67 Apollo Drive, Rosedale, North Shore 0632, New
Zealand (a division of Pearson New Zealand Ltd)
Penguin Group (South Africa) (Pty) Ltd, 24 Sturdee Avenue, Rosebank,
Johannesburg 2196, South Africa

Penguin Books Ltd, Registered Offices: 80 Strand, London WC2R 0RL, England

First published by Penguin Books India 1996
This edition published by Penguin Books India 2008

ISBN 9780143064374

Typeset in Perpetua by InoSoft Systems, Noida
Printed at Thomson Press India Ltd, New Delhi

This one is for my parents, without whose unflinching and generous support I would still have been hacking code in a software house.

Acknowledgements

I did not know writing a book could be such a painful business. Many people helped make it bearable. These include Suresh, Chitra and Aditya; Dr Indira Balachandran and the late Dr V.V. Sivarajan; Yasmin; Biju; Jayapriya and Harish Vasudevan; Rehmat and Nikhil; Dinesh and Satish; David Davidar and Ravi Singh; and last but not least, Leon.

chapter one

In the gathering dark the krait awoke and lay still, its forked tongue flickering, waiting for the earth to cool before setting out on its nightly hunt. This was a common krait, found all over South Asia. It was blue-black, with faint white bands running across its body, about an inch apart: in the dark, when it went hunting, it was almost invisible.

We got them out for the New Year, against all odds, thanks to luck, surprise, and a thunderstorm . . .

On that first Saturday after Christmas, I arrived at the office faintly feverish, ears abuzz, wearied from lack of sleep, just as a watery sun poked its top past the grey clouds on the horizon. I'd been on my feet forty-eight straight hours, being chased by armed men along the ravines, trailing and ambushing them in my turn, and generally causing silent havoc in the course of a war games exercise. In the crimson dawn, in the quiet detachment of my office, the black worm of depression stretched and fattened as I surveyed the bare glass-topped desk and the grey telephone and the ugly straight-backed chairs in my room, and above them the rectangle of cleaner white where I'd removed—much to the dismay of many fellow-officers—the portrait of the Prime Minister.

A wave of overwhelming fatigue turned my knees to water but I walked unsteadily over to the barred window behind the desk to look at the deep green lawn across the gravel drive below. The office itself was a long, low nondescript government building, yellow and characterless on the outside, off-white and sparklingly austere inside, flanked on both sides by car parks. A long, dark corridor led to offices on either side. Mine was near the end farthest from the entrance, the one at the end belonging to my chief. Outside my window, the drive turned sharply away past the lawn, leading arrow-straight to the barricaded gate 200 metres away, where men from companies Alpha and Delta, both on regular duty, filed in behind their JCOs (junior commissioned officers), thoroughly warmed up after an eight-kilometre jog across the rock-ridged hillocks outside the camp.

I felt ancient and used-up, thirty-six going on seventy-seven. The weariness just wouldn't go away: eternal vigilance took its pound of flesh, in my case a marriage on the verge of break-up and years of sleepless nights. For the past year I'd been second-in-command of the Special Operations Force (SOF) headquartered in Delhi, and for two years before that a battalion second-in-command at Siachen, where, crowded into posts seven kilometres apart, we

2

watched warily the crack mountain soldiers of the Pakistani Army as they feinted and skirmished, keeping us on our toes for the war that never came but with the threat always hanging ominously over the blustery grey-white hillocks that bordered the glacier.

A draught brushed icily past my shoulder as the door behind opened once again. Framed in the doorway in the red-tinged sunlight coming in through the windows, his maroon beret slightly askew and sleeves rolled up despite the chill, square shouldered and with the faint beginnings of a paunch, stood my immediate superior and commander of the SOF, Colonel Ismail Qureishi.

Ismail was one of the finest field commanders I'd ever come across. He was an oddity, a faintly worried, immensely intellectual, aristocratic man for whom you found yourself doing things you wouldn't believe you'd do for anyone. On the field he was flamboyant. During the early training sessions, when the men were being pushed to their limits and beyond, Ismail always came along, doing his bit with the younger men on the field. He was, despite his forty-odd years, a remarkable athlete and a fine shot who put himself through a twenty-five-kilometre obstacle course at a pace most men found hard to equal.

Behind the aristocratic gentleness lay a will of iron and a steel-trap mind. No one ever complained of anything being held up for administrative reasons. Ismail was in his element leading this crack unit. He was one of the most decorated soldiers in the Army, and he hadn't got those medals being soft. He drove his men mercilessly when he considered it necessary. But more than anything else the man had quality, and a charisma, a presence you felt the moment he entered a room.

Senior officers, themselves senior commanders, spoke softly around him. But to the juniors—the JCOs, the NCOs and the other ranks—he was like God come down to earth. Distant yet admired, even loved. As his deputy I came in for some inevitable comparisons with him and almost always came off second best.

For all his apparent success and the pleasure he took in his work, there was a sadness to him I'd never been able to fathom. At one level he was the most secretive man I knew. No one ever got a glimpse of his life outside his work. A confirmed bachelor, he never spoke of his family. I'd never met any of his brothers—he'd mentioned once, casually, that he had some—or his parents.

Despite the differences, we understood each other well. In his eyes I saw the same shadows he saw in mine. Between the two of us, in the privacy of my office, we could dispense with salutes and such. 'How did it go?' he asked, stepping into the room.

We'd just taken on thirty-odd fresh men. 'Some of them move like pigs,' I replied, 'like bloody elephants, in fact. Too much noise. The Gurkhas were good, though, and the men from 9 Para.'

Ismail settled into one of the chairs across from me, faintly worried, fingering his beret in his hands, aquiline face dark. 'How much longer will the new men need before we can mix them in with the regulars?'

4

'Another couple of months. Hard months.'

'Do you want to do the review now or do we save it for the afternoon? You look washed out.' His mild eyes blinked rapidly once or twice, a dead giveaway. He wanted the review now.

'Now,' I replied, relieved, dreading the thought of going home to wait for the sleep that came only occasionally, lightly.

In the air was a promotion for Ismail. After building up the SOF he would find life in a mountain brigade dull, but that was the next step towards divisional and possibly higher command. For the past two months Ismail had left more and more of the operational command on the SOF so I could get the feel of things. Now, in the aftermath of the exercise, we went through the performance of each of the new men, marking off the names we thought wouldn't fit into the battalion.

The SOF was only a year old, comprising officers and men selected from those who applied from other branches of the Army after exhaustive tests that defeated twenty-four of twenty-five applicants among the men, and even more among the officers. At the end of the training came the worst of it for the officers: a two-week session on the resistance of interrogation, which effectively broke half those who made it through the rest. Almost half the men had been brought in from 1, 9 and 10 Para Battalions, the crack para commandos of the Indian Army. Others came in mostly from mountain regiments: some Gurkhas, Pahadis, Dogras, Assamese and a sprinkling of short, dark Tamilians.

The officers were an even more varied lot, coming as they did from the infantry or artillery, signals or armoured, or even from the engineers and air defence units. We'd selected people throughout the first half of the previous year, and only now was the battalion's character emerging.

We ground through the review by a quarter-to-nine, the battalion adjutant, Captain Ram Babu—Ramu to his friends, a meticulous mind behind his puckish exterior—joining us towards the end. At half-past-nine I went home, to my first floor quarters in a block of sixteen identical pink-and-cream apartments a kilometre away from the office, near a parkful of screaming, colourfully dressed children.

I sat on the dusty brown-and-white sofa in the heavily curtained, lifeless living room, unable to raise the energy to get up and draw the curtains. With an effort I went to the bathroom to clean up and change into the fresh pyjamas my batman Harkishen had left on the bed, drank the tea he brewed, considered breakfast, then dropped the idea. I lay down on the bed to sleep with the winter sun on my feet and thought instead of my wife. Soon to be ex-wife.

She had packed her bags and left six months ago, complaining of concentrated neglect, of being forced to stay alone in a milieu she didn't like or understand. I'd never stopped her doing anything she wanted, and had said so when she complained. 'I can do that on my own,' she said, 'I don't need to be married to you to do what I like!'

I'd lost my temper at what seemed to be a self-indulgent tantrum and we'd really gone for each other then. She left the next day and while I found myself wishing mildly she'd stay, I was in a sense relieved when she left.

The telephone woke me up from a doze at a quarter-to-two. I dredged up the energy to pick it up.

'Yes?'

'Raja, this is Ismail. Come back. Right away.' His voice bore a hard edge of urgency I hadn't heard before, a note that brought me instantly awake.

'Twenty minutes,' I said, and hung up.

Waiting in Ismail's room when I got there were two civilians in nondescript sweaters, government written all over their faces, the power they wielded habitually in everyday life overlaid now with tension. Open by the two telephones on Ismail's desk was a large brown briefcase with a combination lock, its contents spread out over the rest of the desktop for the three men to study. 'Subhash Gawand,' said Ismail, waving a hand at the older of the two as I pulled up a chair for myself, 'and Arjun Kashinath. From the defence ministry.' He turned in his chair to introduce me. 'Lieutenant Colonel Rajan Menon, my 2IC—that's second-in-command—and the unit's tactician.' They offered brief, limp handshakes and went back to the papers, visibly unimpressed.

Two more colleagues in uniform arrived seconds later: Major R. Venkateswaran—Venky—commander of Bravo company, now on two-hour alert; and Ramu, the adjutant. Ismail waited for them to settle down before turning back to me. 'This morning a terrorist group calling themselves the Free Kashmir Front—FKF—took over a coach on the new Shatabdi Express from Delhi to Madras. Gawand and Kashinath are here to brief us. Venky and I have already been through most of it.'

Gawand riffled through his papers and pushed his gold-rimmed bifocals firmly up his nose before handing me a sheaf of papers stapled together. He was sweating despite the winter chill. 'Go through these,' he said, eyeing me through the top of his glasses, 'and then we'll go ahead.'

Minutes before eight that morning, just outside Basin Bridge station and five minutes short of Madras Central, terrorists had taken over the air-conditioned sleeper coach on the gleaming new train. They had bolted the doors connecting the coach with the ones fore and aft, then locked from inside the four exit doors, sealing the coach off. Inside the coach were thirty-eight passengers, the coach attendant, a travelling ticket examiner—TTE—and an unknown number of terrorists, some or all of whom could well have been among the passengers. The tinted one-way glass in the windows prevented anyone from getting a good look inside.

A porter who had clambered on to the steps slung under the rear door of the coach even before the coach came to a halt at Madras Central had been clubbed ruthlessly down by a big, black-clad masked man who had seemed uncompromisingly competent with the AK-47 assault rifle in his hands. He had then let off a burst from his AK-47 into the air, bringing down the debris of a large electric clock suspended from the ceiling. A few minutes later, this man in black—or someone exactly like him—had shot and killed an armed Railway Protection Force constable edging his way gingerly along the now deserted platform towards the porter lying unconscious two metres away from the rear door of the coach.

'There was no need to kill that policeman,' I said, 'unless . . . unless they did it to prove they're serious. It's the kind of thing a psychopath would do . . . There's a madman in that coach.'

'Keep going,' Ismail said.

'Whoever planned this has put together a very complex operation . . . He's got trained men, he's got weapons, he's got the know-how to pick the targets . . . I'd say they have a man behind the scenes doing all this. He's not on that coach.'

I read uneasily on. At half-past-eight, with the city's transport system jammed, as the local police were beginning to arrive in force, one of the woman passengers, a distraught young woman with a husband still inside the coach, had emerged weeping with a bunch of papers which contained in a mixture of neat typescript and an unclear scrawl the demands of the terrorists. The whole lot had been faxed to us. 'We are the Action Wing of the Free Kashmir Front,' said the first sheet in an inelegant scrawl, 'and have taken several guests. Unless the repressive Indian government does as we demand, we will be forced to conduct reprisals against our guests.'

'We do not, unlike the government, wage war on women,' continued the sheet self-righteously. 'We will therefore release the women and girls remaining among our guests if this coach is placed as we desire before 1400 hours today.'

'There's something mad about this note as well,' I said. No one responded, so I went on.

The second sheet, this one typed, bore their demands, which were simple: the release of eighteen of their comrades now languishing in prison, and the delivery of the released men to Madras international airport by 1000 hours on Monday; the delivery, to the coach, of the equivalent of five million dollars in gold and mixed foreign currencies by the same time; and afterwards, safe passage to Karachi from Madras for themselves, their colleagues, and their 'guests', who would be released at Karachi if everyone got there safe.

The third sheet, hastily handwritten, was a list of hostages in three columns—name, age and sex. No familiar names. The last sheet, which I read very slowly, described how they wanted the coach to be placed.

The coach was to be separated from the rest of the train and drawn away on to a siding on a sparingly used branch line some forty kilometres away, in the midst of a plain. The FKF men would choose the exact location of the coach when they got to the area. A hundred-metre-square perimeter was to be maintained around the coach, the area within to be lit by floodlights placed at the corners of the square. Power was to be supplied to the coach via a pair of cables—one for the 110 volts for the lighting and the other for the 440 volts to run the air-conditioning—from a generator car parked outside the perimeter.

Meals were to be delivered on trays, by one man in underwear carrying one or two trays at a time, whenever the FKF required. Anyone approaching the coach wearing anything more than underwear or carrying anything resembling a weapon would be shot out of hand.

All communication was to be on loudspeakers. The FKF had one inside the coach, and the representative of the Indian government was free to set up another anywhere outside the perimeter after the coach had been shifted out. Until then, they could use the station's public address system.

No secrets, then. Anyone in the neighbourhood would know exactly what was going on. That made political sense.

'We started negotiating with them before they moved the coach out of the station,' said Gawand when I'd finished reading the sheets from the FKF. 'D.S. Chauhan, deputy director of the CBI, happened to be in Madras on an official visit, and had a man at the station at the time. The man called Chauhan immediately, and he went on the station's public address system to try and get through to the FKF as soon as he got those papers from that lady. The FKF responded, through a man standing in the doorway of the coach speaking into a hand-held loudspeaker. He didn't give away much.'

'For what are we negotiating, and with what?' I asked.

'We should try to wear them out,' said Gawand. 'We haven't dealt with this sort of situation before. Cabinet was thinking of bringing in negotiators and maybe a psychiatrist from the US but we have no idea how long that'll take, and how much money.'

'What's Chauhan trying to do?'

'Buy time. That's about all he can do now.' Gawand handed me two typed sheets of CBI notepaper.

Following is a transcript of the dialogue between D.S. Chauhan, deputy director, Central Bureau of Investigation (DD-CBI), and an unidentified member of the Free Kashmir Front (FKF) at 0835 on _th December, 199_. Accuracy cannot be guaranteed since the transcript has been prepared from a recording.

DD-CBI: Good morning. I am D.S. Chauhan, deputy director, Central Bureau of Investigation.

FKF: This is the Free Kashmir Front. You must have received the letter we sent you through the woman. What progress have you made with our demands?

DD-CBI: Why don't you release the passengers first? Then we can all sit down and discuss the matter in peace. I am sure we will be able to work out something satisfactory with you.

FKF: If that is all you want to tell us, policeman, shut up. Our guests will stay with us as long as we like, or until you take care of our demands.

DD-CBI: As you please. I have spoken to the general manager of the railways here. Your coach can be moved out to the location you have described with no trouble at all. However, we will have some trouble with supplying power to your coach once it has been moved away. We have one generator car here that is not powerful enough to supply power for the lights and air-conditioning of your coach and for the floodlights you need. A second one is being made ready but will be available only late in the afternoon. Besides, we will have to put up scaffolding for the lights, which we can start only after you have selected where exactly your coach is to be placed. We will move your coach into position by 1400, but we will have the floodlights and power up only by about 1700. We cannot, repeat cannot, have the lights up before that.

FKF: That is reasonable. We accept 1400 hours as the deadline for moving the coach out, and 1700 for the installation of the lights and power. At 1700 we start shooting the guests if anything is left incomplete. Is that understood, policeman?

DD-CBI: Yes, it is clear. But will you release the women at two, when we move your coach out?

FKF: (Laughter) Sorry, policeman, the women will leave the coach only after the lights are up, not before.

DD-CBI: As you please. There is one issue relating to this that we have to sort out now. We will have a railway crew detaching your coach from the rest of the train, another crew of electricians to take care of power connections, a shunting engine to move the coach around . . . All this will need tools, gentlemen.

Your note says you will shoot anyone approaching with anything like a weapon in hand. What are we to do about the tools?

FKF: Two of your men can carry all the tools you need to the platform here in an open box. We will inspect the box. Your men can take tools from the box while we are here, and then we will take the box along with us. Anymore tools your men may need later, they will be allowed to take only from that box. Is that clear?

DD-CBI: That should be feasible. I will speak to the senior engineer here to confirm that, and get back to you as soon as possible. But there is some trouble with your other requirements as well.

FKF: (Irritated) Tell us everything at one shot, policeman. I'm not going to stand here while you occupy me for the next few hours.

DD-CBI: Today is the first Saturday after Christmas. Most people in this country are on holiday. We will not be able to collect the money you have demanded by 1000 on Monday morning. Give us until Tuesday evening.

FKF: Don't play games with us, policeman. The shooting begins on Monday morning unless we have the money delivered here.

DD-CBI: I am not playing the fool, gentlemen. What I told you is true. The gold is not a serious problem but collecting the other currencies is. We will have to collect it from four or five different locations, and

14

maybe borrow some from the banks. If you will accept the amount in rupees we can make sure the money is delivered to you by Monday morning, but not the foreign currencies.

FKF: (Laughter) Who wants Indian rupees, policeman? (Silence for 88 seconds.) All right, policeman, give us the money in the currencies we have listed by 1400 on Monday afternoon. If you fail to do that we will start shooting.

DD-CBI: I will have to consult the Reserve Bank here before I can confirm that this is possible. I will get back to you as soon as I can.

FKF: What about our comrades in jail?

DD-CBI: I am not yet authorized to negotiate that issue with you, we will have to get Cabinet to decide on it. But from my experience I can tell you this much: Your colleagues will be spread out over several prisons in Kashmir. I think it will take us all of today and tomorrow to trace all of them. Then they will have to be brought to Delhi, and that will take until Monday evening. Which means that they can get here by Tuesday morning or so. I suggest you understand that the logistics of such a transfer are very complicated, and besides that we are losing time because of the weekend.

End of transcript.

'Their m.o. looks familiar,' I said. 'The tone of the letter. Shooting that policeman. The black uniforms. Stripping the

15

hostages down to keep them quiet . . . The Agra case—remember?'

Earlier in the year, kidnappers, black-clad and masked, had swooped down on the industrialist son of a sitting member of Parliament. The kidnappers had collected the industrialist and three of his cronies as they left a bar near their factory at Ghaziabad, put them in a closed white van, and driven off to a safe house in Agra before anyone had a clue to what was happening.

In the safe house the hostages were stripped and their faces painted green, making them totally unrecognizable and making escape harder still. Three hours after the abduction, at eleven at night, a man with a black scarf drawn about his face delivered a small cardboard package to the house of the MP's sister in Agra.

The lady, in all innocence, accepted the box and the man disappeared into the night. The lady opened the box and found, wrapped in cotton wool and with blood clotting the cut end, the little finger off the left hand of her nephew, a coral ring still on it. Under the cotton wool was a note saying that a ransom of five million rupees be prepared for delivery to the kidnappers by five the next evening, and that they be informed when the money was ready to be delivered by means of a banner stuck on to a large poster outside the city's largest movie theatre.

The police, following the industrialist's busy trail from his Ghaziabad office, traced the van, and through the van the safe house, by the next afternoon. But by the time the first policemen arrived quietly at the safe house the kidnappers had fled, taking with them their hostages. The money had not been collected by five that evening, nor had the message been put up. At half-past-seven that evening, a jeep drove up outside a police station some twenty kilometres away from the safe house. A masked man waving an AK-47 charged his way into the police station, left a packet on the table of the station house inspector, spattered all vehicles outside the station with bullets from his rifle, and climbed back into the jeep, which drove away at speed, disappearing by the time the policemen had managed to muster a vehicle in which to chase it.

In the cardboard package left on the SHO's desk was a man's left ear, with an earring still in it; the ear belonged to one of the men who had been kidnapped along with the industrialist. Along with the ear was a note to the effect that the money had to be ready by six next morning, or the hostages would be cut up at leisure into small pieces which would then be mailed to the MP.

The money was collected—the government paid up—and delivered to the hostages in a ravine several miles outside town. The police set a trap for the kidnappers but found that the hostages weren't with them. The kidnappers had got off, and the next day released the hostages, then disappeared with the money.

Ismail had been on leave, away in his hometown near Lucknow, and in his place I had been called in to be consulted on the afternoon the police found the safe house. The kidnappers had seemed too vicious to ignore, the deadline too close. I suggested that since we didn't know

17

where the hostages were and would take too long to find out and mount an operation, it would be wiser to pay the ransom, get the hostages back, and try to get the kidnappers later. I even offered to handle the transfer of the money, far and away the most crucial part of any such negotiation, but was turned huffily away.

The hostages had turned up the day after the money had been paid, by the highway outside the city. They staggered into a police station where a disbelieving inspector took one look at their missing parts and green-painted faces and clapped them in the lock-up, to be rescued hours later by frantic parents.

The calculated doses of ruthless, unprovoked violence had been the same then as now. Also the uniforms and the weaponry. And there was something else similar . . . There was something contemptuous about the abductors. In the first, their note had, unlike most other ransom notes, contained nothing at all by way of warnings not to go to the authorities. The kidnappers had, in effect, been thumbing their noses at the police. As they were now.

And they were remarkably well-informed. They'd known just when to get out of the safe house . . .

Ismail smiled bleakly, the habitual mildness in his eyes replaced by an almost wolfish expression. 'Yes,' he said, 'it could be our friend from Agra. I read your reports. The technique is familiar, but he's escalating.'

'Two things worry me,' I said. 'In the first place, this guy had an informant in Agra. Otherwise he wouldn't have flown the coop like he did. Second, we're dealing with madmen here. There's the guy behind all this, the guy who's written those letters, and planned it all. And there's the front end of the madness, the psychopath who cuts people up and likes to shoot people.'

'I've dug out the police files on Agra,' said Ismail, 'take them along with you.'

'I remember most of what's in them,' I said, 'I wrote most of that material, remember? I was on the spot and had a look at everything the police got. That's why I say this: we have a madman behind all of this, a man with a thirst for attention. I see his signature all over this operation. But Chauhan seems to have hit the right note. Was all that stuff true, about the currencies and everything?'

'I think he was just guessing, but it sounded all right.'

'He should continue to negotiate with them,' I said. 'They might sneer at him and call him a policeman but you noticed they take him seriously. But what do Cabinet want?'

Kashinath answered this one. 'They want to keep their options open,' he said. 'They've started to collect the money. They've started tracing the prisoners. But they're also negotiating, playing for time. And they've called you in. The main thing is that the longer it takes the worse it gets for the terrorists.'

'And for the hostages,' I said under my breath but Gawand heard it. He glared at me.

Kashinath bulldozed past the interruption. 'The Secretary of the ministry of external affairs spoke to his opposite number in Islamabad at noon, asking him to refuse permission to the FKF to land anywhere in Pakistan. I don't know what's come of that. The Prime Minister might follow up with that.'

'What's been done at Madras so far?' I asked.

'I got my last report at 1330,' said Gawand. 'They've got the coach out of the station. They're working on the lights. The next report is due at 1600.'

Nearly a long hour to go, I thought, looking at my watch. 'If we're planning to go get the hostages out of the coach we should be moving soon. There's not much we can plan or do sitting here. Bravo company's on alert.' One of the battalion's six companies was always available at two hours' notice. 'If we start them up now we should be ready to leave before six.'

'General Kelkar was on the phone before you arrived,' said Ismail. Major General Kelkar was Ismail's boss, the director of Special Operations. 'He told me to get back to him immediately after this briefing. I'll call him now.'

The General was on the line in a minute. 'Raja should take a company there,' Ismail said, 'and work out a plan. I'll follow early tomorrow with anything else he needs.' There was a pause. 'Yes, sir. Right away.' He hung up and turned to me. 'It's on. You and Venky go now, with Bravo. Kelkar and I will join you tomorrow, with Delta if need be. Your transport will be ready by half-past-five. Air Force.'

There was a heaviness in the room I couldn't understand. There was no reason for the men from the ministry to be so nervous. I took a chance. 'What haven't you told me?' I asked Gawand point-blank.

'I told you he's sharp,' Ismail said with the ghost of a smile. 'Raja, inside that coach is a nephew of the defence minister.' Gawand and Kashinath looked unhappily away, avoiding my eyes, and Ismail shrugged. 'Life's a bitch, sometimes,' he said to no one in particular.

Outside, under the watchful eyes of the JCOs, Bravo company began the process of readying itself. This was when some of the tricky decisions would have to be made, since the SOF was a multi-role force. We could pick from a fairly long list of weaponry to take along, but I kept it simple since Ismail could bring anything I'd missed the next day. The battalion quartermaster and I counted and checked stores, supplies of ammunition that the men wouldn't be able to carry in transit, communication equipment, gear for climbing and grappling, explosives, body armour—everything packed into metal containers ready for loading into the big Ilyushin-76 craft that would carry us to Madras. Venky, in the meanwhile, briefed his six platoon commanders—five first lieutenants and a captain—on what they could expect in Madras.

There was little enough to go by. We could make our plans only after we did a recce on the site. In the absence of concrete information all we could do was get to Madras as fast as possible, observe, plan and then move if we could.

There was little precedent. The SOF was young, formed as the strike unit against organized domestic terrorism. Earlier attempts to create a national force of this kind had failed. The highly-trained NSG—the Black Cats—had degenerated to a VIP security force, a highly visible effective deterrent no doubt to terrorists, but rather toothless as a strike unit. Besides, there'd been rumbles lately that the Cats, often under the implicit patronage of the bigwigs they guarded, had become unruly. The Rapid Action Forces that each state had developed were undertrained and underequipped to deal with serious terrorism.

Some years earlier, a retiring chief of Army staff had mooted the idea of an Army anti-terrorist unit modelled on the German GSG-9 and trained like the British SAS, an Army unit that would handle domestic terrorist trouble as well. That was how the SOF was born, with General Kelkar playing enthusiastic midwife.

It was now up to battalion strength, a little larger than the standard infantry battalion, comprising six companies and over a thousand men in all. Most of the administrative elements—the tail—in the standard battalion had been replaced with combat elements—the teeth. The normal scout team had been more or less eliminated, with all men trained in many roles. The normal battalion medical team of one doctor and two trained assistants, insufficient even when dealing with injuries during training, had been increased to two doctors and eight trained nurses.

Standard weaponry was the Ingram-10 sub-machine gun, far more advanced than the 7.62 mm self-loading rifle that was now being phased out of the Indian infantry in favour of the smaller, lighter, faster INSAS—Indian national small arms system—that promised so much more. We had much more weaponry, including Milan anti-tank guided missiles and Strela surface-to-air missiles, which we would have to leave behind.

Officers were attached to the SOF—like the Para Commandos—for terms of up to three years. After that they went back to their original units, having to reapply and requalify if they wanted another stint. And you had to keep learning all the time.

We still hadn't got it all together. In the absence of any real experience we could only plan as best we could. If we got the green signal for this operation it could be the proving ground for the force.

The 1600 report came in on the fax in Ismail's office. Two sheets long, containing little of use. They'd fixed up the generator cars, and were even now working on the last of the floodlights, set up on scaffolding made of galvanized iron pipes. The lights would be up in another quarter of an hour or so, just within the 1700 deadline. The hungry passengers had been fed at two, after the coach had been moved out of the station, with meals on trays carried in, as specified by the FKF, by one man, two trays at a time. They'd asked only for thirty-five trays. Strange. With the terrorists and the passengers and the railwaymen inside the coach I'd have thought they needed more than thirty-five.

Another report came in, this time from the ministry of defence in Delhi. It confirmed that one of the passengers included a relation of the Minister, and added that the Minister would be obliged personally if we could do our best. My stomach twinged with tension. Maybe they wouldn't let us in. The FKF had got it right. There'd been

23

that occasion some years ago when terrorists had kidnapped the daughter of a minister, asking for the release of three of their comrades, and the government had caved in without a second thought.

Would it do the same now?

At half-past-five Venky walked in the door trailing sheaves of checklists. Deceptively cheerful and at thirty-four the senior-most of the officers in the unit after Ismail and myself, Venky was far and away the most aggressive of our company commanders. A former 9 Para Commando battalion man, he'd seen service in Sri Lanka with the Indian Peace Keeping Force, and later in Somalia with the UN, and had been on the verge of ending his term with 9 Para when Ismail had plucked him out for the SOF, much to the chagrin of his original unit, the Mahars, who had been waiting to get him back. 'Bravo's ready,' he said, putting his checklists on the desk, 'they're boarding trucks to the airfield now.'

I dialled Ismail's number on the green-and-black intercom. Ismail, as was his habit, picked it up on the first ring. General Kelkar had arrived and was with him, he said, and if I'd finished with Bravo could I go to his room for a couple of minutes, the General wanted to have urgent words with me.

Back in Ismail's room the General had charged the atmosphere with the electricity he generated like an aura. Short and fiftyish, with a pepper-and-salt toothbrush moustache, the General made up for his lack of inches with a straight back, a remarkably powerful voice, and a level of fitness that most men fifteen years his junior would

24

find hard to match. A former commander of 1 Para and a combat soldier to the core, he didn't waste words. He would be at Madras next morning with Ismail, he said, and he expected a proper recce done and a plan of attack worked out in detail, logistics and all. We would review at eleven in the morning.

But that was not what he'd called me for, he said. He had called me for specific advice. I was to behave myself with the civilians and the politicians. No amount of yelling would change them, so I was to conserve my breath for the task of getting the hostages out if we had to. Was that clear?

As crystal, I said, but what about the special hostage?

What special hostage, demanded the General, weren't all hostages special?

There was something on the fax about ministers and nephews in the afternoon, I mumbled, I didn't read all of it. Sir.

For that I got all two thousand volts of the General's crackling glare as he sat straighter still to get a good look at my face before he burnt me out. But the glare dimmed, and he relaxed an eighth of an inch. 'Lieutenant Colonel,' he said slowly, 'I will bring with me specific written orders to the effect that all hostages are equal. Even a hint otherwise and you can go back to your old regiment on Monday. If they'll have you back. Is that clear?'

As mud, I mumbled, but the General missed the words.

I was to report our arrival to Major General J.N. Reddy, the Madras area commander. He had already spoken to Reddy, who would provide any local support we needed.

I would try not to offend General Reddy, too, I said.

All the best, he said, softening a little, go with God.

Ismail's fax buzzed again. A minute later he reached out behind him and ripped the first ten inches or so off the machine, glanced at it briefly, and handed it to the General, whose mouth twisted in disgust. 'They've let off the women,' he told me, 'but they've kept one youngster of five, whose mother was in the coach. There was a misprint on the list they sent us earlier.' He placed the sheet carefully on the table. 'You have your special hostage,' he said meditatively. 'Get that little boy out of there at any cost.'

By six we were on our Ilyushin transports winging steadily south into an ominous greying sky. I couldn't get the contents of that last fax out of my mind. They'd kept a little boy and let his mother go. Bastards. Or were they just thoughtful? In the end it would come down to the politicians and their vote banks. If they lost the little boy they'd lose lots of women's votes. Pile on the pressure. On the flight deck I looked at the flight lieutenant in front of me who flew his lumbering craft with such unconcerned competence.

He must have caught my look, for he turned back with a grin. 'This is just like driving a bus, sir,' he said, 'and as boring. You guys get all the fun.'

I grinned back at him, stuffing down thoughts of hundreds of sleepless nights and the unending tension, and kept back an answer. Out through the window, nearly four kilometres away and silhouetted against a cloud bank, flew the lead craft. I went back to the passenger compartment where the men sat on their pallets in private little worlds of their own, the roar of the engines making conversation impossible unless you shouted. The company havildar major, pen and checklist in hand, went down the rows of men, checking them off against his list. This man was thorough in everything he did. The tension showed on the faces of the men: they hadn't been briefed yet on what they were going to Madras for. All they'd been told was that this was not an exercise but an emergency.

We landed in the dark at Madras airport on the outskirts of the city, where we found in the shadows on the windswept tarmac eighteen trucks waiting to drive us the thirty kilometres out to the coach, which we reached at 2100—it's easier to say nine in the evening but the Army way has become a habit—under a cover of heavy black cloud that hid the moon. It was too dark to make out the surrounding terrain but the area inside the hundred-square-metre perimeter the terrorists had demanded was lit day-bright by the four banks of floodlights at the corners. All around the perimeter, in a shadowy no-man's-land between light and darkness, was a cordon of helmeted men carrying rifles, their menace heavy in the air. The Tamil Nadu RAF.

The floodlights, set atop five metres of scaffolding, lit up the sparse grass beside the four sets of tracks, focusing on the coach in the centre, painted blue and white instead of the normal deep maroon the railways use. The windows showed up as black, opaque rectangles. The black ends of

27

the coach gleamed in the light, the buffers sticking wickedly out on either side of the hook and chain used to connect coaches. Around the coach were scattered rectangles that glinted in the floodlights. Dinner trays, flung out of the doors. They'd have to be cleaned up.

From somewhere north of the coach, well outside the perimeter, came the thudding of engines. I looked carefully in the direction of the noise, made out two looming shapes in the darkness. The generator cars.

As we watched, two men emerged from the far side of the coach, dressed in black, masked, carrying AK-47s. Sentries. They looked remarkably similar. They must have heard the trucks drawing up.

There was something sticking vertically out of the window in one of the four exit doors. A sort of pole. A pole? It was a radio mast! They were transmitting from inside that coach. They had an informant outside.

This was Agra all over again.

Away to the south, past a curve in the tracks, 300 metres from the coach, was a little hillock I could make out faintly, a small sapling struggling to grow at the top. West of the tracks were lights and a large tent. Stretching away north and south were the tracks themselves, their tops gleaming darkly in the floodlights, fading away past the lights into the gloom beyond.

We made our way through a barricade in the cordon to the tent, which turned out to be the command post. Parked by it were trucks, one carrying a generator, the other a tanker. Close by the command post was a cookhouse, where I assumed the hostages' meals were cooked. I hopped out of the truck and walked unsteadily, on legs stiffened by the two rides, to the command post, Venky on my heels.

Inside the confines of the command post the tension was evident. The eastern side of the tent was open, with two desks side by side facing the coach fifty metres away. At one of them sat a pot-bellied Punjabi, probably Chauhan, and at the other, which had radio equipment on it, sat an operator, headphones lowered around his neck. Beside the radio were two telephones, and between the radio and the telephones stood a vast black spool tape recorder. Just inside the tent was another desk, much too large, at which sat a man in the uniform of a deputy inspector general of police, the name tag on his chest saying M. Doraiswamy. Assorted uniformed and plainclothes policemen stood or sat quietly around, most looking down or out at the coach through reddened eyes.

Chauhan turned in his chair as I entered the tent with Venky. 'You must be Colonel Menon,' he said, 'from Delhi.'

'We could have handled it as well from here,' said Doraiswamy. The rising tension was between these two men, not from the hostages outside. Chauhan must have asked for us to be called in, a slight to the local policemen. Chauhan's opposite number in the Tamil Nadu police, the director general, had stayed away, leaving the proceedings to the relatively junior DIG. Which meant that local police support might be less than enthusiastic. Whoever had planned this knew far too much about how the government

29

worked. He'd used his knowledge to create divisions in the opposition, and had now hunched up behind his defences, like a krait hiding its head in its coils in the face of danger.

A fitting name for the man, I thought: the Krait.

chapter two

The krait was a timid creature like all of its kind, moving only in safety, looking warily for enemies, of which it had many: peacocks; its own kind, for it was cannibal; and, most dreaded of all, the mongoose. The krait was mature, four years old, and well over five feet long. Over the years it had learnt to survive, and now it threatened the lives of the small creatures in the vicinity.

I moved past Doraiswamy's outsize desk to take a chair beside Chauhan vacated by an underling relieved to get out of arm's reach of him. 'I was told you'd get here about this time,' Chauhan told me. 'There's a message from a General Reddy.' He fished for something in his pocket and turned up a ragged bit of paper with something written on it. 'Major General Reddy, C-in-C, Madras Area. You're to call him immediately.'

The telephone operator had Reddy holding in a minute. General Kelkar had spoken to him, said Reddy, as sparing with words as Kelkar. His men had arranged for a camp behind the command post and his quartermaster was on call for supplies. I was to let him know what I wanted, and could call him any time, and we'd meet tomorrow. All the best.

I went out of the tension to where Reddy's men and mine had already begun to set up camp. Coming up already were lights, another cookhouse, a lavatory trench, a bathhouse and sleeping tents, of which there would eventually be fifty.

Back at the command post with Chauhan I got a mug of tea and dug for information and got sketchy grains of it. We didn't know how many terrorists there were in the coach. We didn't know how and where the passengers were placed. We didn't know what else the terrorists carried by way of explosives and weaponry besides their AK-47s.

'Can I talk to the women who've been released?' I asked. 'They might be able to help out.'

'They were hysterical when they got out,' replied Chauhan, depression heavy in his voice. 'There were seven of them, two with a husband and a son still inside, another three with husbands inside, one with a father inside and one with a little boy . . . We had them taken to a guest house in Madras, a doctor had a look at all of them. The police and my people are still talking to them.'

'Can I have transcripts?' I asked.

'I doubt you'll get them before midnight,' he replied.

'I'll speak to them. Tonight. We haven't time to spare.'

'I'll call the guest house and find out if any of them's awake. I've been having some trouble with the police myself.'

'I noticed. They want the RAF to go in, if anyone does.'

While Chauhan was on the telephone I looked once again at the coach, thinking of a way in. I'd have to have drawings of the coach. 'That must be a standard coach,' I told one of Chauhan's assistants, 'can we have drawings of the thing?'

He smiled a betel-stained red smile at me, opening a briefcase beside him. 'We thought you'd ask,' he said, handing me sheets from the case. 'We also have on call an engineer from Integral Coach Factory where they make these things. I can have him here in an hour if you want.'

'Later,' I said, handing the drawings to Venky and turning to Chauhan, who had finished his call.

'You can take a chance at the guest house,' he told me, 'most of them have been sedated but you might find someone awake.'

'I'll do that,' I said, and while one of his assistants went out to find me transport to the city I looked at the coach some more. 'Meanwhile you could have a few things done for me. Get those dinner trays out of the way.'

He smiled, the irony heavy in the smile and in his voice. 'We asked. They said no. They've done it on purpose. Will they trouble you seriously?'

'If we want to go in silently we'll have to watch out for them. Anyone stepping on them or bumping one against a rail will make a hell of a noise.'

'What else?'

'Observation platforms. Up behind the floodlights, from where at night we can watch without being seen from the

33

coach. Four of them in all.' They could serve as platforms for snipers as well.

'Done. We have scaffolding for dozens.'

'Those lookouts must be broiling in their black uniforms.'

'I can't understand why they're wearing those masks. I don't think identifying any of them would be useful at this stage.'

'It's not a matter of hiding who they are,' I said slowly. 'If they all look the same, we don't know how many there are.' Camouflage. The Krait. He sat quiet in his hole, trying to lure us in. Dust in our eyes, those masks. 'And one last thing.'

'What?'

'There seems to be a radio mast sticking out of one of the windows. Have a radio scanner van here to try and pick up whatever they're broadcasting from the coach.'

'All right.'

The jeep arrived, driven by a police constable with a stonily silent inspector beside him. I went over to my tent to change into civvies for the trip to town. No one else was to go out of the camp without permission.

I sat in the rear of the jeep while they drove me icily out, first along the highway and then through streets lit with the orange glow of sodium lamps, up flyovers and past movie theatres with gigantic cutouts of stars sprouting outside, to the secluded guest house where the women had been transferred. We drew up by a gate in a high wall outside a colonial tile-roofed bungalow, four armed, camouflage-clad RAF men on guard, their uniforms incongruous in this quiet corner of the city.

The inspector in front spoke to the RAF men, produced his identification, and then we were through, led to a quiet desk in the lobby where a sub-inspector sat, beside him a large, quiet man in plain clothes who turned out to be a superintendent. 'We will give you transcripts of the interrogations,' the superintendent said when I explained that I wanted to speak to the women. 'There is no need for you to speak to the ladies. We have interrogated them in detail.'

No doubt you have, pal, I thought, but it's not you that's going into that coach. 'When can I have the transcripts?' I asked.

He grinned, his resentment now visible and saw-toothed. 'Noon tomorrow. Maybe a little later.'

'That's much too late,' I said neutrally. 'I will have to speak to the ladies tonight.'

His grin widened at my discomfiture. 'The ladies have all gone to sleep. The doctor says they should not be disturbed. I cannot wake them up for you.'

'I was told earlier that one of them had refused her medication.'

'Ah, yes,' he said, the corners of his mouth drooping in mock sorrow. 'One of the ladies made a lot of trouble for us. She just kept shouting at us, refused her medicine. She is angry because her son is still on the coach. I don't think you will get anything useful from her, but you can see her if you like.'

Bastard, I thought, saving up the worst for me, the least useful. 'I like,' I said. 'I'll speak to her. Tell me her name.'

He made a great show of looking through the papers on the desk. 'Let me see,' he said, 'Sandhya Upadhyaya. Age twenty-nine. Her son's name is Kiran, age five years. The inspector will take you to her. Room five, on the first floor.'

Room five was twenty metres down a dark corridor with rooms on either side and a window at the end out of which I could see the street lamps outside. By the door stood two nervous young constables, regular policemen, holding their rifles a little gingerly, obviously unused to handling them. The inspector led me all the way to the door, turned on his heel, and left. I pushed the door open and walked into the room.

In a large cane easy chair opposite the door sat a slim young woman in blue jeans and a yellow T-shirt, her eyes gleaming fiercely above dark shadows of stress in a pale face. On the left side of her forehead was a large red bruise, just beginning to purple. To her left, in a long row of dining chairs, sat a policewoman in a khaki sari, a stenographer now biting the end of his pencil, a plainclothesman, and a sub-inspector.

'I'm sick of this,' she was saying, sitting straight in the chair, very much on edge, but her voice powerful and under control, 'you've asked me the same damn questions fifty times over and not listened to anything I said. Now you'd better tell me what you're doing about getting my son out of there.'

36

'You'd best cool off, ma'am,' I said evenly, 'they're new to this. And we'll be able to get your son out of there only if you get your mind working on it.'

That got her right out of her chair. She took three steps forward and stood facing me, her green eyes level with mine. 'And who the hell might you be?' she flared, looking me up and down.

What she saw wouldn't have been impressive. I stand 170 centimetres—five seven—and weigh just over sixty kilos, and in my civvies have all the personality of an old cushion. 'Lieutenant Colonel Menon, ma'am,' I said. 'If we can't negotiate my men will probably go into that coach to get the people out.'

'God!' she exploded. 'Another of those clowns. What do you want?'

'Information. My men will have three seconds, maybe four at most in which to get those terrorists down. If you can tell me anything that'll save any of my men a tenth of a second of fumbling I'd be grateful. So you'd best get your act together.'

To my surprise, and that of the others in the room, she covered her face in her hands and burst into silent tears, sinking back in her chair. I sat in the chair the plainclothesman pushed my way and waited for her tears to subside. In the shadows and the dim yellow glow of the pedestal lamp beside her she seemed to shrink, her earlier defiance replaced by a deep pathos. As we watched, she stopped crying, sniffed, hunted for a kerchief in her pocket, blew her nose, then sat staring sightlessly at the wall above my head. 'We haven't much time to spare,' I said as gently as I could. 'There's a deadline, in case you don't know.'

She blinked at me, a speculative look coming into her eyes, then a faint, watery smile. 'Funny you should talk of getting my act together,' she said. 'I used to be on stage before I got married.'

'Right,' I told her, 'imagine a set ten times as complex as the biggest you've ever worked on.. In the dark, with no communication. That's roughly what it'll be like.'

'Okay,' she said, 'what do you want to know?'

'How did you get that bruise?'

'One of them hit me with a gun when I tried to take my son along with me. He knocked me down, grabbed my son, and took him away.' Hot tears came welling up in her eyes as she recalled this, and a deep, slow anger.

'We'll get him back,' I told her as steadily as I could. 'Tell me, how many terrorists were there?'

'Six,' she said unhesitatingly. 'I saw six of them. There might have been more I didn't see but that's unlikely. All six in black uniforms, faces and heads covered in masks, all with those ugly pistols with things sticking out underneath . . .'

'Those things happen to be AK-47 assault rifles, ma'am, a far cry from any pistol you'll ever come across. But if the men were all masked and uniformed, how did you know there were six?'

'Body language. I'm a trained actress, remember? They moved differently, talked differently, held themselves differently . . . And they didn't have gloves. I could see their hands.'

'Where did they come from, did you see?'

'I was getting Kiran—my son—ready to get off when one of them just burst into our bay. There was one bay that they kept curtained off through the trip. I think some of them came out of there. I recognized one of them, at least . . . One man strikingly different from the rest.'

'Different how? Physically?'

'He had an extra finger on one of his hands, his right hand, I think. I noticed it a couple of times during the trip. He had reddish hair, long, down past his shoulders, longer than mine . . . And he had this awful look in his eyes. I was wary of him all along. He looked crazy, mad . . .' Her voice cracked. 'God! I can't bear the thought of my boy being with that madman!'

'Mad in what way?'

She pulled herself together with an effort. Shuddered, closed her eyes. Sat silent for a while. 'I don't know,' she said eventually, 'like a psychopath . . . you could see it shining out of his eyes . . .'

Bingo, I thought, the madman in the group. The man who had chopped off a man's finger with the ring still on it, and later another hostage's ear. The Krait's insurance. The thought sobered me. Sick as this man might be, the man who could use him and his illness with such concentrated gall was sicker still.

'Did you get to notice any of the others?'

She nodded, biting her underlip. 'There was one who was the leader. A quiet man, the one who spoke to the police on the loudspeaker. He was very restrained calculating. When he was rough with anyone it was always with the weakest. The most dangerous of them, except possibly that madman.'

'How did the hostages react? The men, especially?'

'Very quietly, on the whole . . . I was surprised. One of them tried to bluster and the leader just knocked him down. After that . . . after that they didn't try anything. One of them even tried to get friendly with the terrorists. Wretched man!'

'What else did you notice about the terrorists? What was their mood like?'

'Confident. They acted as if they knew exactly what they were doing. One of them put a box under our berth, with wires leading out of it . . .'

The penny dropped. A bomb. She must have caught something in my expression because her eyes widened in sudden, tearing anxiety. 'Oh my God!' she exclaimed, the tears starting again. 'That was a bomb! I must have been stupid not to realize it then! They'll blow it up!' She was crying again now, tears streaming down her cheeks, this time making no effort to hide the fact. She crossed the room to grab my collar, almost shook me. 'You mustn't go in there. They'll blow it up. You must do as they tell you!'

I took her gently by the wrists and detached her hands from my shirt. Felt a pang, and then the old darkness reared its head with the familiar warning: Don't get involved. Handed her my kerchief and had to resist quite strongly the impulse to put my arms around her. 'We won't go in there until we're reasonably sure we'll get everyone out safe,' I said as reassuringly as I could.

'I'm sorry,' she said moments later with a measure of regained composure. 'You're the only one that's listened openly to anything I've said. Everyone else behaved like I was hysterical or brain-damaged. But you can't go in there, they'll blow up the coach. Please!'

The plea in her voice would have softened a Bluebeard but I kept my better self buttoned firmly away. 'How were you all placed in the coach?' I asked eventually, when she had got back to her chair.

'They shoved all the women and girls into one bay, and I think they shoved all the men into four bays, crammed seven or eight to a bay. I saw them on the way to the toilet . . . They left Kiran with me until . . . God!' She clenched her hands tight, shut her eyes, leaned back in exhaustion.

I went relentlessly on. 'You said there were six of them, with guns and bombs. Could you see any other equipment they had? Electronic stuff, whatever?'

'I think they had a radio. They kept it outside the passenger area, by a door, with something sticking outside. I think I heard one of them speaking into it. They had headphones so it never made a noise.'

That radio mast. But it still didn't explain why they had to have that radio there. Unless . . . unless there was a leak. 'What else did you see?' I asked, putting the doubts away for the future.

'They had water. Crates of it, all over their bay. I saw them buying it and thought they were crazy. And I think I saw one of them eat out of a box. I think they carried their own food and water.' Indeed. Hence the thirty-five trays.

41

They'd wanted none for themselves. There was no way we could drug them, make them drowsy or panicky.

The Krait was good, whoever he was. I found myself with the shameful wish that he'd been on our side instead.

I stayed with her another fifteen fruitless minutes and then gave up, for she seemed to have run out of ideas as well. At the end of it, as I turned to leave, she came with me to the door. 'Tell your superiors they have a bomb in there,' she pleaded, 'tell them to do as they want, and catch them afterwards. Please. I don't want to lose my son. I'll speak to the home minister if I can.'

'I'll tell them, ma'am,' I replied as evenly as I could, repressing once again the urge to put my arms around her. 'And after that if they decide to send us in we'll go in . . . But if we do, we'll watch out for the madman and the bombs. We'll do that much, I promise.'

'You don't know what that madman is like,' she said, 'anyone else might hesitate before they blow up the coach, and themselves with it, but not that man. Please tell them.'

'Sure I will,' I said, and turned away.

She stopped me with her hand on my shoulder, looking at me with horrified comprehension dawning in her eyes. 'You're just like those terrorists,' she said, 'you're just as dangerous as they are. The more so because you don't look it. You'll go in if you can.'

'I will,' I said, relieved that the need for covering up was past, regretting the need to disturb her with the truth.

She sagged in the doorway, propping herself with her hands on the doorframe, her face twisted in fear and anger.

42

'You bastard,' she said slowly, deliberately, 'you utter, bloody bastard!' And she slammed the door in my face.

Back at the darkened camp I took another look around the perimeter, observing the men at the cordon settle into a deliberate pattern of watching, before moving into the command post, where Chauhan sat amidst a clutter of papers and equipment on the desk, most of his staff having deserted him for the night, Doraiswamy and the police detachment gone. 'What happened to the police?' I asked.

'They pulled out most of the RAF,' Chauhan told me. 'Reaction to your presence. They'll be back tomorrow.'

I sat down at Doraiswamy's oversized desk and examined the drawings of the coach, sipping strong Army tea fetched in from the SOF cookhouse. We had to find a way in.

The coach was a sheet metal shell built on a chassis of steel beams. The chassis itself rested on four axles, with massive box springs to deaden the worst shocks. Inside the coach, the air-conditioning was restricted to a passenger area, a sort of coach within a coach with doors, glass from midway up, placed at either end of the off-centre aisle.

This inner coach had eight compartments, two bunks running along the direction of the train on one side of the aisle and four running across the direction of the train on the other. All were stacked two deep. The four-berth bay could be curtained off for privacy. There were eight such compartments, but one at the far end had only three berths

43

in the four-berth bay, the remaining space being used for air-conditioning equipment.

The air-conditioning vents ran along the top of the coach, with vents in each compartment on the ceiling. At each end, above the toilets, were water tanks. The wiring, too, ran along the top of the coach. Lights were fluorescent, two in each four-berth bay, and one more in the aisle for each compartment, with a blue nightlight.

Each compartment had four windows, two on each side. Each window had two layers of toughened glass, the one on the outside tinted to keep out the glare and one-way to keep out the stares of nosy parkers.

Fifty metres away in the centre of the lit area one of the terrorists on patrol walked up to the rear door on our side, reached up, turned the handle, and tugged it open. As he clambered up the steps into the coach I noticed he had a slight limp in the left leg, as if his left ankle was weaker. When he walked on level ground it looked like a swagger, but turned into a limp when he climbed.

I liked to put tags on people. So far we had the Krait, the man behind all this, the planner I was sure wasn't in this group of terrorists; there was Psycho, the madman; Loudspeaker, the leader; and now Limp, the guard. Three out of six, if you left the Krait out.

Start with the doors, obvious entry points.

'Have these guys been using all the doors or just that one?' I asked Chauhan.

He straightened up in his chair, rubbing tired eyes. 'Only that one,' he replied after a moment's thought. 'I think they've sealed off the rest.'

Booby trapped them, more like, I thought. If they had the bombs and the expertise, putting a booby trap in a doorway was simple. The other three doors would be temptingly open and devastatingly mined, for sure.

The roof was too tricky to cut through, what with the vents and tanks and wiring. The bottom was too strong, restricted by the heavy beams of the chassis underneath.

The doors fore and aft, communicating doors actually, were too far from the passenger area. We'd have to go in through two narrow passages past the toilets to the passenger area, and even then . . . No, too risky.

The windows weren't barred.

The first glimmerings of a plan began to emerge in my mind as I sat looking at the diagrams of the coach. The windows were a little over two metres off the ground from the outside. Add a bit for the filling of small stones under the rails. Two metres and a quarter. Seven and a half feet. Too high for a man to reach, but accessible if he had someone on the ground to give him a leg-up. Then crash through the glass.

Got to get to the windows first, past fifty well-lit metres of open ground. Past the two patrolling lookouts. Without making noise on those dinner trays scattered all over the ground around the coach.

Shoot the sentries out. Snipers on the observation platforms at night would take care of that.

Our snipers were a class apart. They were all outstanding marksmen to begin with, but for a sniper to be really effective he had to be able to operate unseen. The men

45

who'd trained our snipers had put them through hell. They'd had at first to give up their weapons and learn to lie utterly motionless, regardless, being punished for the slightest shift. They'd learnt, by and by, to freeze overnight, often in uncomfortable positions, moving after those hours to aim and fire, and then freeze again. I'd tried their course and given up in the middle. My eighteen precious snipers, only six of whom were here, thought nothing of hitting a six-inch target at a half-kilometre on a windless day. So attached to their long-barrelled Lee-Enfields, that no officer inspecting one of these deadly accurate rifles would ever find a speck of dirt anywhere on it, or a telltale shiny surface to give its presence away.

Four platforms, one behind each set of floodlights, two snipers to each platform. At least two snipers would cover each of the lookouts no matter where he was within the perimeter.

I must remind Ismail to bring more snipers along, I thought.

Bringing down those two lookouts would be a piece of cake for the snipers. And in we'd go.

What if someone inside the coach saw the lookouts go down?

Draw them away to the front or rear of the coach, where they wouldn't be seen from the inside, for just a few seconds. A diversion. Fire, in the dark. A silent fire on the hillock 300 metres away, too far away to be threatening, interesting enough to be worth a second look. Set the sapling on fire.

What about sound? A helicopter flying above would cover most of the noise we made. We'd have to get them used to a helicopter flying over from time to time. We'd time the attack around the helicopter. Light the fire as soon as the helicopter was loud enough.

Where would we go in from?

That was obvious. We'd go in along the track, by the side of the one occupied by the coach. Anyone looking out of the window would see us only in the last few metres of our run-up.

Even that would be disastrous.

But the risk was acceptable.

How many men?

Eight compartments. We'd have to have at least one man on either side, to make sure every terrorist on the coach was within sight of at least one soldier. Two windows to a compartment, sixteen to the coach, two men to each window, thirty-two men.

Thirty-two men. A huge team. To get them fifty metres to the coach silently we'd have to practice. Without practice we'd fumble like drunks in a strange house on a dark night.

Dark. What if the lights were off? The men would wear miners' lamps on their helmets. No problem.

In each of the two-man elements given a window, the lead man would have to turn around, brace his back against the coach wall and give his buddy a leg up. The rails were raised off the ground on a layer of small stones—jelly the railways call it—sloping down away from the rails. The man below would have nothing to hold on to.

Once his buddy got on top he'd have to break through two layers of toughened, shatterproof glass. He'd have to have an opening in the glass at least fifteen centimetres— six inches—square, to poke the muzzle of his gun in and take an aimed shot.

The butts of our sub-machine guns were nothing like the old rifles when it came to breaking glass. We didn't need the bloody sub-machine guns. No one would be pouring a hundred rounds a minute into that coach. A 7.62 mm SLR would have done just fine, but it was now too late to put the men back on them.

We'd have to find out about the glass the hard way. The rest we could manage. The drawing said nothing about how strong the glass was, how hard a man would have to hit it for it to break.

That radio mast worried me. I still couldn't understand why it was there. Maybe the Krait had had it stuck there to put people like me off balance. I wouldn't put that past him.

I took another walk around the perimeter, passing by the men on the cordon, alternating RAF and SOF men, dark shapes crouched watchfully, alertly, following the movements of the lookouts as they walked irregularly around the coach.

They were well-trained, those lookouts. They patrolled carefully, covering everything once or twice every two minutes, but not so regularly as to form a pattern.

That training had sharpened their reflexes. If threatened they would try to hit back immediately. We'd turn their training against them. In the attack, they'd tend to fire at the soldiers in their body armour rather than at the hostages. They'd counterattack rather than blow themselves up.

No, not all of them. Not Psycho.

The lady was right. Psycho was the Krait's insurance. Psycho would go for the hostages in an attack. He'd go for the red button that would blow up the coach.

The Krait had covered everything. For all his madness, his timing was perfect, his choice of location excellent. He'd covered all angles to bring maximum political pressure to bear on the government to get the hostages out at any cost. He'd cut out the possibility of our drugging his men. His defences were impeccable. A formidable man, my adversary. Who was he? What was he like? I had to get into his twisted megalomaniac mind. That was the key to getting them out.

chapter three

The krait was very hungry. On its last hunt it had caught and eaten a small mouse, but that was gone. In its hunger it overcame its natural timidity. In the dark it slipped between the gaps in a pile of rubble and bricks, where it felt safe, waiting for a prey: a small rodent or a tree frog, or another smaller one of its kind.

I slept that night, in my tent in the camp behind the command post, at two. I went out like a light for the first time in years, and stayed out until Harkishen woke me at dawn with a mug of tea just as the faint mist began to lift off the plain. The observation platforms behind the floodlights, now ready and visible from the ground, were unoccupied. The snipers would mount the platforms only after dark, when the FKF couldn't spot them.

At the entrance to the camp, now guarded almost as closely as the perimeter about the coach, men were coming in, some from exercise, others from guard duty on the cordon. The men coming off duty now would sleep, then drill, get their uniforms cleaned in the laundry truck we had borrowed from General Reddy's men. I wondered how worn the terrorists felt, and how apathetic the hostages.

I thought of the little boy alone and helpless. Thought rather longer of his mother, spirited and honest. And eventually, feeling a cool patch of grass beneath my feet, thought of what was happening to me. What had happened very rarely in the past. What I'd promised wouldn't ever happen again.

Ismail rang at seven, just as I got to the command post, to ask how we'd got through the night, if there were any changes so far, and to say he'd been busy but was just leaving and did I need more men or equipment.

We had enough men, I told him, except snipers. I told him to get all the snipers he could lay his hands on.

There were four platforms, each requiring two shifts of two snipers each—that made a total of sixteen snipers, twice the number I had at my disposal. We'd have to make do with eight snipers, which meant that they'd have to make do on catnaps until this thing was over.

I sounded as if I had something in mind, said Ismail, but I was to keep it to myself until I cleared it with him or with Kelkar. God knows what security was available. He hung up.

Venky came to the command post. 'It's getting more political,' he told me, rubbing a hand through his thinning brown hair, helping himself to tea. 'It's escalated out of sight.'

51

'How so?' I asked.

'Would you like to take a walk?' he asked in a tone that said very clearly he would like me to say yes. 'I've got something to show you at the camp.' Outside, out of earshot of anyone, he continued, 'There's a task force now, and a committee running it. I got news of it ten minutes ago and thought I should tell you first.'

'Who's on the committee?' I asked, sipping from my third mug of sweet tea, which I'd carried out of the tent.

'Kelkar's on it, and General Reddy,' he replied, holding back a yawn. 'Gawand, who briefed us in Delhi. They've got some useful guys on it. Mathur, general manager of ICF, and Sundarrajan, general manager of the Southern Railways.'

'So what's the bad news?' I grinned. 'Tell me quick. I can't bear the suspense.'

'Doraiswamy's on the committee, and he doesn't like us one bit. There's Chauhan's boss, D.K. Arya, who got his job only because he promised to collect material on people who could shake the government . . . There are three more members, two from the ministry of defence, one from the home ministry. Watchdogs for the minister of defence, the lot.'

'Where's the committee's office?' I asked.

'At a dak bungalow eight kilometres from here. They're all staying there from this morning on, except Kelkar who'll stay here.'

On the walk back to the command post I wrenched my mind off Sandhya Upadhyaya, disturbed at the effort it took, and tried instead to think of the committee, of the

Minister's nephew. Swore at the values of this country where the wastrel relative of a minister is worth so much.

My mind went again to the little boy I'd never seen. And then, inevitably, to his mother.

If we went in and fucked up, it was the end. Every terrorist group would work up its own new tactics after that. If the government caved in, the results would be much the same. We had to go in, and we had to make it work.

Doraiswamy, the DIG of the Tamil Nadu police, wanted the operation for his men. Tamil Nadu was supposed to have some of the best security men in the country, trained in Israel, said the rumours, but all of them were bodyguards to the fat lady who was chief minister. From what I'd seen of the RAF they were more oriented towards keeping security than breaking it; I doubted they had the offensive skills to match ours.

'What are we going to do?' asked Venky.

'Leave the committee to Kelkar and Reddy. Make the plan as good as possible. And then follow orders, quietly.'

Back at the command post, Chauhan's assistant, who had taken over Chauhan's job, was supervising the delivery of breakfast to the coach. As we watched, one of the policemen, a youngster in loud red underwear, feet bare, stepped carefully out of the command post, carrying two open trays of bread and eggs. He held the trays high, and eyes firmly downward, walked slowly towards the rear door of the coach, avoiding the grassy patches—probably full of thorns—as he went. He left his two trays in the doorway of the coach and turned back. A terrorist picked up the trays from the floor inside the coach and bore them away. The two lookouts lounged around outside, apparently perfectly content, watchful as snakes, and extremely competent. Unless I was mistaken the terrorists weren't at all worn.

Sandhya had got it right. They were confident. To me they looked a shade too confident. Complacent, almost.

That bloody radio mast! They knew that if we were up to something they'd get to know. There couldn't be any other reason for that radio mast.

'What about the little boy's breakfast?' I asked. 'Does he get what the others do?'

'Yes,' said one of the policemen, 'he gets a glass of milk besides, that's it.'

'What's been happening this morning?' I asked Chauhan's assistant, a superintendent of the CBI.

He gave me a cold look. 'We've finished feeding them breakfast, as you can see,' he said. 'Mr Chauhan will have a chat with them when he gets back here.'

'A chat about what?'

'I don't think I am authorized to tell you. Mr Chauhan didn't say anything about keeping you informed. You'd better ask Mr Chauhan himself when he comes.'

'He'll be speaking to those guys over a loudspeaker,' I said evenly, the anger threatening to show in my voice, 'everyone for miles around will know what it's all about. So what the hell are you playing around for? Or should I get Chauhan on the telephone right away?' He looked suitably chastened and I felt a little stab of unease at having been so hard on someone only trying to do his job.

'All the FKF men on their list have been located and are now being rounded up in Srinagar. That should be done by evening.'

'Why will it take so long?'

'Bad weather. Winter. This is the worst part of the year in those areas, and this is the coldest winter they've had in six years. Some roads are completely snowbound, and flying's out of the question. I don't know whether they'll make it to Srinagar by evening.'

'Sounds like the government's giving up,' I said, thinking of nephews.

'Not so,' responded Chauhan, walking into the tent, the weariness gone from his cold eyes. 'They're keeping their options open. They'd like best of all a negotiated surrender, which is now next to impossible. The task force committee will meet later today to decide what's to be done. I'll talk to these fellows now, try to get some more time, and then get back to the committee.'

'I have a plan brewing in my head,' I told him, 'one that I think will work, but only if we get a few trial runs to get our timing straight. If the committee insists on deliberating on everything we might not have the time to set up the practice sessions today . . .'

He gave me a hard stare. 'Come to the committee meeting with me. General Kelkar will be there, and Colonel Qureishi. There'll be people from the railways as well. Put your plan up to them right at the beginning. Present it to them as an option, ask for whatever you need for your practice sessions. That way you won't lose any time.' He grinned suddenly, his cheeks swelling, eyes almost disappearing. 'You soldiers aren't used to dealing with committees, especially civilian ones. But don't worry, Kelkar'll take care of it.'

He picked up the mike. 'This is Chauhan of the CBI, calling the FKF. Good morning,' he said.

The lookouts stopped their patrolling. One of them went into the coach, and a few seconds later emerged. A third FKF man now stood in the doorway, loudspeaker in hand. Loudspeaker, the leader. He looked no different from the others. 'What do you want, policeman?' he asked into the mike.

'I have further information on the money and your comrades,' said Chauhan, his tone carefully friendly. 'The money is yet to be collected. I told you yesterday that we need time until Tuesday evening but you gave us only till 1400 on Monday. That's not enough. We ran around all yesterday for the money and it'll be here, packed and ready, only by about 1500 tomorrow. Make your deadline for the money 1700, to be on the safe side.'

'You should have tried harder, policeman,' said Loudspeaker, 'that's your problem. The deadline stands.'

'I'm asking for three hours,' said Chauhan, in the same friendly tone, 'just three more hours. Do you think I'd waste my time and yours negotiating for just three hours if it weren't something serious?'

56

'All right, policeman, you have your three hours. The new deadline for the money is 1700 tomorrow. Now what about my colleagues?'

'There are snowstorms in your homeland. You know better than anyone else how hard it gets in winter. Eight of your comrades have reached Srinagar, the rest are still in their prisons. We will have everyone in Delhi by lunchtime tomorrow if the weather holds. I repeat, if the weather holds, we should be able to get them here by tomorrow evening, by the time you finish counting the money. But if there's another storm up there . . .'

'Leave the stories for another time,' said Loudspeaker. 'When will you bring my colleagues here?'

'By 1800, but only if the weather holds. I repeat, only if the weather holds.'

'Get them here by 1800, policeman. No more extensions.'

'The weather is not something I control,' said Chauhan, the plea audible even in his amplified voice booming across the plains. 'Please listen to me. You have dealt with me all this while, you know me. You know I'm not playing games.'

'Enough,' said Loudspeaker. 'The deadline for the money is 1700 tomorrow. The deadline for my colleagues is 1800 tomorrow. I will grant no more time.' He slammed the door shut.

'Bastards,' Chauhan whispered, exhausted, wiping his brow, relaxing some of the iron control he'd been maintaining through the conversation. It had lasted only a few minutes but his shirt was already soaked with sweat. I wouldn't have been in his shoes for anything.

57

By half-past-ten, sweating in the humidity—the rains were due—of late December, we were at the guest house, a sprawling old one-storey building left over from the British, with an acre of lawn in front and a henna-hedged, gravel driveway. It was evident the committee had arrived. The parking lot overflowed and the grounds were crawling with policemen. Chauhan's driver had trouble making his way past the crowds at the gate, and as he left us in the porch outside the lobby I could see at least twenty Ambassadors and Contessas outside, and an equal number of jeeps, most with flags or other insignia, both government and military.

The lobby was full of people rushing around looking important. In the centre, behind the reception counter, sat two harried policemen directing people. 'Where's Major General Kelkar?' I asked one of them.

He stared at me blankly, then picked up a list in front of him. 'What is your name?' he asked.

'Lieutenant Colonel Menon,' I said, 'Army.'

He found my name on the list, at the bottom of the second page, and told me to take the left branch of the building. Kelkar would be in Room 17.

Emerging into the corridor, however, I bumped into Ismail, who had come out to look for me. 'We got in five minutes ago,' he said, 'good timing. How far have you got with your plan?'

'Fifteen minutes with you to fine-tune it and we'll be ready for Kelkar,' I said, 'and after that we have some other little things to discuss. What about the snipers?'

58

'I got six more. The rest weren't available. Look, we'll work out a schedule right now, for practice if you think we need any, and for when we can go in. There are men from the railways here, so if you can list whatever you need from them we'll have them deliver everything by two or three in the afternoon. Come on in.'

Inside the high-ceilinged room we sat at an old, scarred rosewood desk by the high windows and I explained it to him, in the sequence it would happen, beginning with the helicopter. The fire would be lit a few seconds after we heard the helicopter. The snipers would go for the lookouts even if they were visible from the coach: I didn't think there'd be a lookout inside the coach as well. With one man resting at any time, two to watch the hostages, and one more attending to the innumerable little things that they had to do—a radio watch, for instance—it was unlikely they'd have lookouts inside the coach.

When the lookouts were down, thirty-two men in four eight-man teams would run along the rails to the coach from the perimeter where they'd be waiting for the lookouts to go down. At the coach they would break up into two-man elements. Each man would wear body armour and a helmet, and carry a miner's lamp as well, just in case the lights inside the coach were off. No one was to go into the coach until all terrorists were down.

Stretcher and medic teams ready by the command post to take care of injuries. A sapper team, borrowed from General Reddy, on standby to take care of bombs.

Ismail picked the same weak point I had. 'The lookouts will be the least of our problems,' he pointed out. 'I'm worried about the time it'll take us to break through the glass. We can't afford more than about two seconds.'

'I think we can have a little more than that,' I explained slowly. 'If we surprise them, they'll try to defend themselves by reflex. And we'll be going in on both sides, so that'll confuse them. We should be fairly safe there, with body armour and headgear. We can get them before they get to the hostages. I'm more worried about the bombs.'

'What bombs?' he demanded, brows drawing together in the beginning of a frown.

'Didn't you read the transcripts of my chat with the woman whose son is still in the coach?'

'No. They gave me nothing of the kind.' Doraiswamy's heavy hand making itself felt.

I explained to him what Sandhya had said about boxes with wires. 'I'm fairly sure one of them—the madman, the one I've tagged Psycho—will be sitting in there holding the detonator. He's the one we should watch out for.'

'Don't the police know about this?'

'She told them about it, all right, and in any case they have the transcripts. They haven't given me transcripts of their interrogations, though.'

'Bloody fools,' he said, shaking his head in disgust. 'They should have sent us copies. I'll make sure we have all of them here in a couple of hours. Bloody idiots.' Ismail rarely swore. I could see he was going to make Kelkar stir up quite a hornet's nest at the next committee meeting.

'The Tamil Nadu police don't like us very much. They want their RAF to do the job. They're just getting their own back.'

Ismail smiled grimly. 'We'll see about that. The committee is meant to take care of people acting small.'

'Another thing. There's a radio in there. I saw a radio mast sticking out of one of the windows, and the lady said she heard someone speaking into one.'

'What about it?' he demanded. 'They probably need to have someone help them with the negotiations. They need to monitor news broadcasts, things like that. As I see it, they have to have one if at all they intend to stick this out. In any case, I'll have a scanner van set up here to catch their transmissions.'

'That's all very well,' I said quietly, 'but I think they have someone here. Someone in the committee, or in the associated staff. I'd be a whole lot happier if we could keep operational details to ourselves.'

Ismail grimaced, looking down. 'We're not telling them more than the minimum they need to know. This is an Army operation and that's it. The man from the home ministry doesn't like it but that's what he's going to get.'

'If we have trial runs the railways and the coach builders and everyone will know what we're going to do. I don't think we can keep the trials secret. That's what I'm really worried about. If they have contacts in the right places they'll know how we're going in, even if they don't know when.'

'We'll think of leaks afterwards,' he said, 'I don't think one radio mast is any reason for you to think there's a leak.

In any case, I don't see a way right now to seal up ICF. So think instead of getting the hostages out safe. Can you make sure they don't spring up in the middle of it all and get themselves shot?'

'We'll drug their last meal,' I said, 'lay them out for eight hours. Let them sleep through the operation. Our men will be told shoot at anyone in black holding a weapon. And no one goes into the coach until all the men in black are down. The leader clears it.'

'How long do you think the whole thing will take?'

'I can only guess now, I'll work it out better after a trial or two.'

'So give me your guesses.'

'Eight or nine seconds to cover the sixty metres from the perimeter to the coach. Three or four seconds to position ourselves. Two more to break the glass. Three more to aim and fire. Sixteen to eighteen seconds in all.'

'I'm not particularly worried about the overall time. It's the gap between the first break in and the firing that we need to work on. That's when we're most vulnerable.'

'The helicopter should be some help in covering up the noise. Any other diversions you can think up would be welcome.'

'We'll see about more diversions. Too many of them and it becomes too complicated.'

'Yes,' I agreed. Most successful operations are simple, and they are brief. The more complex they are, or the longer, the more vulnerable they become. To my mind we had reached the maximum: if our operation became any more complex we'd be putting ourselves at risk, doubly so because we hadn't much time to practice.

'What time would you like to go in?'

'Three or four in the morning. Gestapo style. When they're least alert.'

Ismail looked up from his examination of the marks on the desktop. 'Do you think it can be done?' he asked. 'If you think we can't, just say so.'

There was a discreet knock on the door. I opened it to find Gawand sweating outside. 'I wanted a word with you and Colonel Qureishi,' he said.

'Come on in,' said Ismail, 'Raja and I are through with our confidential stuff.'

'I just want to tell you,' he said, sweating again, 'that the Minister will make sure you have everything you need.'

'We'll make sure of that ourselves, thanks,' Ismail said.

'May I come in?' Gawand asked.

'Sure,' Ismail told him sarcastically, 'make yourself at home.'

'The Minister told me to make sure you have everything you need to get his nephew out of there,' Gawand said. He paused nervously, looking jerkily at the door. 'I've just been promoted. I don't like the Minister, who I think is a prick. I don't like his nephew, who is also a prick. If he dies in there it'll be no great loss. So get everyone out. Ask for whatever you like, and I'll tell the Minister you're asking for it to get his nephew out. You'll get it.'

'And what if the Minister's nephew, ummm, doesn't come through this?' asked Ismail.

63

'Hard luck to him,' said Gawand, 'I don't care . . . The man's a small-time punk who uses Uncle's influence for all kinds of things. Most ministerial relatives are like that. If it weren't illegal I'd ask you to shoot him while you're in there.' He rose to go. 'Keep this to yourselves, right?' he said at the door. 'Otherwise I can kiss my career goodbye. And ask for anything, just anything.'

A constable came to summon us to Kelkar's room. Inside, we explained to him and to General Reddy that we planned to break into the coach through the windows. They listened to us in silence, and that was it. 'All right,' Kelkar said, 'I think it'll work. What do you need for your trial runs?'

'An identical coach,' I replied, 'parked in a place as much like this one, and enough glass to break.'

'You'll have all that. You two wait here, I'll get back to you in twenty minutes.'

He was better than his word. He returned in eighteen minutes, bringing with him a lanky Bengali in a bush shirt and tatty black slippers and a huge, yellow-toothed smile. 'Samir Bhattacharya,' the General introduced him, 'senior manager, production, Integral Coach Factory. He'll get you whatever you need. His boss has spoken to the factory to set up your coach.'

Samir drove nervously back to the camp in the jeep with Ismail and me, and waited patiently for twenty minutes at the barricade while we got B platoon ready and packed into two trucks for the training runs. In another hour, we were at the gates of the factory, grimy yellow buildings looming beyond.

A small convoy of cars had collected to lead us further. We were taken past the small glass-windowed outpost, past the vast administration blocks, past the greying factory sheds, past the workshops with what seemed to be dozens of sets of rails leading out of them, and then along a cobbled road running parallel to half a dozen sets of tracks. On one of the tracks was a small shunting engine pushing a single decrepit maroon coach. They'd picked the oldest of the coaches they had for us to practice on.

Five kilometres along the road, with the shunting engine following us, we came to a flat stretch much like the one where the hostage coach was parked. Our guide, teeth flashing in his dark face, pointed it out. 'This is the place we selected for you,' he told Ismail, 'but we can always shift somewhere else if you think it's not suitable.'

'Looks all right to me,' said Ismail. 'What do you say, Raja?'

'It's fine,' I replied, 'except . . .'

'Except what?' demanded Ismail, looking at me curiously.

'Except around here the ground is flat. The rails lie almost flush with the ground. The sleepers are buried into the ground, if you notice.'

'So?'

'The hostages are in a coach on rails that are raised at least six inches off the surrounding ground on a layer of broken stones, called jelly. That six inches will make all the difference when we're positioning ourselves.'

Ismail shook his head in wonderment at my pedantry, smiled a secret smile, and agreed. 'I'll leave it to Raja,' he told Samir, 'whatever he likes is fine by me.'

We found a level spot more like the one we wanted another kilometre on, bordered a couple of hundred metres away by dark green thornbushes with tiny leaves. I got out of the truck and walked around looking at the stretching tracks, at the sleepers with their greying collection of dust, at the gutters between the rails, for ten minutes before deciding it was all right. Told Samir so.

The new spot was, if anything, even rougher than where the hostage coach was, the layer of stones rising a clear foot above the level of the surrounding area and sloping sharply down away from the rails. It would be that much harder for a man to give his buddy a leg up while sustaining his footing on the treacherous jelly. There were eight sets of tracks, instead of four. The ground had been dug up recently, and the rains that followed had made it muddy, difficult to traverse.

'Could we get a couple of hundred empty metal dinner trays out of your canteen?' I asked the mystified Samir, who hadn't seen the hostage coach.

He blinked at me in surprise.

'Trays. Lunch. Canteen,' I repeated.

He sent off an assistant to fetch the trays, coming back in a minute, thinking obviously that I was crazy. 'You'll have them in half an hour,' he said, his grin replaced by a wary look, 'but what would you want with them?'

'The terrorists have scattered trays all around the coach,' I explained. 'I want the exercise as close to reality as it can be, so we're going to have to run across those trays here.'

The shunting engine meanwhile chuffed its way to the spot we'd selected, slowing to walking speed as I ran alongside and clambered up into the cabin beside the driver. At my signal, he stopped the engine within an inch of where I wanted it. I hopped off the running board, and one of his colleagues detached the engine. He went off with a wave and a flourish, treating it like a sports car instead of a staid old railway engine.

In the heat of the afternoon sun I walked around the coach, eyes shaded against the glare. Found, on inspection, that exactly half the glasses in the windows were cracked. 'Could we fix those windows, the broken ones?' I asked Samir after my tour. 'We have to know exactly how hard it is to break those things. My men have to practice breaking through them.'

Samir looked with growing mournfulness at the grimy old coach standing forlorn in the middle of the plain. 'Changing them isn't easy,' he said, 'we'll need at least half a day for that.'

'How about another spare coach?' I asked.

'We don't have one like this,' he explained, 'air-conditioning on the railways is fairly recent. There hasn't been enough time for these coaches to age. There must be some in the railway sheds in Madras but it'll take some time getting them here. They might have to cancel a service to do that.'

There were sixteen intact windows on this coach, enough for one group of men to practice on. That would do until we got another coach from Madras. 'All right,' I said, 'we'll use this one while you get another from Madras.'

After sending off another assistant—there were hordes of them around, staring open-mouthed at our trucks and the soldiers—with a note, Samir rejoined me. 'I just thought of something else,' he said. 'Safety glass of this type deteriorates a little with age and exposure, especially to sunlight. You don't notice it because it stays usable, but I would think a set of windows on the new coach would be much harder to break than the windows on this old one.'

'How much harder?' I asked.

'I can't really say. The glass in this coach isn't really shatterproof any more. But I'll get you some new glasses, in frames if you'd like to try breaking them.' For the third time, he sent off an assistant to the factory.

We began our first trial at a half-past-one, four eight-man sections led by Ismail, Venky, Sagar the platoon commander, and me. We started from our positions sixty metres away from the coach to the word 'Go!' spoken into a walkie-talkie by Ismail. We found straight away that the dinner trays were more dangerous than we thought. One of the section leaders happened to kick one on to the rails, and it clattered so much we called off the run. We'd have to try and avoid those trays altogether, I thought. Thank God we weren't in standard issue Army boots. Our rubber-soled boots made much less noise when we stepped on trays.

But scratch that eight seconds, I thought, make it ten.

Once again we assembled in eight-man teams sixty metres away, well over the distance we'd have to cover for the real thing, and charged to Ismail's signal on the walkie-talkie. Stepping carefully, we covered the distance to the coach in just over ten seconds, everyone running lightly and easily in the absence of the packs, weighing up to forty kilos, that we carried on the usual practice sessions. At the coach, each eight-man section broke up into four two-man elements, the lead man in each element turning around and bracing his back against the wall for his buddy to climb up on.

I was the second man in the second section. My buddy, the leader of the two of us, got his back to the coach wall ahead of us, and I scrambled up on to his knees, my hands on his shoulders.

My buddy slipped.

With my weight over him, he didn't have a chance. His feet slid out from under him, slipping more on the mud. He landed on his bottom, rolling in the mud, as I regained my feet and stepped away. Scratch that run as well.

It was harder than it looked.

After another hour and three more runs we got the time down to twelve seconds from starting the run to getting in position at the coach, those dinner trays alone costing us more than two seconds because the men had to keep their eyes down while running.

The safety glass stubbornly continued to be the biggest problem. Venky and I experimented with sheets of the stuff fitted into frames while Ismail led the other men on their practice runs, and found it would take four or more blows—far too many—to break through even one layer with the butts of our guns. Samir, watching quietly as Venky and I sweated over the frames, came to the rescue once again. 'Would you like us to make you an instrument to break the glass?' he asked, ambling over.

'Yes,' I replied, 'we need something with which a man can break a hole in both layers of the glass with one or two blows.'

'What size hole do you want? Do you want to bring down the whole thing or only part of it?'

'A hole six inches by six will do. Enough for us to poke our gun muzzles in and fire.'

'We can machine a hammer for you,' he offered after ten quietly contemplative seconds. 'A mild steel hammer with a pointed—not a sharp point—end, weighing two kilos, with a short handle, easy to grip. You can carry it on a sling and drop it after you break through.'

While we broke for lunch brought from the ICF canteen where we had got the trays, Samir got the sixteen hammers machined. They arrived forty minutes later in a small van, the faint grooves of the lathes still showing, stubby handles covered in black insulation tape for a good grip. Back at the frames we found the hammers made all the difference, breaking clean through both layers of glass if swung hard enough and at the right angle. But now the operation was a shade more complex at a critical stage: each man would have to drop the hammer before getting his hands on his gun to aim it.

We did the final run with B platoon at four, with C platoon, who had arrived ten minutes earlier, watching. We finished with a time of fourteen seconds between starting the run up and breaking through, of which three seconds were critical. Then, just to get the teamwork right, we did it once again before B platoon called it a day. They would now return to camp to rest for a few hours, then stand by for the call to go in. If at all it came.

The second coach, a new one this time, arrived as B platoon were climbing into their trucks, tired but confident now, laughing among themselves at the slips made during practice. C platoon, fresh and curious, now took up positions sixty metres from the coach. With the experience just earned from the earlier group's session we tore through C platoon's exercises in less than half the time. Six trials and ninety minutes later we were through, both platoons performing about the same, their timing improving as much as it was likely to in such a short while. Regrettably brief, I thought as I called them off, but it was better not to overtrain them.

We returned to the camp as dusk gathered over the plain, bringing with it a cool westerly wind and later a slight drizzle that cooled us off marvellously after a hot day in the sun, in body armour at that. General Kelkar was waiting for us at the command post. 'We've been told to wait awhile,' he told Ismail. 'We might not go in today. It seems they intend to deliver the money tomorrow before the deadline, build up some credibility, negotiate for another day in which to deliver the FKF prisoners, lull them into

71

thinking the government's given up . . . I wonder what idiot thought that up.'

'That doesn't make any kind of sense,' said Ismail. 'They seem serious about the deadlines, and about . . . about reprisals. Unless I'm mistaken, they won't yield any more unless they get a really convincing reason.'

I sent the men back to the camp. Both platoons would rest now until after dinner. Then we'd have B platoon on alert for the operation with C platoon standing by until about two in the morning, when C platoon would come on alert and B would rest. The snipers hadn't had any practice, I thought, but then they wouldn't need any. Not for something this simple.

Damn the government, I thought, damn that man from the home ministry. He wants to hog the credit.

Damn that Doraiswamy, too, making himself and his men small for the sake of preserving his turf. If he'd had any sense he'd have had scanner vans looking for signals from the coach, and for possible signals to . . . The other end of the radio link would lead us to the Krait.

But Doraiswamy, for all his pettiness, managed to surprise me. As the darkness grew and the shadows solidified, the lookouts outside the coach changed, and then I got a call from Doraiswamy. 'Menon,' he said, 'I think you were right about that radio mast. I sent a scanner van that side this morning and we picked up some strange signals. Then I sent men out looking for the same kind of signals being transmitted from the city. I think we've got something. I'm sending one of my superintendents, a technical man, to brief you at the command post.' The engineer superintendent arrived an hour later, a dark, tall, lugubrious man with an air of helplessness, who kept looking anxiously up at the sky as if he were afraid it would fall on him. 'We came here this morning,' he told me, 'we caught a strange signal from this coach on one of the ham frequencies.'

'What sort of a strange signal?' I asked, hoping for messages in the strangeness.

'An encrypted message,' replied the superintendent. 'There was a pattern to it that we could see but not break. There was nothing else we could do, so we taped what we got of it, and tried to find a similar signal in the city.'

'Did you find one?'

'We didn't. A ham thought he had found one and called us. I'm a ham enthusiast too, so we keep in touch. He called me the moment he caught the signal, passed on the frequency, and I caught it as well. It was the same kind . . .'

'If it was encrypted how do you know it was the same kind?'

'I don't know . . . You see, when you spend many years playing with these things you get a sixth sense for it. Short bursts of noise, like static, but regular . . . I'm sure it was the same kind of encryption. It's not very common around here.'

'Did you catch anyone at the other end?'

'No,' he explained apologetically, 'that was someone else's problem.' He had to get two good fixes on the direction of the transmission, from two different locations, to triangulate it accurately. They'd caught brief bursts, on which they'd got not two but three fixes. The third fix, unfortunately, had been from a completely different direction.

Were they doing it out of a car or something, I asked.

Yes, he explained, his lugubrious air replaced by a lecturer's confidence, they must have been transmitting out of a mobile radio. He'd keep on the trail, he said, until he found something, and when he did he'd come straight to me.

Yes, I said, come anytime, check back with me for anything.

Thanks, he replied with a shy smile, and now he'd like to go home for a while. He hadn't been there for a while, hadn't seen his wife for two days.

He didn't go home. The phone rang. It was Doraiswamy, for my friendly lecturer the superintendent. They spoke for six minutes in rapid-fire incomprehensible Tamil, then the superintendent hung up and came back to me, smiling happily. They were right, he explained, the terrorists had been transmitting from a car. They'd been using a high-frequency transmitter, one of those modern ones the size of a paperback novel, very expensive and very portable.

How had they caught it, I asked, they'd done it pretty fast.

Luck, explained the superintendent, sheer luck. They'd have caught the transmitter anyway if they'd had enough time but they'd caught it so fast because of a lucky break.

What kind of a break, I asked, did someone just stumble on to a car with a transmitter inside?

Something of the kind, he said. A constable going off duty had seen two men in a black Contessa car near the beach behave suspiciously. He'd seen one of the men emerge and twiddle with the dials of something like a radio. The constable had known there was an alert on for something to do with radio transmissions, and instead of going home had called his superior at his police station, who had in turn passed on the information to Doraiswamy. A quickly assembled team of policemen had gone looking for the Contessa in a jeep. The jeep had caught up with the car after an exciting ten-kilometre chase through the city. They'd got the car and the radio but not the men who'd been using it.

How did they know it was the right people, I asked. They'd got exactly the same kind of transmissions, said the superintendent, repeating his lecture on sixth senses. The patterns and the frequencies were the same. Of course, they could have been mistaken but the similarities were too strong for coincidence. Besides, the equipment in the car, expensive, American and unlicenced, and the car itself was a stolen one.

Great job, I said, and he departed, grinning.

After he went away I thought about it some more. If the FKF had money, the loss of the transmitter wouldn't mean a thing. Given time they could replace it easily. But the key factor was time. In this country you don't get to buy high-tech radio equipment across a counter. I doubted they had a backup ready, and if they didn't it would take a day or two to replace the equipment. The question then was, how

75

much did they already know? I'd set up the plan in the morning, and the committee had got the outline from Ismail and Kelkar soon after. And anyone at ICF would have been able to figure it out . . .

Dinner was served, a policeman carrying the food out as usual. More glittering trays on the tracks in a short while. Chauhan came to the command post, weary now from his meeting with D.K. Arya, his boss. He looked at me sideways, a shade of guilt in his eyes. 'You've been stood down,' he said, looking at me sideways. 'We'll have to wait another day. We're supposed to try and negotiate something.'

'I've been expecting this,' I told him, the anger beginning to break out. 'You should have told them that tonight is the best time for it, before they kill someone, before they sink themselves deeper. If they kill one hostage it becomes a very different ballgame. They're committed after that.'

'I suppose they want to find out how serious the FKF are about the deadlines,' he sighed.

'So what do they want?' I exploded. 'A body count in two digits? They've already killed one man, that poor RPF constable at the station. What more do they want?'

The fatigue in his voice when he replied cooled me off. 'I explained, Raja, I explained all that again and again. I think we're caught in a war between bureaucrats, between the home ministry who are behind the negotiations, and behind the defence ministry who are behind you . . . I don't know what else to say.'

After that we waited. Waited while the seconds ticked achingly past. I thought of the little boy, one more night in the coach for him, of his mother, another unbearable night's separation from her son. That wouldn't do. Don't get involved, said a cold voice in my head.

And the seconds trudged slowly past.

chapter four

The krait tensed, first sensing its prey through its tongue, then sighting it through weak eyes a few inches away in the moonlight. Reflexively, it prepared to strike.

At ten the door of the coach opened again and one of the terrorists appeared. It wasn't Loudspeaker, this one's voice was thinner, higher pitched, the anxiety audible. The stenographers jerked into action and the spools on the tape recorder began to rotate. 'One of the men here is a diabetic,' boomed the voice from fifty metres away, 'send three ampoules of insulin and three syringes. Make it quick. The man is unconscious.'

Chauhan leapt for the mike, his voice betraying no sign of nerves. 'We'll get the medicines out to you as soon as we can,' he said, 'it won't take long. But why don't you release the sick man? If he's diabetic and he hasn't had his shots since he left Delhi he'll be in bad shape. He should see a doctor.'

'No,' said the man, Loudspeaker No. 2, 'he stays with us.'

'All right,' said Chauhan, 'keep the man. But let me send a doctor in there. You can search the doctor before he enters your coach. You can blindfold him if you don't want him to see what's inside, in the other compartments. We'll send you an Army doctor willing to go through all that.'

Chauhan was quick, I had to grant him that much. Over the intercom I summoned the unit's duty doctor, Vijay Luthra of the AMC, from the medic's tent, while someone else spoke on another phone, calling for the medicine.

The terrorist hesitated for a while, went back into the coach, returned to agree. 'Send a doctor in,' he said, 'in underwear, carrying only the medicines and a stethoscope. We'll search him outside, blindfold him inside.'

'He might need more equipment,' said Chauhan, 'he might need to take a blood sample. Let him carry all that. You can inspect it as much as you like.'

Luthra arrived. What's up, he asked, a serious young man of twenty-seven, light-eyed and bespectacled, a bookworm to the core.

He would have to go into that coach, I told him, to treat a diabetic. Could he do that, observe what he could past the blindfold, and come back and tell me about it.

Glad to, he replied, rubbing his nose, grinning like a cat. He'd always felt left out while we went out on our jaunts, but now he was going to see the enemy face to face. Face to mask, actually—how interesting. But he needed to take some more things with him. The sick man might need a drip, he explained, if the level of sugar in his blood had

79

dropped dangerously low. Diabetics who went comatose typically suffered from damage to other systems, such as the respiratory system, so oxygen might be required.

He went fifteen minutes later, stripped down to his underwear, carrying his stethoscope and the insulin, a bottle for the blood sample and a bottle of dextrose solution, while we watched anxiously from the command post. Outside the coach, one of the lookouts stopped him, examined the syringes and ampoules and stethoscope, handed it all back, led him into the coach, and slammed the door.

Luthra emerged ten minutes later, still blindfold, waiting in the doorway while a terrorist behind undid the bandage about his eyes. He still carried the articles he'd carried into the coach except the bottle for the drip, and made his way groggily across the floodlit tracks and open ground to the command post. Through my field glasses I saw that his face was unusually grim, and there was a lump on his jaw.

When he got to the command post he was seething with sullen anger, his habitual cheer gone like mist in the desert. 'Don't let the bastards get away with this,' he told me. 'I'll come with you guys and shoot them down if you like.' He paused, swallowed, rubbed his jaw. 'They've stuffed all the hostages into four bays, except the sick man and a little boy. They've tied the kid up, gagged him . . . I was blind most of the time but I saw little bits here and there.'

'What's with the sick man?' asked Ismail.

'He'll be all right now. I got a blood sample out of him and put him on a drip. We'll have to wait for the results of the blood test before we proceed. Nothing much else I could do there, with those monsters around . . .'

'How did you get that lump on the jaw?' I asked.

'I patted the kid, that's all,' he replied, his anger flaring up again. 'Some bloody psychotic in there just clouted me on the jaw.' He brooded, then suddenly burst into a grin. 'When he hit me I fell down and rolled into the aisle and had a look at bits of the coach they wouldn't have let me see otherwise . . . They've got bombs in there, packs of plastic explosive, and the man with the detonator—I couldn't figure out what kind it was—is somewhere in the middle of the coach, in the fifth bay from the rear.'

Psycho had knocked him down, our soft-spoken, highly intelligent doctor. Psycho, sitting in the middle of the coach with the boy and the sick man and the detonator in his hands. We'd have to get to that bay first, if we went in.

If they'd wired up the bombs they wouldn't have a remote controlled detonator. If instead they'd had a remote controlled detonator with the switch in the hands of someone outside . . . That didn't bear thinking about.

I spoke to Luthra again, asking him about the radio and possible booby traps on the doors, but he hadn't had a chance to look at any of that. What he'd had was a worm's eye glance about the coach from the aisle, where he'd fallen when Psycho hit him.

A helicopter clattered high overhead, its lights blinking. The diversion. Kelkar must have arranged with the nearest air base to send a helicopter over at night to get the FKF used to the sound. Both lookouts followed the copter as

81

it moved slowly overhead, their guns raised high in a futile gesture. The coach door banged loudly open, and Loudspeaker stood silhouetted in the doorway. 'What is that aircraft doing here?' he asked.

The stenographer and the tape recorder went into action again, and Chauhan picked up the mike. 'There are several dozen helicopters in the city,' he explained, his tone steady as usual, and friendly, 'I assure you we haven't called for it. I will try to find out what it is doing here, and if this is likely to happen again I will try to get the route changed. But please understand that this could be something completely unrelated.'

The door slammed shut. That sounded convincing. I hoped achingly that Loudspeaker had swallowed the story.

The night dragged on.

The first useful thing I'd learnt about soldiering was that a substantial part of it consists of waiting for something to happen with dramatic suddenness. Soldiers everywhere are trained to wait, patiently, without wasting energy, without panic, maintaining their alertness, just staying awake. I'd developed my own methods of staying awake during training, reciting bits of poetry learnt by heart at school and never forgotten, poems by Frost and Yeats and Blake and Shakespeare, reciting them over and over again, looking for newer meanings that never failed to show up . . .

The patrol of the lookouts had taken on a pattern now. They'd become regular. The first signs of fatigue that would over the hours overwhelm them.

They met towards the centre of the coach, then split, one going clockwise around it and the other anticlockwise, to meet again on the opposite side. They walked unhurriedly, deliberately, taking their time to look around, poking among the trays sometimes, conferring when they met for anything up to a minute.

At a little before eleven there was a small commotion at the cordon, shouting and the sound of running men. I couldn't see what happened but a JCO came up to report to Ismail about it. A man had been caught trying to penetrate the cordon, he explained, a man carrying a tape recorder and a camera. There'd been a little scuffle, because the man had resisted when the men had told him to get out of there. The tape recorder had broken in the scuffle but they had the camera. The man was in the medic's tent, for treating the black eye and contusions he'd acquired during the scuffle. Could Ismail come and sort it out, or should they just call the police in.

Ismail grinned wickedly. 'You go,' he told me.

Inside the brightly lit medic's tent, smelling of mercurochrome and sweat, with a rapidly blackening eye and a bandage on his hand was a stout man with a goatee. 'This is ridiculous,' he was telling Luthra, 'the public have a right to know what's going on!'

Luthra grinned peaceably at the man, his sprightliness in place. 'Sure they do,' he said, 'they'll get to know all about it as soon as it's over, don't worry.' He looked up and saw me and his grin widened. 'Ah! The brass have arrived,' he told the man, pointing at me, 'you can ask him whatever you want.'

'Lieutenant Colonel Menon,' I told the man. 'Who are you?'

Sadanand, he said, a reporter with the Madras office of a major national daily, and what the hell did my men mean by beating him up while he was going about his business.

'There's a cordon outside,' I said quietly, 'and signs warning people off, and armed men on guard. If you choose to ignore all that you take the consequences.'

'I was outside the cordon,' he said.

I looked at the JCO who'd called me. 'He was inside the cordon, sir,' he said. 'He parked his scooter down the road and walked past and then tried to sneak in.'

'I know the home minister here,' Sadanand proclaimed loudly, 'and the one in Delhi. Your men have beaten me up and broken my tape recorder and now I'll make sure you're in hot water.'

'Show me your identification,' I told him.

He fished in his trousers pocket and brought out his Press accreditation card, and a handful of calling cards with his name and the name of the daily printed on them. Fair enough. A reporter looking for a scoop. 'Confiscate all his equipment,' I told the JCO, 'and tell the police.'

A uniformed sub-inspector arrived in minutes, two constables in tow. The reporter seemed to know the policemen, for he greeted them warmly. 'Don't worry about this man, sir,' said the sub-inspector, 'I know him very well.'

'Couldn't care less,' I said. 'Just keep him away from here until everything's over.'

'Sir, could you return his camera?' asked the policeman.

The rage came boiling up and this once I let it go. 'Get the fellow out of here!' I exploded. 'I don't give a damn whom he knows. Just get him out of here and lock him up until we leave, that's all!' Then I stalked out of the tent, to take another walk around the perimeter to try and settle seething nerves.

Went up to the hillock to have a look at the sapling. It stood my height, two inches in diameter at the base, fresh and green leaved and in its spare way beautiful. Looked down at the coach, through my field glasses. The lookouts were conferring by the coach. I could see their lips moving under the masks. One of them stood leaning against the body of the coach.

There was something odd about them.

I kept my eyes on them for all of fifteen minutes before I understood. From this angle they looked disproportionate. Their bodies were heavier than they should have been. Why?

Body armour. Bulletproof jackets, a little older than ours, bulkier, bulky enough to show, protecting their chests. We'd have to go for their heads.

It made quite a difference to the snipers. Instead of a reasonably sure chest shot they'd now have a target one third the size, or less. I must remember to tell them, I thought wearily, and walked slowly down the hillock.

Back at the command post, Venky, who had been napping, was waiting to relieve me. I went back to my tent at midnight, lay on the camp bed, unable to sleep despite the deep fatigue of eighteen straight hours worked. Got up after a while and paced the tent, six steps up, six steps down. Wondered what the police had done with that reporter. Maybe they'd let him off, especially if, as he had said, the home minister was a phone call away. God knows what he'd seen, what he'd heard. If he got on the trail seriously he would end up at ICF, knowing what we were planning to do.

I looked at the scenario, then, in growing horror. Everybody knew the plan. I'd just have to assume that.

We couldn't change the plan. We really didn't have a choice that way. All we could do was play with the diversions. We planned to go in with a helicopter flying overhead, with the fire on the hillock. If someone was feeding them information, they'd definitely know about the helicopter. I knew what to do—we'd go in without the helicopter, with just the fire to draw the lookouts away.

Yes, we'd do that. And we'd go in at any time I felt fit. We'd take everyone by surprise. Even me. That was the only way it was going to work.

I slept.

I slept through the grey dawn, until Harkishen woke me up with the usual tin mug of tea. In the pale green light coming into the tent I came awake with a foul taste on my tongue and the little boy, tied and gagged, on my mind. Went to the bathhouse for a quick wash. The snipers, relaxing after their night's vigil, were collecting outside the cookhouse, handling their rifles gently, lovingly, their limbs stiff from hours of motionless watching. I would let them sleep through the morning and take them for target practice in the afternoon at General Reddy's rifle range. Couldn't afford to have them miss those lookouts.

I wandered over to the medic's tent, to see how Luthra was doing. Found him napping in a camp bed meant for his patients, a book lying across his chest. He jerked awake when I pushed aside the flap of the tent, sat up straight, adjusted his spectacles, and smiled his uncomplicated grin. The bump on his jaw had subsided to a barely visible triangular mark. 'What do you know,' I asked, sitting down in his chair, 'about putting people to sleep?'

'For good?' he asked. 'Or only for a few hours?'

'A few hours. The hostages. Powders in their dinner or whatever, to put them soundly out for the night. I don't want them in the way if we go in.'

'Ah!' he said. 'No problem. We'll serve them dinner from our cookhouse. Make their dinner spicy to hide any taste the medicine leaves. If they don't like the taste we can always blame the cooks.'

'What medicine would you use?'

'Any one of a dozen things. Calmpose, powdered into their curry. Or Alprazolam, which is mildly anti-depressant as well . . . Give you a list, if you want.'

'No, thanks,' I said, 'I wouldn't understand it. But that's a good idea, hiding it in spices.'

His grin widened. 'Not my idea,' he said, 'stole it from Arthur Conan Doyle. Sherlock Holmes. The dog that didn't bark.'

'I forgot,' I grinned back. 'What about the kid? He might not eat the spicy stuff. Kids sometimes don't.'

'Does he get milk or anything?'

'Yes, with every meal.'

'All right, then. He can have his dose with his milk. I'll work up something special for him, poor lad.'

I returned to the command post with the sun in my eye, to organize a practice session for the snipers. We'd built them up well. Ismail had got hold of a Gurkha who was probably the best sniper I'd ever seen. He could lie motionless for hours and hours. I'd seen him do it overnight once, on an exercise, and then erupt from his position to take down a three-man team hunting him. He hadn't settled down well in the SOF because we insisted that every soldier learn at least three languages: English, Hindi and a third of his choice. No wonder Gurung had insisted on returning to his old unit. He could manage only Gorkhali and broken Hindi. To him, learning more languages was work for scholars, not soldiers, and he wasn't cut out to be a scholar.

Many other soldiers had, like Gurung, dropped out because they thought learning new languages had no part in soldiering. Even some of the ones who had remained had learnt under mild protest. But here it was paying off. At least twenty of the men here spoke Tamil, and another twenty Urdu, useful if we wanted to interrogate someone. One man, from Kerala, spoke Arabic. One strange result of all this training was that we had no jawans at all. By the time they qualified they were all Naiks or above. Ditto the officers: they had to have at least three years service before we even considered them, so the SOF had no second lieutenants. It made for a top-heavy force in conventional military terms but it was worth keeping that way given the kind of work we did.

Our snipers had never been called upon to kill a man in cold blood. I wondered how they would react. A windless, clear day, ideal conditions for snipers. They'd have a field day at the rifle range.

Breakfast was delivered to the coach at half-past-seven, by which time I'd arranged for a truck to pick up the snipers and take them to the range for a couple of hours' practice. Bread and eggs went uneventfully by, and soon more trays joined the ones gleaming in the slanting sunrays.

I thought of another session of practice at ICF. Dropped it. Decided instead to have the men off duty go for a route march.

Ismail walked in at a quarter-to-eight, carrying a newspaper: a copy of the daily that Sadanand, the reporter we'd caught the previous night, worked at. 'Did you beat up that reporter they caught?' he asked me.

'I didn't touch him,' I explained. 'The men caught him trying to break in past the cordon. They told me he resisted, especially when they took away his tape recorder and his camera.'

'That's not what he says.' He handed the paper to me, folded to highlight a little item headlined, 'Scribe assaulted at Army camp'. An innocent reporter, said the article in oblique sentences that hinted more than they said, had been grabbed at the cordon and beaten up by a gang of soldiers, who had taken away his tape recorder and expensive camera, the tools of his trade. A Lieutenant Colonel Menon of the Army had refused to intervene, and had in fact encouraged the soldiers to beat him up further. Was this any way to run a democracy?

'Doraiswamy wanted you out of here,' Ismail continued, 'he wanted all of us out of here.'

'So now what?'

He grinned. 'General Kelkar will issue a press statement saying that we're trying to find out what happened. Meanwhile it's business as usual. We can deal with the newspaper afterwards.'

At eight Chauhan picked up the mike once again. 'Calling the FKF,' he announced to the whirring tape recorder and the steno. 'What news of the sick man?'

Loudspeaker stood in the doorway. 'He is better now. He had missed several days of insulin injections, that's all.'

'Can you bring him to the door?' asked Chauhan. 'Let the doctor speak to him, to see if there've been any ill-effects that need treatment.'

'No,' replied Loudspeaker, 'he is all right. If he is not he will tell me. But no more doctors.' He must have figured out what Luthra had done at night.

The morning dragged on. The scanner vans reported no traffic from the coach or from anywhere else. They could, of course, have switched frequencies, but the scanners were watching it closely. We'd cut off the pipeline, for the time being at least, after the horses had bolted.

The trucks came and the snipers left for the range. They didn't think the practice was necessary for the shooting they'd do here but wanted to keep their hands in.

Loudspeaker came to the doorway at noon to ask for lunch. The hostages were getting back their appetites. The knockout drops would work.

At two, just after I'd finished a tasteless cold lunch in my tent, more trucks began to arrive outside the camp, all armoured, all heavily guarded.

The money had come. Policemen unloaded the boxes full of gold and currency notes, stacked them by the command post, leaving the growing stacks in the care of half-a-dozen policemen.

Chauhan took up his loudspeaker once again. 'Calling the FKF,' he announced, the tapes rolling. 'Your money has arrived. How do we deliver it to you in the coach?'

Loudspeaker appeared in the doorway. I was beginning to recognize him, his posture and his gestures. 'How is it packed?' he asked.

'It's in twenty-two strongboxes,' replied Chauhan, 'five for the gold, the rest for the other currencies, roughly equivalent amounts in US dollars, German marks, Swiss francs and sterling.'

'Have one man bring the boxes over one by one. I will watch from here, with one of my colleagues and one of our guests in this doorway. One of my men will be watching from a window. If you fail to follow instructions, we will start shooting.' Psycho, standing beside a terrified hostage with that ugly rifle to his head.

Loudspeaker disappeared into the coach, emerging a moment later. 'We will name the man to bring in the money. Let it be Colonel Qureishi of your Special

Operations Force. That is all your SOF is fit for: carrying baggage. And make sure he wears only his underwear.'

I didn't respond to the barb, but the depth of his knowledge was like a bucket of cold water on the head. How had he known that the SOF was here? Not that the SOF is a secret unit, but it does keep a very low profile. And how did he know that Ismail was here? Did that newspaper report have anything to do with it? Ismail was just a rather obscure officer in a low-key unit.

But Ismail wasn't around. He'd just gone off to his tent for a nap and I didn't want to disturb him. 'Tell them Ismail's not here,' I told Chauhan. 'Tell them I can do it if necessary.'

'Colonel Qureishi is not available now,' said Chauhan. 'We have here Lieutenant Colonel Menon, his deputy.'

'All right,' said Loudspeaker, 'send Colonel Menon, then.'

Chauhan beside me assented. 'All right,' he said, 'Colonel Menon will be with you in the next fifteen minutes with the first box of gold.'

Behind the command post, by the pile of strongboxes, I stripped down to my underwear, feeling vaguely foolish but otherwise unconcerned. I hefted the first box; it must have weighed about twenty kilos, maybe a little more, made of padded metal painted black, like a small safe. It had a folding handle on either side, that pulled out for easy carrying. The lock was in front, built into the box itself, an intricately cut key shining in the keyhole. The box must have weighed close on five kilos empty, and the contents of this one alone were worth more than I would earn in a lifetime in the Army.

I stepped out into the sun, sweating from the heat on my skin, the box heavy in my hands, and began the long, slow walk to the coach, stepping carefully on bare feet to avoid thornbushes. Got to the rails, breathing a little heavily, twenty seconds later. Stepped over the rails and on to the sleepers, three times, until I was within three feet of the coach, the closest I'd ever been to it yet. Looked up into the eyes of Loudspeaker, and saw behind him a short, dark-skinned hostage in blue underwear, sweat streaming down his face, looking as if he'd burst into tears any moment now.

Psycho wasn't by a window, he stood right there, next to the hostage, gun in hand. As Loudspeaker moved back to make room for me to dump the strongbox on the coach floor, I saw the six fingers on Psycho's hand, had a glimpse of the red hair under his mask. I couldn't see his face but there was an unmistakable gleam in his eyes. Psycho was enjoying himself.

The three of them moved back, Loudspeaker to my left, back flat against the wall behind him and his gun aimed with unsettling steadiness at my face, the hostage in front of him and to a side, and behind the two of them, Psycho.

This close up, Loudspeaker had shuttered eyes. I could see what Sandhya had meant. You couldn't tell what he was thinking. The rest of him was black, except his big hands and a strip of suntanned neck between the bottom of his mask and the collar of his shirt. 'Leave the box here,' he said, pointing at the space he'd left, the voice behind the threatening mask neutral, its power restrained.

I heaved the box up, careful not to push it in far enough to touch any of them. 'Where's the key?' he asked.

'In the keyhole,' I said, pointing, 'you can see the head sticking out.'

'Unlock the box. Pull the lid wide open. Take out the gold. Slowly. Do nothing fast.'

The key, shiny and massive, had tilted slightly out of position. I fitted it back in, and it turned easily. I tugged at the lid, which refused to open. Dammit, I thought, what's this. Gave the key another turn, and then the lid came easily open. There, gleaming gentle yellow, was the gold, thirty-two half-kilo ingots stacked at the bottom. They looked surprisingly small.

'Lift those ingots out, one by one,' said Loudspeaker, 'stack them next to the box on the floor in two straight stacks.'

I did so, the two gleaming stacks growing until I'd got all of them on the floor, sixteen to a stack. Loudspeaker stepped forward, peered into the box, said, 'All right. Put the ingots back in, close the lid, slowly, no noise.'

When I had got the lid shut, Psycho came forward, gripped in his six-fingered hand one of the handles at the sides of the box, and dragged it jerkily away while Loudspeaker covered the hostage and me with his AK-47. Psycho returned in a moment with the box empty. 'Pick up the box and take it back,' ordered Loudspeaker. I repeated the process with all five boxes of gold, laying out in stacks the sixteen kilos of ingots in each, putting them back in after Loudspeaker inspected the boxes, waiting for Psycho to drag the box away, and carrying the empty box back, the sun burning on my back all the while. The hostage looked dumbly on, misery in his eyes. I wished I could do something to comfort him.

After the gold was done I carried the currencies to the coach, seventeen more trips with a heavy strongbox, laying out the bundles of currency in stacks, and then waiting while Psycho put it all away inside the coach before carrying the empty strongbox back. 'More money than you'll ever see again, Menon,' said Loudspeaker as Psycho dragged away the last of the boxes. 'Want to join us? You'll be rich.'

I looked up at him, forced a smile. 'No thanks,' I said, 'I wouldn't like to have someone like me chasing me for the rest of my life.'

For a moment the shutters opened and amusement gleamed in his eyes. 'You overrate yourself, Colonel,' he said, 'I'll be quite safe from you.'

Psycho returned with the empty box, and I reached out for it. I saw above me the imploring eyes of the hostage. 'Don't worry,' I told him reassuringly, 'you'll be out of here in no time.'

The utter unbridled ferocity of Psycho's reaction to that harmless little sentence took me completely by surprise. He stepped out to the edge of the floor and swung his booted foot in a kick to my head that would have killed me if I hadn't seen it coming and rolled with it. As it was, the kick knocked me off my feet and I dropped the box with a clatter on the rails, and fell sprawling over it.

The pain followed a moment later, a gigantic hammer blow that left a coppery taste in the back of my mouth, a ringing in my ears. I sat gingerly up, shook my head to clear it, felt the spot where the kick had landed, found my hand bloody.

I was too tired to react. After a while I picked myself up and then the strongbox, and walked slowly back to the command post. It was easy to imagine Loudspeaker telling Psycho to behave as he had. Knock the bastard down, humiliate him, kick the spirit out of him so he won't be able to fight.

The Krait had picked his men well.

At the medic's tent beside the command post, Luthra, his grin now in abeyance, cleaned up and put three stitches in the cut in the side of my head, an inch above my left ear. 'You're not going to find a helmet very comfortable for a few days,' he said as he cut a strip of plaster to stick on the stitches. 'You've been working hard in the sun. I suggest you get to bed and stay there for a long time.'

I shook my head, and that wasn't such a good idea, for the spike of pain it sent through my temple almost made me groan, making me wish for sleep in a painkiller-induced haze. Thought then of the little boy, of his mother's green eyes . . . 'After this operation,' I told Luthra. 'After this I'll put myself in your hands, but you've got to keep me going until then.'

'That would be most unwise, sir,' he said, shaking his head. 'You might be concussed. You'll have trouble focusing your eyes. A blow to the head you can't ignore.'

'After this,' I said with finality, standing unsteadily up. 'In the meanwhile, give me something to keep me on my feet.'

He handed me two dusty white tablets from a brown glass bottle that didn't have a label. 'Have one of these now,' he said, 'the next after a couple of hours. If it gets worse, tell me, I'll give you more.' He paused for a moment, then blurted, 'Listen, sir, you must be nuts.'

I turned and grinned at him. 'You have to be a nut to take on something like that,' I said, pointing in the direction of the coach, and walked painfully out to the command post.

In the slanting rays of the cooling sun I looked at my watch. Nearly 1600. The transfer had taken me nearly a couple of hours, and my muscles sagged with fatigue. The command post was buzzing with activity, crammed now with the staff of all the members of the committee, who had arrived to watch the fun as we reached a deadline. The last of the members of the committee, the man from the home ministry, had arrived when I was midway through carrying out the strongboxes.

Luthra's pills began to take effect. The stabbing pains subsided to a steady throbbing except when I walked.

The main tent was in disarray. Parked firmly inside were the two major generals and their aides, Doraiswamy and his aides, and the other committee members and their staffs. Kelkar's aide elbowed a way through the hive for the General when he saw me. 'How's the head?' he asked, 'We saw what happened. You should stand down now.'

'No, sir,' I replied. 'Unless you actually take me off this I'll stay on. I'll sleep for a week after this, though.'

'Fine,' he said, 'but if you mess this up I'll have you crucified. Right?'

'Right, sir,' I said, 'I'll do my best.'

Chauhan's voice rose above the hubbub inside the tent, clearly audible outside, as he tried to bring some order to the committee. 'Give them a couple of hours to count the money,' he was telling the others, 'we'll speak to them after that, when they know we've delivered the money right, when we can build some credibility. If we talk to them now they'll feel we're pushing them.'

Throb throb throb went my head. Concentrate on something else, anything. Green eyes.

I didn't fit in here. I went out to the camp. My head went stab stab stab in time with my steps. The off-duty troops were taking it easy. For the bulk of them, after the rigours of training, this operation was a bit of luxury. Hot food, regular shifts, no long daily runs in full combat gear, comfortable tents to sleep in. They were scattered all over the ground, squatting in little groups, chatting in quiet voices, the washing hanging on lines at one end in strange contrast to the tension at the command post. I could see at least four card games in progress, the nearest of which halted as soon as the players noticed me and stood up, hands at their sides, faintly apologetic. 'Keep going,' I told them, 'just checking if you're all right.'

A short, barrel-chested Tamilian Naik with a huge toothbrush ad grin answered for the lot of them in slow Tamil which he knew I understood patchily. 'This is like a holiday, sir,' he said. 'I wish we had more operations like this.'

I knew his statement was accurate. This was the closest they'd ever been to urban warfare. They'd been trained for exhausting combat situations in wartime, not small peacetime operations in which there was a small, clearly defined danger zone and safety outside it. The training had been more rigorous than the operation itself.

A few more of the senior JCOs and NCOs came wandering by to where I stood, looking at the strip of plaster on my head. One of them, a B platoon man who had been through the trials with me, finally picked up the nerve to ask, 'Will you come with us, sir, with that injury?'

'Yes,' I said, working up a grin, and moving away. 'Only three stitches. Nothing serious.' As I moved out I heard the group disperse, the buzz of conversation rising with the sound of occasional laughter. Showing them it was business as usual regardless of cracks on the head would go a long way towards keeping morale up.

Those stabs were losing their fire. The dusty white pills worked.

At a quarter-past-five Chauhan took up the mike once again, tense now because the committee was breathing grumpily down his neck. 'Calling the FKF,' he announced, 'I hope you have counted the money and found it satisfactory.'

Loudspeaker appeared in the doorway a few seconds later. He looked tired, I thought. 'We have counted the money,' he said, 'but we still don't know if you've treated

99

the notes with chemicals that will stand out. We can't do that here.'

'Take your time with the checks,' said Chauhan, 'there is no hurry at all.'

'What about my colleagues?' asked Loudspeaker. 'I hope you remember that the deadline is 1800 today.'

'Yes,' said Chauhan, 'we had some problems getting them all here together.'

In the doorway I saw Loudspeaker stiffen, saw his gun come up, all the fatigue in his bearing gone. 'What problem?' he asked, his voice laden with suspicion despite the electronics.

'As you know, the men are scattered all over the state,' Chauhan tried to explain. 'We haven't been able to get all of them together yet because . . .'

'Enough!' roared Loudspeaker, his voice rolling across the plain like thunder. 'The deadline stands, policeman. Get them here by 1800 or the reprisals start.'

'We need some more time,' pleaded Chauhan, 'give us twelve more hours. Just twelve more hours. Getting that many people out of prison and gathered together takes that much time. And I'm not asking for all that much, just twelve hours.'

Loudspeaker's voice rang out over the silent plain with such finality I knew he hadn't the least intention of giving us any more time. He'd probably hand the hostages over to Psycho one by one after the deadline passed. We should have gone in last night, I thought, with the sour taste of regret in my mouth. 'Don't play the fool with us,'

Loudspeaker shouted, the fury in his voice in stark contrast with his habitual coolness. 'The schedule holds. The first hostage will die at 1800.' He shut the door and disappeared inside, to return in a few seconds, pushing in front of him a pathetic, underwear-clad hostage. 'This will be the first man to go. He will speak to you now.' He handed the mike over to the hostage.

The hostage cleared his throat a couple of times, and when he spoke his voice came out painfully high-pitched. 'I am Rakesh Aggarwal,' he said simply. 'These people say that they will kill me if you do not bring their friends here by six o'clock.' He paused, and through my field glasses I saw him swallow hard. 'I am thirty-six years old. I have a wife and one young son. I do not want to die now. Please have their people here by six. Please let me live.'

Loudspeaker grabbed the mike from the hostage. 'This is the man we will shoot at 1800 if my comrades are not here by then.'

Chauhan's chief, Arya, rose in his chair and grabbed the mike out of Chauhan's hands. 'I am Arya, director of the CBI,' he announced, 'I do not speak lightly. We need more time to bring your colleagues here. Most are already on their way to Delhi. Some more are in Srinagar, where the weather is too bad for air traffic. We have no control over the weather. Please understand. Give us time.'

'Don't lie to me, Arya,' screamed Loudspeaker, 'I have a radio here. I know the weather in Srinagar was not too bad for aircraft to fly in and out. This man dies at six if my friends are not here by then! And don't call us again except to tell us they're in Madras!'

Arya continued to plead but Loudspeaker was gone from the doorway. That lie about the weather in Srinagar had destroyed the foundation Chauhan had built so painstakingly.

But now the field had changed. To all of us, soldiers and policemen and civil servants, the hostages were no longer unknown entities hidden in the carriage. Aggarwal had changed all that. They were all men of flesh and blood, who did not want to die. And one small boy. The horror had gotten through to the committee.

The minutes dragged slowly by in helpless silence. The shadows on the plain lengthened, the ground bathed in the red glow of the setting sun. Arya slumped back in his chair, his aura of power gone. No one spoke a word.

Kelkar and Ismail walked out of the tent to my side. 'Do you think they'll start shooting?' Kelkar asked.

'Yes,' I replied, 'I've had a taste of their intentions, and so has Luthra. There's a man in there who's psychotic. I think he'll be the first executioner.'

'The man with the six fingers?' asked Ismail. 'The one your lady friend spoke of so violently? I don't think so. They wouldn't want to show the world the face of their resident madman. It could be their leader who does it.'

The breeze drifted slowly across the plain, raising small eddies of dust that settled in brown patches on our clothes and hair. 'They built their plans around that man,' I said. 'He's the catalyst, the spark that'll light the fire. If the others are too soft, Psycho there will start the killing, and then they'll all be equally committed.'

The FKF didn't respond to pleas, measured or frantic, from Chauhan and Arya. Six o'clock crawled gloomily in with the dusk. The door of the coach opened, and in the doorway stood Loudspeaker. He stood aside then, and the hostage, Aggarwal, was pushed out front. Behind Aggarwal stood Psycho, hair showing in the fading light, rifle ready and aimed. One last shove, and Aggarwal almost fell out of the coach on to the ground between the tracks. He stumbled, then scrambled on to his knees, raising his hands in supplication, but Psycho reached down from the coach and kicked at his head.

In that moment, in perhaps the last minute of his life, Aggarwal tapped unknown wells of courage, and instead of retreating, as he had done all along, found the strength to fight back. He didn't run, or duck, grabbing instead at Psycho's outthrust leg, and pulling hard. Psycho, completely unprepared and already off balance from the kick, skidded off the edge of the coach floor, bumped downwards past the steps under the doorway, and landed on the ground facing Aggarwal, his gun dropping beside him.

Aggarwal ran. While Psycho sat stunned Aggarwal turned and sprinted away as fast as he could on spindly legs, in the direction of the apparent safety of the command post. If he had instead run to the end of the coach and along the tracks, out of the line of fire of the terrorists, he might have saved himself, but this way he had no chance. Psycho, still sitting where he had fallen, picked up his gun, let Aggarwal cross two sets of tracks, then shot him in the leg. Aggarwal fell sprawling on the tracks, then scrambled back to his feet. With a short burst that echoed over the plain, Psycho cut him down where he stood. As the echoes died I heard one of the men in the command post moan. Another ran out and was violently sick. I watched, leaden hearted, holding the bile down in my throat.

I had seen death in Siachen, when Pakistanis across the glacier had cut my buddy down as we sheltered from a snowstorm in the lee of a small hillock. I'd waited until dawn for the storm to clear, to find him dead. With much effort and more grief I'd carried him back to the outpost, but the shock I'd felt then was nothing to this.

Loudspeaker's voice ringing across the tracks broke into my reverie. 'Colonel Menon, come and collect the body,' he said. 'Come alone.' He added, with a touch of macabre humour, 'And this time mind your head.'

Three minutes later, stripped down once again, my head now a solid blob of stabbing pain, I picked my way along the ground, past two sets of tracks, in the glare of the floodlights to where Aggarwal's body lay. I felt his pulse, felt none. He'd been hit once in the leg—that first shot Psycho fired—and at least eight times in the body. I pulled his arms to his side, ignored his lolling head, and with a heave got him on my shoulder in a fireman's lift, feeling the sticky, gritty mixture on his skin of blood and sweat and mud, smelling the stench of fear and blood and two days of dirt, and carried him to the medic's tent where Luthra waited. I dressed again while an ambulance took the body to the police morgue in the city, where it would be put through a post-mortem.

In the camp behind the command post the men fidgeted. The levity was gone, the card games were over. Every man in the camp had seen Aggarwal killed, and it shocked and frightened and angered them, hardened though they were.

I found General Kelkar beside me, his face drawn and grim. 'You go in tonight,' he said, 'we don't wait any more.' He paused for a while, then continued, 'I didn't tell the committee anything more. I just told them we were going in and if they didn't like it they could talk to the chief or the defence minister. They won't spare us if you fail.'

chapter five

The predator came without warning, at the height of the krait's bloodlust. The krait sensed the mongoose almost too late, retreating with a hiss at the last moment into a crack in the earth, by the roots of an old teak.

Towards eight a cool wind sprang up from the mountain in the west, bringing relief from the heat and a cover of heavy cloud. A helicopter flew over again, the lookouts now not bothering even to look at it. B platoon took over the alert at eight after the helicopter left. They would be the ones most likely to go in tonight. I swallowed a dusty pill in my tent and went out to brief them on the attack, just before they went on alert.

They were all good marksmen, comfortable with guns, as only long practice and good eyes and steady hands could make them. We briefed them on identifying and bringing down the terrorists—anyone wearing a mask and a black uniform, carrying a weapon inside the coach, anyone carrying a box with wires leading out of it—without hitting their colleagues breaking in through the window opposite. The first priority was the man with the detonator. Everything else was secondary.

I told them about Psycho, about his long red hair and the sixth finger on his hand. Anyone like that must be neutralized first, I explained, the man is mad. He will press that detonator button with pleasure, I told them, so just concentrate on bringing him down.

No one was to go in until all the terrorists were down, before Ismail or I gave the all clear. Everyone was to stay clear of the doors until they were checked out by an engineer officer who understood bombs and booby traps.

Ismail and I went through the operational details once again with the JCOs who would be seconds-in-command of the four teams. Ismail, Venky, Mahi—Maheshwar Rao, the platoon commander—and myself would lead in. The snipers, their activity much more restricted, were briefed separately as they came on duty, told to lie in wait, and to make sure of a kill with the first shot. Last of all we briefed the team that was to create the diversion, by lighting a fire atop the hillock.

On this first mission of the SOF, Kelkar himself would coordinate with us on walkie-talkies, his position on one of the observation platforms overlooking the coach. His call sign on the walkie-talkies was Scabbard, the sniper team's Rapiers one to four, the attack team's Broadsword one to four, and of the team to set up the fire, Firefighter.

Dinner was served, garnished with Luthra's chemicals. I hoped they would work.

The throbbing in my head increased a few notches. I went to Luthra's tent for more supplies of white pills. He gave me two, garnished with advice—don't have too many of them—and a warning—don't blame me if you black out in the middle of your operation.

Towards nine it began to drizzle. I put on my raincoat and took another round of the cordon and of the snipers perched atop the platforms. As I left the last of the platforms a streak of lightning lit the landscape a flashing blue-green and a huge thunderclap burst out and then the rain came down really hard.

Perfect time to go for it. Catch the bastards off balance. Forget the helicopter.

I ran for the command post, where Kelkar and Ismail sat hunkered down, dismally watching the water flow by the side of the tracks. I ducked into the tent, water streaming off my raincoat on to the earth floor. 'We should go in now,' I said, as another thunderclap followed a streak of lightning in the east.

Kelkar straightened up in his chair and looked out at the coach with unseeing eyes in unnerving silence, while I waited the leaden seconds out. The rain beat a steady tattoo on the tent roof. The wind died except for little gusts, and visibility was under 200 metres in the swirling gusts. Out by the coach I could see the lookouts, fuzzy in the rain, walking together, cheered by the welcome cool that came with the rain. The snipers would still see well enough to bring down their targets, and in every other way the rain was a blessing. 'What about the helicopter to cover the noise?' asked Ismail.

'With the rain and the thunder and everything who needs a cover for sound?' I said. 'We can even play with the lighting system if we want. We can blame it on the storm.'

'No fingering the lights,' said Ismail, 'it'll get them touchy.'

'We'll go in,' said Kelkar, standing up. 'Right now.'

'One thing more, sir,' I said. 'We need to talk to the snipers. We'd told them earlier to play safe and go for the bodies of their targets, chest shots. We should change that. Let them go for head shots.'

'Why?' asked Kelkar.

'I think they're wearing body armour.'

'I don't think so,' said Ismail. 'Chest shots are surer.'

'Not at this range,' I said. 'A football at sixty metres is a piece of cake for the snipers. Even in the rain and the wind.'

'Yes,' said Ismail, but he didn't sound too happy.

Kelkar didn't hesitate. 'Heads it is, gentlemen,' he said, and we sent a JCO off to each of the sniper platforms to tell them. The snipers crouched lower, steadying their rifles. The squads assembled in the rain, swinging their hammers. And the diversion team took off for the base of the hillock. They would go up the hillock at Kelkar's command, use a small improvised bomb to light up the small sapling on top—a bomb with a delayed fuse so they could get off the top before it went off—and get back to the camp. Sapper and medic teams waiting by the command post would move only after Ismail gave Kelkar the all clear.

My head throbbed.

In the rain I sat wishing for courage, the courage to do what had to be done. I have the usual ration of it, no more. The training and the experience had removed most of the dread but now it returned in force. The little boy on the coach, and his mother. I'd never had such a big stake in a raid. I hoped the fear didn't show, hoped with all my heart that my cowardice would disappear.

We were ready at 2155, my JCO second-in-command having inspected the men, checking out weapons, clothing, equipment—the hammers, in this case. He crouched beside me, teeth gleaming in a smile, swinging his hammer in his hand, his dark bulk a large, reassuring presence in the rain. 'Ready to go,' he whispered.

'Broadsword Two to Scabbard. Ready to go,' I said into my walkie-talkie. Over the next few seconds, the remaining Broadswords called in, then the Rapiers, and last of all the Firefighters. I could picture Kelkar, concentrating on his walkie-talkie, crossing each of the teams that reported ready off a mental checklist. Moments after the last team reported in, Kelkar's voice came curtly on, saying, 'Scabbard to Firefighter, go go go!'

Seconds later, just after a lightning burst, at 2159 by my watch, the sapling at the top of the hillock now behind me burst into flame. One of the lookouts saw it, called the other, and we saw them come twenty-five metres away from the coach in the direction of the fire to get a closer look.

The lookouts thought the fire was because of the lightning! As they stood there watching the little flames die quickly under the rain, over the walkie-talkie came Kelkar's voice for the second time that night. 'Scabbard to Rapier teams, go go go!'

The snipers, with the butts of their Lee-Enfields cuddled against their cheeks, must have been following the lookouts. Less than two seconds after Kelkar's signal, the lookouts dropped silently, the silenced Lee-Enfields unnoticed in the rain, their accuracy unaffected by the rain that now swept down in great sheets.

I nearly missed our signal in the throbbing of my head. Ahead and sixty metres away the coach had a misty aura of raindrops about it. I heard Kelkar say, 'Scabbard to Broadsword teams, go go go!' but didn't realize it was for us until the JCO nudged me in the back.

In the dark we rose from our crouching positions and through the splashing rain squelched wetly into the glare of the floodlights, running out of the darkness as fast as we could, picking our way carefully along the centre of the depression between tracks. The body of one of the lookouts was in the way and I hopped soggily over him. The hours of practice took over as we moved steadily out to the still silent coach, hopefully unseen, and the lead men took their positions against the bottom of the coach walls.

We nearly lost it on those stones. The rains had made the layer of small stones appallingly slippery, and the men took almost unendurable extra seconds finding their footing on the unsteady mass—I found during the reviews that it took four seconds—but eventually they did. I put my hands on the shoulders of my leg-up man and heaved, pushing myself up alongside the opaque black window. Three other pairs of men took up their positions, behind me, and four pairs ahead. I gripped my hammer firmly by its handle and swung it as hard as I could at the safety glass in the window. It went clean through. The glass cracked and whitened at the edges of the hole the hammer made. Too small. I swung it once again, the second time bursting most of the cracked glass out of the window, leaving one large hole surrounded by veined glass that would fall out at a touch. All around me was the thud of hammers on glass, the clink of falling splinters. I dropped the hammer, lifted the muzzle of my gun still in its sling, and poked it through the foot-wide hole in the window.

Inside was Psycho. In the beam of the miner's lamp on my helmet I saw him sitting in a seat by the far window, mask off. He was turning around to face Venky, who broke in there just ahead of me, when I shot him in the back. The bullet threw him against the window but he came right off it, reaching for something on a berth close by, just out of reach of his six clutching fingers. A little box, with wires leading out of it. The detonator.

Without conscious aim I shot him again and again, the two bullets flinging him away from the box, and then Venky shot him from behind, turning him around. We had to get him off that little box.

I broke my own orders that day. I swept the rest of the glass out of the window with my gun butt, scrambled on

112

my buddy's head, and was inside the coach, boots crunching on the bits of glass, firing again, before Psycho got back on his feet. I hit him once but this time he had his rifle up and knocked me down with a three-round burst in the chest before Venky shot him down again.

I had dropped my gun but when I fell the detonator was within reach. With a desperate tug at the wires I ripped it right off and flung it across the compartment as Psycho, now unarmed, came swarming at my face, going for the head. He must have recognized me, and decided to try and get me in the same place he'd hit me earlier.

I didn't wait for him. Instead, I went for him low, grabbing him by the legs and lifting him right off the ground and then throwing him backwards on to the floor, winding him. Jumped on his chest, kicked him on the head, delivering poetic justice. Then picked him up by the collar and thumped his head against the hard corner of an upper berth, the anger billowing redly up my chest.

When I let him go he came staggering back at me. And then he collapsed in my arms, limp as a dead fish, his weight forcing me back and down.

Ismail had shot him in the head. As I raised my eyes to see what had happened I saw his eyes shining under his helmet. For a brief, elusive moment there was an expression in them that I found threatening . . . I was seeing things, it was just a trick of the light. Also breaking orders, Ismail had burst in next door, found a sleeping terrorist, finished him off, and had come across to investigate the prolonged series of shots in the compartment.

113

All along the coach we could now hear more glass being broken as the rest of the men clambered in through the windows. Ismail raised his walkie-talkie and spoke clearly into it, 'Broadsword one to Scabbard. All hostiles down, repeat all hostiles down. The coach is secure. Bring in the medics.'

A great wave of relief engulfed me. I dropped Psycho's body, straightened up, found my head throbbing, knees shaking. Felt a wetness about the head. That cut had started bleeding again. I took off my helmet and sat on a berth. Out of the corners of my eyes I saw a strange shape on the upper berth facing me. Stood up and looked, and found curled up there, gagged with a strip of plaster across his mouth, wrists and ankles tied, eyes shut in restless sleep, a thin little boy. Reached out for him, brought him down, sat down to cut the ropes at his wrists.

He came awake when I was midway through, looking expressionlessly up at me through sleepy, large eyes, his hair tousled, a lock sticking spikily up from his forehead. 'It's all right, son,' I said, 'I've come to take you home to Mama.' He lifted up his now freed arms, put them around my neck, tucked his head under my chin, and went back to sleep.

In the bluish glow of the fluorescent lamps in the coach I tried to take stock. I tried several times to hand the youngster to someone else, but each time I did that he woke up and clung like a limpet, until Ismail told me, 'Sit down, Raja, we're leaving you holding the baby!'

114

From outside came the roar of engines and the whoop-whoop of sirens on ambulances preparing to tear the wounded to hospital, and through the broken glass of the windows I saw the glare of their headlights approaching the command post and the medic's tent.

The JCOs reported. They had checked all doors. Connected to the handles of the three unused ones by tripwires were improvised anti-personnel mines, rather like the Claymore mines the Army uses. The doors fore and aft, connecting doors with other coaches, were clear.

Use the connecting doors to evacuate the coach, Ismail said, let the medical teams all go there. Carry off the hostages on stretchers regardless of what their condition is. Each of them goes to Luthra for a quick check before being handed over to the police.

Reports kept coming in a steady stream, delivered by men with light hearts and serious faces, all floating high on sudden, incredible success. The flush of adrenaline would keep them awake the rest of the night.

There had been six terrorists in the coach. Five, including Psycho and Loudspeaker, were dead. The sixth had been shot thrice in the pelvis and would be taken to hospital as soon as possible.

The hostages were all safe. Three had been cut by flying glass. One had a broken bone in his hand where a heavyset commando had stepped. Another two had bruises from bumps in the dark. The rest were unscathed. All were being checked out by Luthra. Their next of kin had been notified, and they would soon be transferred to a civilian hospital.

The young hostage's mother had been informed that her son was alive and well, and told to collect him at the command post.

The commandos were all unhurt. No casualties.

The terrorists had been prepared for a stay of a week, judging from the amount of water and food they had stocked. And there were five kilos of Semtex in a suitcase in the bay they had used as a storeroom.

The gold and the money had been found and were being transferred to the command post. The radios worked. We would take them along, and hand them over to the signals to figure out.

The sappers were looking at the bombs in the doorways.

The cleaning up had begun, and it would go on for a while. My head throbbed abominably now. The men would manage quite well on their own. 'I'm off to the medic,' I told Ismail.

'Go ahead,' he said. 'Take your time. And the boy.'

'Thanks,' I said, and walked away down the aisle.

I leapt off the coach floor on to the tracks, landing on unsteady knees in the drizzle, and set off towards the medic's tent. Outside stood a growing knot of men dressed in ill-fitting clothes, some with towels wrapped around their waists. The hostages had no clothes, and had borrowed some from my men. The fatter ones hadn't found trousers that fit, and had had to make do with towels. Some were already asking about their baggage still on the train, the questions a sure sign of returning normalcy.

Luthra, in the middle of examining a hostage, turned to me and said, 'Could you wait until I finish with these guys, sir? It'll only take five minutes.'

'Sure,' I said. 'But give me something to get the plaster off this kid's mouth.'

'Sorry, I forgot,' he said, and tossed me a bottle of fluid.

I rubbed the liquid in the bottle into the skin about the boy's mouth with a bit of cotton, then began gently to peel the plaster off. He woke up then, large eyes blinking at the unfamiliar tent, the uniformed men passing by. 'Does it hurt when I pull at that plaster?' I asked.

He shook his head without making a sound, and I peeled the whole thing slowly off. 'Want some milk?' I asked.

He nodded, still stubbornly silent. A nursing assistant found me some milk in the cookhouse and brought it to me. The boy drank it quickly while I changed out of my clammy body armour and combat fatigues, then curled up again to sleep. Luthra came over, grimaced over the burst stitches in my head, replaced them, the boy still in my lap.

I went to my tent and lay on my camp bed, the boy atop me. I felt a warmth along my midriff and found the boy had, in his sleep, wet his pants. I took them off, wrapped a towel from my kit about his waist.

A soldier came to say the lady had come to collect her son, and was waiting at the barricade. I shook him awake, told him we were going to his mum, and set off in the drizzle under a borrowed umbrella.

They hadn't let her into the camp. I saw her at the barricade, standing by the sentries, a police jeep waiting, a

117

halo of light around her in the drizzle. She saw us fifteen metres away and came running, getting damp in the slight drizzle. She took her son wordlessly from me in the near dark and he wrapped his arms and legs around her and hung on for dear life. Both wrapped up in each other, ignoring the drizzle. One of the SOF guards, who had followed her, came to lead her back to the jeep.

In my watch it was almost midnight. The end of the year was only thirty minutes away. I ignored my growing urges and said to her, 'Happy New Year!' Then turned around, and headed back to my tent in the rain.

There I found another message, from the hospital where they'd taken the wounded terrorist. He was dead, from haemorrhage and shock, when he arrived. Our last link with the Krait was gone.

chapter six

The krait had withdrawn almost unhurt from its first encounter with its enemy. It retreated into a crack in the pile of brick and rubble, invisible in the dark, safe from the predator, safe from all except its own kind.

Nothing like a thorough debriefing to get your spirits down.

My new year had danced in unnoticed. The ache in my head had become unbearable so I finally swallowed Luthra's dusty white tablet, which brought sleep immediately. I awoke in the orangey daylight after dawn, to the sounds of the unit preparing to leave. I stumbled out of bed, found Harkishen waiting by the flap of the tent. Drank the tea he brought, then went to the bathhouse to find half the tents down and the rest on the way down, the plain returning slowly to normal.

On the tracks the coach stood suddenly forlorn in the bright morning sunshine, its windows gaping now, having been cleared of broken glass during the night. The rain had washed the air clean and it smelt incredibly fresh as I stood there watching the men prepare to leave for home.

Ismail and Venky had prepared the company for the trip back to Delhi. We sneaked through the city along separate routes to Avadi Air Force Base, where our transports were waiting. I faked smiles at every holding-the-baby joke tossed at me, held my peace, and ignored the aches in my chest and head.

The debriefing took three long, grey days, during which everyone on the operation was confined to quarters. I did nothing but sleep—thanks to more doses of dusty white tablets—or talk in the company of the two Intelligence officers, a fat, greying lieutenant colonel with a handlebar moustache and a young, nervous captain, who had come to debrief us.

They peppered us with questions and listened with blank, unsettling neutrality when I spoke of tactics and explosives. They sat up when I told them of the windows, and what had made me choose to break in through them.

The captain fidgeted when I spoke of the Krait and his methods, while the colonel just yawned and fingered his moustache. When I mentioned the Krait for the third time, the colonel tapped his pencil on the table and said, 'Can we leave that for the time being, old boy, and get back to work instead?'

'But that's the most important thing to tell you!' I persisted. 'Sure it is, old boy,' said the colonel, 'psychological profiles and whatnot. Why don't you prepare a separate report about it, and send it along to us in due course?'

They ignored the possibility of a leak. The radio mast? To keep in touch with the outside world. They had someone outside feeding them information, not necessarily a leak.

I held my peace for the duration of the debriefing, as did Ismail. On Friday the Intelligence men went away, lifting the security clampdown as they left.

The defence minister called personally, to speak to General Kelkar, to Ismail and to myself. Small pats on the back. I successfully concealed my detestation of the man who was more concerned with purchases of equipment from West European suppliers than with the effectiveness of the Army.

Of all the soldiers on the operation, the most seriously affected were the snipers, who had had to shoot down two men in cold blood. In peacetime it eats into a soldier's mind to have to do such a thing, even when the targets are terrorists and murderers. We hadn't yet learnt to handle the bouts of depression that followed the shootings, and the best we could do was make sure that the snipers' buddies stayed with them for at least three days after the shooting, the length of the debriefing. I spent time with them immediately after the debriefing, found them depressed but under control, left them to deal with their ghosts after telling them they'd done exactly the right thing.

I got two letters in the mail that day, one from the uncle who had been my legal guardian after my parents died, the other from Jayanti, my soon-to-be-ex wife. Both were about the divorce.

How could I drag the family's name in the mud by taking a divorce, demanded Uncle. I was to visit him at once in my hometown in Kerala and afterwards sort things out with my wife.

Did I now see that divorce was the only sensible thing to do, asked Jayanti in her letter, and wasn't it obvious.

I did what I like to do when I'm upset. I tinkered with my bike. I had a Norton 500 single-cylinder machine nearly my own age, bought eight years ago for a song. I hadn't been able to use it much, because of being away most of the time, but found myself going to work on it, often machining new parts myself for ones worn away by age, and over the years it had matured into sedate, reliable middle-age.

The range of reactions it raised was amazing. I'd often used it as a refuge from my wife in her stormier moods, and she had resented it passionately. Ismail curled his upper-class lip at it and called it 'that ghastly wreck', much to my private amusement. Venky, who had spent much of his youth thumping around hillsides on a single-cylinder bike with his brother, was frankly envious.

After dinner I read the letters again, then put both of them away in a drawer and thought instead of Sandhya Upadhyaya. Wished with all my being to see her again.

Reached for the phone to call her, drew back at the last moment. Take your life in both hands, and you get clobbered, I thought.

The phone rang and her voice floated across the wire. 'Colonel Menon?' she asked. 'Hello!' I sat silent, speechless at the coincidence, until she repeated, 'Hello, may I speak to Colonel Menon?'

'Speaking,' I said, a tightness in my throat.

'This is Sandhya, Sandhya Upadhyaya,' she said nervously. 'I've been trying to get in touch with you all day, ever since I got back from Madras.'

'I was being debriefed. We were restricted to quarters. No calls, nothing. We just got through with it.'

'I called to apologize, and to thank you . . .'

'You're welcome,' I said, trying to keep my voice light. 'Anything for you.'

The sound of her laughter floated across the wire, the nervousness gone. 'Do me a favour, then . . . Are you very busy?'

'Quite the opposite. I have a few days leave in which to lie around and get over the bruises I collected in Madras.'

'What happened to you? You looked all right when I came to take Kiran, and no one there told me you'd been hurt.'

'Concussion from a kick to the head, a cut from broken glass, and a huge bruise on the chest where I got shot.'

'You must be kidding! You get shot and all you have is a huge bruise?'

'Bulletproof vest. Without it I'd have been a goner. As it is, it feels like Mohammed Ali clobbered me on the chest.'

'Why aren't you in hospital, then?'

'Nothing serious enough for that. I can just lie around and catch up with my reading while the bruises change

123

colour. And how's your head? There was a bruise purpling on your forehead when we last met.'

'Oh, that's almost gone,' she said. 'I collected it two days before you got yours. Come to lunch tomorrow if you're free, then.' She paused. 'Bring your wife along.'

'I'm free,' I said, with a lightness I hadn't felt in a long while. 'My wife's out of town. And what was the favour you said you wanted?'

'There's been . . . I've been having trouble with Kiran . . . Could you spend some time with him?'

'Of course,' I said, 'will noon tomorrow be all right?'

By next morning, the pain in my head had subsided to a dull ache I could ignore, and the stitches no longer shrieked for attention. The bruises on my chest, five days old now, were colourful but didn't hurt at all, and I knew they were getting better all the time.

I dressed in my best casual civvies, blue jeans, Adidas, and a black sweater, and presented myself at her Gulmohar Park flat at five minutes before noon the next day, hoping my feelings didn't show. 'You look terrible,' she said, welcoming me into her airy, bright home, the bruise fading on her forehead, the little boy still clinging silently to her, 'You haven't been sleeping well. And that bandage . . . Are you sure you should be moving around?'

'Yes,' I said, smiling, ashamed of my thudding heart. 'Never felt better.'

I sat on a cushioned cane chair in her sunlit living room while in the kitchen, still carrying her son, she made coffee. The furniture was all light cane, the walls a soft yellow, the cushions with geometrical shapes in pastels. A glass window ran the entire length of the east wall, the sunlight coming to highlight a row of black-and-white sketches on the other walls. A small blue ceramic vase held flowers, purple and white, on a glass-topped, circular table. On the floor a blue-and-tan carpet with a flowery design. In the corner nearest the door, on a black acrylic and steel stand, a big TV set.

She brought coffee one-handed on a tray, balancing it gingerly while her son rested against her with his thumb in his mouth. 'What's with him?' I asked. 'Hasn't he got over it yet?' She shook her head, her hair dancing like a gleaming brown bell about her face. 'He hasn't spoken a word since,' she said. 'He hangs on to me all the while, he won't go to the toilet alone, he can't sleep in the dark . . . I have to keep a light on for him all the while. He wakes up if I turn it off at night. And he's been wetting his bed every night. I took him to a psychiatrist, and he told me to get you . . . He was comfortable with you that night.'

'Remember me?' I asked him. 'I got you off the train that night? And sat with you until Mama came?'

He straightened himself and looked at me in wide-eyed, searching appraisal, then nodded a half nod before lowering his head back down on his mother's shoulder, from where he looked at me out of the corners of his eyes. 'Come here,' I said, stretching out my arms at him, 'You can't stay with your mum all the time.' She nudged him, saying, 'Go!'

He came, in a short, stumbling run across five feet of flowery carpet, arms out towards me, and I caught him

125

when he got within range. He scrambled up on my lap, standing on my thighs, put his arms around my neck, and hung on with all his strength. I put my own arms around his thin body, pulled him close, feeling his heart beating wildly, smelling chocolate on his breath. He let go with one of his arms, leaned away from me, put his thumb in his mouth, looked at me out of serious, liquid eyes.

'Want to go out?' I asked. 'Play in the sun?'

He looked out of the window for a moment, then back at me, and shook his head, his thumb in his mouth all the while.

'Are you hungry?' I asked.

Again the shake of the head, his arm wagging with it, and the silent appraisal.

'Did you have any breakfast?'

A nod this time, and the beginnings of a banana-shaped smile around the thumb.

'Why do have your thumb in your mouth, then? Take it out.'

Still very serious, he unplugged his mouth for a moment, inspected his thumb, wiped it on his sweater, and put it back in. Unless I missed my guess Psycho would have been at him. Shut up, you little bastard, or I tie you up, he would have said. Kiran wouldn't have been able to shut up and Psycho had bound and gagged him. 'Do you remember,' I asked him, holding him closer, one hand behind his head, 'the man with the red hair and the funny hand? The man on the train?'

He put his arms around me, stamped his feet up and down on my thighs, and screamed, again and again, his face tucked into the crook of my neck. I waited for his screams to subside, and still holding him tight, put a finger beneath his chin, pushed his face gently up until he was looking me in the eye, his face red and screwed up and wet and terrified. 'The man's gone,' I told him, freeing a hand and cocking it like a pistol. 'I shot him dead. Bang-bang. He won't ever come near you again.'

He looked at me a long while with teary, protesting eyes, wiping his cheeks with one hand, and put his thumb back in his mouth. 'If anyone like that even comes near you again, your Mama will call me and I'll go bang-bang at them. Promise I will.' When he stayed silent, I asked, 'Don't you believe me?'

His gaze travelled all over my face before he nodded once again. 'They won't get you again,' I said. 'No one's going to tie you up ever again. No one's going to tape your mouth up. No one's going to lock you up in a toilet. Right?'

He nodded again. Only then did I notice Sandhya kneeling by my side, her eyes full of tears and distress. She shook her head in mute, tearing sorrow, took her son back from me, and disappeared with him into a bedroom.

I listened for a while to the faint sounds of Sandhya talking to him in the bedroom, and sipped at my cooling coffee. When she emerged nearly twenty minutes later she was subdued and not quite subdued, though trying hard to be. She sat quietly in her chair, gripping the arms hard.

127

'They were animals. Bloody animals.' She shivered, remembering. 'I'm glad that madman's dead. You could see it shining straight out of his eyes . . . Did you kill him, in the end?'

'No,' I replied, 'Ismail did. My boss. I ran into him—I gave him a name, Psycho—on the coach and managed to pull the detonator off him, the one with which he was going to blow up the coach. He went for a gun after that but Ismail came up on his side and shot him down . . . He was a madman all right. He just wouldn't give up. He and I scrapped over the switch for the detonator and I hit him a few times but he just wouldn't stay down. They post-mortemed him and found I'd broken his jaw and cracked two of his ribs but he just kept coming back for more.'

'Did he shoot you?'

'Yes. Earlier in the day he nearly kicked my head right off. And he knocked down a doctor who went in to treat a diabetic . . .'

'I'm just glad he's dead,' she said, shaking her head in pain. 'Kiran'll have nightmares about him for the rest of his life, poor thing.'

'I'm having my nightmares right now because Psycho's dead,' I said unthinkingly, the truth emerging, taking me by surprise.

With the disbelief almost welling out of those magnificent eyes she looked at me. 'You can't be serious,' she said at last, slowly. 'You can't want a man like that alive.'

'I do. Think of the greater madman behind this, the one who's willing to use a madman like Psycho. Now I don't have a single lead to him. To the Krait, hiding in his hole.'

I shouldn't have told her all this, but after three days of having my thoughts on the Krait dismissed by a bitter, ageing desk officer. I was ready for anything.

'What do you mean, the guy behind this?' she asked. 'You killed all of them, didn't you? I thought you killed the leader, the dangerous one.'

'We did. We killed all the FKF men on the train . . . The point is that the guy who planned this wasn't on the train. There are two men involved here who weren't on the train: the planner and the turncoat. The one that slipped them bits of information that nearly got us all killed.'

Her jaw dropped and her green eyes widened in surprise. 'What do you mean, the planner? And what's this about a traitor? I never heard of them before.'

'Those men had guns, ammunition, explosives and some very slick electronic equipment. You can't buy that kind of hardware in this country across the counter. You have to have a network of suppliers, smugglers, informers, bent policemen and the like. You can't just sit down one day and decide to take a railway coach. You have to plan for it, get your timing straight, get your geography straight . . . I get the feeling after the review that this was planned like a regular military exercise . . . I'll lose my job and probably end up in prison if anyone hears I told you all this . . .'

'Don't worry, I won't tell anyone,' she said. 'But what about the traitor? How did you work out there was one, in the first place? And who could it have been?'

'I've no hard evidence there was a traitor,' I said slowly, collecting my thoughts. 'Just a lot of little things. They asked for Ismail by name to deliver the money to them. In the first place, how did they know a low-profile unit like the SOF had got to Madras? In the second, how did they know Ismail runs it?'

'But I thought you delivered the money.'

'Ismail had gone to his tent for a nap after thirty hours on his feet. I went in his place.'

'What else?'

'I don't know, really . . . It's just a vague disquiet now.'

'Who could it be?'

'I haven't a clue . . .'

'So what are you going to do about it now?'

'Wait. There's a planner, there's an organization. The planner's a madman . . . A megalomaniac, judging from his letters. It won't be long before they try something else. And they'll have learnt from what we did in Madras . . . I wish I could look into the Krait's head.'

'I talked to some of the men who'd been kept hostage,' she said after a longish and companionable silence. 'They told me they'd all been made to strip down to their underwear, to stop them escaping. Did you know, they made all the hostages sit at the windows when you took in the money? They wanted everyone to see how helpless you were against them. They saw you deliver the money, helpless. And the way they shot that hostage . . . It was terrible.'

'Did you find out how they selected the first hostage to be shot?' I asked, curious.

130

'Remember, I told you one of the hostages tried to get friendly with them? The biggest coward among the hostages? Well, they picked him. For maximum effect.'

'In the end he fought back, did you know?' I said slowly. 'He died bravely. He panicked at the end, but before that he did what he could on the spot.'

'Why, what did he do?'

The hostages inside the coach wouldn't have been able to see Aggarwal bring Psycho down, and no one outside would have told her about it. 'He got down on his knees to beg them to let him go. Psycho instead tried to kick him down, like he did with me. And Aggarwal caught his leg and pulled him right out of the coach. If he'd had a little training he'd have been able to grab Psycho's gun and let loose . . . but he ran instead, and Psycho cut him down . . . I was a little worried after that Psycho might fly off the handle and let the other hostages have it.'

'He wouldn't have,' she said very definitely. 'Their leader had him well under control. I don't know how he had that control but he had it. I remember, he used to let Psycho just a little loose once in a while to keep the hostages quiet.'

'It was good they stayed quiet. It lulled the terrorists . . . And besides, if they'd tried anything when we went in they'd only have got in our way. We drugged the last meal we sent into the coach to make sure all the hostages would be asleep when we went in. We even doped Kiran's milk . . .'

A high-pitched wail from the bedroom jerked her to her feet. She ran, hair bouncing, to his side, and emerged a few minutes later with him hanging on to her as before, his thumb still in his mouth. He'd wet the bed again, and woken up after. I held him while she changed the sheets, tossing the used ones in a laundry basket, and afterwards fed him lunch with a spoon while he sat quiet in my lap.

After lunch she put him back to sleep on the big double bed, under a warm blue quilt with a large Mickey Mouse across the top. 'I've to go out for a short while,' she told me when Kiran was asleep, 'could you sit with him while I do that? He won't stay with anyone else, and I don't want to take him along . . .'

I lay on her bed then, next to the little boy sleeping under the quilt, and with an odd sense of delight at sleeping in her bed—even though she wasn't in it—tried to understand what was happening to me.

There had been little time for women so far, little time for anything but work: I'm from a very poor family. My father, a clerk in a small tile factory near Thrissur in Kerala, died of an unexpected and misdiagnosed heart attack at forty-one, when I was eleven and my brother eight. For the next five years, until she, too, died, Mother had brought me up, assisted by a municipal scholarship that paid my fees. When she died, I continued on the scholarship, eked out by some largesse from an uncle who had taken over the house when Father died, and my brother, until then erratic, had blossomed into the brains of the family.

Uncle had set me up at the NDA, the money given in minuscule doses, accompanied by lectures on his own magnanimity. After having borne Uncle's painful and unwilling hospitality for fifteen months, my years at the

NDA had been lean but sufficient, and from the time I graduated from the IMA I'd taken over the education of my brother, who was by then doing his degree in electronics engineering at IIT, Madras. During the last two years of his stint at IIT, though, he'd paid his own way—thanks again to scholarships—and left me to live life as I saw fit. He had later gone to the US on another scholarship, a bank loan paying his fare, and from there completed a doctorate with honours and now earned more than he knew to spend properly. He called when he remembered, infrequently but with affection, talking mostly of his girlfriends—whom he changed every three months or so—and of his work at Bell Labs, of which I couldn't understand a word.

After I joined the NDA I hadn't gone back home much. The hardest part of life at the NDA had been the cramped weeks during my summer and winter vacations spent at Uncle's bleak house. The only real catch at the academy had been the total absence of pocket money, which I'd long learnt to do without. Later, in a line infantry regiment, I kept the austerity of earlier days because by then I'd come to prefer it over clutter and useless socializing. My background hadn't helped, and though I acquired the minimal social graces required by the Army, I largely remained the insignificant, clumsy yokel in many ways.

I'd applied for and got my secondment to 9 Para as soon as I completed the two years they insisted you spent in the Army before getting in. Then I'd gone to Siachen and returned with a bullet in the leg and a lifelong aversion for the snowy wastes. A tour in Sri Lanka with the IPKF had followed. There we'd learnt the hard way that our weapons were outdated: the 7.62 mm SLR was too slow to deal with ambushes. We'd learnt then to file the sears off the breech blocks of our rifles, converting them from semi-automatic into automatic rifles, overheated barrels being preferable to a slow rate of fire.

There'd been no time at all for women, and no opportunity. Most of my service life I'd spent in areas where families weren't permitted. When Uncle wrote me that it was time I got married, and that he had found a suitable girl, I agreed on impulse. For me, that had been a lifetime's commitment, and now she said she was leaving . . . I closed my eyes, trying to deal with the new reality. I slept.

A small movement at my side brought me awake. The little boy had woken up and was lying staring at me, a thumb in his mouth, his free hand on my shoulder. I prised it gently out, saying, 'Wouldn't you like to play something now, instead of lying around?'

He nodded, putting his thumb back in. 'What?' I asked.

He answered, silently and with only lip movements around his thumb, 'Lego.'

His mother returned at four, letting herself in with her latchkey, to find the two of us on the living-room carpet with bits and pieces of his Lego set scattered between us, building a red and blue jeep. Her sombre face lightened as soon as she saw us. 'What would you like for tea?' she asked him.

I didn't hear his answer, for he whispered it in her ear, but saw the tears in her eyes and her assenting nod. 'You'll have that,' she promised him, then turned to me. 'This is the first I've heard him speak after you got him back,' she said. 'He's whispering now, and soon he'll be all right.'

Over tea, at which she presided with joy and poise, the old feelings of social inadequacy returned with redoubled force. What was I doing so far away from my element, I wondered, and left soon after, ignoring the plea in the youngster's eyes and the hurt in his mother's.

Alone in the flat I watched the sun set, listened to the children chirping in the park downstairs. When dusk came I watched the lights come on in the houses around, and wondered how to spend the desolate evening. I dined at the mess, where the chatter of the young bachelor officers made me feel even older.

Walking back to the flat from the mess, I understood at last what Jayanti must have felt all those years we'd been married. If this was what she'd had to go through while I was away . . . No wonder she wanted out. I'd give her that divorce.

chapter seven

In the pile of rubble the krait rested. It needed time to recover from the shock of its encounter with near death.

On Monday I went back to work, nearly as good as new. Luthra removed the stitches early in the morning, a day earlier than they were due to come out. The bruises had faded, and with them the pain. With disturbing effort I kept my mind off Sandhya and concentrated on the FKF and the Krait.

Chauhan called Tuesday, and I met him at his office late that evening. The CBI had tried to trace the source of the explosives and the electronics but had run into a brick wall. The chances were, he explained, that everything had come into the country from Pakistan, through what we call POK—Pakistan Occupied Kashmir—and the rest of the world considers part of Pakistan.

The FKF men had all been identified. All except Loudspeaker and Psycho were youngsters. None had a record with the police. The police were worried: six hitherto unknown men with the training that these men had been through meant sources of big money they knew nothing about. The CBI was going to beef up its team in Kashmir.

How about infiltration, I asked, the SOF could provide men.

Not yet, he said, let's try other methods first.

Had he any idea who was behind it, I asked.

There were suspicions, he replied, but no evidence. The trail ran dry at a certain point. The FKF had created independent networks to supply arms and ammunition, to dig for intelligence, and for infrastructure—safe houses, vehicles, whatever—and for electronics. From what he'd learnt so far, only one or two men knew how and where everything tied together. And there was one big difference between this group and others: this group had professionals. They depended on smuggling networks rather than Muslim sympathizers, paying five times the price for a service delivered by professionals.

So what, I asked.

So they had someone with a big budget behind them, he replied, and if we broke any of the networks they could set up another without much effort.

In other words, I said, we could expect more trouble from the FKF.

Maybe, he replied, and maybe not. It could reappear with a different face. He was looking for facts that would fit patterns.

On other fronts, things seemed to get better. The Minister was happy with the SOF and in return for his nephew's life we got more money for ammunition, for the newest parachutes and training. Requests for joint exercises with the special forces of other countries would be examined more liberally. With any luck we'd soon have trained hostage negotiators. The government was trying to work out a rule book to cover the handling of political kidnappings, based on what the American FBI was doing. From now on the government would take a much harder line.

The snipers had shaken off their depression, at least for the time being. Bravo company, floating on the intoxication of success, had returned to exercises with vigour. The other companies, fired by Bravo's success, were competing hard.

Rakesh Aggarwal's wife was contemplating legal action against the government. I was tempted to write to her, telling her what had happened, and how her husband had died, but didn't.

After that it was back to the grind, interrupted on Tuesday by Sandhya. Kiran was better, she said, to the extent that he now spoke aloud to her. Softly, and rarely, but he had begun to speak. His grandparents had arrived from Calcutta to help her cope with him, and could I visit again.

I would, I said with lifting spirits, on Sunday this time, because I worked Saturdays.

Fine, she replied before hanging up, but I was not to leave abruptly as I'd done last time.

On Wednesday I reread the letters from Uncle and Jayanti. After some thought I wrote to Jayanti saying I'd visit her in Bombay, where she had moved, sometime soon so we could settle whatever was to be settled. Then I wrote to Uncle telling him I'd visit Jayanti and then him as soon as I could get some leave. Then I got myself booked on a train to Bombay for the following Monday, arranging with a friend to stay with him for a couple of days. Booked myself onward to Thrissur where Uncle had settled. I got my leave, ten days, without fuss, because all other officers were in town during the period, and because I hadn't taken any leave for three years. Ismail warned me that in an emergency he'd have me back immediately.

At ten on Sunday morning Sandhya's parents treated me with enough gratitude to last me the rest of my life while I sat tongue-tied with their grandson in my lap. They left at eleven, much to my relief, to visit old friends they hadn't met for decades. 'That wasn't too bad, was it?' she asked after they'd left. 'They're emotional people, and demonstrative. They picked it up in Calcutta.'

'Different from my lot,' I said. 'Mine rarely even smiled. But I don't mind in small doses.'

'Wait right there,' she said, mischief shining in her eyes. 'Hold your position for fifteen minutes.'

'Why?' I asked, Kiran squirming in my lap.

'I want to sketch you,' she replied, 'with that hunted look in your eyes.' She produced A4 size sheets of art paper and a box from which she produced two pencils, three strange-looking pens, a couple of brushes, a bottle of Indian Ink and a palette. Last of all, she took from a case a pair of spectacles that, when she put them on, made her look five years older.

'I didn't know you needed spectacles,' I said.

'Only for sketching,' she replied. Settling herself at the dining she drew on the paper with a pencil for about ten minutes, looking at me from time to time with eyes turned inwards in concentration. 'All right,' she said then, 'you can move around now, but I'll have to look at you again after a while.'

I wandered over to the table to watch her work. She poured three drops of Indian Ink out the bottle into a slot in the palette, dipped a pen in it. She shook the excess off the tip, and began to darken the faint lines she'd drawn with the pencil. 'What's all this paraphernalia for?' I asked. 'I thought you just sat down with paper and pencil and went ahead with your sketch.'

She looked at me over the spectacles, which had slipped down her nose. 'You might do that for a rough,' she explained, 'actually some people do it like that all the time. I prefer to do a rough with a pencil, HB, so it's faint enough to be rubbed off easily, and then darken it with a pen.'

'Why not a standard pen, a good one?' I asked. 'Using those pens must be a pain.'

She took out another sheet of paper to demonstrate. 'Indian Ink is much darker and longer lasting than normal ink. It's also thicker: you can't pour it into a pen. If you put Indian Ink in a pen it'll be clogged in no time.

'The harder you press these nibs down the wider the tips splay. When you want a thick line, you press hard. For a thin one, don't press.' She demonstrated, drawing a line that started narrow at the top of the page and broadened gradually downwards until it was nearly a millimetre thick at the bottom of the page.

She put down the pen and picked up a brush. 'You use pens for lines, but larger areas of black, like with hair, you fill in with a brush.' She put the brush down. 'And now shut up and let me finish. I'll answer questions afterwards.'

She worked fast, drawing over the pencil marks with firm, sure strokes, filling in first the eyes, pupils and irises followed by the eyelashes, done with quick, short strokes, then the eyebrows, and the line of the nose. With faint, almost invisible lines she shaded the dark side of the nose, with slightly darker lines for the wrinkles on the forehead. Then she did the mouth, and the ears, and, last of all, the hair, an outline filled quickly in with a brush. She left the paper flat on the table when she was through, weighing down the corners with spoons. 'It needs to dry out properly,' she said, 'I'll rub out the pencil marks after that, and that's it.'

It was me all right in the picture, but at the same time it wasn't me. The features were all there, familiar from years of looking in the mirror, but there was a keenness to the eyes that the mirror never showed. 'This looks like me, all right,' I said, 'but you've added a character that mightn't be there. This guy in the picture is all focussed . . . Like a hunter. I'm not focussed like that most of the time.'

'Yes, you are,' she said. 'That's what I saw when we first met in Madras, and when I tried to stop you from going into that coach. You're a hunter all right. You're confused only when you're not on the hunt.'

'Let's not quarrel,' I said. 'May I keep this?'

'Sure,' she replied. 'It's for you.'

'Are all those your work?' I asked, waving at the uncluttered black-framed sketches that lined the walls.

'Yes,' she replied, taking off her glasses, 'I did them all in the past year and a half, after . . . after my husband died.'

'Didn't you do any while he was still around?' I asked, curious about the strange note in her voice when she spoke of him, eager to know about her.

She shook her head. 'Not after the first six months after we were married.'

'Why not?'

'Yash—that was his name—was . . . He was violent. I didn't know about it when we were married, he was so sophisticated. You see, he was rich, with inherited money. He got a huge farm from his parents that he sold. He invested the proceeds in blue chip shares, and lived on the interest. He pretended to play the stock market, but he was never serious about it. He . . . he did nothing at all. He just sat around and did nothing at all and that ate into him. He must have felt utterly useless.'

'Did he ever hit you or anything?'

'Never. He never got physical with me, or with Kiran, but the threat was always there. Always. And he used to get drunk. He was an alcoholic. He used to get drunk every evening. Not drink, but get drunk.' She shivered. 'He must have found himself very hard to bear . . . He used to get

142

the whole house all tensed up trying to persuade everyone he was doing something useful. He used to drive us crazy, and the servants . . . I just couldn't work, not in that atmosphere. It was like being inside that coach. I was . . . sort of locked in.'

'Why did you stick around, then?'

'Mostly for Kiran. Look, no one ever believed me when I said Yash was violent. On the surface he was so cool, so smooth, so very civilized . . . For a while I thought there was something wrong with me because he never did anything overtly violent . . . But towards the end you could see. Whenever we had a problem he'd talk of fixing it violently. I'll kill that guy, he'd say, or, I'll burn him out . . .'

'How did he die?'

'Someone at a party told him he was drunk. He said he wasn't. He said he'd climb on to the railing around the balcony to prove he was still in his senses. They tried to stop him but they were all too drunk. So he climbed on to the railing, holding on to the wall . . . and his hand slipped. He fell five floors on to concrete.' Suddenly there were tears in her eyes. 'I was so relieved when he died, and so ashamed I was relieved . . . It took me a long while to get over it. I stayed out of things for a long while after that. Everyone thought I was grieving for him but I was only trying to get to grips with being so happy he was dead . . . I don't know why I'm telling you all this. I'll get you some coffee.'

As she went off to the kitchen Kiran looked up from the carpet where he'd been playing with a battery powered, remote-controlled police car. 'You'll drain the battery in no time if you run that car on the carpet,' I told him. 'Play on the floor. It'll go faster if you run it there.'

He left the car where it was and instead produced a large picture book. Peter Pan, it said in colourful letters across the cover, and, in the distinctive script, Walt Disney. He handed me the book and sat down, waiting expectantly for me to read it out. 'Nothing doing,' I said. 'I'll read it out to you only if you ask me properly.'

He started to pout, then changed his mind halfway. 'Read the story out to me,' he said silently, mouthing words slowly so I could make out what he was saying.

'I can't hear you,' I said, mouthing the words silently, exactly as he had done. 'Speak up.'

He giggled, the first sound I'd heard him make, aside from those screams when I'd spoken to him of Psycho. He repeated the words, this time in a whisper barely audible. 'All right,' I said normally, 'you got it.'

His mother returned with the coffee to find me trying to read—it was much harder than I thought—to Kiran from his book. 'Watch out,' she warned me, 'he's fine now. He's learnt that he gets more out of people if he mouths his words instead of speaking normally. Everyone falls for it.' She handed me my coffee. 'If he pulls it on you, just ignore it.'

'He just did,' I replied, 'and I didn't fall for it.'

'Good,' she said, turning to him. 'You'd better get back to your car while he drinks his coffee. And don't play the fool with him ever again. Right?'

'How did you know?' I asked her as he scrambled off my lap with the book.

She reached down to tousle his hair. 'I've known him all his life,' she replied. 'He does this kind of thing every time he falls ill. He recovers quickly but tries to stretch the special treatment as long as he can . . . You're awkward with children. Don't you have any of your own?'

I shook my head. 'My wife can't have any. We checked.'

'Oh . . . Is she still out of town?'

'Yes. For good.'

'What do you mean?'

'She wants a divorce . . . I suppose I never did spend enough time with her. She was alone for a long while after we discovered she couldn't have children, because I was away in Siachen. She must have taken the worst of it on her own . . . And now we don't have much in common.'

'Will you give her the divorce?'

'Yes. I expect she plans to marry again. She isn't the type to push for a break unless it's essential.'

'Have you told her you'll agree? Asked her plans?'

'I'll meet her this week. I'm off to Bombay tomorrow for a couple of days, to see her, and after that I'll go on south. To my hometown, to meet the clan. Or what's left of it.'

'They won't like it, will they?'

'They most certainly won't. I got a letter from Uncle last week asking how I could allow the family name to be dragged in the mud . . . You see, he fixed up my marriage and doesn't want it to break up because if it does he loses as much face as I do.'

145

'So what'll he do if you do take a divorce? Kick you out of the clan, or cut you off with a rupee or something?'

I laughed out loud at the thought of inheriting anything from him. After Mother died he'd taken our house, everything we'd had. In return we'd got dribbles of money, given grudgingly with sermons. I didn't want to have anything to do with him any more, or with the clan. Might as well use the divorce to cut unwanted strings, I thought. 'Nothing he can do to me,' I said. 'When we were young he could but now he can't touch me. Or my brother, for that matter.'

'What's your brother like?'

'Three years younger, very bright, and he's done well for himself. He's an engineer, settled in the US, working at Bell Labs on something I can't understand.'

'And your wife, what's she like?'

'I never really got to know her,' I said slowly. 'Her family is well-off. Lots of land, a plantation somewhere . . . I think that's why we got into trouble. She'd never had to lift a finger before we got married, and I'd had to work hard right through. There's never been the time nor the money for self-indulgence. She couldn't stand that, while I thought that her wanting to go off on holiday and so on were just weaknesses . . .'

Sandhya's parents trooped back then, laden with gifts of fruit and sweets. Lunch followed shortly after, uncomfortable and noisy, with the old folks fussing equally over Kiran and me. I sat through it with determined patience, looking up once or twice to see the shadowed amusement

146

in Sandhya's eyes, going back to the food, which though splendid tasted like ashes in my mouth.

I left as soon as I gracefully could, after coffee. 'When will you come again?' she asked at the door.

'I'll be back in town towards the middle of next week because I've got only ten days' leave,' I said. 'I'll call you as soon as I get back.'

She smiled. 'They'll be off in a week. They get fidgety out of their home in Calcutta, and now that they can see Kiran's on the mend they won't worry about him.'

'All right, then, I'll call you as soon as I get back.'

She sobered up a little. 'Do that,' she said. 'And don't mind them. They mean well.'

The next afternoon I took the Paschim Express from New Delhi and spent most of the first hour or so avoiding the company of the hearty Sardar who occupied the other berth in the coupé they'd given me, and who took a bottle of Glenlivet out of his suitcase as soon as the TTE finished checking our tickets. In the half-hour that followed he told me between large gulps of whisky and water that he worked in customs at Delhi airport, got lots of 'tips' and presents while on duty, had developed a taste for scotch and an aversion for his wife of fifteen years, and was saving up to start an import–export business of his own which he hoped would run well because he knew everyone. When I told him I was in the Army, he hiccupped, then announced in slurred Punjabi that he liked all Army men, they were bloody good guys, and his own brother was in the Army.

When he went to the toilet I opened my own small suitcase to retrieve a book, and turned eight pages without absorbing a word. I refused the Sardar's persistent offers of a drink, and watched him settle morosely into his seat for a snooze. Looked out of the window at the reddening dusk and found my mind returning to the coach, to what I'd seen when I burst in through the window, and what had been wrong about it. I looked then at the napping Sardar, and with a little internal jerk of insight, understood what it was: the sight of Psycho napping.

There was no way he should have been napping at the time we went in. He should have been up and about, or at least watchful. Unless . . . unless he'd known that the attack wouldn't come at that time. He must have thought the attack would come early in the morning, as we'd originally planned it. Or he'd been waiting securely for the rhythmic whack-whack of the helicopter's rotors, the sound around which we'd built the plan. He'd been napping to build up reserves for the hour when he thought the attack would come.

Ismail, too, had caught his man asleep. The two remaining terrorists in the coach, too, had been caught with their guard down. Only one man other than Psycho had even managed to get off a shot, and that had gone wild. The attack had taken them all by surprise. They must have known it would come at some other time . . . That thunderstorm had saved us from a massacre. There was no way they could have figured out our plans on their own.

Someone must have told them. There had to be a leak somewhere.

It seemed too strong a conclusion to make from a radio mast, a man's ill-timed bit of sleep, and some relaxed men. But those men had been trained to stay awake. Psycho, in particular, would have enjoyed any chance to cow the hostages down, and make them sweat. It didn't fit.

I sat up with a jerk. But for a quirk of nature we'd have been massacred. Not a comforting thought, that. The one that followed was even worse. The next time round we wouldn't have luck on our side. Not if the Krait had the brains I thought he did.

So who was his informant? He must have had a friend on that committee. Or . . . or was he himself on the committee, hunting with the hounds and running with the hare?

chapter eight

The krait was patient, like any good hunter. It would wait invisible until its prey came within striking distance. Then it would strike, biting repeatedly, injecting its venom into its victim's bloodstream through the grooves running down the length of its foremost fangs.

Even in January Bombay sweltered in the afternoon sun when the train arrived at Victoria Terminus. The Sardar, who had continued drinking late into the night, had broken off for a sketchy dinner of bread and eggs at ten. He had then returned to the bottle, and spent most of the next day snoring in his berth, surfacing occasionally for another swallow from his bottle or a dose of whatever junk food was available closest the coach when the train halted.

I had my suitcase packed and ready well in time, and was the first off the train at VT. I looked around at the streams of people pouring in and out of the dusty station and hoped the Krait would never attack here: Bombay depended entirely on its infrastructure and if he managed to knock out any one system for a few days . . . Time to stop thinking of that.

Outside at the taxi rank I took a yellow-and-black cab to Colaba, where Ajit, my friend, lived. He had done well for himself in the corporate world after two years at business school and now lived in a flat in a seven-storey coop a kilometre away from the Hotel President.

He was in when I arrived, having got back from work a couple of hours early to let me in. In the years since school, he'd acquired a great deal of polish, fifteen kilos about the middle, an active wife and a fund of worldly knowledge that he used to great effect in his work as an investment advisor in a bank. The last time we'd met, six years ago, at my wedding, he'd still been working his way up. Now he had become quieter, more relaxed, almost content.

His polish made me feel rough about the edges, his expensively tailored clothes and smooth haircut in stark contrast with my own workaday outfit and Army crew cut. In his flat he had surrounded himself with quiet luxury, air-conditioning, an exquisite stereo system, crystal ashtrays, the works. 'We read about what you guys did at Madras,' he said when he'd got me settled into an overstuffed armchair with a cup of tea. 'I never thought you'd end up doing stuff like they do in the movies.'

'Why not?' I asked.

'You were too serious. Too quiet to make waves. Too thoughtful.'

From the solid upper-middle-class comfort of his home the railway coach in Madras and the Krait seemed aeons away. 'You have to think a fair bit,' I explained. 'You have to figure out how the other guy's thinking, and outthink him if you want the rescue to work. You have to learn to wait, and get your timing straight. And there's endless preparation, mostly aimed at quelling your fear. You do things over and over and over again until you do them without thinking and leave your mind free to work on outsmarting the other guy. That's what it's all about. From the outside you get to see only the hit, but that's actually the easiest bit. Knowing when, where and how to hit are far more important but then no one cares. Nobody would find anything interesting in my boss sitting on an observation platform for two hours understanding the patterns that their sentries observe.'

He shook his head, bemused. 'I don't pretend to know enough about what you do to understand all of that, but I get a sense of it when you put it that way. Like reading up as much as possible about stocks and bonds before deciding when, where and how much money you're going to invest.'

'I think so,' I replied, grinning, 'but I don't know enough of your work to say for sure.'

He grinned back. 'You're right, they're the same. But the difference is that in my business you can cut your losses and hedge your bets. You guys can't do that.'

'Sure we can,' I replied. 'It's like a war. In any war you lose battles but they don't matter as long as you win at the

152

end. It's often a matter of style, of a quality that goes beyond competence. But in something like we did at Madras, yes, you're right, we can't cut our losses and run . . .'

'What makes you tick?' he asked. 'Not that you aren't doing well in the Army, but you could have done well for yourself anywhere. What got you into the Army, and into your unit in particular?'

I'd crushed such questions in my own mind as soon as they came up, but now I let it float and an answer emerged. I liked the hunt. Had acquired a taste for it. As others had a taste for making money or movies . . . Life without the hunt would be disastrously boring. 'I don't know,' I replied, unwilling yet to pass on my new-found insight. 'It's always easier to see why others do the things they do than why you yourself do what you do.'

His wife walked in from work just then. Early thirties, wilting a little in the heat but hair still miraculously in place, dressed in blindingly cheerful chiffon, a breathless little girl of seven or thereabouts in tow. The ladies offered us poised, tired smiles and retreated to their bedrooms to emerge some fifteen minutes later, freshened up and even more colourful in their casual clothes. The girl settled down in front of their TV set to watch cartoons, while her mother lowered herself gracefully into a couch across from us. 'Ajit's told us so much about you,' she said. 'It's a great pleasure to have you here. But what brings you here?'

The question Ajit himself had avoided. 'Came to meet my wife,' I said.

'Does she work here?' she asked.

'Yes, she does, but . . .' my voice trailed off.

'But what?'

'But we're breaking up. We haven't got along too well for some years and now she's been asking for a divorce.'

'What do you think?'

'Much the same as her. I came here to tell her to go ahead with the paperwork. Shouldn't take long.'

They both took it in their stride, not probing any further but obviously available if I wanted to talk, willing to leave me to face it on my own. I looked around once again at the evidence of their orderly, comfortable life. Thought to myself that I'd probably enjoy it for a few days, and then find a way to escape from it . . . To each his own.

Later that evening I called Jayanti at her flat. 'Could we meet tomorrow?' I asked. 'I leave the day after and I do need to meet you before I go on.'

'Where are you?' she asked, her voice wary.

'Colaba, with a friend.'

'I work that side of town. Can we meet for a quick lunch?' She named a Goan restaurant somewhere near the Regal theatre, not too far from Ajit's house.

I met her at the restaurant the next day at a quarter-past-one, five minutes later than she'd said. We sat at a table covered with a red-and-white chequered cloth, on low-backed chairs that encouraged one to sit straight and eat quickly and not linger in the restaurant over coffee or to chat. It must have suited her to a tee: there was no way we were going to spend hours here.

'Did you get my letter?' she asked when the young, grinning waiter had collected our orders.

'Yes,' I replied. 'I came to tell you I agree with you completely . . . And to say I'm sorry we couldn't make it work out better.'

'If you expect to make up for six years of neglect with one casual sentence saying you're sorry you must be out of your tiny mind,' she replied, her anger surging to the surface.

'I don't expect anything at all,' I told her. 'Take it any way you wish.'

She glared at me across the table. 'I've often been tempted to take you to court for a divorce, and scratch all I can out of you by way of alimony, to scratch your eyes out in public . . . Then I realized it wouldn't bother you. You've learnt to live on the bare minimum, and other peoples' opinions just don't bother you.'

'Revenge isn't sweet,' I told her, 'it usually turns to ashes in your mouth when you've got it.'

'Thinking about revenge is sweet, all right,' she said. 'That's all that kept me going for a couple of years. But then you're so . . . so self-sufficient. There was no way I could touch you ever.'

'Does it matter any more?' I asked, wondering how she would react if she knew about Sandhya, and grinned at the thought.

'Not any longer,' she said, eyeing my grin with suspicion. 'You go your way and I'll go mine.'

'There's a difference,' I said slowly. 'I've got nothing against you . . .'

155

'Oh, shit!' she exploded, leaning forward on the table, closing her eyes in disgust. 'There you go again. So bloody self-righteous. I wish you knew what a pain in the bum you are sometimes.'

Lunch arrived then, a steak for me, spicy pork for her, a large cucumber salad on the side. We crunched through it in uneasy silence. 'What would you like,' I asked when she had finished and laid her fork on her plate, 'by way of alimony?'

'Nothing,' she said, her anger cooling visibly, 'I don't want a thing from you . . . Not even revenge.'

'And what do you plan to do now?'

'Keep working . . . I'm doing rather well now.' She bought cotton clothes all over India and sold them in Europe, and when I last heard anything about it, was planning to sell some in France. 'I'll be clear of my debts in another couple of years.'

'Plan to get married again?'

'How did you know?' she asked, eyeing me narrowly. 'I never wrote to you about it.'

'You wouldn't have harped so much on the divorce if you hadn't.' I felt a faint and entirely unjustified twinge of jealousy at that, that she had preferred another man. Kept it down.

'I will, by and by,' she said. 'He works here, in Bombay. He's as different from you as chalk from cheese, thank God. He's there when I need him, and he's not addicted to his work.'

'Good for you,' I said, knowing her need for comfort and order and solidity. 'I hope it works out this time.'

'Oh, it will,' she said airily. 'I'm not going to repeat the mistake of marrying a stranger and regretting it afterwards.' She smiled and sat as far back as the chair would allow. 'I thought you'd come here to talk me into coming back to you. Snapping at you was pointless.'

The bill arrived, and she insisted on paying for it with her credit card. 'This is the first credit card I've paid for,' she said, revelling in her new-found independence. 'I could never afford anything like this when we were together, so this one is on me. The last time.'

'All right,' I said. 'Just send me the papers to sign, as soon as you like.'

She looked down at her plate in silence. 'You're a good enough man in your own way,' she said at last. 'Yes, I'm sorry too that we couldn't make it work.'

Six years, I thought, watching her stride purposefully down the crowded pavement towards a cab rank, is a hell of an investment to write off over lunch, but that was what we'd just done. It had been easier than I thought. Now for Uncle.

I wandered all over Bombay that afternoon, wondering at the crowds, thinking once again of the ransom to which the Krait could hold the city if ever he felt like it. He could strangle this city quite easily, with a handful of men.

I returned to Ajit's well-ordered house at four, well ahead of the terrifying peak-hour crowds, and let myself in with the latchkey Ajit had lent me, sat in the living room with its comfortable, lived-in look, and wished for the first time that I had some place like this to go back to. From the hunt.

Ajit's daughter arrived at ten past, led in by a young ayah who would sit with her until one of her parents returned. She came in like a small, ink-stained whirlwind, cranky with hunger, quietening down with a pretty smile when she saw me. Pausing only to change into jeans and down a glass of milk, she went down to the yard to play with the other kids in the block.

Ajit arrived at five, still fresh as he'd been when he left in the morning. I told him so. 'Air-conditioning,' he explained, 'and a quiet snooze at my desk after lunch. A chair comfortable enough for me to sit in for hours at a stretch. That's the secret. And how was your day?'

'All right,' I replied. 'I met Jayanti. We, umm, decided to split. Peaceably, of course.'

'What are your plans?' he asked. 'Will you get married again or something?'

'Or something,' I said. 'Right now I have no plans, only wishes. Talking about them would be premature.'

'Tell me, then,' he said, 'how you deal with physical risks in your work.'

'There aren't too many,' I replied, 'and there are tools to take care of them. Training, weaponry, body armour, things like that take the sting out of it.'

'Not that bit,' he explained. 'Now that these terrorist blokes know you were the guy who went in after them, won't they try their best to eliminate you personally? Like they did with General Vaidya?'

158

'Not really. I'm a small fry. They go for the chiefs, for people whose assassination would shock the country.'

'The papers said you're with this special unit, whatever it's called. Wouldn't knocking off the head of this special unit tie it down for a while? It's not as if you were with any old battalion or regiment or whatever.'

'It's possible,' I replied, 'but it hasn't ever happened before.'

'Neither had the kind of stuff these people from the FKF or whatever did in Madras. There's a first time for everything.'

'That puts my boss on top of the hit list. I'm only the deputy head.'

'These terrorist types have long memories. They killed Vaidya after he retired, remember? That was pure revenge.'

'So what?'

'The way I look at it, pal,' he said slowly, 'you're stuck for life with a price on your head. If I were in those terrorists' shoes I'd go for you or your boss before doing anything else. I'm sure substitutes for heads—or even deputy heads—of units like yours must be fairly thin on the ground. And without a good head your unit would be useless.'

'Thanks for that,' I grinned. 'Now you'll have me looking over my shoulder all the while until I get back to base.'

'Your problem,' he said with untouched equanimity, 'I just pointed it out.'

'Actually it's not so easy to kill a serving soldier,' I said. 'In the first place it's not so easy to get into a base, and in the second, it would spark off intensive investigation. If anyone happened to knock off my boss we'd move heaven and earth to catch the bloke who did it.'

'Don't fool yourself, pal,' he said. 'They killed two Prime Ministers and look what happened. Look at what happened to the men who killed Indira Gandhi. One of them lived several years on death row and became something of a public figure, the other one's widow ended up in the legislature.'

'I know all that,' I said. 'But I still don't think they'll try anything of the kind.'

'That's up to you,' he said, 'but just keep it in mind. You never know when you'll end up in someone's sights.'

He dropped me off at the station the next afternoon, and insisted on seeing me to the train. A couple of minutes before the train was to leave he said, 'Look, Raja, if you want to get out of your job in the near future, get in touch with me. You learn quickly, you can deal with large numbers of men, and you have common sense. That's saying a hell of a lot. We can use you any time. And if there's any kind of threat you can always go abroad.' He grinned mischievously. 'To Bangladesh.'

The train, leaving Bombay in the afternoon, passed through the Western Ghats on its way to Pune just an hour or so out of VT. I sat juggling things in my mind through the most beautiful bits of the Ghats. Sandhya. The divorce. Uncle. The clan. My job. My future if I left the Army. The threat Ajit brought up was always at the back of our minds, and was a very real one, despite all I had told him. It came with the territory.

I found then, with a certainty I never had before, that I wanted my job. And wanted, with an intensity I'd never felt before, Sandhya. And I slept on the train, much better than on any other night after the operation.

Back in Thrissur I faced Uncle squarely. His anger was now pathetic. I told him Jayanti and I were getting divorced, and he could take it or leave it. He took it: his other nephew, my brother, still sent him money each month. I'd never even have thought of asking Gopi to stop that, but Uncle wasn't to know that. So he played safe, and held his peace. But he obviously didn't want me about the house, didn't want curious visitors to find out what had happened, so I hopped on the train to Delhi the day after I got there, and with great luck and a small bribe to the TTE managed to find a berth.

I returned to Delhi Tuesday afternoon, eight days after I left, to the empty flat now with a coating of grey dust over everything. With a decidedly lighter heart I called Sandhya. 'You're back early,' she said. 'You said ten days. When did you get back?'

The gladness in her voice lifted my spirits further still. 'Just this minute,' I replied, 'I dumped my suitcase in the bedroom and called you. How's Kiran?'

'He's fine. He went back to school yesterday and did fine . . . If you're not too tired you could come to tea and tell me about the trip.'

I arrived at her warm and welcoming home minutes after Kiran got home from school. In the bright sunlight I found myself thinking of her flat as home. Home . . . a dangerous word, that, weighted with bondage, laden with responsibility. I thought of the Krait on my trail just as I was on his, and found the old warnings resurgent. Look life in the eye and get kicked in the teeth, said the voice in my head. Trust to fate and get clobbered. And so I retreated behind a bald account of what I'd done with my days away from Delhi, and returned to my silent flat as soon as I could.

chapter nine

Again the krait sensed a possible prey. It was rested and fresh and its hunger was mounting. It slithered out of its shelter to attack the field mouse that scampered past the rubble in the moonlight.

All through the end of January and most of February I kept myself busy. I visited Sandhya twice in February and came away with dissatisfaction lingering on afterwards.

With spring came an American Ranger team for a week-long joint training exercise, led by Lieutenant Colonel Dick Williams. In the course of the first six days Dick and his men outshot, outmarched and eventually outdid us in every way. On the last day of the exercises, though, in a tactical jungle exercise, we outfoxed them, ambushing twenty of his men, taking them completely by surprise.

At the farewell dinner at the mess Dick and I made friends and afterwards I broke a rule and got tipsy with him in his room at the quarters. When it was time to leave, he enfolded my small, brown hand in his large, red one, saying, 'You guys are terrific. If I had to make do with the equipment you guys have I'd have a mutiny on my hands at the end of the first week.'

The weekends at Sandhya's Gulmohar Park home receded slowly into history. The divorce agreement arrived and I signed it and sent it back to Jayanti as soon as I could. In those grey winter evenings I braved the drizzles and went for long walks alone, struggling to fill in the free hours that now seemed as long as days. With All Fool's Day after a hard winter and a beautiful spring came the summer heat, but we went on with scarcely a change in schedule. Temperatures went up into the thirties and the forties, and tempers climbed appropriately. Sleep, always a rarity, came even more seldom, and never for very long. Sandhya called a couple of times and sensed that for the time being at least I would prefer to be left alone and did so.

I called on Chauhan a couple of times. Distributed over the hour or so that I spent with him he told me that the CBI had found another network that might have supplied the FKF their arms through Gujarat or Rajasthan. There was nothing definite on the Krait. There were no new patterns in the gunrunning across the border. There was nothing definite on the Krait.

In the lengthening evenings I found the Krait occupying my thoughts increasingly. Where would he strike again, I wondered, and when? Somewhere in Tamil Nadu, a second time? The state's police were largely demoralized. With the LTTE moving around more or less freely in the state, the state government would be happy to have something drastic happen, so it could point a finger at the Central government. And no one in the state could care less about Kashmir.

On a warm morning early in May, as I sat in my office working on a review of a new type of light machine gun that we had been asked to try out, the phone rang: it was Chauhan, calling from his office. 'The FKF seem to be on the move again,' he told me hurriedly. 'They've chosen Bangalore this time. I just got the news.'

'How do you know it's them?' I asked.

'They said so, for one thing,' came the reply. 'They referred to bits of the Madras incident that they are unlikely to have got unless they knew how it was planned. The modus operandi this time is much the same. You should have official confirmation from your ministry in minutes.'

'Are you going out there now?' I asked.

'Yes. The Karnataka police chief called us the moment he heard it was the FKF. I'm taking an Air Force craft to Bangalore within the hour. Chances are I'll do the negotiations.'

'Do you think they'll call us?' I asked, hoping this time we would arrive at the scene sooner.

'Unless I'm mistaken they already have. Your ministry should be in touch with you very soon now, they've got copies of everything I have.'

'Tell me what you know, then.'

'Four men rushed a hotel in Bangalore at half-past-nine this morning. The local MP was there, inaugurating a seminar on software technology parks. They grabbed him—he didn't have any security—and at least eight of the leading businessmen attending the seminar. And a foreigner, a white man, probably British.'

'Are they holed up at the hotel, then?' I asked, because penetrating a large hotel would be relatively easy.

'No way. They'd organized a bus for themselves. They stuffed the hostages into the bus and drove off to God knows where. My reports say there was a policeman following them on a motorcycle, but not where they went. I suppose they've headed for an easily defensible position around town. Exactly as they did last time.' The Krait picked his defensive position for himself.

'They'll do it better this time if they're half as bright as I think they are,' I said. 'Any casualties so far?'

'One that we know of. A hotel security man was shot when he got in the way of the kidnappers. I don't know how he is. There might be more casualties, we don't know. Listen, I have to go now. The flight's waiting. You'll get all this in a few minutes in any case.'

The news arrived on the fax ten minutes later. At twenty-past-nine, four black-clad men in masks and armed with AK-47s that they waved threateningly around, had burst out of the first-floor gents toilet near the Vijayanagar hall in the Taj Residency hotel in the heart of Bangalore. They brushed past or knocked down the few people between them and the hall doors. They then took over the Vijayanagar hall where the seminar was being inaugurated by one M. Siddalingaiah, the local MP. A hotel security man who tried, perhaps foolishly, to stop them was shot in the chest.

Inside the hall, three men covered all the doors leading to the hall, front and back. The fourth, hearing the screams of some of the women in the room, fired a burst from his AK-47 into the air to frighten them. A chandelier hit by the fire crumbled and fell, bits of it injuring a steward. In the silence that followed, the terrorists ejected fifty or so of the sixty-five people in the hall, including hotel staff. The remaining fifteen, all wealthy and influential businessmen, were kept inside the hall at gunpoint, but not for long.

Almost as the echoes of the burst of gunfire in the hall died away, a large bus with darkened windows drew up outside the gates of the hotel. Buses do not usually enter the hotel premises, and when a guard tried to stop the bus at the hotel gates he was ignored and knocked over. The bus scraped through the gates—which are a little narrow for a bus—and along the driveway, which loops backwards to the entrance to the lobby of the hotel. The bus driver was either inexperienced or casual—or terrified, if he had a gun to his head—and the bus scraped and bashed at least four cars on its way.

Two more masked and black-clad men emerged from the bus waving their AK-47s, and pushed their way into the lobby past the stunned crowd that had collected there. They fired another burst into the air, which did no damage but cleared the lobby almost magically, the guests heading for the rear exits which led to the car park behind the hotel. One of the men stopped by the security chief, who had just arrived. 'Keep this place clear while we move our friends to the bus,' he said, 'otherwise we start shooting.'

The terrorists then transferred the hostages to the bus in groups of two or three, hustled along by two terrorists, handing them over at the entrance to an unknown number of terrorists waiting inside the bus.

A single jeepload of police arrived in response to the urgent summons from a receptionist at the hotel and another from the security chief, as the last of the hostages were transferred to the bus. The police stopped their jeep in the gateway, hoping thereby to block the bus, and jumped out of the way.

The terrorists pushed the jeep backwards on to the road, and then took off as fast as the bus would go. A traffic policeman at the lights outside the hotel took down the number of the bus as it charged out of the hotel along the wrong side of the road, clipping a three-wheeler and a taxi as it came. The bus then bumped across the divider on to the right side of the road, jumped a red light, and roared off along the road to the airport.

Another traffic policeman, an inspector sitting fifty metres away on his Yamaha, kicked the engine of his bike into life and took off after the bus. He spoke to his station on his radio as he went, telling them that the bus was going past Air Force Command Dental Hospital, past the Manipal Hospital, and eventually past the airport itself towards Whitefield. Then the transmissions came to an abrupt end.

A second report followed on the fax a few minutes later. The traffic policeman following the bus had had his motorcycle shot from under him a kilometre past the airport. Other police teams who had joined the chase found him lying on the pavement, the motorcycle a few feet away. He was taken to hospital with severe head injuries as a result of having taken off behind the bus without waiting to secure the strap of his helmet.

The MP who had been kidnapped telephoned the chief of police of the city to tell him that he and his fellow hostages were at a farmhouse in Whitefield, several kilometres past the airport. When the MP had established his identity, another voice took over on the telephone to give the police chief the address of the farmhouse, and to warn him not to penetrate the wall which enclosed the three acres or so of land surrounding the farmhouse.

Gawand, the man who had briefed us on the Madras operation, arrived a little after noon, bearing his large, brown briefcase and a little more news. The FKF had driven to a farmhouse belonging to a Bangalore-based doctor-turned-businessman who lived weekdays in his flat in Langford Town in the heart of the city and spent weekends on his farm. He was out of town just then: he was, in fact, in transit from London to Moscow, and the police were trying to get in touch with him.

Close on Gawand's heels came General Kelkar, who had been dragged out of a meeting. Ismail had already called Venky, Hari—Major Hariprasad Deora, commander of Delta company which was now on two-hour standby— and Ramu, the adjutant. The fax buzzed again, this time producing four sheets.

The FKF had arrived at the farmhouse to find the gate locked. They had driven the bus right through the gates,

169

tearing them off their hinges, and parked the bus midway down the sixty-metre driveway. They shot and killed the two barking Dobermanns chained by the farmhouse, and then went on to the servants' quarters at the rear of the grounds. There they dragged the four servants—a cook, a maid who was the cook's wife, a handyman and a gardener—out of their rooms and forcibly took from them the keys to the house. They then threw the servants out, terrified but unhurt, bearing a letter they were told to hand over to the police.

The servants, being almost as terrified of the police as they were of terrorists, had given the letter instead to the next-door neighbours, who didn't believe a word of the servants' story until they took a look over the wall and found masked, black-clad men roaming the grounds. They handed the letter over to the local police station, who took some time over delivering it to the commissioner because they were unaware of what had happened in the city.

'We are the FKF,' said the letter, included in the fax. 'We lost a battle in Madras but not the war. We will continue our struggle against the Indian government. We will also try to make up the losses we incurred in Madras, though our dead colleagues are irreplaceable.' This time, they wanted the equivalent of fifteen million US dollars worth of gold and mixed currencies, to be delivered by the following morning. They also wanted the release of thirty of their comrades in jail, these released comrades to be brought to Bangalore by the morning following that. And finally, they wanted safe passage for themselves and their colleagues and the hostages, this time to South America, where they would release the hostages.

They hadn't sent down a list of hostages. 'You can find out on your own who our guests are,' ended the letter.

'This has all the salient features of the Madras operation,' explained Gawand. 'They picked a low-security area, grabbed hostages, most of whom are fairly important but would tend not to have any personal security around them, and have now retreated to a good defensive position. From what I have, they are all dressed the same way they were in Madras: black uniforms, black masks, all big, well-trained men working smoothly together. Oh, and this time they're wearing gloves.'

'That's what worries me most,' I said. 'There's a pattern now. Like I've been saying all along, there's one man behind all this, planning it out, setting it up. He keeps getting better. His men are acquiring polish now. Until this fellow came along you wouldn't have thought any Kashmiri militant would fit into a five-star hotel. Until we get him he'll keep at it, and since he's learning as he goes along, the day's not too far off when he'll strike hard and successfully.'

'So what are you leading up to?' asked Ismail.

'Catch the bastards alive, as many as we can manage.'

'Let's have whatever you've got on the farmhouse,' said Ismail, suddenly thoughtful. 'Let the police get hold of the architect and his drawings for the house. There must be a map of the property and drawings of the house with the municipality. Get those as well.'

'I have a description of it here,' said Gawand. 'We haven't been able to get in touch with the owner but the police have already traced the architect. The drawings are now in Bangalore, but the architect sent me a description.

'It's a three-storeyed building, built on stilts: there's a car park where the ground floor should be. The owner likes parties, socializes every weekend he's there, calls friends over for quiet drinking sessions and cards, and he's made sure there's enough room under the house for at least six cars. There's more room on the driveway.

'Behind the house is a swimming pool, twenty metres by ten, with a deep end twelve feet deep, that's now dry. It's normally used at this time of the year but the owner's away for a long while.

'Around the house is about three acres of land, in a square, with the house almost in the middle, about sixty metres up a curved driveway. There's a four-foot-high wall all around the property. The owner grows coconuts on about a third of the land, some more at the back, behind the swimming pool, is set aside for vegetables. There's a patch of lawn and decorative flower beds along the front, and a henna hedge along the driveway. There's a well in one of the rear corners of the compound.'

'Now for some bad news,' he continued after a pause, laying his glasses on his briefcase. 'The owner was worried about security after a spate of dacoities at the outskirts of Bangalore some years ago. He installed lights all over the property controlled from inside. That compound is going to be well-lit.'

'This one's been planned by the same guy, then.' I said.

'Who's negotiating with them?' asked Ismail.

'Chauhan of the CBI is on his way there now,' replied Gawand. 'Until then it's the Bangalore commissioner of police, C. Dhandapani. But they haven't begun yet. We tried ringing up the farmhouse—the number's in the directory—but they seem to have left it off the hook. We haven't been able to contact them yet.'

'So what's been done so far?' I asked.

'That farmhouse has been cordoned off. There's a company of Karnataka RAF around it now.'

The fax buzzed again. The terrorists had rung up the commissioner's office and had been patched through to his command post outside the farmhouse. The FKF would now be available on the telephone, the same smooth voice had said, in English, and wanted to know what had been done about the delivery of the money and the imprisoned FKF men.

The commissioner, far out of his depth, said he wasn't empowered to say anything except that the money was being collected and would be ready for delivery the next morning, as required by the FKF.

All right, said the voice, the commissioner had sixty minutes in which to get back to the farmhouse with someone who was empowered to negotiate. Failing that, one hostage would die straight away.

The commissioner had called the state's home minister, who had in turn contacted the home minister in Delhi, only to be told that Chauhan was on his way to Bangalore and would get there by about two, past the hour's limit the FKF had given.

The commissioner then called the farmhouse. He told the FKF spokesman that Chauhan was on his way from Delhi but would arrive at the farmhouse only at about half-past-two. Off his own bat, he told the FKF that the government was considering the logistics of getting thirty prisoners together and out to Bangalore.

Fine, said the voice, Chauhan was to ring up the moment he arrived. And in the meanwhile, the hostages had to be fed.

What, how and when, asked the commissioner.

South Indian food, said the voice, idlis or dosas or whatever, on disposable paper plates, with plastic spoons, no knives or forks. Enough food for twenty people. No vessels, no metal objects, no loose liquids that could be hurled at the faces of the captors, no pepper or salt besides what was already in the food. All the meals would be collected at the farmhouse gate by a man from the FKF, who would check everything. The commissioner was to call as soon as the food was ready at the gate. Any attempt to endanger the FKF man sent out to collect the food would cause the death of at least one hostage . . .

The police had traced the bus in which the FKF had taken their hostages out to the farmhouse. It had been hired from a hire firm near Richmond Circle. Two men had collected it early in the morning, with the driver. The driver was missing.

Delta company would have to get to Bangalore, said the last sheet of the fax, they were to get ready to move.

A task force had already been set up. It was much the same as the committee for the last one, comprising people from the home and defence ministries, the state and city police forces, and from the Army the local Army sub-area commander—whose offer of troops to set up a cordon about the farmhouse had already been turned down—and General Kelkar. Also included this time was the head of the Bangalore Air Force establishment and a general manager from Bangalore-based Hindustan Aeronautics, just in case air transport of any kind was required, or if anyone wanted things dropped on the farmhouse.

Kelkar brought things into focus immediately. 'There is a deadline. Those guys are serious. We have enough evidence of that. We should do exactly what we did last time: get there as quick as we can and figure out a way in. We can't do that sitting here. Ismail, Raja and I will leave today with Delta company. If we need anything more Venky can bring it along tomorrow, or we can borrow from Bangalore sub area.'

Hari and Ramu left immediately to make sure Delta was ready on time, while Kelkar got on the phone to arrange our transport. Gawand sat back looking at the activity, relaxed a wee bit, smiled weakly at me. I went back to my office and called Sandhya. 'Just called to tell you I'm going out of town for a while,' I told her.

'You should be ashamed of yourself,' she replied. 'You haven't come over or called for weeks. You've been avoiding us. Where are you going?'

'I'm not allowed to tell you,' I said.

'And when will you be back here?' she persisted.

'I don't know,' I said. 'Not more than a few days.'

'Is there trouble somewhere?' she asked slowly, sensing the tension in my voice, worry showing in hers.

'Ummm, sort of,' I said. 'Can't tell you any more than that just now.'

There was a little pause while she absorbed what I'd said. 'All right, then,' she said, 'I won't dig. Take care, and make sure you get back in one piece . . . And listen, call me the moment you get back. Okay?'

'Sure I will,' I said, and hung up.

Hari was the youngest of our company commanders, and the least experienced. He'd topped out of the IMA eight years earlier and joined the Bombay Engineering Group, been seconded to 10 Para Battalion as a captain, going into Sri Lanka a month after his training with 10 Para was complete. But he'd spent less than two months in Sri Lanka before his unit was pulled out of there. He was a brilliant engineer, and probably the most intelligent man in the unit, but he somehow left me a little uneasy. Under that perfect cover lurked a weakness I hadn't been able to pinpoint. I was sure he'd joined the SOF only because it was a terrific career move.

He tended to drive his men too hard and too long. I'd begun to hear faint rumbles over the last six weeks, over exercises, but his company always did well on the field, whether training or exercising, and the best men at infiltration were in his unit. He himself was a fitness freak and drove himself as hard as he drove his men, which was to my mind the only reason they accepted what he gave them. He was uniformly pleasant with his superiors, never lost his head, the perfect soldier on paper if ever there was one. But hidden in there was a weak spot . . . I had to find it.

I debated whether to get Bravo ready as well, from their six-hour alert status which would be upgraded to two-hour alert by the time Delta moved out. They'd been tested in the field and that made all the difference. And Venky I was sure would bend and massage rules and drive his JCOs crazy to get his men ready in far less than the six hours I could give him. Venky himself had mileage, and a fund of common sense, and was a good man to have around. I was thinking of making him 2IC when Ismail moved on.

But Hari wouldn't like it, and neither would Delta. Getting Bravo along at this stage would be a clear sign of lack of faith in Delta, which I couldn't afford. Delta would have to grow up very quickly indeed, and I'd have to ride herd on them, making sure Hari stayed in line, watching for possible weaknesses, nipping them before they generated failures.

This time the equipment list was different. I'd asked Hari to take climbing gear along, grapnels, ropes, suckers and the like. If we had to climb the walls of the farmhouse we'd need every bit of help we could get out of our equipment. The heavy weaponry stayed behind, like last time.

We landed at Bangalore, at the civilian airport run by HAL and not the Air Force field at Jalahalli, at half-past-five, with a good forty-five minutes of daylight left in which to study the lay of the land. Awaiting us on the tarmac were Brigadier J.S. Kalra, the Karnataka sub-area commander, and by his side a superintendent of the Karnataka police.

The farmhouse turned out to be only twelve kilometres from the airport, straight down the road away from the city. Twenty minutes after touchdown, while the equipment was still being unloaded from the aircraft under the supervision of Hari and his JCOs, the lead jeeps were drawing up at the broken gates of the farmhouse. The trucks with the rest of the unit would follow in their own time, but Kelkar, Ismail and I wanted to observe as much of the farmhouse as we could before sunset.

Chauhan had set up his command post to the west of the farmhouse, three metres outside the compound wall, from where he could watch the house at ease across the vegetable garden and the swimming pool. He'd set up another post by the gate, manned by the RAF contingent, used for deliveries to the farmhouse.

'Shit!' exclaimed Ismail after his first sweeping look at the farmhouse through his field glasses. 'That house is surrounded with jungle but there's a clear area at least twenty feet all around it. And it's set on stilts. If we try to go in along the ground they'll be able to chew us up.'

Indeed they would. The house stood on pillars three metres high. Through my field glasses I could see the open bit of lawn in front—the eastern side—of the house, the green ornamental poles rising more than waist high, with white globes on top that would light up at dusk. Behind the house was the swimming pool, now dry, surrounded by a concrete apron. On either side of the house itself was a concrete apron at least twenty feet wide. Two men patrolled the apron and the parking area under the house.

A brief message arrived from the home secretary of the state. A British citizen attending the conference had been taken hostage. The British government were in on this one. Take all precautions, the note said, to ensure that the hostages are retrieved safe.

The men arrived in their convoy of trucks, to be led to a clearing 400 metres to the rear of the farmhouse, where Brigadier Kalra had made provision for our camp to be set up. I went along with them, and then, when Kelkar and Ismail went off with Kalra to meet the task force, took a walk around the perimeter wall, now patrolled by alternating SOF and RAF men, looking for clues on how the FKF had organized their defences.

The house actually faced backwards, away from the road, facing the swimming pool. A balcony ran around the western and southern sides of the house, with a single staircase up to the first floor from the west. From the landing the staircase continued upwards to the second floor balcony as well. The balconies had a waist-high railing that looked solid. In the north-west corner of the compound were the servants' quarters, a row of whitewashed rooms with sloping, red-tiled roofs, now empty. One of the lookouts caught sight of me watching them over the wall by the servants' quarters, and half-raised his AK-47 in a warning.

In the fading sunlight a black box at the top of the stairs to the first floor caught my eye. It didn't belong there. Through the field glasses it looked a foot wide, six inches high, three inches deep . . . an improvised anti-personnel mine hooked up to a tripwire across the steps somewhere on the staircase? We'd have to watch the lookouts negotiating the staircase: that would tell us where the tripwire was, if there was one at all.

The windows on the first floor were all firmly barred: I could see the aluminium bars against the yellow curtains. There was no way to get a peep into the rooms. We didn't know how many men the FKF had in there, or how the hostages were disposed.

Above every window ran a sunshade, sticking maybe eighteen inches out of the wall and about a foot beyond the edge of the window. On each floor, a wooden door to the west opened on to the balcony. Another glass door opened on to the south wing of the balcony on each floor.

A small cabin between the pool and the house had a pipe leading to it, probably for a shower or tap inside it. On the roof of the house was a TV antenna, and beside that a small dish antenna for Star TV. And beside the dish, weapon ominously raised, watching me intently through field glasses, stood another FKF man. Three lookouts, then, two on the ground and one getting a bird's eye view from above. In the dark the man on top would be impossible to see from below.

I took a closer look at them, first at the man on the roof, then the ones below. All wore helmets, and, unless I was mistaken, body armour. They were offering much smaller targets this time. The lookouts below kept on the move, changing positions every few seconds, disappearing behind a pillar now and again, or behind the bathhouse. The one above had retreated out of sight. Difficult targets, the lot of them, even for my snipers.

I see you, Krait, I thought, you've learnt to protect your lookouts better. If you'd had them protected like this last time we wouldn't have got past your perimeter.

He'd taken the high ground this time. We wouldn't find it so easy to go crashing in through unprotected windows. I didn't trust that garden. We had a reasonably clear approach to the farmhouse from the east and the west but to the north and south were trees, mostly coconut palms. Lots of cover there for us to infiltrate, I thought. The FKF hadn't asked for any lighting there, and the owner hadn't installed any as best I could see. I couldn't believe he'd left it open. He couldn't have. So where was the catch?

In the growing dark I went back to the command post, looking for the head of the RAF detachment. I found him standing by Chauhan, a short, thickset, tough-looking deputy superintendent in James-Bond-style Ray-Bans that hid his eyes. 'Did you see any of those men planting wires or mines in the garden?' I asked him.

'No,' he replied. 'We arrived here about three hours after they took this building. They haven't come out of the house since we arrived, except for those lookouts. But we don't know what they did in those three hours before we arrived. I scanned the garden from outside but saw nothing. The only mine I saw was the one at the top of the staircase, on the first floor. Did you see that?'

'Yes. I hope that's the only mine but the fact that they have the know-how to build and set mines makes me suspicious.'

'I'll tell my men to watch.'

Chauhan interrupted us. The architect had been traced, and had arrived with drawings of the house. On each of the two floors was a large, long hall, the main entrance to each, the wooden door to the west. The glass doors on the south face, too, opened into the hall. Off the hall, on the first floor, were three bedrooms, each with a bathroom attached, and a kitchen to the east, its window facing the ruined gate.

Seven bedrooms, then, and a kitchen, all off two long halls. The owner liked light: he'd specified that a window should run along almost the entire length of every bedroom. The south face of each hall was almost all glass. This was an airy house behind all those curtains. 'Did the police talk to eyewitnesses about how many men there are? Has anyone cross-checked statements?' I asked Chauhan.

'We've been through all that,' he replied. 'But it's still a black box, just like last time. We don't know how many men they have in there. They asked for lunch for twenty people—too much for the hostages alone, and not enough for hostages and terrorists—and we can't figure anything from that. We only know they have at least fifteen hostages, including the MP, from the lists we got from the hotel and the association that organized the seminar. We don't know if they picked up a casual visitor as well. We have no idea how the hostages are kept . . .'

'I'd like to speak to the hotel staff, and some of the others involved in this,' I said.

'Sure,' said Chauhan. 'The police are still at the hotel and if you get there right away you should be able to catch most of the staff before they leave for the day. If you get anything more out of them share it with me.'

At the hotel things were limping back to normal after the horrendous day. Many of the guests had, after informing the police, checked out and moved into other hotels, or moved in with friends or relatives. But surprisingly enough, the majority had taken the kidnapping in their stride and stayed on. The broken glass doors and the chandelier and some other debris had all been cleared up and there was at least a superficial air of business-as-usual about the place when I walked into the lobby. A receptionist led us to an office just off the lobby, where in a few minutes we were joined by the front office manager and the steward who had been in charge of the Vijayanagar hall that morning. 'How many men came into the hall?' I asked him.

'Four, sir,' he said unhesitatingly. 'Four of them came in, two or three fired into the air, and while we were still trying to get our wits together they shepherded everyone they didn't want out of the hall. They kept a waiter with

183

them, just in case they needed to know the back ways, I suppose, but they let him go when the bus arrived here.'

'Where were you after they pushed you out?' I asked.

'I was in the lobby, to a side, because they wanted a clear path to the entrance. I got Krishna—the security man who was shot—on to one of the couches in the lobby and called a doctor.'

'Did you see how many men got off the bus to transfer the hostages?'

'Two, sir. They marched into the hall and took three hostages out to the bus. They never gave the hostages a chance to look around or anything. There was one man who kept prodding at them with his gun, telling them to move.'

A cowboy type. 'Did you see how many men there were in the bus, waiting for the hostages?'

'At least two, sir,' he replied. 'We couldn't see into the bus because the windows were all closed, and darkened. There was a driver, and at least one man to take the hostages in. But you can talk to our guards about that. They might have got a better look into the bus.'

The guard who had been at the gate had no clear recollection of the inside of the bus. 'I saw the driver,' he told us. 'The driver didn't get out of his seat at all, and behind him I saw at least one other man before they brought the first hostages into the bus.'

'That makes four inside the hotel,' said Ismail, 'two in between shuttling back and forth with the hostages, and three in the bus. A minimum of nine men, if they didn't pick up anyone else on the way.'

'Did you notice anything about how they took the hostages to the bus?' I asked.

'Each time they came to the door they did something threatening,' he replied. 'There was one man in particular who was jumping around waving his gun. They terrified us. When I thought about it afterwards I realized they must have done it on purpose, to keep everyone in line, to discourage people from getting too close. I thought it was a good idea. Otherwise they might have had to shoot more people.'

That cowboy again. Keeping people away. 'What damage did they do?'

'They broke one of the glass doors at the entrance, sir. They brought down a chandelier in the hall. They broke the glass doors of the bookshop, which was closed: it opens only at ten. They knocked down some signs and broke a coffee table. Nothing very much, just enough to keep people away.'

'Where did the men come from?' Ismail asked.

'One of the waiters saw them charging out of the gents' toilet. He went inside the toilet to investigate, sir—he's a very brave man, you see—and found another guest tied up in one of the cubicles. The man who had been tied up identified one of the four.'

'Who was he, the man the guest identified?' Ismail asked.

'Another guest. The receptionist will be able to tell you all about him, sir. I don't know.'

The girl who had checked him in the previous afternoon, a twenty-fiveish, poised young lady, gave me her impressions

185

of the man, her shoulder-length hair bobbing as she spoke. 'He made a reservation here himself two weeks ago, sir. He paid in advance, in cash, for one night. The cash payment was strange, because most people pay by credit card, or by cheque if they're companies. We didn't bother too much about it because we thought it was someone burning off some black money, and the amount wasn't very large.'

'What did you notice when you checked him in?' I asked.

'He checked in on schedule, at three yesterday afternoon. We brought out the records of his reservation then. He had three visitors this morning, before nine, and the housekeeping staff on his floor said that the do-not-disturb sign was up all morning.'

'What was the man like?'

'He looked like a Punjabi, sir,' she replied. 'We get used to seeing these things. He spoke with a slight Punjabi accent, but he was quite polished. He was very fair, with brown hair, brown eyes and he was carrying Ray-Ban glasses. To me he looked very different from our usual guests: he was very fit, very strong. Most of the people who come here are middle-aged but he looked very young, very strong. The bellboy told us his suitcase was very heavy but he carried it without any trouble. He had no rings, no jewellery . . . Nothing to identify him.'

'Have you checked his name and address?'

'I gave it to the police, sir, and I heard later that it was all false,' she replied, 'but you should be asking the police about that. But I can't get over it, he was so polished, so civilized, and pleasant, smiling all the time . . . I couldn't believe the man's a terrorist.'

'That's why no one's caught him yet, ma'am,' said Ismail. 'What were his visitors like, did you see?'

She sent us to another girl to answer that question, the one who'd been on duty that morning. 'Three young men, sir,' said the girl, 'two with briefcases and one with a suitcase. They looked like businessmen. A bellboy thought they were guests and offered to carry the suitcase . . . They were quite rude to him, that's why I noticed. They went up the stairs instead of waiting for a lift. They must have been carrying the guns.'

The police had no idea where the men had come from, but had discovered that three young men matching the description the lady at the Taj had provided had checked out of a much more modest hotel in Shivaji Nagar only half an hour before they arrived at the Taj. More to the point, the names and addresses the young men had given the smaller hotel had proved false.

The man at the bus hire concern was rude, to say the least, and not in the least concerned about his driver, who seemed to have vanished. The driver could, of course, have been one of the terrorists but it was unlikely because he had been in service for over a year. 'What are you people doing?' the man protested when we visited him. 'Someone steals my bus and my driver disappears and I don't know anything about it, but instead of trying to find my bus and my driver you come and harass me while the thief gets away. How can a man run an honest business like this?'

Unlike the hotel staff, I thought, this man ran his own business, the mainstay of which was his commandeered bus, but while the hotel's staff had been mostly cooperative, this man was going out of his way to get rid of us. He should have been falling over himself pleading with us to get the bus back. I didn't understand until the local police inspector explained to me in a whisper, grinning, 'This man runs lots of businesses out of this office. His transport business isn't doing very well . . . He hopes the terrorists will destroy his bus so he can claim the insurance and wind up without making too much of a loss. He doesn't want the bus back.'

At the farmhouse we found the lights on all over the garden. The concrete apron about the house was brightly lit. There was little that the lookouts on top and below would miss. There was something odd about the lighting, though—the car park wasn't lit. It was impossible to have a good look at the lookouts stationed below. I looked up at the terrace and found it similarly dark as far as I could see. With all the lighting around, it would be hard to see the lookouts even with image intensifiers. I went back to my tent and from my kit dug out an image intensifier. I could now make out the lookouts but not well enough to put them out of action with a single shot. And they all wore night-vision glasses, too.

Out to the east of the house the globes in the garden lit up the lawn and the hedges. But to the north and south of the house, past the apron, where the coconut trees were planted, there were dark patches. Enough for a careful man to slip through. Further up by the servants' quarters was another dark patch.

The area was well lit but the lookouts were in the dark. We wouldn't be able to take them out as we had done at Madras. The feeling deepened that the same man had planned both operations. The Krait had learnt to take care of his sentries.

The dark areas about the house were a mystery. The FKF had explosives enough, and expertise. Had they planted mines amidst the coconut palms? Was this a trap that the Krait expected us to walk into?

chapter ten

This time the krait was aware of the predator earlier. In the face of the unknown danger the krait first curled up, its head in the middle of the curls of its body.

A cool breeze sprang up towards half-past-seven, the moon disappearing behind clouds from time to time. Dinner was delivered to the hostages, one terrorist coming to the outpost at the gate to collect the boxes of food while another stood guard, gun at the ready, some twenty metres up the driveway next to the bus. Here, too, the Krait had learnt. He had come in with more men this time, and could afford to have one of them come up to the RAF post at the gate to collect and deliver food and messages. There was no risk at all of an outsider seeing what was happening inside the farmhouse.

Hari and Ismail joined me at the gate as the FKF man walked away up the drive with his boxes of food. 'What do you have so far?' asked Ismail. 'Do we have a way in?'

'No,' I told him. 'We don't know a thing about what's going on inside. I need more time.'

'Don't forget the deadline,' said Ismail, turning to return to the command post. 'Find a way tonight. We'll have to go in tomorrow.'

One of the lookouts under the house emerged from the shadows in the car park on to the apron, looked around, then headed for the staircase. I took out the night glasses again. The other sentry was still in the car park, lurking behind a pillar. I couldn't see him clearly. There was no way we could snipe both of them out from the perimeter: too little of their bodies was exposed, even for our snipers. They moved around too much.

So we'd have to go in close, to the edge of the apron. The open areas east and west of the house offered no cover so we'd have to go in from the north and the south, under cover of the coconuts, and part of the hedge bordering the driveway.

Hari stirred beside me. 'The boss seemed edgy,' he said, 'I've never seen him so wound up.'

'Yes,' I replied. 'Kelkar must be putting the heat on him. And the committee must be putting the heat on Kelkar. And so on.'

'I think we can go in,' he said. 'I had a good look at the place while you were away.' He paused, pointing in the direction of the servants' quarters. 'We should be able to get in from the north-west corner, over the wall, squeeze between the wall and the servants' quarters and on to the coconut palms, and make it to the edge of the apron. If you'd like to come around the place with me I'll show you. We should be able to make it to the edge of that concrete apron around the house.'

We walked in silence, clockwise around the perimeter until we came to the servants' quarters. On the face of it Hari was right, that was the best way to go in. 'And how do you get past the apron, into the house?' I asked.

'We'll assemble in the shadows at the edge of the apron,' he replied. 'From there we can take out the sentries . . . With night glasses at twenty-five metres it's not a problem.'

'Both lookouts? At the same time? I'd say you have a rather large problem there.'

His back straightened at the rebuke, but he plodded on. 'We can wait for the time there's only one lookout. I've been watching these guys all evening and every now and then one of them goes up for God knows what reason.'

'Did you watch them going up the stairs?' I asked.

'Yes. The tripwire for the mine at the top of the stairs is on the third step from the top. They stepped carefully over that.'

'Did you check how long the fellow stays upstairs?'

'Minimum of two minutes. Maximum a little over five minutes. I couldn't make out whether it's the same man that comes down or another. I think there was a change of guard at dusk.'

'How many men would you take in there?' I asked.

'I had a look at the plans. I'd say most of the hostages are in the two halls, the biggest rooms in the house. If the FKF have nine men, with one off duty all the time and three lookouts, they have five men inside. I'd have the hostages distributed over the halls, two men watching each hall, and one free.' He paused, looking at me for approval.

'Go on,' I said.

'We should have two men for each terrorist in the halls. If the numbers are right, we'll have five men for each hall.'

'And the bedrooms?' I asked. 'The men resting will be in the bedrooms, won't they? And we don't know which ones?'

'We'll have to take each bedroom,' he replied. 'We'll take them through the windows, with men standing on the sunshades. One to each bedroom. There's a lookout on the terrace, we'll have someone go up there as well. Seven bedrooms, seven men. Add ten for the halls and one for the terrace, that makes eighteen men.'

'And how do we get into the building in the first place?' I asked.

'We'll assemble in the car park when the sentries are down,' he said, 'and we'll use grapnels and ropes to go up to the balconies and the sunshades. We'll go into the hall through the glass door, and have a couple of men at the windows of the hall as well.'

'Why can't we penetrate the perimeter after the sentries are down?' I asked.

'They keep talking to the guys above,' he replied. 'It's almost continuous. We can't afford to have a twenty-minute silence there.'

'Let me understand what you're saying, Hari,' I said. 'You want to infiltrate the compound with seventeen men, assemble at the fringes of the apron in the dark, shoot down the lookouts, assemble again under the car park, and then go up on ropes and break in through the glass doors. If we get a slot when only one of the men is on duty in the car park, so much the better. Is that right?'

'Yes,' he said.

'Do you know what I think, Hari?' I said slowly. 'Those lookouts—don't forget the one on the roof—will almost certainly spot eighteen men going in from a corner of the compound. One or two might get past but not eighteen. The sentries are well trained, remember?'

'We could do it from two corners,' he said. 'They needn't all go in from the same corner.'

'Even if we do that,' I said, 'it's going to take each man a couple of minutes to make it silently to the apron. If they go in two at a time, that's a minimum of eighteen minutes, if there are no gaps in between. Do you think they can stay unobserved for that long, Hari? And what about when all those men collect outside the apron? Do you think you can hide eighteen men in the shadows there? I don't. It's going to be very hard indeed.'

'Yes,' said Hari, now standing stiff and straight, looking past my shoulder at a point light years away. 'We'll have to cut down those numbers.'

'That we will, Hari,' I said, a bad taste slowly building up inside my mouth. 'And do you know the worst, Hari? Ismail and I and anyone else who works on this plan won't be able to improve it substantially, because you can cut the

194

number down only by five or six, if that much. Trim any more and the risks inside the house increase dramatically.'

'Yes,' he agreed. 'We don't seem to have a choice.'

'Fine,' I said, 'if we have to go in that way we will. But give me some timescales first.'

'From the time the men begin to go in to the time they assemble outside the apron shouldn't be more than half an hour. From there on it gets finer. Two minutes from that point to getting rid of the lookouts. Once the lookouts are down, five seconds to assemble under the car park. Three seconds after that for positioning, four to get the ropes up, and four to five more to climb up. Sixteen seconds after the lookouts are down we're ready to break in.'

'Those grapnels will make a noise. Enough to warn the man on the terrace, at least.'

'We'll cover that with a diversion. An aircraft flying by at the time. Or preferably a helicopter hovering overhead.'

'We'll see what we can do about diversions. What happens once the men are in position? That's the trickiest bit, and I want it as clear as possible.'

'We'll have to be careful about that,' he said. 'This is one thing I'm not very clear about. Those curtains on the windows . . . They could ruin everything.'

'Exactly. So how do we handle that?'

'The men go for the sections where you can see the curtains overlap . . . they can push the overlapping bits out of the way. With at least two men going in through each of the glass doors to the southern side of the halls—that should give everyone a reasonable chance of making it.'

I didn't think so but couldn't well say so. Besides, there didn't seem to be any other way in. 'All right, Hari,' I told him, 'you work on the details some more and we'll present it to Ismail and when he's been through it, to Kelkar.'

'All right,' he said, 'I'll walk around a bit more, have another look at the plans, and take a closer look at the garden.'

'Do that, Hari,' I told him. 'And listen, I wouldn't take too long over it. I'd like to put in a trial run before daylight.'

'A trial run?' Hari turned right around in his tracks. 'At this time of the night? How are we going to organize that?'

'I don't know,' I said, 'but I will. I'm not having our men go and do something this complicated without some practice. I want those grapnels to go up silently. I don't want the men to grope in the car park.'

Over the next hour Hari worked on his plan, trimming the team size to fourteen: one to each bedroom as before, seven men there; one man at one of the windows to each hall with two each going in through the glass doors, six men there; and one man for the terrace. He found that we could use two more corners to enter from, for the men to sneak in between rows of palms, which meant the men could get to the apron in twenty minutes max. But they'd all have to walk silently as cats.

Cats! We'd use animals as a diversion. Catch a few cats and let them loose over the walls of the compound. Get the FKF used to the sounds of small animals moving around amidst the coconut palms. We could get on that straight away.

196

I went to the cookhouse. I hadn't eaten since breakfast and for a change was hungry. The men had eaten and the cook himself was just sitting down to eat. At such short notice he could only provide fried eggs and salad but that was enough. I sat munching, trying to figure out how we could work cats and dogs into the plan while Hari worked some more details into his plan. Then I went to the command post to ask Kalra if he could get us half a dozen cats in a couple of hours. Bemused, he asked why I wanted them. 'Diversions,' I said, and he left it at that.

Hari joined me half an hour later, with the plan as he'd worked it out afresh. It was almost identical to what we'd worked out earlier, except that he'd based it now on getting in through three corners, and taking out both lookouts if there were two in the car park. Ismail heard us out in silence while we explained it to him, then said, 'I suppose that's the best you can do if you assume we have to go in along the ground, but I'm not very happy with it. It's risky.'

'We don't have a choice,' I told him.

'I can understand that,' he said, 'but tell me, Raja, what are the chances we'll get in there unchecked? Compared to the Madras operation?'

'I'd say about half as good as Madras,' I told him. 'If we use that cover properly we have a good chance of getting in unseen. We'll have to pick our men much more carefully than we did in Madras. And we'll have to have lots of dummy runs. The terrain will be different, of course, but I want them to get a feel of what we're going against.'

'What time do you plan to go in?'

197

'About three in the morning would be best.'

'On balance I'd say it's not worth risking an attack. I'll tell General Kelkar that.'

'I'd tend to agree with you,' I told him. 'But it's worthwhile waiting to see how the men do in the trial runs before we tell Kelkar anything of the kind.'

The trial runs were a disaster from start to finish.

Even at that late hour, Brigadier Kalra, a former 9 Para man who had served under Kelkar a few years earlier, waved a magic wand and uttered a few brusque words and got us a patch of land where we could see if the attempt was feasible.

The ground he'd organized for us was a four-acre, coconut plantation, a little larger than the grounds around the farmhouse, and it had in the centre a broken-down, old building which the owner was planning to demolish. Better still, it had electricity, and we could leave our own men as lookouts in the building while others attempted to get past them.

Ismail, leading the men in on the first trial, made it to the clearing beside the house, and so did two men following close behind, but one of the watchers spotted the next man in.

On the second run, Ismail again led the men in, slipping silently over the wall as before. This time, ducking for cover behind a shrub, almost sightless in the dark, he and his buddy fell fifteen feet into a disused well that had been more or less covered with undergrowth. The second man had landed on Ismail, and when we got the two out of the

198

well Luthra found Ismail had twisted and sprained an ankle, dislocated a shoulder and possibly cracked a rib: more than enough damage to put him out of the operation. We didn't wait for an ambulance but instead put him in a jeep to be driven out to a hospital, where X-rays confirmed the cracked rib.

On the third and fourth attempts, both with me leading, six men made it to the clearing. In each case, the lookouts got the seventh man as he cleared the wall.

Hari and I returned to the command post with the dismal news for Kelkar. Despair sat heavy on our shoulders as I reported to him that a ground attack was infeasible. Midway through, one of Brigadier Kalra's men arrived with a box. It contained a cat, the man said, a cat that I'd asked for earlier in the evening.

Kelkar looked at me as if I'd gone mad. 'What the hell are you doing with a bloody cat?' he exploded.

'I thought we'd let a few loose in the compound,' I told him. 'Let the lookouts see them. Get them used to hearing small noises out of the compound. Diversions, I thought.'

Kelkar grinned. 'You come up with crazy ideas sometimes,' he said, 'but since we can't go in on the ground we'll drop this one. Get rid of the cat.'

We opened the box outside the command post to let the cat out. A small striped ginger and white fury tipped with claws at the end of thrashing limbs burst out of the box, crouched for a moment by the tent, slashed at the man who had released it from the box. Before we could do anything about it, it streaked for the fence, and with a smooth leap for which it didn't even break stride, swept up to the top of the compound wall.

It ran along the top of the wall, looked over its shoulder, found no one in pursuit. It stopped then to clean itself, settling down on the wall to lick its bottom.

Moments later we saw it tense and straighten up, looking straight ahead along the wall. Some ten metres ahead of it, faintly visible in the wash of light from the bulbs in the compound, stood a big, scarred, white tomcat. As we watched, the tomcat advanced majestically on the newcomer, back slightly arched, tail twitching, ready to eject the intruder from his territory. He stopped a metre or so from the ginger cat, by which time the ginger cat was standing on its toes, back arched in anticipation of a fight, growling softly. The two cats regarded each other with hackles raised for maybe five seconds, and then the ginger cat broke away. It turned tail and jumped off the wall into the compound, away from us, presumably to the shelter of the coconut grove, with the big tomcat on its heels.

I walked up to the wall to see what was happening beyond. For a moment the ginger cat halted when it heard me come up to the wall, and then the tomcat was on to it. The ginger cat shrieked once, fought back with teeth and claws, and the cats disappeared into the pit in the middle of the coconuts. The lookouts below, who heard the noise, stepped out on to the concrete apron, watchful and tense. Then they saw the two cats, and retreated. Then we heard the cats fighting, the tomcat in full, threatening cry, and as we watched they emerged from the shadows by the swimming pool, crossed over to the trees north of the house, disappearing into the dark. The lookouts crossed with them, watching intently.

They stopped again for a scrap behind the trees. For a moment we heard the sounds of feline combat, and then one of the trees blew up. There was a flash and bang and a cloud of grey smoke as a mine went off, probably set off by a tripwire the cats ran into. In the house above more lights came on and from the halls emerged a guard, gun at the ready, torch in hand, calling to the lookouts below. One of the lookouts went into the trees carrying a torch, walking very, very carefully, and emerged a few minutes later, carrying by its tail the corpse of the white tomcat. Through my field glasses I could see that it had been hit a couple of times by shrapnel.

That was the end of the plan. There was no way we could go in along the ground if the FKF had mined the grounds. When had they done it, I wondered. If we'd gone in through the gardens we'd have been massacred. I looked up at the building now quiet again. We had to find another way in. There had to be a better way.

There was. We'd hit it from above. It was so well secured from the ground, that was the only way we could afford to go in.

The telephone at the command post rang. A soldier came out to call me in. Chauhan was on the telephone, the tapes rolling, saying, 'We'll get a doctor out to you in an hour.'

On a speaker set up on one of the walls came the FKF man's voice, educated and English-speaking, saying, 'Nothing doing, policeman. No doctors come here. We've learnt that much.'

'You must let a doctor see him,' pleaded Chauhan. 'You can't afford to let him die.'

'Don't tell me what I can do and what I can't, policeman,' said the FKF man. 'Two of my men will carry the sick man down to the car park. Your doctor can treat him there.'

'Give me some time,' said Chauhan. 'The man has a history of cardiac trouble. I'll have to arrange a doctor and some equipment: a portable ECG machine.'

'All right,' said the voice. 'Call us when you're ready. And don't take too long over it.' He hung up.

Chauhan turned to me. 'Look, it seems that MP had a heart attack when the mine went off. He has a history of heart disease and after the blast in the garden he complained of pain in his chest, and threw up. Then he lay down and wouldn't wake up.'

'Did you ask them to send him out?' I asked.

'That man laughed at me when I asked,' replied Chauhan. 'I've been trying to get him out of there ever since I started speaking to the FKF but he laughed and said the MP was his chief guest, how could he let the man go. He said he was willing to exchange the man for another MP. I offered him a soldier or a policeman in exchange but he refused.'

'What's the trouble with getting a doctor out to the MP?' I asked.

'He doesn't want anyone to go into the house. I told him they could blindfold the doctor, check him out, do whatever they did to Luthra when you sent him out to check that diabetic on the train, but he insisted that no one comes into the house. He agreed eventually to our sending a doctor to the car park to check the MP out. I told him that just moving the sick man down could kill him but he wouldn't listen to me.'

'So now what?' I asked.

'I hope your doctor's a good cardiac man, because he's going into the car park to treat the MP.'

But this time Luthra refused to go in unless we couldn't find a specialist to do it. 'I'm primarily a surgeon,' he explained, 'I know as much about the heart as the average doctor, which is certainly not enough to diagnose and treat a patient on the basis of limited tests, limited equipment, bad light, and in a high-stress situation like this. I'd tend to give the fellow something to sleep until it's all over one way or another. So get a specialist, and I'll go in if you can't.'

Chauhan traced a willing specialist, a consultant from St John's hospital, who was willing to treat the patient but only if he had a soldier accompany him. Chauhan called the farmhouse. 'I have a doctor ready to come in,' he told Smoothie, the FKF spokesman. 'He's willing to see the patient in the car park, under your supervision, and meet all your conditions, but he's not willing to come into the car park alone.'

'He comes alone, policeman,' said the voice, 'or the deal's off. I couldn't care one way or another.'

'The longer he stays alive the better it is for you,' pleaded Chauhan. 'If he dies he's got no hostage value.'

'Only if you know he's dead,' said the FKF man. 'As long as you think he's alive you'll continue to deal with us . . . Hey, that's a good idea! We'll kill him and stick him in the freezer and we won't have to worry about him any more, and you'll continue with the good work . . . By the time you find him it'll be too late.'

Chauhan's voice hardened slightly. 'We'll need evidence that the hostages are all alive and well before we pay you anything,' he said. 'You'd better keep him alive.'

'And what will you do if we show you only half the hostages alive, policeman?' taunted the voice on the telephone. 'Do you think you can force me to do anything?'

'It makes no sense for you to kill a hostage or have one die on you at this stage. We've missed no deadlines, we've made no mistakes in dealing with you, and you've made no mistakes, so keep him going as long as you can.'

'All right, I will,' said the voice. 'Send the doctor into the car park. He should be dressed only in his underwear. He can carry his equipment on a trolley or an open box. One of my men will come to the gate to check out the equipment and lead him in. The soldier—let it be Colonel Qureishi—should also strip down to underwear.

'Since we don't know enough to check the equipment out thoroughly, let me tell you that I will ask my men to connect a detonator to a small bomb which we will put around the colonel's neck when he comes in. I'll have the switch in my hand, and if anyone does anything I think suspicious, that's the end of the soldier. We'll have one hostage down in the car park as well, with a similar bomb around his neck. Insurance.'

'Colonel Qureishi is not available now,' said Chauhan. 'It'll have to be someone else.'

'Strange,' said the FKF man. 'The good colonel's never available when we want him. I begin to suspect something fishy. Is he hiding from us, or what?'

'The colonel is in hospital with injuries sustained during training,' said Chauhan. 'Now tell me, who else could we send in with the doctor?'

'Your Colonel Menon will do just fine,' said the voice after a pause. 'He did something of the kind in Madras as well, didn't he, policeman? Well, you just give him my compliments and tell him that we'll be pleased to give him a porter's job in Free Kashmir if the Army don't want him.'

It was getting on for five in the morning when we all assembled at the gate, the doctor in his underwear, shivering a little in the cold wind, his box of tricks loaded on to a trolley, and me. Chauhan called the farmhouse from the command post and a black-clad FKF man walked down the driveway in the light of the globes in the lawn, his gun in his right hand and in his left a crude necklace of insulated electrical cable, its pendant a fist-sized lump of plastic explosive taped up in black insulation tape. He came up to me and wordlessly stuck the muzzle of his gun in my mouth, and the necklace around my neck. From the pendant hung a wire attached to a little box which he continued to hold. He signalled to me to move on, and I pushed the trolley along the driveway, getting into the compound for the first time, with the doctor following close behind. We walked slowly past the bus, standing forlorn in the middle

205

of the driveway, most of the glass in its windows broken, its tyres deflated: they'd made a barrier of it.

The lights in the car park flashed on when we got there. By the staircase, a terrorist beside him, stood one of the hostages: the Briton. He was young—thirty or so, not more—and clean-cut, and even in the bad light I could see the dark rings under his eyes. He was dressed as I was in underwear, around his neck a necklace of plastic explosive which lead to a box in the terrorist's hand.

To the western end, the patient, now awake, lolled miserably on three chairs laid side by side, shivering under a sheet. The doctor stepped up to him, inspected him, checked his pulse and respiration, put his stethoscope to his chest a few times, percussed him firmly in the ribs. Then he opened his box and removed from it the portable ECG—a box the size of an average video cassette player with nine leads. Coating the electrodes with a gel to make them pick up electrical signals better from the skin, he began to attach them to the patient—six to the chest and three to the limbs, nine in all. In a moment there was a buzz from the machine and a tongue of paper appeared in the ECG's printer.

I looked around. The hostage by the staircase was the only one whose eyes weren't riveted on the ECG machine. He was staring at me most peculiarly, as if trying to say something. I saw a flicker of movement by his side, then saw something white drop to the concrete behind the hostage. A wadded piece of paper.

The man was trying to send me a message. It lay on the grimy concrete floor a metre away from me. It might as well have been a mile away; I couldn't reach it. The hostage coughed hard, a dry, smoker's cough, and bent over. He stepped back on to the paper when he bent down, got his foot over the paper, and managed to scrape it towards me. It travelled to within twenty-five centimetres of my feet, close enough for me to pick up on my way out.

The doctor finished his examination and straightened up. 'This man should be in a hospital now,' he said.

'No one goes out of here,' said the terrorist standing guard by the staircase. A harsh voice, not the smooth one we'd heard on the telephone.

'In that case,' said the doctor, 'this man will need regular medication. He will need a special diet, and rest. He shouldn't get out of bed at all. When you take him back upstairs let him just lie in bed. I'll send you his medication with instructions in a few minutes, and the police will bring you his food as I tell them to. Please cooperate with us. Please follow medical instructions carefully. This man is extremely ill.'

As he spoke I took a small step back towards the box. The little wad of paper, now directly under me, I covered with a foot, and managed to get it stuck between the first two toes of the foot.

A tall, masked man in black stepped out of the shadows to the north of the car park. 'Strange,' he said, coming up to me, 'how adversity breeds invention. I never thought someone would try to pass you a message, Colonel. Give

207

me that little piece of paper.' The same smooth voice on the telephone. The same smooth man who had so impressed the receptionist at the hotel. It wouldn't do to play games with him.

I stepped back, revealing the bit of paper. Smoothie took a few steps forward, prodded me in the stomach with the muzzle of his AK-47, forcing me back two steps, the lead from the bomb on my neck to the terrorist going taut. He stooped, picked up the wad of paper, unfolded it and read it, a smile appearing on his face as he did so. He looked at the hostage, now sweating in fear. 'Very observant, aren't you?' he said conversationally. 'Where's the pencil with which you wrote this?'

From the waistband of his underwear the hostage produced a small stub of a pencil, no more than an inch long, and another small folded sheet of paper, apparently torn from a spiral-bound notebook. 'You put these aside in the bus, didn't you?' asked Smoothie. 'When we made you sit with your heads down?'

The hostage nodded. In the chill morning, with the sun just beginning to show, he found a reserve of courage. He swallowed, nervous but no longer afraid. He held himself erect, prepared now for anything.

'Is anyone else involved in this trick?' asked Smoothie.

The hostage shook his head. 'No,' he managed to say from a throat gone dry. 'No one else.'

'Very brave of you,' said Smoothie, still sounding calm. 'I think I believe you, but we must make sure.' I could detect a new note in his voice, though, something menacing in the background. Very quickly, he shifted his sub-machine gun to his left hand, and a knife, a large commando knife, appeared in his right hand. His right hand flew forward and up in a blur of movement, and the hostage cried out in surprise and pain, a hand to his cheek, blood dripping between his fingers from a gash below his eye. Without giving the hostage time to recover, Smoothie hit him backhanded on the other side of his face. The hostage staggered back, and fell, a bruise appearing redly on his cheek. 'Who else?' repeated Smoothie.

The hostage lifted himself on his elbow, shook his head, then spoke through a dry throat, his voice a harsh whisper. 'No one,' he said. 'I'm an accountant. I'm trained to look carefully. I needed no one.'

Smoothie turned to one of his colleagues. 'Get another of them,' he said, 'from upstairs.'

The terrorist ran up the steps to the first floor. I heard voices above, and then he reappeared in the car park, dragging another hostage, whom he led to Smoothie. Smoothie held out a hand, helped the new man straighten up, and kneed him in the groin. The hostage doubled up with a gasp, and found Smoothie's knife in his face. Grey faced, the hostage straightened up. Smoothie held the knife to his throat, and turned to the hostage who had tried to pass me the message. 'Tell me who else, or I take out this man's eyes. Slowly.'

The British hostage shook his head in exhaustion. 'Do what you like,' he said, 'I did it alone. That's the truth.'

Smoothie nodded, smiling. 'I believe you,' he said. 'We respect courage. We must give you some recognition for yours. Take off your necklace.'

As the Briton, unnerved by the smooth man's calm, took the necklace gingerly off his neck and handed it to the terrorist standing by him, I realized what was going to happen. 'Keep that necklace on!' I shouted hoarsely at him. 'Keep that bomb and hug the man next to you!'

The smooth man moved behind me, kicked me hard on the base of the spine, and I went down on my knees in shock and pain. He drew his foot back and kicked me in the ribs as I knelt speechless, throwing me forward on my face. 'Quiet, Colonel!' he hissed. He turned back to the hostage, still standing confused, a hand still on the necklace. 'Go on,' he said, 'hand your necklace over and leave. For you it's over. Just walk out of here. You've earned it.'

I raised myself on my elbows to tell him not to but hadn't time to get a word out before the terrorist by me stepped forward and kicked me in the ribs. I watched helpless as the hostage let go the necklace to the man beside him, looked at me, then walked slowly down the driveway towards the gate and the slowly lightening day, towards what he imagined was freedom. As he left the car park, Smoothie raised his gun and cut him down with a single, sharp burst from his AK-47. He turned to me. 'I really couldn't let the man get away with it, could I?' he said. 'That man thought he'd get away with it because he was British. I can't afford to have this sort of thing going on among the guests.' He paused, and I tensed, thinking he was going to shoot me next. But he only shook his head, smiling again, seeming to read my mind. 'I'm going to let you go this time, Menon,' he continued. 'No other guest will dare try passing you a message now. And you do understand I won't hesitate to do what I have to with the guests.'

I turned over on my back and fingered the scratches beginning to show where I'd scraped my chest in the fall. I was getting too old for this. There'd be bruises on my chest, where they'd kicked me. My breath rasped a little and I wondered if I'd broken a rib. I lay back, let the pain wash over me. Let someone else do all this, I thought. I want a nice, safe job, I've had enough of being hit and shot at and threatened and now I should spend some time in the sun watching the grass grow. I picked myself gingerly up, felt nothing broken, and joined the doctor on his way out, pushing the trolley along, a terrorist escorting us along after removing my necklace. 'Come back in ten minutes for the body,' called the smooth man.

'What was wrong with that guy?' I asked the doctor. Anything to take my mind off the thought of the hostage being shot, off the pain rampaging through my body.

'Nothing,' he replied, still getting over the shock of seeing a young man shot down in cold blood. 'Just scared, that's all. I think he was trying to get out of that house on the strength of his illness. His faint might have been real, but the rest is probably just acting.'

Kelkar and Chauhan both waited grim-faced at the gate, ringed by an SOF contingent. 'What was that?' Kelkar demanded. 'Why did they have another hostage there? And why did they kill him?'

'They kept him there for insurance,' I said. 'They put a bomb on his neck. He tried to pass me a message written on a slip of paper somehow smuggled in inside his underwear, with a tiny bit of pencil. One of them—the man who talks on the telephone—caught him doing it, and shot him.'

'Why did they knock you down?'

I stood leaning on the gatepost in fatigue before answering. I didn't give a damn any longer. 'I figured out what they were going to do,' I said. 'I yelled at him to keep the bomb and hug the terrorist next to him.'

'Who was he,' asked Chauhan, 'and is there any chance of him being alive?'

'He was the British hostage,' I replied. 'I don't know anything else about him. I don't think anyone could have survived that burst. He must have been hit at least ten times. And now I've to go back there to fetch the body.'

I handed the doctor's trolley over to one of the policemen at the gate and returned to collect the dead hostage. I found a terrorist standing by the body, holding some clothes, a wallet, a few pathetic remains of the man. The corpse was heavier than I'd thought, and very pale. The terrorist standing by stepped forward to give me a hand when I staggered under his—its—weight. I eventually got him—I still thought of the corpse as a man—on my left shoulder in a fireman's lift, then took the clothes and the rest of his stuff in my right hand, and walked down the driveway back to the police post, wanting to do nothing but leave the corpse there and walk away to somewhere quiet . . .

At the gate an ambulance and stretcher team were ready to take the body of the hostage. A young medic came grim-faced to my side and gently took the body. In the dead silence I heard the scrape of boots on the ground as one of the RAF shifted position. I handed the clothes over to the police, dressed, and retreated in the rising mist of early morning to the command post behind the farmhouse. The operation hadn't begun and already we had a hostage dead.

Luthra walked in carrying a box of stuff. 'The General told me to have a look at you,' he said. 'Where have you been hit?'

I told him. He made me take off my shirt and poked and prodded for a while. 'Nothing broken,' he said, purposely cheerful. 'Not much damage apart from some rather impressive bruises.'

'Your bedside manner leaves much to be desired,' I said.

'You should see me handling old ladies,' he laughed, proceeding to stick medicated dressings over some small cut on my chest. 'Would you like to be treated like one, sir?' He handed me some pills, told me to see him again in a couple of hours if anything began to hurt and left.

Kelkar stumped wearily in some minutes after, followed by Chauhan, the commissioner and Kalra, and behind them a uniformed police stenographer. 'We're going to take a detailed look at what happened when they shot that hostage,' Kelkar began as the others gathered around me. The way

213

they sat it looked as if they were all ranged against me, until Kelkar and Kalra noticed and drew their chairs aside, dissociating themselves from the CBI and the police.

'You could leave this to us, General,' began the commissioner.

Kelkar didn't think so. 'We'll get on faster if you understand that until the operation's over and the Army debriefs Colonel Menon the only way you get to speak to him is in my presence,' he said firmly. The commissioner subsided, and Kelkar turned back to me. 'Tell us in detail what happened, and the steno will take notes.'

I told them. I told them about the hostage catching my eye, about his dropping the scrap of paper on the ground, and the terrorist coming out of the shadows where he'd been hidden.

'How much did he see?' asked Kelkar.

'All of it,' I replied. 'They were in position before I got there, and no one arrived after I did.'

'What did he say?' he asked.

'He said he couldn't permit this kind of thing to happen . . . Very smooth guy. I think it was the guy on the phone. He seemed very much in control . . . put up a hell of an act.'

'What do you mean?'

'The smooth man pretended he was letting the hostage go free. He told him to take off the bomb he was wearing around his neck, to walk out . . . And when the hostage was walking away he shot him.'

'Did you interfere?'

'Yes. The moment he told the hostage to take off the necklace bomb I knew what was going to happen. I yelled at the hostage to keep the necklace on and to hug the terrorist standing next to him . . . He didn't understand . . . There was nothing else I could do.'

'Why did he kill the hostage?' asked the General.

'To make an example of him,' I replied. 'At least, that's what he said.'

'And why didn't he shoot you? You had the paper for a while, didn't you?'

'First off, he wanted someone to come back here and make it clear they're serious. Second, if he had a go at me he'd probably provoke the SOF into something disastrous for him. Third, there was no need, since I was only responding to the hostage: I didn't start anything. Finally, I think they picked on him because he was British. They thought we'd be more careful that way.' The pain in my side was growing, and I sat back to ease it.

Kelkar looked at me strangely. 'All right,' he said. 'That's enough for the time being. I suggest you get some rest. But you do understand, we'll have to review it several times because the dead man is a foreigner.'

'All right,' I said, and went back to the camp, to my tent near the perimeter. Washed and dressed, drank some tea, looked out of the flap of the tent at a kite circling low overhead. Lay down on the camp bed. Forced the dead hostage out of my mind. And reflected on going in from above.

That was the only way we could do it.

215

No one was going to know about it. I'd have to tell Kelkar, of course, and the Air Force men who would drop us out of the sky, and the men who would be in the operation, but not a word to anyone else. If the committee or Kelkar demanded we tell anyone else I'd damned well leave.

My chest throbbed mercilessly. I got up from the camp bed and turned to the flap of the tent to find Kelkar approaching warily. 'How's the chest?' he asked. 'What did Luthra say?'

'Nothing very much,' I replied. 'I was thinking.'

'About what?'

'The leak. Now I'm sure there's one.'

'Why?' he demanded.

'They didn't let the doctor go into the house because they knew what Luthra did when he went into the coach in Madras.'

He started to say something, then changed his mind. None of the terrorists had survived the Madras operation. Luthra's little bit of playacting hadn't been mentioned anywhere except to the intelligence men at the debriefing, and the committee. All other accounts stopped with his having been knocked down. The FKF had gotten it from someone on the committee or among us . . . It was possible, of course, that the informant hadn't known at the time he was passing on sensitive information, and it made a good story . . . Given the other pointers, though, I didn't think it likely the informant was innocent.

'What do we do about it?' he asked eventually, examining the floor. 'It might not matter for now because we might not go in at all, but we need to know who the informant is.'

'Does it matter?' I asked.

'Yes,' he said. 'We've lost a foreign hostage and if we have a leak as well the risks will be unacceptable.' His head was bowed and his shoulders drooped slightly under the uniform. He sounded as if he were on the verge of cancelling the operation. 'They want to slaughter you. They think you should have saved that man, the Briton.'

'There was nothing I could do.'

'I know. That's why I've kept the others off your back. But now . . . If there's no way in . . .'

I took a deep breath. 'I think there is a way in, sir,' I said slowly. 'I've been thinking about it since I got here.'

chapter eleven

Once again the mongoose struck hard, leaping down from the high ground of a rock several feet above the snake. The krait uncoiled to flee. It was a little slow retreating. The mongoose nipped at its tail, leaving two long gashes in the smooth, blue, scaly skin of the reptile.

His head came up. 'From the air?' he asked, seeming almost to read my mind. 'I knew it. I wanted you to come up with it, for you to believe in it. I'd have planted the idea in your mind if it hadn't struck you, but this way is the best. Tell me how.'

'We'll jump from a helicopter at 2000 metres,' I said, 'open our chutes at 200. One man comes in early to take out the sentry on the terrace. I'll need some more time to work out the details.'

'How many men do you think there'll be on top?' he asked. 'If you're going in from above that's most important.'

'I've seen only one so far,' I said. 'There might be two at most. Assuming they have nine men, or even ten, with two lookouts at the bottom and two on top, that leaves only six men on two floors inside the house. If they rest in shifts, with at least one man out at any point in time, there shouldn't be more than two on top.'

'The sentries were carrying night-vision glasses,' he said. 'I saw them last night.'

'We need a diversion, sir,' I said, 'a really good diversion. Maybe you can pull it off.'

'Try me,' he said, grinning, his mood switched completely. 'If it's something the Army can do I'll have it done.'

'Nothing like that,' I said. 'What I'd really like is a civilian airliner nosing around among the trees east of here. It's in the normal flight path of commercial airplanes coming in to land. If we have one of those limping in, a genuine commercial aircraft from one of the private airlines, they'll tend to believe us if we tell them it's not a stunt we're pulling. Do you think you could fix that?'

'You don't ask much, do you?' he said. 'It'd be hard to do without telling them why. But I have friends with one of the private air-taxi operators. I'll try. Let you know by evening.'

'The weak spot,' I explained, 'as you rightly said, is clearing the sentries on the terrace. If we can catch them early enough while they're watching the airliner nosing about at treetop level . . . It'll also get the sentries' attention off the helicopter that we're going to jump out of.'

'Why don't you jump from higher up?' he asked. 'Less noise that way.'

'Right,' I agreed. 'We can do it from anything up to 5000 metres up. That should cut down the noise quite a bit.'

'Practice sessions?'

'None,' I replied. 'The point is to clear the terrace without being seen. Then the others can land there. What we'll do afterwards will be fairly routine. We can use ropes to come down to the balconies outside the halls.'

'How many men will you land on the terrace?'

'The absolute minimum. Fifteen. Seven for the bedrooms, two each for the halls, and two more to take the men in the car park. We'll use the best of the climbers for this one. The men going into the car park can carry grenades, there's not much risk of a hostage being down there.'

'What if they spot you?'

'Olive drab chutes against a black sky, sir?' I asked. 'It's not likely. And if you can't get hold of an airliner, sir, it could be any old plane. A small one with a noisy engine buzzing around the airfield, with a bit of fire stuck out of the window would be terrific.'

'I'd be happier with practice sessions,' he said. 'Especially for the men who'll clear the terrace. That's when you'll be most vulnerable.'

'The leak's what I'm most concerned with now. If we hold trial runs we'll have to tell many more people about it.'

For once Kelkar put his foot down. 'We'll handle the leak one way or another,' he said, 'but we must have a dummy run.'

'All right,' I said. 'We'll set it up separately. Dummy runs only for the men who'll go first. No one else must know what they're doing. Nobody leaves the camp. If anyone does they don't come back in. We don't tell the committee what we're doing. We'll quarantine the Air Force men who deliver us as well. The only people out of the quarantine will be the liaison guys.'

'You don't ask much, do you?' snorted Kelkar. 'And what do I tell the committee?'

'Tell them about the leak. Explain why you're doing it this way. Watch while you tell them. Tell them this is the only way we'll work on this operation. Otherwise . . .'

'Otherwise what?' he demanded.

'Otherwise I pull out, sir. Of the Army if necessary.'

'We'll consider that unsaid,' he replied bluntly. 'Say that again and you really will be out. I don't like threats.'

'That wasn't a threat, sir,' I explained, 'just a statement of fact. I do not see the need to tell people what I am going to do when there is a strong possibility that one of them is going to tell the enemy. And it's not as if they contribute anything to the plans. They wish to persuade themselves there isn't a leak but I'm not risking my neck on that wish.'

Kelkar rubbed his chin, hand rasping over the stubble of nearly twenty-four hours. 'Okay,' he said at last. 'I'll go with what you say. We'll check the plan with Ismail once— see him in the hospital, probably this afternoon—when you have the details ready. But if you screw it up or if we find afterwards there wasn't a leak I'll have your head . . .'

'Sure,' I said, 'I'm game.'

221

'What else?' he asked, preparing to leave.

'We need chutes, those special Korean ones. For precision drops. Can we have them by evening?'

'I'll have them delivered to you by four,' he promised, and stalked off.

Outside, the morning sun brightened and the last trails of mist disappeared. An airliner banked overhead, turning in to the airport ten kilometres away. It seemed almost to brush the treetops as it descended to the runway. A few cumulus clouds in the sky, and patches of high cirrus. Nothing like rain-bearing nimbus yet. The breeze would bring more clouds. The weather forecast had said partly overcast, whatever that means. Lots of clouds at night and thankfully not much of a moon. We'd be much better off under a dark sky. I hoped fervently for heavy clouds and no rain.

Breakfast was delivered to the hostages, to the gate, including the special one for the MP. A terrorist came out to collect the boxes with another watching, as usual.

I thought then of the parachute jumps in the dark. We'd be jumping without packs—which can weigh up to forty kilos—and with only weapons, so the jump would be easier. Our standard chutes, round, silk, static-line umbrellas, were clumsy: you could lose control and at the altitudes we were going to jump from could drift a hundred metres in a strong wind. With the new Korean ones— rectangular chutes with two layers and with a multitude of vents—we could control drift, rate of descent, horizontal movement with ropes that hung on either side of the

222

parachutist. With these chutes we could touch down in a circle just a metre in diameter. Most of the trouble when jumping was due to the packs, which hung below the jumper during the descent, landed first, and being heavy and inanimate often dragged the jumper along a few yards, especially if the landing were on a sloped surface. Without packs it would be a breeze.

The first man down would have to clear the sentries on the terrace. He'd have to land silently and hopefully unseen in a corner of the terrace, farthest from where the sentry—or sentries—stood. If there were two of them, he'd try to land so that he and the two terrorists would all be in line, so the terrorist farthest from him wouldn't be able to get a clear shot immediately. He'd have to release his parachute—a single button would do that—unsling his rifle, and bring down the lookouts. He'd come down with night glasses, as would everyone else, to see the sentries as clearly as possible.

For the kind of precision jumping we needed here the man would have to land very slowly, on his feet. He'd be vulnerable during the descent. If they saw him as he descended, he'd be a sitting duck, and if they heard shots, the others would have to land outside the perimeter. One of our better marksmen would need only a couple of seconds with a silenced rifle to bring them down. A pistol would have been much easier to use but our standard 9 mm pistols with their muzzle velocity only a third or so of the rifles might not be accurate enough across the possible range of twenty metres or so . . . No, we had to

223

have that diversion. We had to have that sentry with his back to the lead man as he came in.

The lead man, armed with a rifle, would have to stay on top. The men going to the two floors of the house and to the car park would be armed with sub-machine guns.

I wished we had more practice with the chutes, especially at night. Parachutes are expensive. Even in the regular para units—not the para commandos but regular infantry trained in jumping—each soldier gets to jump only five times a year. Unlike civilians, paras never recover their chutes for reuse—they might recover them to conceal their tracks—so the chutes are meant for one-time use. The Indian Army can barely afford even the five annual jumps per soldier with the regular chutes. And the ones we were going to use in this exercise were Korean ones, much more expensive than the standard ones. Unless I was mistaken, only about half of Delta company had ever jumped at night . . .

The money began to arrive at a little after ten, in armoured trucks, unloaded at the police post at the gate. I walked past as policemen stacked the strongboxes by the gatepost. This time, for the equivalent of fifteen million dollars, they were using more than sixty strongboxes. A dozen policemen sweated in the sun, unloading the boxes and carrying them to the gatepost, where a pair of terrorists watched as the boxes were stacked neatly on the ground. Another terrorist stood near the bus midway up the drive. He had grenades in pouches on his belt. In case of trouble he could lob a couple of them at us, or into the police post. On the top floor of the house a curtain jerked. There was another terrorist watching us from up there. They were taking no chances. According to Chauhan, they had said they would carry the money up to the house. There must have been close to a quarter-ton of bullion, notes and specie in them.

A policeman opened the first of the strongboxes for the terrorist to inspect. The terrorist offered the policeman a black plastic sack like a garbage bag. The policeman transferred the contents of the box—gold bars—into the sack, which the terrorist took away. The process was repeated with the second terrorist, who waited for the first to return with an empty sack before starting off for the farmhouse. These men were painstaking, like accountants. They checked everything.

The third time round, the policeman tripped. Walking backwards, dragging the box along, he tripped on a small bit of stone sticking out of the ground, and fell sideways on his hands and knees. The FKF man watching him dropped his sack, and before anyone could do anything, took his gun off its sling and fired once at the fallen policeman. The rifle was thankfully on single shot, and the bullet hit the policeman on the chest, grazing him across the sternum. The RAF men at the gate, too, had their guns at the ready and in that second the atmosphere of the post changed from wary neutrality to hair-trigger tension.

The policeman who had been shot made it to his feet on his own, stunned, not quite believing that he had been shot. I had one of our men lead the injured policeman, still

225

dumbly holding his chest, to the medic's tent behind the command post, from where Chauhan rang the farmhouse. 'One of our men tripped and fell as he was delivering a box of currency to the gate,' he said. 'I suggest you send someone else to supervise the transfer, someone who's not so nervous.'

'Are you telling me how to run my kidnapping, policeman?' sneered the smooth voice on the telephone. This was the dangerous one, the one who had caught the hostage with the bit of paper, and shot him. 'I'll put whoever I wish on whatever job I choose, policeman. Just tell your club-footed colleagues at the gate to be more careful. If their guys get killed that's their problem.'

'I'm trying to avoid a bloodbath that's no use to either of us,' said Chauhan, a hard edge to his voice. 'We're delivering the money now, and we intend to deliver your comrades as well, so you win this one. But if one of your colleagues overreacts and Colonel Menon's men react to that, especially after you killed that hostage . . . Your man in the driveway has grenades, and I'm sure you have other explosives. So do we. You don't want to blow everything up when you're on the verge of victory, do you? I don't know who you work for but if you threw everything away at this stage I don't think he'd be very pleased with you.'

There was a long pause at the other end. When the reply came, it was the same smooth voice but now there was a tinge of anxiety to it that hadn't been there before. 'All right,' he said eventually. 'I'll tell my men to keep their cool.'

This was taking a turn for the worse. The terrorists, who had all been very collected until the doctor incident, were becoming progressively more nervous. I wondered, was it because they'd found a hostage almost succeeding in passing a message out to us? Or was there something I hadn't caught?

The man on the telephone, the leader of this band, had been shaken by something. From the way he had shot down the hostage earlier in the morning I could see he was like Psycho in that he wouldn't hesitate to blow things up if he panicked. He wasn't as psychotic as Psycho had been, but under that façade of civilization he was quite barbaric. And there was that other man, the cowboy. When he hung up I tapped Chauhan on the shoulder. 'I'd ease up,' I told him. 'Press him too hard now and he could turn violent.'

'I sensed that,' replied Chauhan, wiping his brow with a soiled kerchief. 'That's why I told him they had almost made it this time.'

Back at the gate the delivery of the money had been resumed. The injured policeman had been given first aid and taken off to a hospital by a colleague, and two others had replaced them. They carried the boxes together now, one at each end, walking on eggs and extremely slow. One by one the sixty-five boxes were unloaded, their contents transferred to sacks and then to the farmhouse. The sun rose higher and we sweated.

The transfer took three hours, give or take, averaging nearly three minutes a box. Into the relief at the end of the transfer came a new demand from the terrorists. The MP had fainted again while the money was being transferred. The FKF wanted a doctor inside the farmhouse. An extra hostage, in effect. 'The man who treated the MP earlier should do,' said the man on the telephone. 'We will take him inside with his equipment and he can stay here to look after his patient.'

'I'm not giving you another hostage for you to threaten me with,' said Chauhan. 'If you want the man treated, give him back to us. We'll arrange for someone else to replace him, like I said before, but we're not giving you a doctor. Otherwise we can send you the doctor along with the colonel, as we did before.'

'What stops me from taking the doctor hostage once he's here, policeman?' rasped the voice.

'I hope you don't do anything of the kind,' replied Chauhan. 'We're releasing your comrades and paying you the money because the government believes you do intend to release the hostages once you're safe. If you break your word, pull something like that now, we'll have to stop negotiating.'

'All right, then,' said the voice, the fatigue now showing clearly, 'send the doctor in. But send him in alone. I don't want a repeat of what happened earlier. If the doctor needs help he can use one of our people. I'll send someone along to the post at the gate to help with the trolley or whatever.'

'I can't afford to send the doctor in without some assurance that you'll release him when he's done,' said Chauhan.

'I can't give you any such thing,' said the tired voice on the telephone. 'You'll have to take my word for it.'

'All right,' said Chauhan, 'but just remember that if you do anything funny now . . .'

'Do you think I'd forget, idiot?' said the man on the telephone. 'Just send the doctor in.'

Chauhan turned to me when he hung up. 'You were right,' he said, 'that man's losing it. He's been on edge ever since you and the doctor went in. What the hell did you do to him, Raja, to get him so upset?'

'Nothing I can understand,' I said. 'I told you what happened. A hostage tried to pass me a message and he killed the hostage. After that I just came back.'

The doctor went in again to see the MP, his trolley this time pushed along by a terrorist. From the post at the gate we saw him go through the routine again in the car park, this time in good light, in the heat of the afternoon sun, and return twenty minutes later with his trolley, sweating but intact. 'The man's a bloody swine,' said the doctor when the FKF man had retreated back to the farmhouse. 'I don't know why I voted for him. All he's looking for is a way out of that mess in there. He's just playing sick.'

Kelkar joined us at the gate to call me away. He led me to the committee's office, a row of tents sandwiched between the command post and the SOF camp. 'I've got everything you asked for,' he told me in his improvised office. 'I told the committee about the leak. The man from the home ministry protested, just like he did last time, and I told them I wasn't about to tell them the details of the

229

operation, and that if they insisted I would ask the chief to pull us out. Your chutes are on the way. The para outfits here in Bangalore don't have anything like the ones you need. None ready for use, anyway. The Air Force have agreed to give us a helicopter for you to jump out of, both for the dummy run and the real thing. They'll have a Mi-8 ready courtesy HAL. They've even agreed to quarantine the pilots. The Indian Airlines guys refused your diversion— something about it being against their association's rules— but I got a private airline to agree. They'll send a Dormer down to treetop level for you.'

'Why exactly did IA refuse?' I asked.

'It's against the pilots' association rules. They don't have sanction from the civil aviation people. It violates safety regulations. All excuses, of course, but what do you expect from them?'

'And the private airline?'

He grinned. 'I found that Gawand—remember him—is related to the man who runs the group to which that air-taxi operation belongs. I rang Gawand up and he spoke to his cousin. Gawand said his cousin'll send his pilots here for us to brief . . . When I asked him how much it would cost he said it was on the house. When I spoke to the cousin an hour later he said every pilot around volunteered . . . They've got some conditions, though: they won't fly below radar height, and they want at least two thousand feet between themselves and our helicopter.'

'That's all right,' I replied. 'While the operation's on, they can stay between 500 metres and 1000 metres, and we'll stay above 2000. We should set it up so that the aircraft comes in to land, aborts the landing and comes in a second time, as if it's in real trouble, coming in on a failing engine or something, circling a few times . . . If the FKF ask we can give them a story that the aircraft is in trouble, its electricals are kaput and the pilot's bringing it down visually instead of on the ILS. What about the airport guys, though?'

'We won't tell them anything. Gawand spoke to someone in the Airport Authority and fixed it up. No problem.'

'I hope they swallow it. Some fake signals in the air would help.'

'Yes, we'll do that,' he grinned. 'My friend even offered to have his pilot send out Mayday signals to Air Traffic Control, so if the FKF bump into those frequencies on their radio our story will hold water.'

'Have you found a place where we can do our dummy runs?' I asked. 'We have to have one with a roof in darkness, with at least twelve metres by fifteen on which to touch down.'

'Yes,' replied the General. 'There's a farmhouse, an old one, on the other side of the city that we can use. We'll keep two of our men on the terrace to see if the others can come in undetected.'

'Could you have red lights set up at the corners of the perimeter?' I asked. 'One red light outside the command post. That way we have our orientation straight all the way down.'

'Sure,' he said.

'One last thing. Have a medic team at the gate, with Luthra in charge. Have them prepared for shrapnel, gunshot and blast damage. Get hold of that cardiac specialist for the MP in case he needs it. Let them assume ten casualties.'

By late afternoon the news of the Briton's death was out. The high commissioner himself was on his way from Delhi. The BBC, who had learnt that the hostage had been shot in the presence of an Indian Army man, speculated on our competence or otherwise. 'Don't react,' Kelkar said, 'we all saw what happened. There was nothing you could do. Just concentrate on what needs to be done and leave the rest to me.'

The day dragged on. Kelkar and I had decided to keep the plan to ourselves until the last possible moment. Hari and I would pick the fourteen men—twelve excluding the two of us—by half-past-four, and take them off to the HAL factory, where we, along with the two pilots, would all stay until the operation. Three of us, Hari, the lead man and I would take off from one of HAL's helipads in a Russian Mi-8 Hip troop carrier, from which we would drop for our practice session . . . We'd have just the one practice session, to see how long the lead man would take to get the sentry down. I thought once of sending a two-man team ahead, then decided it wasn't worth it risking fouled-up lines: that close, the risk of a mid-air collision was far too high because both men would have to land together. It would have to be just one man.

We would all wear night-vision glasses on the way down. Land in the south-west quadrant of the terrace—the diversion would take place to the east—cross over to the north-east quadrant immediately after releasing our chutes, clearing the way for the next man in. Lower nylon lines anchored to the little shed on top of the terrace or to the parapet itself, and rappel down, the men timing their descent to arrive at their targets at the same time. Break in, bring down the targets . . .

Who were the targets? For the Madras operation I'd begun to get a kind of handle on Psycho and Loudspeaker, the most important targets, and Luthra had managed to find out where Psycho would be. We'd known there'd be six men all told, and hence four inside the coach. Here we had nothing of the kind, except that the prime target, Smoothie, was unlikely to be among the sentries. Since he spoke on the telephone, and the telephone was on the first floor, the chances were that that was where he too would be. I had an idea about two of them, Smoothie and Cowboy, who had hustled the hostages out of the hotel. Cowboy was the twitchy one, liable to go off at half-cock. Smoothie was losing it, he'd be close to panic. He had become nervous when I'd gone into the car park with the doctor . . . Had he become nervous after he told Chauhan about Luthra?

That must have been the reason. He must have realized when he told Chauhan about Luthra that I'd have understood about the leak. He must have realized that I'd try to fix the leak . . . And I had. He wasn't getting the information he'd expected. No wonder he was nervous. He must have been kicking himself.

The police delivered lunch for the hostages. I went out to my tent and sent for Hari at half-past-three. Time to brief him, at least, if not the others. He listened to me silently, disapprovingly, making it clear in his own, quiet way that he wasn't at all happy with the change of plan, that he thought the ground attack had a better chance of success. When it came to picking the men, though, I began to see the quality of his preparation. I didn't even think of changing any of the fourteen men—two extras, just in case—he picked for the assault, and in particular the lead man, Subedar Arvind Joshi.

We assembled the team at the entrance to the camp a little after four. The chutes were already at the helipad in HAL, two spare chutes per man, forty-two in all. Chutes and sub-machine guns aside, the leader of each of the three teams—car park, first floor and second floor—carried walkie-talkies. The lead man, carrying his rifle for silenced, aimed fire at the sentry on top, would be redundant after clearing the terrace and would stay on the terrace and keep an eye on the proceedings from above. Everyone would wear night-vision glasses into the attack, taking them off if necessary after landing.

Chauhan sent a policeman for me just after we'd got the men all together. The doctor had returned from another trip to see the MP, who was still malingering. The other hostages were fine. I told him to get in touch with Luthra about getting all the hostages knocked out for the night. 'What're you planning?' Chauhan asked.

'I'll tell you when it's over,' I said. 'Just remember to get those guys down.'

In the silence of the command post I heard the change in the tone of his voice. 'You suspect even me?' he asked.

'I suspect everyone,' I told him, 'I have to. That's our only chance of coming through the operation alive. I'm sure you understand.'

'Are you going in yourself, this time?' he asked. 'What about those blows you got when you went in with the doctor?'

'I'll get by,' I told him, 'nothing serious. A couple of bruises, a couple of aches.'

'I suspect you'd say that even if you'd broken both arms and legs and had your kneecaps knocked off as well. I've heard some stories about you.'

'Sure,' I said, 'you can discount the more arresting stories straight away. And the colourful bits of the rest. But you'll have heard I don't talk unless I have to. That much is true.'

'I believe that,' he said. 'I can see it. All the best, then, you chaps just don't go mess it up.'

General Kelkar arrived at the command post just as I was leaving. 'Tell Hari to take the men out to HAL,' he said, 'you and I are going to the hospital to see Ismail. We must sound him out. I'm sure he'll have something to add.'

At the hospital, only six kilometres from the airport, we found Ismail looking gloomily out of the window of his room, his head bandaged, his ankle in a cast, thoroughly

235

fed up with hospital routine and medication. 'I wish I could come with you,' he said, looking even more haggard when we had told him the plan. 'But I still think a ground attack is more likely to succeed. Here you've cut the period of risk down to the minimum but I'd say the risk itself is far higher. Unjustifiably so.'

'I think it's justified, Ismail,' I said. 'Assuming we're going in from the air, what changes would you make to the plan?'

He rubbed his eyes with his thumbs. 'I don't know what to say, Raja,' he said finally, 'except that I'm sure you can make it work. But watch your flanks this time. Keep your security tighter than ever before.'

'Of course,' I said, 'we're doing that. The committee don't know a thing and we won't tell them until it's over. By the way, I'm almost certain now there's a leak: one of the FKF men made a small slip.' I told him that Smoothie had mentioned Luthra's doings inside the coach.

He nodded. 'Good, good,' he said. 'That might help us plug the leak. All the best.'

We ran the practice sessions, for just Hari, Subedar Arvind Joshi—the most experienced jumper in the company, and one of the best marksmen—and me, out of an old and now unused and musty farmhouse with broken doors and windows. We drove out there at six to inspect the place and set up lights outside so it would look like the real thing from up above, with lights all around the building but not on top. Over three run-throughs we found that Joshi, the lead man, would have enough time to land, release his chute, aim and fire only if the lookout didn't spot him first. Any attempt by Joshi to cut seconds by releasing his chute while still in the air and dropping the last few feet with his weapon ready wouldn't work: unless he could judge the drop exactly he'd run the risk of landing too hard, alerting the sentries.

From there on it was easy. Hari and I fixed grapnels to the parapet around the terrace and slid down them to the ground in under four seconds. With the whole team it would take ten seconds, no more.

We couldn't, of course, practice all of it. Even with the most experienced of soldiers, rehearsals with mockups make all the difference to morale and timing. Here, without the rehearsals, we were all wound up, and Hari in particular. I'd have to do the briefing myself to make sure Hari's nerves didn't get through to the men.

I thought once more about the four groups going in. Most of hostages would be in the halls, as would the terrorists. My nightmare was of a terrorist in a bedroom, in a corner outside the sight of the man at the window. The architect had said the windows ran along almost the entire length of the wall but . . . If I were sure there'd be no hostages in the bedrooms we could have the men at the windows lobbing grenades in at the first sign of resistance. But I wasn't sure.

The lead man and the groups going into the car park would be the most vulnerable. With no hostages there, the terrorists on the terrace and in the car park would be able to concentrate on the attackers. We'd issue them grenades, though if the lead man had to use his the operation would be a washout. God, if only I knew what the FKF had on that dam' rooftop . . .

With the teams going into the farmhouse we couldn't afford explosives: the chances of a hostage being hurt or worse were far too high.

We'd go in at three in the morning. The kidnappers would by then have been on the alert for at least forty-two hours. Not enough by itself to wear out a trained man, forty-two hours with an average of two or three hours per man. We'd all done it ourselves. It was the stress that got to them, the stress of being on guard all the time, and at night of not knowing what lay in the shadows beyond the light. All said and done, the presence of a few hundred armed men at the perimeter was for them a threat. They had to be extra careful with their hostages, for hostages were after all their own resources, and killing or hurting hostages ate into their own resources. Any kind of roughness with the hostages would, in the long run, cut down public support for their political motives.

Our biggest advantage was time. The FKF, in upping the stake from the Madras operation, had guaranteed that they would have to stand guard at least forty-eight hours. They were more vulnerable at night, and in those forty-eight hours were two nights. To my mind, they'd have improved their chances five hundred per cent if they'd kept their demands small enough to handle over a single night, giving us no time to prepare. Instead they'd worked on their defensive position.

Of course they would. With an informant in the committee that was the logical thing to do. I couldn't fault their strategy, really. No wonder Smoothie was panicking: he must have realized I'd cut off their source of information after I heard his little slip about Luthra.

What would he do with his informant cut out of the picture? Was he still in touch with the Krait? If he was really panicking I'd have thought he was out of touch with the Krait, too . . . In that case the chances were that his informant and the planner were one and the same . . . the Krait was on that committee, then, or somewhere close to it. Running with the hare and hunting with the hounds.

The MP was Smoothie's key hostage. The Krait would have locked him up separately, invested a man for that. Would Smoothie? He probably would. I'd have to assume that he would. Where would he keep the key hostage? In one of the bedrooms. Since they seemed to be on guard against a ground attack it would be logical to have the MP on the upper floor, as far away from the point of attack as possible, in the bedroom at the north-east corner. Given the MP's 'failing' health, they wouldn't want to risk having him climb stairs. The chances were, therefore, that he'd be on the first floor, not the second. If that were the case, the FKF would concentrate their defences on the first floor, and keep the MP in the bedroom farthest from the staircase, if they expected us to attack from the ground. The upper floor would therefore be lightly defended: with the strength the FKF had here, they wouldn't be able to guard more than one or two rooms at the top. Two or three of my men, therefore, would be able to work their way around to the first floor balcony from the sunshades . . . But it would take them ten to twenty seconds to do that, and unless something went disastrously wrong, I expected the action to take less than ten seconds. My effective strike force was three less than the count . . .

When would we go in? We'd have to go in when the sky was at its darkest, the best protection for the lead man. About three in the morning, with the moon low down on the horizon would be best. If we had cloud cover so much the better, but we couldn't bank on clouds to arrive as we wanted them. I found myself wishing hard for another thunderstorm. Back in the closed-off atmosphere of HAL the tension grew as in my mind I made the dispositions. One man for the terrace, six for the second floor, five for the first floor—we'd ignore the kitchen—and two for the car park. Fourteen men. We'd stick to that. I drew Hari aside to a corner for his views. He listened in silence, agreed.

I briefed the men, then. Joshi, alone on the rooftop, would be out of the operation as soon as he'd cleared the rooftop for us. Hari would lead the team on the second floor—designated Team Upper—and I'd lead the one on the first floor, Team Middle. Subedar Madan Lal Yadav, one of our most promising JCOs, would lead the two-man element in the car park, Team Car Park.

Thanks to the FKF's policy of keeping the hostages in underwear the terrorists were clearly identifiable. The men in black would stick out against the walls. Our men would go for the guys in black, aiming for the faces and the limbs, areas most likely to be left uncovered. Given the possibility of mines on the stairs, the teams would have to stay on their own floors until all team leaders had said their respective areas were clear.

We took off from HAL at a quarter-to-three, swinging west towards the farmhouse. We took a wide arc outwards to get away from the airport, well out of earshot of the farmhouse, to stay away from the airplane that would take off soon to give us our diversion. The big Mi-8 troop carrier clattered its way swiftly up to 2500 metres, where it would stay until we were all out. Six minutes later, the aircraft confirmed to the helicopter pilot on the radio that it had taken off from Jalahalli Air Force Base, and would be approaching the HAL airfield at 1000 metres in eight minutes. The tension grew, as it does for a batsman going to the crease when he is the last hope of the team.

Eighteen minutes later on the dot it appeared below us, two kilometres away, going in for the first of its four planned attempts to land, and the helicopter again swung towards the farmhouse, which we had identified on the way out.

As I watched from the helicopter, the airplane banked towards the runway, descended and almost disappeared before reappearing, climbing slowly before coming round again. Less than two minutes later, just as the helicopter climbed and positioned itself three kilometres above the red light it came around for its second attempt, which too

241

was aborted. I tapped the pilot on his shoulder, and the jump lights at the front of the fuselage turned green, and the lead man, already at the door, stepped out into the chill, dark night. There was a twenty-second wait, and then one by one the twelve others followed, and then it was my turn to walk into nothingness.

Going straight down without aerobatics it took a long, breathless minute or so to free-fall the 2750 metres to 250 metres, at which height the parachutes opened automatically. Down below, through my night-vision glasses and against the lights of the city I could see several other rectangular chutes opening against the street lamps below, and then felt the hard tug of my own chute as it opened out against the sky and then I was drifting slowly in to land in the south-east corner. In the green lenses of the night-vision glasses I could see the men assembling at the north-west corner. Joshi had done his work well, and then I was drifting in, less than a foot away from the parapet, with almost pinpoint precision.

Then it nearly went askew. A stray gust of wind blew me a foot off course, inches outside the parapet of the terrace. The nylon lines of the chute snagged and hissed and scraped against the edge of the wall and the chute itself collapsed. In a kind of reflex I reached out and grabbed the sunshade above the staircase as it went past, hanging on one hand, hitting the waist-level release catch of the chute. I clambered silently on to the sunshade on the west face of the house just as Hari arrived at the edge to find out what had happened to me.

The grapnels and ropes for the descent were ready, anchored on the parapet, the men waiting to drop the ropes and go. I raised my hand in a thumbs up, pushed my night-vision glasses up on to my forehead, over my helmet, gripped the line on which I would descend one storey to the second floor, and down we went.

I came down with my feet on the railing in front of the half-open, glass door of the balcony, light streaming out to the left, just as a terrorist emerged, gun in hand, obviously unsuspecting because he was looking back into the hall as he emerged. He sensed a presence on the balcony and as I saw his head come round and his rifle come up I was on the floor, swinging my own rifle in a wide arc to the left, bringing it down on his neck and shoulder with a soggy thump. Even as he dropped his weapon I had him by the shoulder, dragging him forward and propelling him unarmed over the railing on to the concrete apron below. The other man on the second floor, who landed a second after I did, saw that I was occupied and forced his way in past the terrorist and into the hall, and as the terrorist fell on the concrete I heard him open fire in the hall. There was more firing downstairs but I shut it out of my mind and concentrated on the job at hand.

My buddy had moved two metres into the hall to leave my path unobstructed and as I followed on his heels I saw the terrorist he had shot slumped back against the wall, his helmet off, half his face shot away. Sprawled on the carpet in the middle of the hall were the startled hostages, seven of them woken by the sound of gunfire in the enclosed space. 'Down!' I yelled. 'Stay on the floor!'

There were more bursts of automatic fire from down below. Probably from the car park. I hoped desperately it wasn't from the first floor.

Then the nightmare came true. From one of the bedrooms emerged one more terrorist, the third on this floor, dragging in front of him the ashen-faced MP, a gun to his throat. The MP was sagging on his feet, the terrorist with his arm around the MP's throat half carrying the man along.

From downstairs came the crump of a grenade, startling the terrorist. For an instant his grip loosened and the MP sagged another few inches, leaving the terrorist's face exposed.

I took a chance then that I have often told my men never to take. In that split second I raised my gun and shot the terrorist in the face once, the bullet missing the hostage by inches, knocking both on to the floor. Most important, the terrorist dropped his gun, and then my buddy, several feet closer, dived for the gun, kicking it into a corner, well out of reach of the man on the floor.

The dive was unnecessary. The MP had fallen on the disarmed terrorist, and rolled off, leaving the man in black writhing on the floor. We later found that that single shot had hit him in the lower jaw, shattering it, penetrating his throat just above the adam's apple and passing on to lodge in the spinal column.

From below came the sounds of heavy crossfire, and then the thump of another grenade. In the silence that followed, I lifted my walkie-talkie to hear the voice of Naik

Joginder Singh. 'Car park to leader. Car park clear, four hostiles down and out, repeat four hostiles down and out. One hostile fell down, fell from above. One friendly is down. Repeat one friendly is down. He needs assistance. Over.'

A bitter regret lurched in my gut. I'd planned for two sentries in the car park, but the two men who'd gone in there had run into four of them. God, what a mess! I couldn't call the medic unless the first floor was clear, too. To my relief there followed on the walkie-talkie Hari's voice saying, 'Lower floor clear, repeat lower floor seems clear, all hostiles down. Now checking bedrooms and toilets. Over.'

The men at the gate would be listening in. 'Leader to base,' I said into the walkie-talkie, 'Leader to base, all positions clear, checking the bedrooms. One friendly down in the car park, one friendly down in the car park, repeat car park. Send a medic team through the driveway, repeat send medic through driveway. Medic to collect one friendly. Stick to the driveway and the apron, repeat stick to the driveway and the apron. Over.'

'Base to leader, medic on the way. Medic on the way,' came the reassuring reply. Then, in a breach of radio protocol, 'Hang on, sir, we're moving. We thought there'd be trouble. A few minutes ago we saw two more hostiles in the car park. Too late to tell you. Over.'

A big commando, one of the men at the windows, came into the hall from the balcony. Without waiting to check, he kicked the doors of the bedrooms open one after the

245

other and looked around. When another man assigned the windows came in, he checked the toilets, and a minute later reported all bedrooms and toilets clear. And then, on the walkie-talkie, came Hari again from the first floor, saying, 'All bedrooms clear, all toilets clear. Repeat lower floor clear. Two hostiles down, two hostiles down and out. All hostages clear, all hostages clear. Over.'

Outside I could hear the wail of the ambulance as the injured man was driven to hospital in one of the ambulances. Luthra would stay at his post until we confirmed all friendly casualties were handled. Down the driveway to the house came the rest of the company, sticking to the apron, surrounding the house. I felt empty, and vastly tired. 'Leader to base,' I said into the walkie-talkie. 'All positions clear, repeat all positions clear. Maintain the cordon outside. Stay outside until we check for bombs. All teams stay in position, all teams stay in position until bombs cleared. Over.'

Hari, himself an engineer officer, cleared the booby traps, the mines and tripwires, on the staircase to the first floor, removing first the battery that would set off the detonator, then removing the detonators themselves and finally removing and rolling up the spring-loaded tripwires. He moved up the staircase, torch in hand, and found an identical mine on the third step of the staircase, and likewise disarmed it. The way down was clear. The operation was over.

'Leader to base,' I said, 'staircases clear, repeat staircases clear. Bring in the medics.'

With the driveway and the staircases cleared, we heard the sound of running footsteps down below and then on the staircase as the medics rushed in with stretchers, removing first the hostages and then the kidnappers.

Havildar Laxmikant Yadav, who had led the car park team, died, shot in the neck almost as soon as he had landed in the car park, and again in the foot in the course of the vicious firefight that had followed. The pillars were pockmarked with bullet holes, and two grenades had exploded there. A gentle breeze slowly blew away the smoke but the pungent smell that exploded plastic leaves behind stayed.

Yadav and his buddy had been seen almost as they touched down, even before they had released their chutes. Yadav had been hit in the first fusillade from the terrorists, but had managed to keep his head and maintain covering fire while his comrade, who had spoken to me on the walkie-talkie, sneaked behind the pillars to counter. Seeing his comrade swamped, Yadav had managed to lob a grenade at the terrorists, killing one and momentarily stunning the others. His buddy had then stepped out and brought down two others, and when the fourth began to fire back, finished him off with a second grenade.

Only two of the men among the terrorists had night-vision glasses, one of whom had been killed by the first grenade. The second, armed with an AK-47, had been the last to be cut down in the car park, when Yadav's buddy tossed him the second grenade.

The medics found two terrorists alive. One was the man I'd tossed down from the balcony. The blow on the neck had wrenched his neck and the fall had broken several of his bones. He'd been shot in the leg when he arrived by the lone SOF man left in the car park. The medics carried him away, still conscious and in pain, but taking it stoically. The other was one man on the ground floor who had been shot in the face and had a broken jaw. He had lost his rifle and Hari's buddy had kicked him in the groin after shooting him half a dozen times in the area of the chest. None of the bullets had penetrated his body armour but he'd been flattened against the wall, winded; being shot in body armour is like being hit by a strong man.

The man on sentry duty on the roof was dead. He'd been concentrating on the traffic in front of the house—the last of the ambulances was arriving at the time we went in—turning around only when he heard the click of Joshi releasing his parachute twenty feet away, by which time Joshi's rifle was on the way up. Joshi had got him in the face with the first shot.

A total of six other terrorists had died: four in the car park and one each on the two floors of the house. Smoothie was the man who'd emerged from the bedroom covering himself with the MP. In the end he had decided to hold the key hostage himself.

And we hadn't lost a hostage in the rescue.

Havildar Yadav's buddy was led away to the camp, speechless and a little shocked in the aftermath. Someone would stay with him till he began to get back to normal.

Most people who have just lost a buddy are bitter and prefer—or at least think they prefer—to be left alone but that wouldn't be permitted. For at least the next day or two someone would hold his hand from time to time, help him exorcise his ghosts.

The hostages were whisked away to a hospital for a checkup and then to a police station for eventual release. The MP was rushed off to a private hospital where he made many telephone calls about the callous treatment he had received, about the two days he had had to spend in custody before anyone rescued him.

Brigadier Kalra's engineers entered the garden and found tripwires all around the building except along the pool and in front, in the driveway. Even the hedges had been booby trapped. The terrorists had then run out of explosive, and in places rigged up tripwires that would set off lights instead of mines.

The FKF men had come prepared for a long stay. They had provisions for themselves. They had brought food for themselves, loaded perhaps in the bus, and had stocked it in the freezer.

I retreated to the crowded command post, where Hari turned up, face flushed, faintly intoxicated from his triumph. In his eyes I could still see the faint disbelief that it had all actually happened, that of all the people in the world he had survived in an operation in which people had used lethal weapons on him. He wouldn't be able to sleep for some time yet but by tomorrow he'd steady out and the debriefing would bring him firmly back to earth. I could see he was not going back to his old self. I didn't think he'd ever be the same again.

The bus was recovered without much damage. The glass in the windscreen and the windows was gone, the seats had been ripped up, and the tyres slashed to make it an obstacle, but the owner would get it back as soon as the police were through with it.

As mission commander, I carried the responsibility for Yadav's death. If I had predicted accurately that there would be four men on guard in the car park, waiting for an attack, we would have used a different strategy and picked them off comfortably. At the very least we would have sent more men into the car park, to attack from different directions. God, I thought, we should have ignored the men in the car park and instead kept men on watch in the balconies to keep them trapped downstairs . . . then we could have driven them into the cordon from inside, instead of risking lives on a surprise attack that was blunted at the beginning. If only I'd thought of four men in the car park. If only I'd thought a little harder. But I hadn't and now Yadav was dead. The words kept going round in my head.

chapter twelve

The krait is a creature of the night, common enough but rarely seen. It often approaches human homes but is almost never seen because its deep-blue colour blends well with the blue of the night . . . In the still night, the krait lay curled up while the hunger and the pain mounted. When it could no longer bear the stillness it moved, wriggling crookedly, for its tail was burning from the bite of the mongoose.

The intelligence men who came for the debriefing this time were both young and sharp and very persistent, and they listened with untroubled patience and unshakable neutrality to all that we had to tell them—about information being passed to the other side, the Krait; the tactics we'd used to handle security, Yadav's death, Smoothie and Cowboy . . . about everything on the mission. The death of one of the men made them that much keener; a few minutes into my first session with them they had homed in on my mistaken estimate of the FKF's strength in the car park.

How come there were so many men there, they asked, and how come I didn't see them?

Because we'd isolated ourselves hours before the action, I said, and because no one on the cordon had seen them in time to tell the helicopter pilot. In the shadows under the car park it was hard to tell, even with night-vision glasses. They must have been lurking behind the pillars. They might have known when the attack was planned . . . They nodded, sceptical but not disbelieving, and came back to my troop dispositions. Had I based all my dispositions on the basis of poor intelligence and speculative psycho-profiles?

Yes, I replied, there'd been no choice. I'd banked on surprise.

Why hadn't I left the car park for afterwards, they asked. Why hadn't I taken the first and second floors and then moved downwards with more support?

Because the lookouts in the car park might have come up on to the balconies along ways I hadn't been able to see, I replied, and if they'd come up in the midst of our operation, before we cleared the floors, they would have complicated matters no end.

Was I always willing to send men into rescue situations armed with grenades, they asked, when the information I had was sketchy? Had I considered the risk?

Yes, and yes, I replied, and on the basis of the information I'd had I'd do it again.

They changed tack. That incident in which the hostage had been killed, they asked, what could I have done to prevent it?

I could have ignored the hostage, I said, but maybe that wouldn't have made a difference. Smoothie had been watching from the shadows, and would probably have killed him whether or not I'd moved to take that bit of paper. Come to think of it, they'd picked him because he was a Jew.

They came eventually to the Krait. Did I have anything more to tell the police, they asked, and was there any evidence—hard evidence—that the Krait was on the committee?

No, I said, it was just the sequence of events that led me to believe that the Krait was on the committee.

Ah, yes, they nodded in their hard-headed fashion, and went their way, four days after they began.

A team of British diplomats grilled General Kelkar, who called me in occasionally to answer specific questions. I got a very limited view of what went on in that inquiry but afterwards got from Kelkar the opinion that they had absolved us of incompetence.

I called Chauhan immediately after, to ask about the terrorists we'd got alive.

Lay off, he replied, they're in no shape to talk.

Give them to my men, I said, we'll make them talk.

Bloody gorillas, he snapped, then laughed. He wished he could, he said, but there were laws and such.

Did he think there was someone on our side feeding them information, I asked.

The laughter vanished. What prompted that question, he asked warily.

General principles, I replied, it was hard to conduct operations on the scale the FKF were doing without an insider's involvement.

And who could it be, he asked.

I thought it was the Madras cops, I replied, but after the Bangalore operation I doubted if that was the case.

I was holding out on him, he said flatly.

No, I replied, just intuition. Little facts that registered in my head without my noticing them.

Tell me when you do notice them, he said.

What could be behind the FKF, I asked.

Topaz, he replied, the General's legacy.

What was that again, I asked.

General Zia ul-Haq, he replied, made friends with the Yanks and got them to fund his ISI. Then he launched Topaz, which was aimed at separatists in Kashmir and Punjab.

What evidence did he have, I asked.

He laughed. None, he said, and if he had any he wouldn't discuss it with me. Everyone knew about Topaz, so that much was all right.

I'll come over, I said, and dig it out of you.

No, he replied, he'd keep in touch.

That evening it rained and in the welcome fragrance of rain-wet earth I called Sandhya. 'Hi,' she said, 'it's been a long while. You got into all the papers again.'

My spirits leapt at the gladness in her voice. 'Not the best of things to happen,' I said unthinkingly, remembering what my friend Ajit had said. 'Now the FKF will come after me.'

254

She went serious immediately. 'God, what are you going to do about that?'

'Nothing,' I said equally seriously. 'Actually I'm too small for them to chase.'

'Good,' she replied. And then, with creeping concern, 'Are you all right? No little injuries this time?'

'Nothing now.' The bumps on my chest had subsided to a dull ache, and the marks were almost gone. But there were other burdens. Ben Goldstein, the Briton who'd died, gunned down possibly because I'd tried to take the bit of paper he'd smuggled out to me. Yadav, gunned down helplessly in the car park because I'd trusted to luck once too often.

'Come on Sunday then,' she said. 'You sound . . . different. What's wrong?'

She had picked up the vibes on the telephone, across the miles, hearing not just the words but the feelings behind. 'I'll come Sunday,' I told her, 'about eleven. Tell you everything then.'

On the way out of the camp in a light drizzle the following Sunday I bumped into Ismail, going in the same direction. 'Where are you going?' he asked, guessing. 'I can give you a lift if you're going visiting your girlfriend.'

'Thanks,' I told him, 'but that's wishful thinking.'

'All the best,' he said, smiling. At the gates to the apartment block where she lived he hesitated. 'I'd like to see the youngster,' he said. 'May I come in with you?'

'Sure,' I said. 'Don't see why not.'

When I rang the doorbell she was finishing a late breakfast with Kiran, who'd been watching cartoons on TV. The sight of her in a bright yellow outfit was by itself enough to lift the darkness considerably. 'You look terrible,' she said when she saw me. 'Stunned.'

'Reaction,' I said. 'Here's someone else to meet Junior.'

She saw Ismail looming up behind me and her smile froze, then widened. 'Hi,' said Ismail diffidently, 'I was concerned about your little boy. How is he?'

'Ask him yourself,' she replied.

We got to know without asking. In the weeks since we had last met he had changed from a silent, withdrawn and vulnerable little boy to one very imperious, occasionally rebellious, and voluble, like any other kid his age. Over the next twenty minutes he told me how he'd been, besides showing me pictures, gifts, a Lego airplane, things he'd just got. 'He seems all right,' Ismail told her when he ran off to the bedroom to fetch something out to show me. 'Not yet,' she said. 'He still has nightmares, still wets his bed from time to time. The psychiatrist said the nightmares might continue for quite some time—years, he said—but he'll grow out of the bed-wetting soon. He can't say about the fear of the dark.'

'How long does he think it'll take?' I asked.

'He says counselling will have to continue another three to six months . . . But it's been worth it, seeing the shrink. Kiran sleeps by himself now, in his own room.'

'It's all right,' said Ismail. 'I'm glad there's no permanent damage done.' He excused himself after that, refusing coffee, claiming a prior engagement elsewhere.

'And how have you been?' I asked after he'd left.

'All right,' she said. 'Busy. Lots to do illustrating a magazine. I got a couple of good contracts. I don't need the money but it helps. Best of all, I can work here. I can go see the people I work for in the day, when Kiran's at school, and get back here for him. Now tell me what happened to you, and why you disappeared for so long.'

I told her about Yadav and Goldstein. Told her that I was in some ways responsible for what happened to both of them. Told her what the reviews had said.

'That's nonsense,' she said forthrightly when I was through. 'You're imagining things.'

'What do you mean?' I asked.

'You're responsible to some extent,' she said, 'but there's no need for you to carry on about it like it's the end of the world. You're just putting yourself down.'

'How so, ma'am?' I asked.

'Look, this hasn't happened to you before,' she said, 'or it's happened only once or twice. You're just making it worse by dwelling on it and not telling anyone about it. Everyone knew the risks involved, and you can't blame yourself if someone died.'

'They needn't have,' I said.

'You expected too much,' she replied. 'In Madras you didn't lose anyone and you expected the same thing to happen in Bangalore and it didn't. Besides . . .'

'Besides what?' I demanded.

257

'You're overdoing the macho-male bit,' she said slowly, 'carrying responsibility all by yourself. See what a great guy I am, and all that nonsense.' She bowed her shoulders and put on an overly serious look that mirrored my feelings exactly.

For a moment the anger rose high in my chest, then turned into laughter. That bit of mimicry had been marvellous. 'All right, Wise One,' I said, 'I'll take your word for it.'

'Maybe I shouldn't have been so blunt about it,' she said. 'But you shouldn't mind.'

'Don't worry about that,' I said, the clouds lifting. Time to get going one way or another, I thought. I could either spend the rest of my life with her or get out of here before it became too late.

She brought out more sketches to show me, and the more I looked at them the clearer it seemed somehow that the important things weren't the ones that forced themselves on one. The first was a sketch of a temple. Where I'd seen only crowds, grime, beggars, petty traders trying to make a living out of tourists, and all kinds of false godmen, she saw tall, clean-cut columns and a strange cool quiet, an inner character I'd missed. 'I've never looked at these places the way you've sketched them,' I said in surprise. 'You've left out all the nasty things I saw.'

'Don't you know?' she asked. 'What you leave out is as important as what you put in. Otherwise you get confused.' She changed topics. 'Umm . . . I don't like your boss much.'

I laughed. 'What's he done to you?'

'There's something about him that isn't right.'

'What?' I asked.

'He seems sick,' she said bluntly, apologetically. 'My skin crawls when I see him . . . Wait! I'll sketch him for you as I see him. That's better than trying to explain.' Before I could stop her she was off to her room to fetch paper and pens, and I had to wait impatiently for ten minutes while she put on her glasses and sketched him from memory, the faint lines darkening swiftly as she filled the details into the outline she'd started with.

She'd got the features right once again, the broad brow and the aquiline nose, the thin mouth and the gaunt cheekbones, but in place of the aristocratic quality I saw on his eyes she had drawn a hate-filled madness, and about the mouth played a wolfish smile. Just the expression I'd seen on his face that night in the train in Madras. 'You've made him some kind of a loony,' I told her. 'He's not like this at all.'

'I don't know,' she replied, 'but that's how I see him.' She paused. 'He's a killer, Raja, thank God he's on your side.'

I laughed and let it slide, and over lunch some of the comfort returned, that splendid comfort I'd felt on my first visit here. I could get addicted to this very easily, I thought, stretching luxuriantly. 'What are you thinking about?' she asked.

'Nothing much,' I said. 'Comfort. Being at ease. Things like that.'

259

'You like it here, don't you?' she asked, looking up from her plate and putting her fork down. 'You like it here and you seem to be warming up but then you suddenly grow distant. Why?'

I looked away, the comfort destroyed by that question. 'I don't like being dependent,' I said. 'When it gets too comfortable I get the hell out . . . Get too close and fate kicks you in the teeth.'

'That's the most stupid thing I've heard you say so far,' she said. 'You sound as if you've made up your mind to be unhappy with your life. Yes, you can survive on your own, you don't have to prove that any more . . . I can understand why your wife walked out on you.'

'I also don't like to owe anyone anything,' I said.

Her eyes narrowed in anger, and I remembered helplessly the anger in her eyes when we'd first met. 'Nasty middle-class mind you've got there, Colonel,' she said. 'Making debit and credit entries in your little book of accounts . . . maybe I should bill you for the time you spend here.' She paused, breathing hard, her eyes beginning to get wet, then she turned her back to me. 'I don't know why I'm saying all this to you,' she continued. 'I should have called you and said thank you very much, and sorry about the hard words, and left it at that.'

I sat there looking at her stiff back, mulling it over for the next few seconds and when understanding came it came with a sudden incredible lift of the heart. I looked at her, found myself smiling. Walked over to her side of the table, turned her around, put my arms around her, drew her close, bent forward to kiss her.

It worked as advertised. She wound her arms around my neck and clung with surprising strength, tears running down her cheeks and on to mine. I pushed her backwards into the bedroom, the passion rising overwhelmingly, more strongly than I'd ever felt it before.

In uncharacteristic haste I took the lead, undressing her and myself, taking breaks from undoing hooks and buttons to explore with fingers and mouth, as I'd never done before, while she lay back in what seemed to me complete contentment.

It was too good to last. In bed, my arms twined about her I felt a sudden reserve in her, a withdrawal, as the passion that flared up in her turned suddenly to ice. I let go of her, raised myself up on an elbow to look at her, and found with surprise her eyes swimming in tears. I bent down to kiss them away and she put her hands on my chest and pushed me firmly away. And as I watched, once again she turned her back on me.

This wasn't what she'd wanted. I'd misread the signals. I took my hands off her, moved back, wondering what had changed her mind so completely in those few minutes between the dining room and the bed, and hoped with a sudden intense tightening in the chest that I wouldn't lose this. Managed with a suddenly dry throat to ask, 'What's the matter? I thought you wanted to make love!'

She took another deep breath, shook her head. I saw again the wetness in her eyes, said hoarsely that perhaps I shouldn't have pushed so hard.

She looked me straight in the eye. 'Of course not,' she said, having regained her control, 'don't be silly.' When I kept silent, she continued, 'I'm sorry, this is my fault. It's my turn to apologize.'

'What for?' I asked.

'I did want you to make love to me,' she said slowly. 'It began for me the moment I saw you. Just like it did for you. But . . .' She turned away to hide her brimming eyes.

'But what?' I asked.

'But it's hard to square the man who comes in here and plays with my boy and worries all the while about whether he's doing the right thing with the other man, the man who shoots people and throws bombs and talks of body counts and the Krait . . . I told you I can't handle violence and there's so much of that in you . . . I just can't handle it.'

'So where do we go from here?' I asked, drawing back.

'I wish I knew,' she replied. 'I wish I could make up my mind. It's not fair to you.'

'Leave the fairness bit alone for the time being,' I said. 'Take your time over it.'

She looked up at me swollen eyed. 'I don't want to keep you in suspense,' she said, dabbing at her cheeks. 'It's not on.'

'Try me,' I said, remembering the new, overwhelming passion. 'I've never been in love like this before. I never even had the time to think about it and now that it's happened I don't want to lose it. Take your time, and when you can square the two men, let me know.'

'All right,' she said. 'And in the meanwhile?'

'I'll wait. Stay away, if you like. Leave you to think it out without any pressure at all.'

She thought for a moment, and agreed. 'Yes,' she said gratefully. 'That would be fine. But keep in touch.'

chapter thirteen

The krait's venom is very powerful, upto ten times as powerful as that of its better-known cousin the cobra; a droplet is enough to kill a full-grown man.

After a particularly hot summer, fall came early that year. The earth, softened by the summer rains, caked hard again, the sun beat down, and water and tempers ran short on the field exercises. We struggled with our exercises through August and September, looking forward to the beginning of winter in October.

Yadav was given posthumously the Param Vishisht Seva Medal, the highest peacetime award the Indian Army gives. Cold comfort, I thought, to his widow and sons: they wouldn't be too badly off, the Army would take care of that, but the family would now never be complete.

Ismail was finally cleared for his brigade, after a gruelling series of meetings with assorted generals and people from the defence ministry. I was cleared for full colonel shortly afterwards, thanks largely to recommendations from General Kelkar and Ismail.

More than a month after the debriefing, unexpected but welcome, came a report from military intelligence. Bits of it would end up in a rule book for handling kidnaps and hostage rescues—never exchange one hostage for another, never risk a hostage's life for information the way I'd done. Though the report was neutral, and my evaluation reports from both Kelkar and Ismail unchanged, in my mind there hung a faint question mark over the wisdom of what I'd done: it had cost two lives that I thought could have been saved.

Hari flaunted his book learning a little less and became gentler with his men. The operation seemed to have given him something that had been missing so far, I didn't know what. He'd kept his head during the Bangalore operation and earned the good feeling of the troops. In those few minutes in Bangalore he had aged ten years. His men surprised him by doing even better than they had when he had driven them hard.

At three on a sunny October afternoon, militants from the Peoples' War Group in Andhra Pradesh descended on a busload of Yugoslav tourists outside the Salar Jung museum in Hyderabad, and waving murderous-looking pistols and rifles, drove the bus out of the city. Police managed to track the bus to a vineyard fifty kilometres out of town, from which the PWG men evicted its occupants. A panicky state administration, dreading an 'international

265

incident', called the home ministry in Delhi, who in turn called the Yugoslav Embassy and then us.

Soon after dark, unknown to the police, two large and adventurous men among the tourists managed to overpower their PWG guards, who they discovered later were armed with World War II vintage .303 rifles and crude 'country-made' pistols backed up with explosives made from nitrogenous fertilizer and diesel fuel. The two men then led the rest of the hostages through the vineyard and over the back wall, unobserved even then by the policemen setting up a cordon around the vineyard. In the dark the twenty-four escapees stumbled cross-country to an ill-paved road and thence to a near-deserted bus stand where the manager had the sense to call the police, and where they waited to be collected by the authorities. Meanwhile, the company of SOF that we had despatched to Hyderabad with the embassy's agreement landed at Hyderabad airport and proceeded to the vineyard, where they found the police taking the place apart: the PWG men had fled. The officer commanding the detachment prodded the police into finding out where the former hostages were, and was told that they were at the bus depot, where he took his men, to find them all slightly inebriated with relief and Golconda wine. The detachment then returned to Delhi, feeling faintly foolish but waving colourful handkerchiefs that the erstwhile hostages had presented them.

Someone took a potshot out of a car at General Kelkar as he and his wife drove home from a friend's house on a weekend. The General, driving himself, alert as he had ever been, instead of braking swerved and fishtailed his car, taking the would-be assassins off balance, and continued home in a vehicle sporting three bullet holes, including one through the rear windshield. The police were told, and he was ordered to take a bodyguard, which he did, from the SOF. The CBI found the car from which the shots had been fired, but no more.

Sandhya and I spoke to each other at least once a week, with reserve on her side and a fierce hidden longing on mine, but met only twice, briefly, at her flat. The second time I went on foot instead of on my bike and Ismail gave me a lift. 'Visiting your lady friend, eh?' he asked, and I nodded. He smiled knowingly but didn't mention it afterwards. I wanted to meet her again but held back because I was afraid that to push her now would only put her off. I settled instead for looking for signs of change in our telephone conversations, but found none.

On a Sunday some three weeks after the Hyderabad incident General Kelkar got a call from the chief secretary of UP. Breaking all protocol, the chief secretary had spoken directly to the defence minister after someone kidnapped for purely financial cause the son of a leading Lucknow industrialist, a generous contributor to party coffers. The industrialist had with remarkable presence of mind ignored the kidnappers' warning not to contact the authorities and called the chief minister. Some unusually quick legwork and intelligent guesses by the police had shown up the house where the captive had been taken after the kidnap: the kidnappers, working purely for money and local men all, had drugged the lad and carried him away to a bungalow in Hazratganj, a residential area, one of the posher bits of the city. A platoon of SOF under Venky left immediately for Lucknow, where the RAF, after consulting Venky, went in on their own and emerged a few minutes later carrying the hostage, unhurt but still unconscious, as well as two of the kidnappers.

Some things emerged very clearly from these encounters. I'd prefer any day to deal with kidnappers working purely for money. They were much more predictable, and though they often had local political connections, could be depended on not to sacrifice themselves in a confrontation.

Chauhan and I kept in touch over the weeks and months, meeting occasionally in his office, where I went to collect snippets of information about the FKF. One of the FKF men we had captured in the Bangalore operation—the man I had hit and thrown over the railings—had died in hospital three days after. The other, who had survived the firefight with Hari's team, was still being interrogated. His capture had generated so much publicity that he had become something of a public figure, with the attention of several human rights agencies, including Amnesty—since he turned out to be a Kashmiri, from the Pakistani side of the Line of Control—and several Indian ones. The police could no longer afford to interrogate him as they would have liked to, Chauhan told me. He wished some terrorist group would go after someone in Amnesty so they'd learn that terrorists couldn't be handled with kid gloves and a rule book.

So what were they doing with the man, I asked. Asking him the same questions over and over, replied Chauhan, in the hope that he would either break or give inconsistent replies. A high-priced lawyer had most uncharacteristically offered to plead the terrorist's case when it came up for hearing.

What about the CLA bill that had replaced TADA, I asked. The man was caught in a regular operation, he'd been armed, and he'd fought back.

That was what the police had booked him under, said Chauhan, but all they could do was keep him in his cell and talk to him.

And what of the Krait, I asked, bringing out what was uppermost in my mind.

The trail had once again run cold, he explained. From the interrogation of this FKF man and the dead one it was clear that he had put a distance between himself and his operatives: they dealt only with the leader of the team, who himself, presumably, was in touch with the Krait. Which meant that the team leader himself had to be alert during communications with the Krait . . . It made his job very hard indeed, but it kept the Krait protected. And the methodical way they'd set it up pointed at lots of training.

From whom, I asked.

Topaz and ISI, he said, where else.

A week later he had more snippets. The weapons and explosives used in the Bangalore operation had all come into the country through Kasargod in north Kerala, of all places. There was in those parts a flourishing smuggling

269

network as well as many Muslims with distinctly Pakistani sympathies, many of them supported by the fundamentalist Peoples' Democratic Party of Kerala. Bringing their goods in this way was much more expensive than bringing them in via the traditional drug-smuggling routes through Rajasthan and Kutch which were so popular with the Pakistanis.

'Isn't it possible to trace the money?' I asked.

'There is a drug-smuggling route through Rajasthan,' Chauhan explained, 'passing through the border and on to the university town of Pilani, then on to Delhi or wherever else. The smugglers themselves are almost all young Indian or Pakistani Muslims. The drugs earn profits which are in turn used to finance the gunrunning. Since both sets of transactions are entirely in black money, the profits never show up in any set of books. Since the Americans have stopped helping the ISI it needs more money that the drug-smuggling networks provide. Brilliant operation.'

'How do you know the drug network in the north, is related to the gunrunners in the south?' I asked.

'The set-ups are similar,' he said, 'the types of men used are similar, and there are references to each other. The same man must have built up both networks. He had used different ends of the country so that state police forces, which rarely communicate with one another, would know only what is happening in their own state. It has taken a stroke of luck to tie the two together.'

'It must be the Krait,' I said.

'Probably,' he replied, 'RAW (Research and Analysis Wing, India's spook agency) says it's with Pakistani help. Smuggling drugs and weapons on this scale without the connivance of the Pakistani border forces is next to impossible. If not connivance, at least a conveniently blind eye.'

'So what,' I asked.

'RAW says ISI's involvement is more or less confirmed,' he said, 'this is just their style.

'So they have lots of money besides what they earn from the drug-smuggling,' he continued, 'and lots of trained men. Many of the men they had used to penetrate Afghanistan, with American support, have nothing to do, and stirring up trouble in Kashmir is as good a way as any to keep them occupied. Pakistan now has a relatively—relatively, mind you—stable border with Afghanistan, and hence free resources of men and money and weapons. The men, especially the ones like "Major" Mast Gul, they use. They don't use the weapons because that would give us a direct lead from the terrorists to the Pakistanis, but they have the money to pour into purchases from Eastern Europe of weaponry and explosives. And the ISI has much less to worry about on the domestic front: they concentrate on cross-border operations.'

'How about a covert operation against them?' I asked. 'The SOF should be able to do it.'

'No way,' he said instinctively. 'The ISI are on a high right now. They're running operations in Afghanistan besides India, funding and arming the Taliban. All of it on the money they earn from drugs.'

'We can bust up their drug operations good,' I said, 'we have the desert experience for it.'

'It's a good thought,' he said, 'hold it for a while.'

'Not just that,' I offered, 'we could even get into Afghanistan. Peshawar is not too far from Faisalabad, on the border. From Peshawar we'd be able to infiltrate the drug- and gunrunners all the way.'

'Hold it,' he said, 'don't get carried away. Besides, we don't do stuff like that.'

'Oh yeah. What about Sri Lanka?'

'Look, the Tamil Nadu state government could be doing some stuff, and we're trying to stop it.'

'Okay, okay. And did RAW tell you why the Pakis are into Afghanistan now that the Russians are gone?'

'No, but it is obvious.'

'Because it's good for business?'

'What else?' he said, despondent. 'The Yanks sell F-16s and fast breeders to the Pakis because an arms race here means more business for them, less unemployment, the works. Likewise, the Pakis sell food, weapons and vehicles—Range Rovers and old Land Rovers are popular—in the Hindu Kush and the Pamirs when there is trouble with the guerrillas.'

Ismail's promotion came through, and his brigade, late in December, in the last few days before Christmas. It came more than six months after he'd been cleared for it, mostly because Ismail himself, General Kelkar and I had all wanted him to stay longer. He was to join his brigade on 16 February, said the orders, giving him six weeks to hand over to me. My own orders, promoting me to full colonel and giving me charge of the SOF, arrived at the same time. Ismail called me to his office. Considering he'd just got a crucial promotion, he seemed washed out. 'I need a couple of weeks off,' he told me. 'I'll tell them I'll hand over to you on 16, but I'll join my new unit only on 1 March.'

'You need it,' I told him. 'Leave early if you like. Take a month off. You know I can handle it, and so does Kelkar.'

'A fortnight's good enough,' he grinned. 'Besides, I want to stay back here, as long as possible.'

In the midst of it came cricket fever, the build-up to the World Cup. I'm a cricket freak but rarely got to see any: the job got in the way. But this time, thanks to satellite TV, I watched bits of the better matches.

That January the FKF man in custody broke down after seven months of intensive questioning. Chauhan rang one afternoon to ask me to attend a session with the terrorist. 'We'll have him talk about training and plans,' he said. 'You might pick up a hint about what they plan to do.'

'Right,' I replied. 'What's he said so far? Has he said anything about who's behind all this?'

'No,' replied Chauhan. 'He's been talking mostly about his training, and his background. You'll have to lead him on.'

I went, that evening, to Tihar jail, where they'd kept the terrorist in a special cell, away from the other undertrials, down long, gloomy, stale, stone-flagged corridors along which we heard the echo of our footsteps as we walked. I found him, a pale, young man with three days' stubble on his face, sitting on a stool alone in a small, darkened room

273

with one window high up. He was sweating profusely despite the chill in the bleak room, elbows resting on the rough table bolted to the floor in front of him. He looked dully at us as we entered and a warder switched on the light bulb in the ceiling, and watched expressionlessly as we all ranged ourselves around him: Chauhan, a prison guard, another warder, a stenographer and me. I stayed in the shadows so the man wouldn't see my face clearly. The warder, with practiced watchfulness, had his staff out and ready while we spoke, and I, too, knowing that the FKF man might be suicidally minded, was watchful.

In the seven gruelling months since the man, Hassan Obaid, had been caught, he had put on weight. He moved listlessly all the while we were there, looking a very sick, young man with his crew-cut and pale eyes and prison pallor and fat. I thought he must have been disenchanted with the FKF: when they recruited him they had probably promised him they would have him released if ever he were caught, and now they hadn't come. Obaid would probably have preferred death to the limbo of a grey prison cell.

'Tell us about what you did in Bangalore,' said Chauhan in Urdu. 'Where you lived, what you did at the farmhouse, everything.'

'I have told you many times,' Obaid sighed. 'But since I have nothing better to do I will tell you. I came to Bangalore from J & K three days before we started. There was one other man with me, who is now dead.'

'What did you do in Bangalore those three days?' asked Chauhan.

'I was briefed. The team leader met us in our hotel—we stayed in a small hotel in Shivaji Nagar—and briefed us. We went twice to the Taj to look around the place. We went on drives on the outskirts of Bangalore trying to pick a site at which to keep the hostages. When we settled on the farmhouse where we took the hostages we stood watch on it for a couple of nights to make sure it would be all right to take it . . . We were very busy.'

'Were you alone?' Chauhan asked.

'No, we always moved in pairs. We got close to each other but in general we were discouraged from getting friendly or asking personal questions. To keep the others safe if one is caught, you see . . .'

'What did you do during the operation itself?'

'I was in the bus. We had to go to the fellow from whom we hired the bus, get rid of the driver, and be ready to reach the hotel at the time we had been given. We were behind the hotel, actually, on Ulsoor Road, waiting for a radio signal.

'I waited in the bus for the hostages. After we started off I stood guard on them. Later, in the farmhouse, we all shared the work. The hostages got their food from outside, but we cooked ours in the kitchen . . . that was safer.'

'Tell us once more about your training,' said Chauhan, 'about your camp, about your trainers.'

'I have told you already, many times,' replied Obaid in the same language, a mixture of defiance and fear in his voice, 'I don't want to tell you all over again.' With his sparse beard and stubble, his light eyes turned downward,

275

he looked perhaps nineteen or twenty years old. I felt for a moment a fleeting pity for the man that disappeared with the recollection that he had been willing to participate in a massacre, and had a hand in killing one of my men.

'Do you know who I am?' I asked, leaning forward into the glare of the lamp overhead so he could get a good look at me.

He looked me in the eye, a hint of defiance still lurking in him. 'I know,' he said, flatly and definitely. 'You needn't have stayed in the shadows. They used to show us your photographs. You're Colonel Menon. You and that traitor Colonel Qureishi. I saw you in Bangalore when you came with the doctor. They say you're the planner, but you're not just a planner . . . It would be an honour to kill you.'

'I have nothing against you,' I said. 'We could have finished you off in Bangalore. My men would have been happy to do it. You killed my comrade. I held them back.'

'You kept me alive to ask me questions,' he said, his voice rising in accusation, 'to find out about my comrades. Not out of kindness. I know your type.'

'No one's forced you to speak,' I said. 'I could have kept you with me and let my men have their way with you. You would have talked, then, you would have sung songs for me through the night.' This was pure falsehood. We did understand the basics of interrogation; we had all been trained to interrogate hostiles during combat, and everyone in the SOF could apply pressure when required. But there was no way I could keep a man like Obaid in SOF custody for weeks, or have him tortured. But then, Obaid wouldn't know that.

I saw a flicker of doubt in his eyes. Chauhan had told me before we went into the cell that Obaid hadn't been ill-treated—not physically, at any rate—though they had used two men to interrogate him, a hard man and a soft man, and deprived him sometimes of a few hours of sleep. Obaid had finally given way to the soft man, his youth and inexperience leading him to seek solace, which was more or less what Chauhan had expected.

I pressed on. 'I make no promises,' I told him. 'You will get a fair trial, whether or not you tell me anything about your organization. But if you tell me more about your organization and your trainers I will do what I can to make your life a little more comfortable.'

He gave me a ghost of a smile. 'Will you let me go?' he asked, his voice grating. 'What comfort can I have in a prison? All my people are outside.'

I leapt at the lead he'd given me. 'I'll try to get news of your people,' I told him, 'if you tell me who they are, and where they are.'

Suspicion darkened his eyes for a moment, then they returned to their normal listlessness. 'How do I know you won't put them in jail?' he asked. 'How do I know you won't use them to trap my friends? How do I know you won't punish them, to make an example of them?'

'I'll have them brought to you,' I replied. 'You have my word on it that as soon as I can have them traced you will meet them. In this very room. I'll make sure they're not unduly harassed. We can see to it that they are here during your trial, that you see them in court every day.'

'All right,' he said, the suspicion abating. 'Get my people here. Your Army killed my father and my brother years ago. My mother and sister live thirty miles from the old Chrar-e-Sharief shrine.' Their names followed, and then the address. I could ask the Army commander in the area to trace these people and have them sent to Delhi.

'Give me a letter for your people, in your own writing,' I told him. 'If my men call on your people without a letter like that they might refuse to come.' On a sheet of paper the steno offered him Obaid scribbled a brief note in Urdu. 'I can't read or write Urdu,' I continued, 'but to be on the safe side I'm going to have that letter read out to me. Just to make sure.'

'All right,' he said, dispirited, 'I've written nothing wrong.'

Bit by bit he told me about himself. He came from a family of shepherds, his grandfather having been a vassal of the maharaja of Kashmir. They were very poor. The money in the region was mostly with the Hindu traders—the pandits—and Muslims who were in the good books of the Indian government. False Muslims he called them, apostates who drank and chased women and ignored prayers while the true believers got nothing at all. Until eight years ago, his family had done nothing. Then, one evening, a recruiter from the Hezbol Mojahiddeen dropped by. 'He changed our lives,' Obaid said. 'Your government promised us everything and in the end gave us nothing. This man brought us enough to take away our hunger, and after many generations we had respect. We held our heads high in the village. Do you understand that, puppet?'

I nodded. 'Go on,' I said.

'By and by, some six months later, my father agreed to work for the Hezbol, instead of just sheltering their men. Then my elder brother, too, joined. Your men killed my father first, then managed to catch my brother alive. They killed him, too. They tortured him through a whole night, then killed him. And they said he had been killed in a fight, even though there were the marks on his body of the beating they had given him, and his bones were broken . . . Then I joined. It was a . . . it was a matter of honour.'

'What did you do in the beginning?' I asked.

'I used to carry messages for them at first,' he said. 'When I became full-grown I used to go out raiding with them. We used to harass your Army. We tried to ambush patrols. We tried to ambush your convoys. We tried to hit police stations . . .'

'Where did you get your weapons?'

'The Hezbol gave us weapons,' he replied. 'They gave us Kalashnikovs. They gave us AK-47s and AK-74s. A few of the groups got RPGs, and anti-tank missiles. They gave us wire-guided anti-tank missiles, and heat-seeking ones.'

'What about training with these weapons?'

'They used to make us carry those weapons. They made us carry our rifles so long our arms felt as if they'd fall off. They never allowed us to rest the rifles in their slings: we had to carry them in our hands, no matter what we were doing . . . When we got used to them we could handle them as if they were matchsticks . . . They taught us to aim and fire, how to judge the light and the direction of a moving target. They taught us about bombs, they taught us to get away from the site of a bombing . . . It lasted more than eight weeks, all of it in Pakistan.'

'What else did they teach you?'

'They taught us to hide, to use cover while preparing an ambush and to prepare an escape route for ourselves as we planned the ambush. They taught us to use knives to kill people, how to strangle people with a piece of wire. They taught us how to recognize targets. They taught us to go for the officers in a group of soldiers, and for radio equipment.'

'How did you make out the officers?' I asked.

'From their badges,' he said, 'and from the tabs on the collars of the senior ones, like you. And officers carry pistols. We would go for the lead vehicles in the convoys, for the cabs of the lorries, next to the driver, which was where you could find the officers. Or we would go for the jeeps.'

'Where was this camp of yours?' I asked.

'Three hours' march from the border, in the Ranbirsinghpura sector. About twelve miles from the border, in the hills, on a plateau. The surrounding country was very rough. We used to walk up the camp in groups, not less than ten or twelve, in the dark, carrying lanterns. Otherwise people got lost.'

'That must have been what everyone learnt,' I said, 'handling those weapons, and making simple bombs, and offensive and defensive techniques. You must have learnt some more for this Bangalore operation.'

'Oh, yes, we all went through special training for this one, at the same camp but with different trainers.'

'How were you picked for the special training?'

'I spoke English. They wanted men who were good and who spoke English. That was all.'

'And what did you learn in these special training sessions?'

'More about weapons. More about patrolling. How to stay awake and stand guard through the night and the day following. Getting along with little food and water. Survival. Not being caught . . . There was an Afghan there who could move without being seen. We used to call him the Ghost. We had to stand guard in the dark while he tried to approach us, and we had to spot him. Most of the time we failed. This man had once managed to kill some Spetsnaz troops— Russians, in Afghanistan—and we all wanted to be like him . . . We learnt to pick targets, to attack. We learnt to use radios, some codes . . . But this special training was only for a few of us.'

'How many of you were there?'

'For the basic training there must have been forty or more men. For the advanced training there were less than ten . . . We started with ten but three dropped out during the training. It was very difficult.'

'What language did you speak there?'

'Mostly Urdu. When we went through the special training we had to speak English all the time. The instructors hit us if we spoke Urdu. Some of us learnt much more English from a white man. I don't know where he came from.'

'How did they treat you in the camp?'

'They used to lecture us all the time, about what you people are doing to us Kashmiris. They used to tell us how we are Islamic, and would be better off with an Islamic country like Pakistan. They said the Hindus would never let us free . . . They told us we were fighting a jihad. We were heroes, though the Indians called us terrorists. They gave us good food and warm clothes, and kept us comfortable except for the training itself. The training was painful . . . There was another element to the training. They gave us good clothes to wear, all made in India. They taught us to use knives and forks and spoons to eat, to talk politely. That was part of the preparation for Bangalore.'

'Were all of you in the Bangalore operation trained together?'

'No. I told you, only seven of us were in the group for advanced training. Only two of us were in Bangalore, eventually. Others must have been trained elsewhere, or in other batches at the same camp.'

'Did you all live together? In the same buildings?'

'There were only four buildings, we all lived in tents. Even the instructors.'

'What were the buildings for?'

'I don't know . . . One of them had a radio, a big radio. Another was used for meetings. Once in a while people came in jeeps to the foot of the mountain and then stayed in the camp. They never spoke to us, only to the instructors. They stayed in that building. A third building . . . that was the arsenal. They guarded it heavily. I don't know what was in the fourth building. Some kind of stores, I think. I saw them carrying cylinders into it, and cans of something, and a boiler. I don't know what it was for. They never told us, and never let us get near it.'

Something went click in my mind. Cylinders. A boiler. Cans of chemicals. Poison gases? Chemical warfare? As in Japan?

'All right,' I said to Hassan Obaid, 'I have to go now. I will see to it that if I can trace your people you will meet them.'

'Do that,' he said. 'I don't mind dying. I would like to meet my people before I die, that's all.'

The next day I called Chauhan. 'That guy Obaid,' I said, 'I think he was talking about a store of chemical weapons. Poison gases. What do we do about it?'

'I don't think they'll use poison gas, Raja,' he said. 'They've got to have training for that.'

'If a religious group could store chemical weapons in Japan and Australia why can't these guys do it here? Or store them across the border and deliver them here?'

'I'll see what we can do about it,' he replied, not sounding very convinced, but I went ahead and ordered some protective gear anyway, from the US. General Kelkar and I got into a long argument with accountants from the ministry, and ended with them ordering just ten sets of gear, with respirators.

Ismail threw a party at the mess that week to celebrate his promotion. As I left the party he stopped me in one of his rare, sociable moods. 'I'd like you to come for a drink

283

sometime,' he told me. 'Informal. Bring your girlfriend along if you can.'

Things are beginning to look up, I said to myself on the way home from the mess.

chapter fourteen

The krait's mouth opened wide. The long, grooved fangs at the front of its upper jaw, held almost flat against the jaw when the snake's mouth was shut, extended, readying to squirt venom into its prey. The krait's venom glands, now full, contained enough to kill several thousand of its prey.

I couldn't have been more mistaken. We never did have that drink together. The FKF struck again, viciously, where we least expected them to. I woke from a light doze at two one morning, in the midst of a power cut, to the sound of the telephone bell. Still half-dazed, I listened to Venky's urgent voice on the telephone—he was the duty officer for the week—say, 'You'd better get down here quickly. It's our old friends again.'

I shook off the last, clinging vestiges of sleep and fatigue, dressed in the dark and ten minutes later found my way down the dark staircase to the jeep Venky had sent to fetch me to the office. Outside the office, I could make out the dark shapes and moonlit glints of at least ten cars and jeeps in the parking lot. Far too many, I thought, hopping out of the jeep before it halted, breaking into a run along the asphalt to the entrance to the building.

Ismail came up seconds later, dark shadows under his eyes, and we made our way down the corridor to the last room at the end, formerly his and now mine, where we found, to our surprise, Chauhan sitting in one of the straight-backed visitors' chairs. His hands, pushing papers on the desktop, trembled, and his chubby face bore an uncharacteristic bleakness. I slowed down, went over to my chair. 'What happened?' I asked as Ismail took a chair. 'Venky just told me the FKF hit again.'

Chauhan looked at his hands as if forcing them to be steady. 'They let off poison gas inside a theatre,' he said eventually, his voice forced into steadiness. 'An hour ago. Of those who got out, more than thirteen people were dead from the gas, and another four died in the stampede to get out of the theatre.'

My mind went chill at the thought. Those containers Obaid had seen in his camp had indeed contained poison gas, or chemicals that went into them. They must have been concocting it up there, in the quiet of the mountains. 'What gas?' I asked.

'They're not sure yet,' he replied. 'We haven't been able to get a sample from the theatre. The doctors say from the symptoms that it could be any of the three major nerve gases, sarin, tabun or soman . . . So far they've been administering drugs called atropine and pralidoxime—some

286

names like that, I'm not sure—to everyone who showed symptoms of the poisoning. But that's generic treatment for anyone who's been poisoned by malathion or parathion—common pesticides.'

'What's happening at the theatre?' I asked.

'I don't know, it's a little confusing. One of the men working at the theatre said that someone came out leading a child with blood all over her face, and then there was some screaming, and then everyone stampeded for the door. A policeman in the audience spread the word that it was a poison gas and after everyone who could get out of that theatre on their own got out they locked the doors to keep the gas in.'

I was already reaching for the phone. I called the quartermaster to get the protective gear out of storage, the operations officer to get A platoon of Alpha company ready to go, and General Kelkar, to get his presence to help with the bureaucracy, before responding to Chauhan. I still found it hard to swallow. 'You mean . . . You mean there could be people in there? They locked the doors of the theatre with people maybe still inside?'

'Yes,' he said. 'They called the fire brigade, who in turn called the police. The police in turn called the forensic labs, who said that the gas could attack you through the skin, or whatever, and it wasn't advisable to go into the theatre without protective gear, and we haven't yet been able to raise anyone with the gear. It's a bloody mess in there.'

'You talked of body counts,' I said, 'the truth must be much worse.'

'We don't know,' he said. 'We won't know until you go in and find out.'

'Why the hell didn't you call us earlier?' I exploded. 'It's over a couple hours since it started and I don't think there's anyone left alive in there. Shit!'

'Cool it, Raja,' said Ismail. 'Take it easy!'

'We didn't know what it was . . . I got the news only half an hour ago and told my people to call you and headed straight down here . . . I didn't know. I just didn't know.'

'How do you know it was the FKF?' I asked.

'Someone rang up my boss on his unlisted residence number about the time this thing started—he hadn't got the news yet—and told him the FKF had left a little message for him at the Priya theatre. That was it. Arya went back to sleep and half an hour later he got a call from the theatre . . .'

Venky, who had just walked in, interrupted. 'Sir, I think Hari's in the theatre. He told me yesterday he was planning to take his girlfriend there tonight, after dinner. He seemed very keen about it.'

'Find out where he is,' I said. 'Try the hospitals, his quarters, his parents' place, his girlfriend's place . . . The morgue, too. If he's been there and he's alive and in any shape to talk I want to see him right after we get into that theatre.'

'I'd like to come in on this,' said Ismail.

'You're welcome on the case,' I told him, 'but we have only ten complete suits, with respirators and everything. The police will want some, and maybe a technician will have to go in as well. We haven't enough suits. I'm sorry, you can't come into the theatre.'

'I understand,' he said. 'As you wish.'

'My men have got a command post up near the theatre,' Chauhan said, 'about half a kilometre away. We didn't want to get any closer . . .' He gave me the address.

I remembered photographs in *Time* of Japanese soldiers going into Aum Shinryoko premises with a canary in a cage . . . A natural alarm. 'Get hold of someone from the forensic lab,' I said, 'tell them to meet us at your command post as soon as they can. Someone who knows about these dam' gases, to brief us on what we need when we go in. Ask them to send equipment to collect a sample of the gas . . . and a small animal or a bird that we can take in along with us, a sensitive creature that'll fall over if there's gas in the air.'

Chauhan reached for the telephone with something approaching relief at having something better to do than sitting around chewing his fingernails off.

The quartermaster came running up. The protective suits were ready, loaded into two jeeps, where were they to go?

Near the Priya theatre, I said, handing over the address of the command post. Get there and wait for me.

Venky returned. No, he said, he hadn't been able to trace Hari but he'd got someone else working on it now, and the platoon was ready and where were we going?

289

Half an hour of dark roads—the power cut was still on—later the boffins from the labs met us at the command post, in thoroughly unromantic candlelight. One was a chemist, a thin, bearded man with a faint lisp and a tendency to blink rapidly when asked questions, and the other a doctor, fat and jolly, with shoulder-length grey hair and an alcoholic's nose. Two men utterly dissimilar in appearance but in some subtle way identical . . . Tweedledum and Tweedledee. 'We traced some of the patients at the hospitals,' the chemist, Tweedledee, who seemed to be the senior of the two, said to the ten-man team assembled outside the command post. 'They'd had their stomachs pumped out—gastric lavage is standard with cases of poisoning—and we got some samples out of them. We had a look at the metabolites and now know it's either soman or sarin, not tabun. We can't say for sure because we didn't have large enough quantities, but we'll confirm with samples of air.'

'Keep the technical details for later,' I told him. 'Right now just tell me what we need to do when we go in there, what we need to watch out for by way of precautions. We're going in first to bring out any people who might still be inside. We'll go in again for anything else, but right now I want to know what we need to watch out for.'

'Nothing,' he said, blinking behind his spectacles. 'Your gear should take care of everything. But remember that the gas could enter you through your skin, your eyes, everything. Under no circumstances may you take off any part of your protective gear. You might be tempted to take your gloves off to handle something. Don't.'

'Sure,' I said. 'Anything else?'

He brought forth a cage, containing a little, brown bird with a reddish beak. 'This is a muniya,' he said, 'a fairly common pet around here. Under a milligram of the gas will kill it in minutes.'

'Right,' I said, 'we'll take one of these into the theatre, and we'll leave one in the lobby, with the door open, so you can see if it's alive. If there's anyone inside the theatre we'll bring them out to the lobby. If the bird in the lobby survives, we'll leave the bodies in the lobby for the medics to collect, otherwise we'll bring them out here.'

Chauhan produced a hand-drawn map of the theatre for the rest of the briefing. 'The main door to the lobby is here,' he said, pointing a stubby finger. 'This big key lets you through that. Inside, first room on the left is where they sell tickets, and past that, past the gents' toilets, is the room where they keep the main switch. Somebody switched off the mains as they left. The first thing you do there is turn the mains on. In the same room you'll find a small diesel generator. If there's no power when you go in there, start the generator: you pull a cord to do that.'

'I'm familiar with that kind of generator,' I said. 'Keep going.'

'These three doors,' he pointed at the three theatre doors closest the lobby door, 'seemed to be where they let off the gas. We're not sure. There's a total of eight doors downstairs and four doors upstairs.'

'We'll have one man to each door downstairs, then,' I said, 'and I'll have two men cover the balcony.'

'Cover the ground floor first,' said the man from the lab. 'This gas is much heavier than air and it would take some time to reach the top.'

The protective gear, bought from the US Army, blue PVC-coated suits with yellow helmets that had large visors, came in three sizes—small, medium and large. I picked the smallest size they had and found that it flapped irritatingly loose around me, the gloves were a size too large, and the awkward rubber boots were roomy enough for me to walk around in. The respirator, a cylinder which strapped on to the back, had a tube coming out front into the helmet, and at the rear a small valve. Built into the helmet were a speaker and a microphone, for us to hear clearly past the visor. Loops for a belt at the waist hung loose, for we had nothing to put into them.

In the light of powerful torches we found our way past the small crowd that had collected—even at this hour—at the police cordon, to the theatre lobby and then to the switchboard. I turned the generator on and then switched the circuit to run off it, and in the lobby outside the lights came reassuringly on.

We waddled clumsily on through the lobby from door to door, a man stopping by at each door after I opened it, until I came to the last, which I would use. I handed the keys to the two men who would go up the stairs to the balcony, took a deep breath, opened the door, and walked into the theatre, shutting the door behind me as I did so.

I almost tripped on a body in the red-carpeted aisle, just past the curtain, lying asprawl in death just inside the door.

A girl, in her late teens as far as I could tell. Blood on her cheeks below her eyes, a trickle of it out of the side of her mouth. Short hair askew. She'd almost made it, then collapsed just short of escape. She'd been badly bruised. Caught in the stampede. With her body already failing from the nerve gas, she must have been helpless when she was trampled to death.

By her, his head resting partly on her stomach, was a young man. I put down the birdcage in my hand and from one of my pockets I took a mirror to check for traces of breath—it's well-nigh impossible to feel a pulse through a PVC glove—and found none in either of them. Heard a chirp, and looked around to see the bird in its cage collapse.

I picked the girl up clumsily, opened the door, carried her out to a spot just inside the lobby doors where we'd left the muniya in its cage. The bird at the lobby door was still alive, pecking at the bottom of the cage in casual unconcern. One of the teams of stretcher bearers waiting at a safe distance would run in to pick up the body. I watched the bird for a few seconds to make sure it wasn't affected by the gas, then went back in for the man.

On the carpeted aisles in the theatre we found five more people, one a young boy of ten or so, all dead. Five minutes later we were all outside the theatre, being hosed down with water from a fire engine that had just arrived to wash off any traces of gas sticking to the clothes.

Back at the brightly lit command post—the power had returned—General Kelkar was eyeing the boffins and their equipment suspiciously while the boffins themselves tried to make themselves as insignificant as possible. 'When next you go in, use this,' said the chemist, pointing a box on wheels, rather like a vacuum cleaner, a hose coiled up above it. 'Take it along with you to collect a sample of the gas. Remember to take the sample from somewhere low down: like I said before, this gas will be much heavier than air.'

'What do we look for by way of sources of the gas?' I asked.

'This gas is tricky to handle,' he replied. 'The chances are they would have dissolved it in some industrial solvent, like acetonitrile or just plain alcohol, and rigged up a vaporizer with a tank—like a giant bottle of perfume— with a motor attached. We don't think the gas would have spread as fast as it did unless it was blown out of whatever it came in. The people at the theatre wouldn't have noticed the buzz of a small blower or the hiss of escaping gas with the sound track on loud. So you're looking for a small package, not bigger than a briefcase, certainly, and not smaller than a kid's lunchbox, containing a blower, vaporizer and a container for the solvent. And watch out: there could be more than one.'

'And how do we handle the theatre?' asked General Kelkar. 'How long does it have to stay sealed? How do we get rid of the gas in it?'

Tweedledum resumed his lecture-hall tone. 'These gases are all unstable. They degrade very quickly in the presence of sunlight, and they hydrolyse—react chemically with water, that is—into relatively harmless components. Once you get the samples and figure out the source we'll wash the theatre down in water and leave it open to sunlight in the morning . . . It should be safe by late evening.' He grinned, and continued, 'And we'll have a cordon of muniyas to tell us if it's safe.'

'You can't do that,' said Chauhan. 'We need to search the theatre for clues on who did it, and washing it down will destroy them.'

'All right,' said the chemist. 'If we wash it down you lose your clues and if we don't you can't go into the theatre at all for at least a couple of days or so. Take your pick.'

'We'll open the doors,' said Chauhan, 'and we'll turn on the fans in the theatre, and wash the outsides of the theatre, while Colonel Menon's men and mine in protective gear search the insides.'

'Fine,' I said, turning to Chauhan. 'Could you please find the men who were on duty here? We'll speak to them after I get back.'

Back into that clammy, menacing theatre we went, looking now for clues under the seats, finding mostly debris— empty packets of popcorn and wafers, bottles of soft drinks, and closer to the doors shoes, slippers and some pathetic belongings abandoned in the stampede. Six hundred panicked people rushing for five doors in the dark had left generous traces of the violence of their flight.

Near the main door, tucked firmly away under a seat, I found a black briefcase that rattled when I shook it, and had holes cut into a side. Next to it, curled up on the floor, was a strip of black insulation tape, and a slight tackiness about the holes made it clear that the tape had been used to seal the holes temporarily. The briefcase was locked, so I took a screwdriver out of one of the pockets and forced the locks open. Inside, amidst a few feet of tubing, was a small blower, the size of a hairdryer, pointed at the holes in the case, and a clear plastic lunchbox-sized container with a liquid swishing about at the bottom. The gas, its solvent and a vaporizer.

Taped to the container was a clear plastic envelope, the black writing on the white paper inside visible: 'To the Government of India,' it said. With clumsy gloved hands I got hold of a corner of the plastic envelope, ripped it off the container, and put it into a pocket on the leg of the suit.

We found two more briefcases near exits, all identical, all with the note inside, addressed to the government. I locked the doors of the theatre once again and returned to the command post. From now on I had little to do in the theatre. Chauhan's men would borrow some of our gear, and while they searched the theatre they'd leave four doors open, with four men on the outside, also in protective clothing, standing by with hoses pointed at the doors.

At the command post the big brass had begun to arrive. First in was the Secretary of the home ministry, who had control over the federal law enforcement machinery, with three aides for whom there wasn't room in the post. The Secretary himself came quietly in and found himself a chair, calling Chauhan to brief him. Others arrived at intervals, until I wished they'd go away and leave us alone with the boffins to get the work done.

Out of the clear plastic envelope when it was ripped open came another white envelope, inside which was a letter. I opened it, dreading what it might contain.

'This is the FKF,' said the letter in a Roman font, obviously printed on a dot-matrix computer printer. 'The Government of India has continued to ignore our demands for a free Kashmir for too long. What you have just seen is a demonstration on a small scale of what we can do to the government if we choose to.

'First, all political prisoners in Kashmir must be released. They must be brought to the border and permitted to cross into Pakistan, or go free, as they choose.

'There is a little more than a day in which to do this: all prisoners must be at the border crossing by 0600 tomorrow, failing which we will demonstrate once again, on a slightly larger scale, the might of our weapons.

'Second, all military and paramilitary forces are to be withdrawn from Kashmir. This withdrawal must begin in earnest by 0600 tomorrow, and must be complete within a week. A failure to start the withdrawal tomorrow, or any serious interruption, will give us cause for yet another demonstration.'

I handed the letter to General Kelkar—the other copies of the letter were now in the command post, being read by policemen, and one copy was with the men from the lab. 'These men are nuts,' said the chemist.

'That we know,' rasped the General, 'but in what particular sense do you mean nuts?'

'Stupid.'

297

The General frowned. 'Why?'

'The gas is hard to make. Unless you're very careful you could make a mistake and gas yourself while making it. It's unstable and biodegradable, which means it's not easy to store. If you do store it so it can't degrade, it could leak. It's hard to handle, again for the risk of gassing yourself. It's hard to make, hard to store and hard to deliver. A bomb would have been easier.'

'All right, so they're mad,' I said, 'but tell us some more about the gas itself, sarin or whatever.'

'There were three possibles, sarin, soman and tabun. Sarin's chemical name is isopropyl methylphosphono-fluoridate. Soman is pinacolyl methylphosphonofluoridate. and tabun is . . . Umm . . . ethyl n-dimethyl-phosphorocyanidate, if I remember right.

'They all belong to a group of chemicals called organophosphates, to which also belong pesticides such as parathion and malathion. The Germans came across a pesticide, one of the earliest organophosphate pesticides, called tetraethyl pyrophosphate, TEPP. They tried to make a nerve gas out of it later. The difference is that the pesticides are solids, while the nerve gases are, well, gases.

'The pesticides are popular because they leave no permanent toxic residues. They degrade quickly, especially in sunlight—ultraviolet light, actually—and in humid air. That's why they're so popular.

'Like pesticides, you ingest nerve gases through the skin, the eyes, lungs, everywhere. I'm not too sure about their action on human beings but I know it interferes primarily with the nervous system. Dr Garg,' he said, waving his hand at his colleague, 'will be able to tell you more about it.'

Tweedledee came to his feet and in the same lecture-hall tone that Tweedledum used, began, 'Organophosphates affect the transmission and reception of impulses along nerves. Adjoining nerve cells are not really in contact with each other: there's a tiny gap between nerve cells called a synapse. To get the impulse across the synapse requires a chemical called acetylcholine esterase. The body normally keeps producing this. Nerve gases are acetylcholine esterase inhibitors. Impulses don't travel along nerves as they should. Your involuntary functions are hit first—except the cardiac functions, the muscles in the heart are another type altogether.'

That name, acetylcholine whatever, rang a faint bell in my mind. Where had I come across it? The answer came, surprisingly: it was while talking to a doctor who treated one of my colleagues who had been bitten by a snake. 'Doesn't snake venom work the same way,' I asked, 'by inhibiting acetyl-whatever-it-is?'

Tweedledee smiled, as if at a good student in a class. 'Some kinds of snake venom do. Cobra and krait venom typically contain acetylcholine esterase inhibitors. I don't think viper venom contains anything of the sort.'

'In that case, isn't there an antidote?' I asked. 'Can't we inject something into people to prevent the action of the gas?'

'No.' The reply was flat, definite. 'The action might be the same but the agents are different. We don't have a prophylactic.'

'Is there some protection from pesticides that we can implement here?' I asked.

'No. The difference between the action of pesticides and these nerve gases is because of differences in the way they are ingested. Pesticides go in through the skin, nerve gases mostly through lungs and eyes. You need protective clothing against a nerve gas. A lethal dose should bring on death in minutes.'

'You read that note,' I said to Tweedledum. 'Where do you think they'll . . . they'll do those other demonstrations?'

'Wait,' the General interrupted, 'there are three things we need to know. What we need to do about the theatre; what we can do to stop the gas being made, if it hasn't already been made; and what we can do to stop them delivering the gas if it's already been made.'

'We'll let you know about the theatre as soon as we figure out what gas they used, and how much of it,' replied the boffin.

'Don't you have gas detectors?' I asked. 'I've read somewhere that there are such things.'

'Let me explain,' said Tweedledum, the chemist. 'That depends on the concentration. When we're measuring something spread out fairly thin, we use something called a gas chromatograph to separate out the components of a gaseous mixture. It's essentially a thin glass tube—its inside diameter is no more than half a millimetre—but it is very long, upto thirty or forty metres. Inside the tube is a coating of neutral material to which components of the gas stick: that's called adsorption. When you pass the mixture through the tube, different components are adsorbed at different stages through the tube.

'When you heat the tube and then pass an inert gas through the tube, the bits that were adsorbed are desorbed into the inert gas at different temperatures, so you time the passage of the inert through the tube, so different batches of it pick up a different section of whatever has been adsorbed. Then you can put your inert gas into a spectrometer—if you have a mass spectrometer you can theoretically detect even one molecule of a substance.

'We don't have a portable mass spectrometer yet, but we have other kinds of gas analysers, which are possibly less reliable and need higher concentrations of gas in the air to work. We haven't got that kind of equipment, though we might get it soon.'

'So what do we do about the gas in the theatre?' asked the General.

'Wash it out, like I said,' replied the boffin, 'and use these birds to find out how dangerous it is.'

'Why a bird?' I asked.

The boffin smiled. He was in his element now. 'Birds use up energy much faster: they have to, if they want to fly. Their metabolic rates are much higher than those of humans, so they're that much more sensitive to poison gas.'

'How much gas do you think they let off in the theatre?' asked the General. 'You should know, now that you've seen the containers.'

301

The boffin looked pityingly at the General, as if he were a retard. 'I don't,' he said. 'This gas isn't pure. It's dissolved in some solvent: this gas is lipid soluble, which means in effect that it will dissolve in most organic solvents, like carbon tetrachloride, acetonitrile, petroleum ether, chloroform . . .'

'Wouldn't the gas go up into the air?' I asked.

'All these gases are heavier than air,' he replied, 'they'll spread along the ground. They degrade in the open, and I can't tell you offhand how long that'll take.'

'Doesn't it smell?' I asked, remembering that the gas let loose in Tokyo had had a horrible smell, like burning rubber.

'Not really. They have a faint smell.'

'The magazine accounts of what happened in Tokyo said there'd been some kind of a smell.'

He looked at me pityingly this time. 'That's the smell of the solvent,' he said, 'not the gas. Umm . . . Like pesticides. They don't have a strong smell: what you smell is the petroleum ether in which the pesticide is dissolved . . . You don't have a choice. Keep this area evacuated for at least a day. That's all I can tell you with what we know.'

The telephone in the corner rang, one of the policemen took the call. He handed it over to the boffin, and the boffin after his hello listened carefully to it for two minutes and then hung up without a word. 'It's sarin,' he said, 'sarin dissolved in chloroform. Chloroform evaporates easily, and is itself a poison in large quantities. They just confirmed it from the samples of air.'

I handed the boffin the letter. 'What do you think all this adds up to?' I asked. 'Where will they strike again?' He read the letter slowly, twice over, and blinked expressively at me. 'I haven't the faintest idea but I can tell you what kind of a place I'd look for if I were in their boots . . . I'd go for an enclosed space, from which the air wouldn't escape. I'd go for a space where air is recirculated: where you have central air-conditioning. I'd look for a crowded place from where you can't get out very easily. A place away from sunlight, to slow down the degradation. A dry place, where it won't rain and there won't be too much moisture in the air, to keep hydrolysis under control.'

'That subway in Tokyo fits perfectly,' Chauhan said. 'The Calcutta Metro fits even better. It's as crowded at peak hour, the ventilation is not as good, and exits are worse. But that's in Calcutta, thank God, not here.'

'What stops them from striking in another city?' I asked. 'They could hit anywhere in India, not just in Delhi.'

'Wait,' said Tweedledee. 'Let's get some more basics clear. There must have been a total of something like five kilos of solution in those briefcases. Not more than a third of that would have been sarin itself. Less than a kilo of it. It would have taken some time to evaporate, and it was diluted by the chloroform.

'There's a measure of toxicity called LD 50: the concentration, in parts per million, that would kill half— 50 per cent—of the population ingesting the toxin. Based on what we have for sarin, they'd need something like three or four kilos of pure sarin to inflict severe casualties over an area of a 100 metres square. Maybe more, depending on the weather and wind and the time of the day.

'If they dilute it by dissolving it in acetonitrile or chloroform, they'll need at least five times that amount, probably more, to do the same. They'll also need some kind of a delivery system to spread the gas in that area. What they used in the theatre isn't really sufficient to cover larger areas.'

'What if they use a completely different delivery system?' I asked. 'What if they stuff the gas into a cooking gas pipeline, like they have in Bombay? What if they mix it in LPG cylinders and distribute them all over?'

'The Bombay gas pipeline is out of the question,' replied Tweedledum, stepping in to support his colleague. 'It's not in use as best I know. Besides, any system for the distribution of gas would have large tanks and miles of piping. You'd need far too much of the gas to use a pipeline like that. Ditto the cylinders. If people notice anything wrong with the flame the first thing they do is shut off the cylinder.'

'So where else would you strike?' I asked.

'I'd go for a centrally air-conditioned building, preferably a high-rise, at peak hour. A couple of kilos in the central air-conditioning mechanism would do the trick . . .'

Out of the blue came a new, chilling idea. 'If the terrorists who are doing this have a little money and basic technology they could well have set it up already: a small case of the fluid stuck into the air-conditioning somewhere, to be set off by remote control . . .'

'We should prepare a release for all television and other mass media,' said the boffin. 'Tell them to watch out for symptoms, to see a doctor if they have any of those symptoms . . .'

The home Secretary spoke to the group for the first time since he'd entered. 'We'll look at news broadcasts in a little while,' he said, 'let's first decide what's to go into it.'

'Another thing,' said Tweedledee. 'The chances are that they've had to synthesize the stuff somewhere nearby. You can get the chemicals that go into its making—precursors, they're called—quite easily, but making it without enough precautions is risky. Check among doctors in Delhi if they've come across cases of pesticide poisoning in areas where there's no agriculture. You could get some leads that way.'

'How would you treat nerve gas poisoning?' I asked. 'Can we do something by way of stocking up for treatment?'

'Treatment is in theory simple but complicated in practice,' said Tweedledee, the doctor. 'You have to wash the patient, first in water, then if possible in ethyl alcohol. Pump his stomach out. Then administer atropine, which counteracts the effects of sarin but is itself a poison . . . You administer a tiny dose of atropine every hour until the patient begins to show signs of atropine poisoning. You can use pralidoxime as well. If the patient begins to convulse, use diazepam to calm him down. No morphine products.

'The point is that we have enough stocks of drugs to handle casualties. It's the care and the infrastructure— hospital beds, trained nurses, sometimes even IV equipment—that might run short if we have to face a serious poison gas attack.'

'All right, gentlemen,' said the home Secretary, 'let me recap. We have to find and stop this criminal who wants to let poison gas loose in this country. We have to anticipate where he will attack, if at all he decides to attack. We have to make sure that people are informed of the signs of poison gas so in case of an attack they will know what to do. We have to set up the infrastructure to handle an attack, wherever it comes.

'Gentlemen, in these matters, prevention is far and away the best thing to do. We will look for possible locations where sarin might have been synthesized. As Dr Garg here says, we will look for unusual cases of reported pesticide poisoning in the past few weeks in this city. We will work out guidelines to identify vulnerable locations, and inform people likely to be in these places on getting out in time. We will concentrate on the large cities, because I think it is unlikely this man will go to the villages or to small towns.

'Whatever the CBI has will go into this investigation. Likewise, I will ask my colleague, the Secretary of the ministry of defence, to keep his resources available for relief work if required anywhere, and to keep the SOF ready for any offensive operations we might consider feasible.

'We will now form a control room to take care of public response, which will be towards finding out where the terrorists have synthesized their stocks of sarin. We will announce a substantial reward for information on the whereabouts of these terrorists, but we will announce along with the award that approaching the terrorists or the gas is extremely dangerous.

'We will soon have a crisis management task force, which will meet in my office twice a day to review the situation. Thank you.' He left for his office, leaving a wake of sweeping resentment for having taken control so smoothly.

chapter fifteen

A tenth of a second before it struck the krait sensed the mongoose dance in, dipping and weaving. It swerved from its prey, but instead of retreating, reared back and struck at its foe, fangs still extended.

The first break came at eight in the morning.

I spent the first hours after the home Secretary left speaking with the theatre staff, and the watchmen who had been on duty in the general area, who had all been rounded up by the police.

The man at the entrance to the lobby had seen three men leave the theatre together a few minutes before the stampede. He didn't remember them come in, couldn't remember their faces . . . They were all large men and they had been in a hurry, that was all he remembered. There was little the theatre staff knew that was of any help.

One of the staff remembered that a door burst open and a young woman stumbled out, leading a child with her face bleeding. That was when the panic began, for a woman outside saw the blood and began to scream. A schoolboy ran out of the open door, red eyed, looking for someone to whom he could complain of having smelt chloroform.

The police found Hari in a hospital. He'd managed to get his girlfriend out of the theatre and then fought his way back in, against the stampede, to help. He had collected a larger dose of gas and emerged on his feet, only to collapse just outside the lobby. His girlfriend took him to a doctor uncle twenty minutes away, but by then his lungs had already begun to give way. He was comatose in the morning, on atropine, but the doctor said the prognosis wasn't encouraging.

The Army began to prepare mobile hospitals, tents and equipment packed and crated and ready to be flown out anywhere a gas attack was threatened—if the FKF attacked on a large scale the hospitals wouldn't be able to handle the load—and medical teams ready to board aircraft at an hour's notice.

Chauhan's control room came up with blinding speed, considering the pace at which the government normally works. But this was something different. This was a whole country united by the fear of an insidious, undetectable gas let off by a madman.

From six in the morning the media began its campaign, warning people of the dangers of a gas attack, telling them about the first symptoms, telling them what to do if they felt the symptoms. After the warnings came the requests, asking doctors around Delhi to report unusual cases of organophosphate poisoning, offering a telephone number to be called toll free by anyone who had information to offer.

A doctor in Mehrauli rang up Chauhan's control room in response to the hourly broadcasts on all electronic media—government and private TV channels, and All India Radio—on the gas attack by the FKF. Two men had brought in a third, he said, suffering from all the signs: salivation, lachrymation, incontinence, emesis, slowed reactions, everything. He had started the man on 0.2 milligrams of atropine every hour, but at some stage in the proceedings the patient had pulled the needle out of his arm, dressed himself, and sneaked out of the clinic, never to return.

When had all this happened, asked the inspector who took the telephone from the constable who had taken the call in the first place, and what did the man say was the source of the poison.

Six days ago, explained the doctor, and the man had said pesticide though it was hard to see how pesticide could be ingested through the eyes and lungs as it seemed to have been in this case.

Did he have the man's address, asked the inspector.

Of course, said the doctor, but it seemed false.

Did he have descriptions of the two men who accompanied the patient, asked the inspector, and could he help a policeman build an identikit picture.

Of course, said the doctor, anyone who committed crimes like this needed to be found as quickly as possible. He'd be there as soon as possible.

Not to worry, said the inspector, the police would come to him shortly. They would also scout the area, talk to the doctor's receptionist, and so on.

Just two hours later, at ten, the hourly status reports on the poison gas included also identikit versions of the faces of three men, built up based on descriptions supplied by the doctor and his receptionist. If you see these faces in the street, said the accompanying narration, go, as inconspicuously as possible, to the nearest police station.

The police, meanwhile, left the doctor's clinic after concealing two armed plainclothesmen outside, just in case the patient or his companions revisited the doctor.

The second break, a bolt from the blue, actually, came also from Mehrauli, almost immediately after the identikit faces went on the air. The owner of a small computer service centre rang up to say that three men, one of them almost certainly one of the men in the portraits, had dropped in two days earlier with a malfunctioning ink-jet printer. He'd been out of spares for the printer but had offered to have it set right in two days.

We need a printer right away, the men had said.

The computer service man had offered them a standby printer he had, a small dot-matrix printer.

Let's see how it works, the men had said, but had been unable to understand how to install the thing and to reinstall their word processor to use the dot-matrix printer.

They had eventually struck a deal. The men agreed to bring their computer—a small notebook—out to the service centre, where the service man would attach the

311

standby printer to it, and reinstall the word processor if required. The men would then leave a deposit and their own malfunctioning printer behind for repairs and take the standby printer home.

As luck would have it, the constable who took this call remembered vaguely that a computer printout had been involved in the gas attack and had called the nearest sub-inspector.

Do you have the address of those men, asked the policeman.

Of course, said the computer service man.

Stay right where you are, said the policeman, we're on our way.

An hour later, the doctor and the computer service man were together with a police artist, offering further descriptions. The man had violet eyes, the doctor remembered, and a mole at the side of his forehead. Possible, said the computer man, who remembered the eyes but not the mole, but there was something wrong with one of his ears.

Ah, yes, exclaimed the doctor, there was a bit missing from his left earlobe.

Right, said the computer man.

Bingo. We had the general locality. The address given to the computer service man was different from the one given to the doctor. In any case, both addresses, as the doctor had said, turned out nonexistent.

Back we went to the boffins, Tweedledum and Tweedledee, who, never before having followed a manhunt of this magnitude, had decided to camp at the command post. 'What kind of a place would these men need to store or synthesize the gas?' I asked.

'It's poisonous,' said Tweedledum the chemist, 'so they'd try to keep it clear from other buildings. If you're looking at an area like Mehrauli, you could look for farmhouses, with some area around them, with sheds a little distance from the farmhouse itself, so they don't poison their own living quarters and the neighbours as well.'

'Any idea what size?' asked Venky.

'At least two acres,' said the Tweedledum. 'Less might excite suspicion among the neighbours. They need several tons of supplies which they need to mix, and so on. Deliveries might seem suspicious.'

'Eliminate houses where there are women and children,' said Tweedledee. 'This group wouldn't bring their families along for the joy ride.'

'They'll have rented a farmhouse,' I said, 'they wouldn't own one. We should check all farmhouses that have been rented out any time in the last six months or so.'

Luck was against us. Delhi's tenancy rules are so weighted against the landlord that getting a farmhouse on rent, unless it's for a corporation or something of the kind, is next to impossible without a huge cash deposit. The police made a round of all the estate agents in the area without result, then started on a longer and infinitely slower search of all the agents in the city. Another team looked at farmhouses in the area, driving past to check for signs of activity.

By two in the afternoon they had found two possible farmhouses in the area: owners of both of them were out of town at the moment. By three in the afternoon the police had spoken to neighbours and more or less eliminated one of the two, leaving just one, that had all around it a four-foot wall surmounted by a barbed-wire fence . . . Too much protection, I thought.

By four o'clock eight police watchers were in place. One of the men who emerged from the farmhouse seemed to match an identikit portrait that the doctor had generated. Half an hour later, while the doctor watched with binoculars from behind a hedge in the company of a plainclothesman, an SOF commando walked up the driveway to deliver a package addressed to the house up the road.

The doctor identified the man who opened the door as one of the men who had accompanied his patient. We had at last found the lair of the Krait.

The command post went up first, in another farmhouse half a kilometre and two streets away, men moving discreetly in unmarked vehicles, the watchers at the Krait's lair reporting that no one had entered or exited the gates.

The police went again to the houses nearby, in ones and twos, dressed in plain clothes, to find out what the neighbours knew. At the next house to the west, a serious, young inspector found a boy of eight, the tree-climbing champion of the neighbourhood, who had in an adventurous moment climbed the wall around the Krait's lair and been caught by one of the men inside. The inspector brought him around to the command post where he sat staring pop-eyed and breathless at the armed men around him.

'I climbed the wall three weeks ago,' he told me.

That fence on top of the wall was at least seven feet high, and this kid, pale, bony, undersized, wouldn't have been more than four feet tall. 'How did you manage to get up that wall?' I asked him.

'I climbed a tree next to the wall,' he said. 'I get on to the wall and sometimes I fall off on the other side and sometimes I get cut on the barbed wire.' He pointed at scarred knees and calves as evidence. 'The men chased me off,' he continued. 'They had guns. I told Mummy but she doesn't believe me.'

'I believe you all right,' I told him. 'I'm going to look out for those guns. If I show you pictures of guns will you be able to show me what kind it was?'

He looked scornfully up at me. 'I don't need pictures,' he told me. 'They had AK-47s. I didn't tell Mummy because she doesn't know anything about guns and she didn't believe me anyway.'

'Did you see what's behind the farmhouse, the parts you can't see from the road?' I asked.

'Of course I did,' he replied, 'I climb the wall all the time . . .' He realized he'd just let away the fact that he'd been going in regularly and his voice faded out.

'Tell me, son, how many times have you been in there?'

'Umm . . .'

'Tell me the truth,' I told him, 'this once I guarantee your mum's not going to whack you for it.'

'Five times, or six,' he said. 'I heard some of them talk in a strange language and I wanted to find out what they were saying . . . That's how I started.'

He'd seen men in a shed behind the farmhouse, and white plastic canisters. He'd seen two of the men talking over a gas mask, trying it on, laughing. He liked to climb up a tree in the corner near the well and pretend at being the good guy hiding up a tree from the bad guys. Then one day he was caught when he dropped his catapult. The next time he tried to climb the wall a dog come slavering and tried to jump up the wall, and he fled. He didn't like dogs very much. Ah, and finally, he was sure he'd heard, sitting in his tree, noises from the attic. There were men in there.

I sent him back ten minutes later, to his relieved mother, promising to let him examine my sub-machine gun later, and turned back to the Krait.

Flushing him out of his lair was another matter altogether. The FKF's deadline expired at six that morning. Unless I was completely mistaken, he would have made preparations already for at least his first attack. We'd have to go in there and grab him and his men early enough to find out what he'd set in motion, and to stop it. And we'd have to take them completely by surprise, or face the possibility of a lungful of sarin.

The Municipal Corporation of Delhi, which was supposed to have a plan of the farmhouse, said they couldn't find the drawings, and could the police get back in a week or so.

I rode slowly by on the bike a couple of times, anonymous behind an enormous blue helmet and a black leather jacket, hoping I wouldn't be noticed, looking for answers to the usual question: what lurked behind the closed doors of that farmhouse?

It was set in roughly an acre and a half of land, a tarred driveway leading up to a sprawling one-storey house with a sloping, tiled roof to keep the rain off. A well in the eastern corner of the compound, the wall around its mouth broken and collapsing in parts. A pumpset in a small shed next to the well, raised electrical cable and piping along the ground identifying its function. Electrical power to the farmhouse was from a pole near the large wrought-iron gate. By the farmhouse itself were trees—mangoes and guavas and a tamarind that I recognized, at least three others I couldn't. A lawn, unkempt and patchy like an old man's stubble, spread to a corner of the compound. A shed behind the house, away from the well, windowless: for storage, perhaps, of fertilizer and pesticides. The shed the boy had talked about.

The media campaign continued. The broadcasts seemed desperate, as if none of the earlier ones had turned up anything. While they might have lulled the FKF, side effects began to erupt. Across the Yamuna, a man resembling one of the faces flashed on TV and coincidentally a Muslim, was beaten up and dragged to a nearby police station. The police beat him up further before verifying his identity, found he owned a small restaurant and hadn't been away from it for many years. By five in the afternoon, the

317

restaurateur's angry friends, most of them Muslims, had caught one of the policemen at the police station as he came off duty. In the scuffle that followed, the policeman cracked a head or two before he himself was stabbed and brought down.

Six o'clock came, and dark with it, early in the cold winter months. I wished for an extra couple of hours of daylight in which to watch the farmhouse but settled for night-vision glasses. The police watchers reported to the command post. They'd seen two men outside the house, in the lawn in front, chatting. One man had gone to the shed sometime in the afternoon, carrying a sack, and returned empty-handed to the farmhouse ten minutes later. They couldn't be sure because the trees around the farmhouse screened large parts of it from view but the watchers didn't mind because they figured it screened them from the farmhouse as well. They finished their reports, stretched and grinned, and went home.

The plans arrived at half-past-six from the architect, whom the CBI traced with remarkable speed after the municipal corporation refused. The farmhouse was just what it seemed to be, a one-storey villa with walls and foundation solid enough to last another couple of generations, built some twenty-five years ago. The entrance faced west, opening on to a large sitting room, and past the sitting room a living room, and beyond that a corridor off which opened four bedrooms, two with toilets attached. Two toilets off the living room, and one more off the corridor.

All these rooms enclosed an open space in the centre, a sort of small central courtyard, where there was storage space for produce, a small granary, and on the far side a long dining room with a kitchen and large pantry attached.

From a corner of the corridor a wooden staircase led up into an attic, a large, L-shaped single room lit in the day from skylights set in the roof, providing more storage space. The architect, who was a friend of the patriarch who'd had the house built, told me that the attic was meant to store furniture and timber in, and was therefore higher ceilinged in the centre than one would expect such a space to be. Also under the corridor was a cellar, its entrance a solid iron door, rather like a hinged manhole cover, in the far corner from the staircase to the attic. Two places where the Krait's men could hide from unwanted visitors. I was sure by now that the gas was in the shed behind the house: they wouldn't have been comfortable enough with it to live with it. The cellar, if it wasn't too damp, would be a terrific arsenal . . . The shed at the back was a blocky, squarish, windowless concrete structure a few years newer than the house. In the Krait's place I'd have used the shed for the gas, with only men who actually needed contact with gas or its precursors allowed inside.

But how many men did he have in there? There were the three who had been at the theatre, three more at the doctor's clinic, and three more at the computer service centre. Of these nine, we knew from the testimony of the theatre staff, the doctor and the computer service centre man that two had been common to at least two groups: that

319

meant at least seven men, possibly with one out of action, the man who had sneaked out of the clinic. The doctor had said he had been affected quite seriously, and was unlikely to survive long without expert medical attention.

Seven o'clock. Eleven hours to go.

The FKF's six o'clock deadline drew relentlessly closer. We'd have to go in before midnight to have any chance of catching some of them alive, interrogating them and preempting their strike. They'd be prepared, too: they wouldn't have missed the television and radio broadcasts, and they'd have heard the request for unusual case of pesticide poisoning and seen the identikit pictures of their members. They would have figured out that by now we knew the neighbourhood in which they were hiding. They wouldn't know about the computer service centre man, though, or about their neighbours, about the youngster who'd helped us zero in on their farmhouse so quickly.

As I watched through the night-vision glasses two men emerged from the front door of the house, carrying torches, leading two silent dogs. Dobermann Pinschers, I saw, straining at their leashes, bouncing on ankles like springs. The men had the same air of competence we'd seen in the other members of the FKF. They seemed unarmed. One of them wore a shawl about his shoulders, the other a jacket . . . There could be a machine pistol underneath the shawl, a sidearm behind the jacket, but that would show only to a trained observer watching them for some time. Pistols or revolvers at the very least.

We would cut the power. The residents had told us that the power could go off without warning at any time of the day or night. Night-vision glasses in the dark would give us the edge. But cutting off the power would also warn them . . . No, we'd go in with the lights on.

Two prongs, at least, to the assault. One to isolate the shed in which I thought the gas was stored. We'd have men in protective gear cut that off first, so the FKF wouldn't be able to use that gas against us. The second prong would target the farmhouse itself.

Have fire engines around to spray the farmhouse and its surroundings with water under high pressure in case they let off gas. Check if there was a sprinkler in the lawn.

The attic worried me. The cellar was airless, and most likely damp from the winter rains, a terrible place to hide out. They would have men in the attic. Was there any way we could go in on top? An air strike, as we'd done in Bangalore, was out of the question: landing on the sloping roof, slippery with moss, would lead to a disaster.

The worst possible surface to land on. Dammit, there had to be a way along the top.

The kid who'd climbed the wall provided the answer. The trees. If there were a couple of trees close enough to the house we'd have men go in along those, break straight through into the attic. They'd be able to get their bearings from the skylights, visible in their night-vision glasses.

Five men for the shed, in protective gear. We'd asked for more suits to be shipped out to us from the US Army, which had stockpiled huge stocks in case Saddam Hussein had decided to use chemical or biological weapons against the coalition that eventually drove him out of Kuwait, but they wouldn't arrive before lunchtime tomorrow, too late for this assault. Just hours too late.

The Navy had rigged up equipment for us to try out, but their gear was modified diving gear, scuba gear and boiler suits borrowed from factories nearby. It had turned out safe but far too heavy. The Navy thought in terms of weight under water, where a scuba suit weighs next to nothing, but out in the air it would weigh the men down. We'd go in wearing body armour. Face the FKF on level terms. The Kevlar would at least keep the gas off our skins. The assault hinged on surprise. If the lead team managed to isolate the shed we'd be much safer.

I wished I'd ordered more chemical and biological warfare kits. If only I'd insisted on fifty instead of agreeing on ten.

If only the queen had balls she'd be king.

Half-past-seven.

Four men or five, as many as we could manage, on the trees, to go into the attic. Fewer than that would make them vulnerable to the men inside. The two prongs had grown to three.

I retreated to the command post to talk to the watchers and consult Ismail and General Kelkar. Assembled there while I'd been away were the committee, most of them the same we'd faced earlier, in Madras and Bangalore. I tagged on to the General. 'We haven't the time for the committee,' I told him. 'We have to get moving right away.'

'What have you got so far?' he asked.

'We haven't the faintest idea how many men there are in that farmhouse,' I said. 'I still don't know where we'll go in from.'

'What about the police watching the house?' he demanded.

'I came here to talk to them but the committee's taken over this place.'

'We'll have that sorted out in a minute,' he said, and did, by the simple expedient of telling a group of large SOF soldiers to clear a room of its furniture. They moved the furniture out and the occupants, mostly hangers-on of the men on the committee, followed. 'You've got your room now,' said the General. 'Proceed.'

'We have to go in,' I said. 'We have to go in tonight, and we have to go in quietly.'

'Tonight, yes,' he said. 'But why quietly?'

'They might gas us on the way in if they know we're coming. They could be the suicide types, ready to kill all of us and themselves to avoid getting caught. They might even kill themselves and not us, if they know we're coming in. That's why.'

'All of them?' he asked. 'I don't think so.'

'Sir, we know they plan at least two gas attacks: that's why they've given us two deadlines. They don't let their lower orders into the details of the strikes they plan, so we have to go in and make sure we get the leaders alive. Since we don't know who the leaders are we have to get everyone alive.'

'So what do you plan to do?' he asked. 'Go in as early as possible, interrogate the terrorists, find out where they'll hit first, and then preempt the strike?'

'Exactly. They've got the first strike set up already, unless I'm mistaken, so we'll have to interrogate them, find out where they'll strike. They probably haven't got the machine for their second strike in position, so we might just be able to cut it off now.'

'Tell me what you have so far about what's inside there,' he demanded.

'They have at least seven men in there who have been seen outside the farmhouse. They most likely have at least as many more. They have dogs running loose in the compound at night, and at least two men on sentry duty. There's a small shed away from the main house, behind it, where they probably keep the gas. My feeling is that they keep their arsenal, whatever it contains, in the attic. There's a cellar under the house but in this weather it's probably damp and airless: they might hide in it when we go in but I doubt they have anyone there all the time.'

'Can't they keep the gas in the cellar?' he asked.

'It's probably too damp. The gas reacts with moisture, sir.'

'How do we go in?'

'We'll have a five-man team in protective gear take the shed first,' I replied, 'and another team go for the farmhouse in three groups. One for the front door, another for the back door, a third to blow the wall near the corridor, from where they get to the attic and the cellar . . . That attic is their stronghold. If they make it up there they'll be able

324

to hold us off for quite some time and we can't afford to have the operation take more than a few minutes at most.'

'What'll you do about it?' he asked. 'I'm not very happy about the attic. Or the cellar, for that matter.'

'I had a good look around the garden,' I said. There are trees growing close to the house. There's a mango tree at the side which has branches growing over the roof of the house, and at the far side is a tamarind even bigger.

We could have men go in along the branches of the trees and blow their way through the roof. A couple of grenades would do the trick.'

'How many men?'

'We can have maybe five men in all go along the top like that . . . We can't send in less: they'd be far too vulnerable.'

'So that makes a total of five teams,' he said, 'one for the shed, one each for the front and rear doors, one with beehives for the walls of the corridor, and one for the attic.'

'Right,' I said.

'Two points,' said Ismail, who had joined us. 'What will you do if they let off gas during the attack? How will you know? And what about the sentries, and the dogs?'

'We'll have an advance team take out the dogs and the sentries,' I said. 'We know how many there are. We'll have the advance team—maybe three men, or four—stay in position outside the farmhouse as a supporting force.'

'What about gas?'

'We'll have someone go in behind the advance team . . . Maybe ten men, with portable gas detectors, or birds in cages. If they find anything untoward you can set off sirens, do something to get us out. And have fire engines ready nearby to water the gas down if they let it out. They could save a few lives. In fact, if people around here have sprinklers in their lawns you could tell them to start sprinkling.'

'Anything else?' asked Ismail. 'I remember the boffins talking about sunlight. Can we have floodlights around?'

'No. Sunlight has lots of light in the ultraviolet range that we can't see,' I explained, 'and that's what breaks the gas up, not the light in the visible range. Floodlights emit very little in the ultraviolet range. If you could get back to someone and find out if it's possible to rig up a huge source of ultraviolet light . . . that'll come in handy wherever they plan to attack, actually, not just here.'

'What kind of armament do they have?' he asked.

'Lots of small arms,' I said. 'Some AKs, that little kid saw them and recognized them. We should assume they have some heavier arms as well.'

'So what will you take in with you?'

'The usual sub-machine guns for the farmhouse teams, and flash-bang grenades for a sound and light show. Concussion grenades for the men going in along the top. Silenced pistols and rifles for the advance team. Beehives for the shed team and for one of the farmhouse teams, to bring walls and doors down . . . I'm worried about the attic. If they manage to hole up in there they might be able to run a good defence . . . They could pick us off at will, and if they have grenades up there our treetop team will be in trouble. I think the attic is their arsenal. The men going in on top should have something heavier. They can carry grenade attachments to their rifles.'

'Grab the men downstairs right away,' said Kelkar. 'Have the men on top go in immediately after you blow in the doors. That way those men on top will concentrate downwards and backward at the shed and that's the time our men the trees should attack.'

'Right,' I agreed, 'we'll have several firefights going on at the same time: one in the attic, another at ground level, maybe one around the shed . . . We must try to get control of the corridor in that house, from where we can control access to the attic and the cellar.'

'What did the architect say the attic floor is?' asked the General.

'It's wood,' I replied, 'supported underneath on heavy beams. We can kill the fellows there all right but we have to take them alive. Another thing is that we shouldn't destroy anything: they might leave clues around, bits of paper, letters, signals, whatever. They've been there more than two months now, long enough for each of them to put his stamp on the place.'

Few Army men can think in terms of having to take an enemy alive, or a place undamaged. By and large your focus is on getting where you want without taking too many casualties . . . And to hell with the enemy and the site.

'When do you plan to go in?' asked Ismail.

'About midnight,' I said. 'That'll give us enough time to find out what they plan to do, and stop it.'

'I'd be happier if you went in about three,' he said, 'they'll be easier to catch off guard then. And it still leaves us with three clear hours to stop them.'

'That might not be enough if it's outside Delhi,' I said. 'What if they pick a smaller place, like Ahmedabad? Besides, we have to get one of them to talk. What if they refuse? From what I've seen of the FKF so far I don't think they'll talk easily. Those few hours might make all the difference.'

'Shouldn't we leave that to the police?' asked Ismail.

'I don't know,' I said. 'I think we should take the responsibility for the whole thing. Going in, breaking the terrorists, and stopping them. Unless someone takes overall charge we won't make it in time.'

'How are you going to break them?' asked Ismail, smiling grimly. 'Torture?'

'I don't know,' I said. 'I just hope we get the farmhouse intact, and its contents, with some clues to what they plan to do. Otherwise . . . I don't know. But I do know I'd be willing to use torture on them.' I knew then the lengths I'd go against the Krait. Yes, I would break them, just one of them, if we had no choice. The corpses in the theatre were strong enough incentive, and Hari in hospital. 'Yes,' I continued, 'I'll do all I can to get information out of them. This poison gas thing is something no human does to another.'

'Repercussions?' asked the General.

'If you have any qualms I'll take it on myself, sir,' I said, suddenly disgusted at the sight of my seniors covering their asses, 'and I'll take the repercussions. Right now what's uppermost in my mind is cutting off the gas attacks.'

'I'm with you,' said Ismail, sensing what was in my mind. 'Nominally I'm still your commander. I'll back you.'

I looked at him gratefully. The General broke in, 'Let's not quibble about that,' he said. 'I'll give you authority to do whatever you think fit. Within reasonable limits.'

'And what might those limits be?' I asked.

'Whatever think reasonable, Raja,' grinned the General, his eyes crinkling. 'Just do it. I'll take the flak. I'll cover with the committee. I'll keep them off your back. Just get it right, that's all.'

chapter sixteen

*The krait was blindingly quick but the mongoose was even faster.
It leapt back on its feet, and the snake had to withdraw. Again
it struck but its grooved fangs failed to penetrate the thick fur
of the mongoose. The mongoose sidestepped and moved in, and
soon had the krait by the neck, just behind the head.*

A quarter-past-eight. Under four hours to midnight.

I turned to the telephone to call Chauhan. 'I want to talk
to the men you put on watch around the farmhouse,' I told
him. We'd lent his men eight of our night-vision glasses so
their plainclothesmen could watch the house: my own
men were too obviously services men, with their crew-
cuts and watchful eyes. The terrorists, accustomed to such
men, would have little trouble picking them out of a crowd.

Three of the four CBI men who had been watching the
house since we identified it trooped in, one of them slightly
awed, the other two defiant at having to report to someone

outside the investigative agency's hierarchy. 'How many men have you seen in there?' I asked them.

Their answers were very flat, definite. 'Not less than eleven,' answered one of the defiant ones, speaking with calculated insolence, carefully leaving out the 'sir', which I couldn't care less about as long as he told me whatever he knew.

'Did you see that many?' I asked.

'Yes. We saw three chatting outside, of which two men went into the shed at the back. We saw three more through the windows before dark, by the curtains, and one more after dark. Two more came out with dogs, after dark. And two more took a walk about the garden just ten minutes ago.'

'Are you sure they were all different?' I asked.

The defiant one looked at me pityingly. 'Of course,' he said. 'That's the minimum. If they have regular guard duty there'll be at least four more men asleep inside. I'd assume at least fifteen men, closer eighteen, of whom at least a dozen will be alert at any point of time. There are those two men outside, in the grounds, and the two dogs. I'd say there are more men watching from inside, from the windows. We can make out silhouettes against curtains. After the lights go off they can sit in there and watch and we won't know they're watching.'

'Lights in the compound?' I asked.

'Nothing much,' replied the awed one, his voice soft. 'There are lights fixed to the building itself, at the corners, and there are two on the gateposts, and one outside the shed. That's all we've seen so far. Neighbours say they don't have anything on outside at night other than these.'

'Anything else?' I asked. 'Any arms?'

'One of the men we saw outside had a rifle,' said the same quiet man, 'probably an Armalite. Another had a shotgun. I think one of the rest had a pistol in a shoulder holster but I'm not sure. Such weapons aren't unusual in these parts. I didn't see any regular fighting weapon like AKs or anything.'

Half-past-eight. Three hours and a half.

News arrived, on the telephone, of the first of the fights between Hindus and Muslims, beginning across the Yamuna and spreading to the city. The police were out in force, angered by the death in hospital of their colleague who had been stabbed earlier in the day.

I summoned Venky, whose company was now on alert, and whose soldiers had already taken up positions in the vicinity. 'Who's out there now from your company?' I asked.

'D platoon are on guard now,' he replied. 'They'll be relieved at midnight.'

'Relieve them at ten, not midnight,' I said. 'Have A platoon out here, ready to go. We'll work out the teams when the men arrive. Make sure there are enough demolition men around.'

'When are we going in?' he asked.

'Midnight. Earlier if we can make it.'

'Tell me what you need and I'll tell you if we can.'

I did. At the end of it he shook his head. 'Even midnight is cutting it a bit fine. There's no way we can be ready before that.'

'So get moving,' I said.

The men, on fighting alert at base, would arrive in minutes. I went back to make a cautious circle about the farmhouse. What that kid had said about men in the attic—there must have been half a dozen of them, to make noise audible outside—seemed to make sense. Kids don't lie, and their senses haven't been tampered with like those of adults. So why did they have so many men in the house? Their second string of men for their attack, just in case the first string failed. The men who would carry out the second attack, which might still be days ahead.

I'd break the bastards.

That damned attic worried me. If they were suicidally minded they could get up there and slaughter us all. One large bomb would bring the house down about our ears. And if I'd made a mistake and they had gas up there, or in the cellar . . .

I wished I'd ordered another dozen suits.

When you look at anything over and over patterns begin to emerge. There was moss growing on parts of the tiled roof, showing up as darker patches in the glasses. There were patches of new tiles here and there, showing lighter. One of the beams stuck out a bit under the eaves. The roof sloped sharply down, at over forty-five degrees. At its extremities its edge was about eight feet off the ground. With a man below to help, would my mountain men be able to climb up on it? No, not one at a time. They'd be horribly exposed. God knows how many terrorists were in there.

333

Up the trees, then, as planned. I took a closer look at one of them through the night-vision glasses, a tamarind tree growing right next to the house. The lowest branches started three or four feet above the edge of the roof. The trunk wasn't too thick to grip, and the branches stuck out over the roof. No problem sending three men in on this tree.

A concussion grenade on the roof would blow enough tiles out for the men to get in. If one grenade wasn't enough they could use three or four. The roof would take most of the blast. The men inside would be relatively safe from serious injury, but the explosion would blow a hole in the roof large enough for a man to clamber through. The attic was one large room, the architect had said, and any partition would give the terrorists a defensive advantage. We'd have to have another group of men go in along another tree.

Better look for one. Identify them all now.

Have the men go for the edges of the attic, rather than the middle. The roof sloped towards the edges and if men were indeed sleeping inside the attic they would tend to be near the centre where the roof was higher. The trapdoor to the attic was in its centre, and the men would prefer to stay close to the exit. They'd leave the edges free.

I took another walk around the farm, outside the fence. Yes, there was another tree at the back from which it was possible to jump, a mango tree, a little smaller than the big tamarind out front . . . Two men here, a total of five attacking from two angles on the rooftop.

When would they go in? Last, I thought. Everyone would attack at roughly the same time, within a range of half a minute. The first wave would be at the shed, the next at the walls of the farmhouse, with beehive bombs to blow holes in the walls, and then together the assault on the front door and the attic. When the men in the attic were sure the assault was on the ground the five men on the trees would burst in on them through holes in the roof. It was looking better now.

Five-man teams everywhere. Six assault teams and one watcher team, thirty-eight men in all, thirty in the assault itself. Only the team at the shed would have protective gear. Twenty-five more suits. I'd have given my arm for that. My three prongs had grown to five.

I'd go in with the team at the front door. By rights I should have gone for the treetop, where my lack of inches and weight would have made all the difference.

There were men patrolling the garden now, two of them, whom I could see clearly with the glasses. They took their cues from the dogs for some time, then left the aggressive, silent creatures to nose about amidst the shrubs. There might be others behind those heavy curtains . . . I couldn't see any silhouettes behind the heavy tan curtains in the windows, but there were several unlit windows. We could get the dogs easily, they didn't bark.

Did the FKF have night-vision glasses? They'd equipped some men in their Bangalore operation with those glasses but only two. Chances were they didn't have any, because they would have planned to finish their job and flee, not to face a frontal attack.

But for the gas it would have been easy.

The lookouts kept moving around all the while, too often ducking behind trees for a sniper to get a clear shot. I'd assumed five men would be required to take those lookouts, and the dogs. Ideally the team going for the shed would have taken them but hand to hand combat clad in a PVC suit with a respirator at the back would be suicidal.

There was plenty of cover in those grounds. We'd infiltrate with ease. We'd have the lead team take the dogs first, then the lookouts . . . The dogs would go for the infiltrators, and if at all the dogs got within range their teeth would fail against Kevlar body armour. Then the lookouts. In the dark, in those grounds, it would be a breeze. Our eight lookouts would then follow, carrying their loads of birdcages, position themselves around the farmhouse. If there were gas in the air they'd warn the shed team, the one with protective suits, who would then concentrate on getting their colleagues out.

The cellar . . . No problem. One of the teams in would blow the corridor walls and block off that iron trapdoor. I doubted they'd have anyone posted there, or keep weapons in the damp.

Nine o'clock. Three hours more. The plan was firmly in place in my mind. I went back to the command post to clear it with Ismail and Kelkar. 'I know how we're going in,' I explained. 'Six assault teams of five men each, and one group of eight men with birds, to pull us out if they let off gas.'

'Where do the six teams go?' asked Kelkar.

'The first—we'll call them Team Black—will take out the dogs and sentries,' I explained, 'and the second goes to the shed, in protective gear. That's much as it was when we spoke earlier. The others go the moment the shed team— Team Blue—blow the door. Yellow for the front door, Red for the back door, White for the walls, Green for the attic . . .'

'That's thirty men in the assault teams,' said Kelkar. 'And how many others?'

'Eight, around the farmhouse, with birds. A total of thirty-eight.'

'What kind of backup do you want?' he asked.

'We can't afford to kill the whole lot of them,' I replied, 'otherwise we could have an RPG (rocket propelled grenade) team at the perimeter to blow the house sky high if we fail . . . We'll have a platoon outside to follow-up if things go wrong.'

'What else do you need besides the fire brigade?' he asked.

'Nothing. We'll take the farmhouse, clear it and interrogate the terrorists right there.'

'Once again, shouldn't we leave that to the police?' Kelkar asked.

'Let the police come in after us, after we clear the place. I don't want to waste time shifting them to police headquarters and so on. Chauhan can send in some men the moment we sound the all-clear.'

'What about the cellar?' asked Ismail.

'It's a trap, for them. The architect said the floor's solid, and there's this whacking great iron door that should stop bullets. If we get in quick enough we'll catch enough of them alive for questioning. If any get down into the cellar we'll just wait for them to give themselves up. Or we can punch a hole in the door and tear-gas them . . .'

Ismail considered a moment. 'I'd still be happier if you went in a little later. By then the dogs will be tired, too. If you go about three they'll be slower, and those little fractions of seconds could save you being gassed . . . And if they let off the gas, remember, they kill themselves. You'll have no one to interrogate, then, even if you make it.'

'I won't argue with you over that,' I told him. 'My only thought is to prevent them letting off the gas while we're on our way in . . . For that we go in early, and interrogate them in the farmhouse.'

'All right,' said Ismail, 'we'll interrogate them right there. I'll be there.'

I was about to agree when Kelkar interrupted me. 'Yes, we'll go in early,' he said, 'like Raja says. We'll have the CBI right behind us, and the police, and we'll talk to the terrorists right there.'

'What about the committee, sir?' I asked.

'They don't have a choice any longer,' he replied, 'I'll tell them roughly what we can do, and that if they don't like it it's up to them to come up with an alternative . . . This time there's nothing to negotiate.'

Ten o'clock. Kelkar left the room for the committee's conference room—the big drawing room—while I got on with the job of getting the men ready to go.

Bravo company's B platoon were already on guard around the farmhouse, shadowy black, moonlight-striped shapes invisible unless you knew they were there and looked for them. I walked over to a clearing next door where C and D platoons stood ready, their sixty-two men silent, at attention in parade-ground order and black combat uniforms. With Venky and the platoon commanders I picked the teams out of the group, a total of thirty-four men—the remaining four would be the platoon commanders, Venky and myself—while the rest stood by, their unspoken disgust at being left out almost palpable. Venky would lead Team Blue—hitting the shed—and I would lead Yellow, to the front door. The lightest men went to Team Green for the treetops, and the most silent into Team Black, the advance team.

Kelkar returned, his face a fraction less grim than it had been. 'The committee agreed to everything I said. One man dissented but the others overruled him. Go in, with the police behind you, and interrogate the terrorists in the farmhouse.'

We were ready to go, briefed and kitted up, by a half-past-eleven in the moonlit night, and again for the umpteenth time I wished for courage, the courage you need to cool jumping nerves, butterflies in the stomach, the kind of courage you need to keep your mind clear in a crisis. Out in the grounds there was silence, and little movement visible to the naked eye: the FKF had had to maintain their cover, and hadn't therefore been able to mount a full guard. Just when 2335 glowed on my watch

339

I whispered into my walkie-talkie, 'Yellow leader to Blacks, go!'

They went silently, slithering over the wall and the barbed-wire fence, disappearing into the shadows in the grounds. Moments later I heard the dogs run through the bushes, and hoped they hadn't alerted their handlers, and waited, ridiculously tense, for the beeps on my walkie-talkie that would signal the removal of the guards and the dogs.

The beeps came, three heart-stopping minutes later and less than a minute apart: four men signalled in, two for the dogs, two for the sentries. Standing by the wall I'd seen one of the sentries go down, thanks to the glow of a cigarette he was smoking, but had no inkling what happened to the others. 'Yellow leader to Black, report,' I said in response to the beeps.

'Black leader to Yellow leader, one hostile down, repeat one hostile down but alive, one hostile down and out. Repeat one hostile down and alive, one hostile down and out. Two dogs down and out, repeat two dogs down and out.'

'Confirm all friendlies okay, confirm all friendlies okay,' I said. If one of the terrorists was dead he must have put up a fight and perhaps injured one of my commandos.

'One friendly has very minor injuries, repeat very minor injuries. No medic now, repeat no medic now,' came the answer.

'Yellow to Black, where are you now?' I asked.

'Clear of the farmhouse, thirty metres west. We'll take the live hostile out over the west wall, repeat take live hostile out over the wall. Get the medics there.'

Even as he spoke, the next detail who would form a close cordon about the farmhouse, accompanied by muniyas in their cages, began to disappear over the wall one by one, crossing over and then reaching across for the small cages they had to carry. They, too, dispersed immediately to select points, night-vision glasses fixed on their eyes like frogs' eyes on stalks. With the sentries and the guard dogs down they moved much more quickly than the lead team had done, and less than two minutes later they signalled in, each man taking careful cover behind a tree trunk or a thick shrub, ready to move in towards the farmhouse to deliver emergency support to a failing comrade.

2344 on my watch. 'Yellow leader to Blues, check your suits, repeat check your suits,' I said. The Blue team, in their gloves and gear, wouldn't be able to check their buddies: someone else had to do it. In the clearing five men lined up behind the Blues, checking each Blue member's heavy protective gear, helping them shrug clumsy respirator packs into position on their backs, checking the armament slung on their chest harnesses.

2346. The spare men broke off, leaving the Blues checked and ready. 'Yellow leader to Blues, go!' I said into the walkie-talkie, and they flapped off in their loose gear, helmets shaping their heads into grotesque bulbs, a buddy helping each man over the fence. They would position themselves around the shed, then call us. The rest of us would then move inwards and when everyone was in position the Blues would go for it.

It took too long. I came close to biting my nails as the seconds dragged by. Team Blue had no night-vision glasses: we couldn't fix the glasses to their visors. Travelling inside their suits they felt none of the things they needed to get a bearing; no wind on their cheeks, no small insect sounds, none of the creaking of the trees. They had to make their way in the dark, led by a soldier from the advance team, with whom they rendezvoused just inside the fence. The minutes ticked by, five, then eight, then ten, and I was on the verge of breaking the rules and calling up on the walkie-talkie when the guide called in. 'Blue guide to Yellow leader, Blue guide to Yellow leader, team in position,' he said, then after a pause continued, 'there's a ditch around the shed. I suspected a tripwire, so we checked it all round. Watch out in the area of the shed.'

'Yellow to Blue guide, thanks,' I said, glad for news of the tripwire. 'Blue guide, pull out to perimeter, repeat pull out to perimeter.'

2358. Even as I finished speaking Team Green were on the move. I saw the leader's teeth gleam briefly in his blackened face as he moved silently past, the only bit of him easily visible in the dark. Green, lightly loaded men, all smaller than average, moved quickly, making their way to the trees they would climb in under two minutes, almost running their way to their targets.

Two minutes past midnight. With me in the lead the fourteen other men of Teams Yellow, White and Red moved out of the clearing and separated for points along the wall where they would cross over into the grounds. The ground was soft underfoot from the winter showers, easy to move along. After the heavy training runs in the forests of Garhwal, weighted down with full packs and rifles and radios, this run was child's play and the night-vision glasses showed the area clear as day, although slightly blurred, like a green and white TV set slightly out of focus.

The attacker came silently, from the side, bringing me down before I knew what it was. A dog. There was a third dog somewhere in the compound and it had come unseen for me. I'd been concentrating so hard on the farmhouse I hadn't heard it leap out of the shadows at me.

As I went down I drew my knife. The Dobermann got it's teeth on my left forearm, uncomfortably painful even through the Kevlar, its forelegs defending its throat. I slashed upwards from under my trapped forearm, got through to the dog's neck, and still the creature wouldn't let go. I could feel it losing blood, its hind legs weakening, but it just wouldn't let go. I slashed it again and again, and after it collapsed had to pull it off my arm. Eight minutes past midnight. We were late. The Blues had been waiting over twenty minutes now. On the walkie-talkie came signals from the other teams: all were in position at least three minutes ahead of Yellow.

It seemed an age before I reached the hedge bordering the lawn in front of the house, past the corpse of one of the dogs that Team Black had taken out.

Nine minutes past midnight. 'Yellow leader to Blues, go for it!' I said into the walkie-talkie, and waited for the blast of the shed's door coming apart. It came seconds after my go-ahead, followed by the sounds of running and shouting from the farmhouse, and lights coming on in the hallway. Simultaneously I heard ambulance and fire-engine sirens from the road outside: the medic team had come up to the gate and would break through it up the driveway after us.

From behind the hedge I straightened up and ran down the driveway to the front door less than ten yards away, moving aside as Venky, directly behind, brought his sub-machine gun up to bear on where he thought the bolts would be. He squeezed off three two-second bursts that nearly emptied his magazine, moving himself out of line as I kicked the door in and rolled a flash-bang grenade in along the floor.

The grenade went off in the sitting room with its usual spectacular flash and deafening bang, and then I was in the sitting room, a terrorist facing me, his AK-47 well out of position and one arm about his eyes. I dropped flat on the floor, cut loose at his legs from my machine gun, and then heard an explosion in the corridor. Not the muffled crump of a beehive or the higher-pitched bang of a grenade. Not one of ours, I knew as soon as I heard it, and went for the source of the sound, past the terrorist on the floor, kicking his AK-47 out of his reach as I ran for the corridor, past the drawing room.

From above came more explosions. The men on the treetops were moving in. There were confused voices from the attic.

The drawing room itself was empty. I vaulted a mattress on the floor—the man I'd shot in the sitting room must have been sleeping on it—and was in the corridor just to see a man lower his legs into the trapdoor to the cellar and another emerge from the attic. From behind someone opened fire at the man coming down the stairs as I took three quick steps and slammed the door of the cellar shut, on to the legs of the man going down. From above came the sounds of more gunfire, and then more commandos came in through the hole in the wall. I kicked my man in the face, dragged him out of the trapdoor, and tossed in another flash-bang grenade, then slammed the door shut.

Inside the cellar the explosion of the grenade must have been terrific. I felt the floor tremble beneath, and when I opened it and shone a torch inside there were two men cowering in the corners, holding their ears, eyes shut tight, stunned.

It was all over.

In seconds, the men behind me had gathered their prisoners in the sitting room. From Team Blue outside came the first report, 'Blue Team leader to Yellow leader, shed taken, one hostile down, no friendly casualties. Sir, this place is full of drums and canisters and there's a great big boiler in here, and a compressor. It's pretty dirty in here.'

'Yellow leader to Blue, two of you stand guard at the shed, the others bring the hostile to the front door.'

'Roger, Yellow leader. Out.'

Next came the treetop team. 'Green leader to Yellow, four hostiles here on their feet, one hostile down and out, repeat, four hostiles on their feet, one hostile down and out, no friendly casualties.'

'Bring the hostiles down,' I said, 'White Team will watch the bottom of staircase. Lead them down right away.'

Two commandos down in the explosion in the drawing room, one dead, another injured. A bomb had gone off just as they came in through the hole in the wall made by the beehives.

My team and Team Red fanned out into the rest of the rooms on the ground floor, taking the kitchen and the dining room, and found two more men hiding. From outside came the sound of more sirens and bells as the medics moved up the driveway. 'Yellow Team leader to base, farmhouse cleared, attic cleared, shed cleared. We need medics. Two friendlies down.'

In the two big bedrooms off the corridor we collected the captured terrorists, the ones who didn't need immediate attention. The one I'd shot on the way in had been hit in the legs and passed out from loss of blood. The one who'd been shot in the attic had died by the time the medics arrived to take him away. The one in the shed had lost a finger to a bullet, and was holding his bandaged hand and swearing continuously in Arabic. In all, we had fifteen men to interrogate.

Chauhan joined us.

'We'll pick one of them,' I told Ismail, 'one of their leaders. Their toughest-looking man. We'll take him down to the cellar and there I'll break him.'

In the master bedroom Ismail and I stopped before the dirtiest looking of the men, crouched in the middle of the group, obviously one of the leaders of the group, shaven headed, light eyed, hook nosed, with three days worth of stubble on his great jutting prow of a chin. I touched him on his shoulder, and he looked up at me through those pale eyes with a hint of madness shining out of them. 'What is your name?' I asked in Urdu.

The terrorist hesitated, glared defiantly at me. 'Not telling me your name is not going to help you,' I told him.

'Fazluddin,' he replied, 'Fazluddin Ahmed.'

'Fazluddin,' I said, 'do you know who I am?'

'Menon. We will get you one day.'

Without warning Ismail clubbed him from the back, in the kidney, and he collapsed on his knees, his forehead on the floor, in an agonized kowtow.

'Don't threaten,' he said, his usual relaxed air gone as if it had never been. 'We intend to talk to you, Menon and I. You would be wise to listen to us.'

Ahmed brought his head slowly up and spat, missing my feet by inches. Ismail kicked him at the base of the spine, and Ahmed's back arched upwards, and his head lolled sideways. 'Take him down to the cellar,' Ismail said to one of the soldiers, 'tie him to a chair and wait for us. Make sure there's light.'

In my watch it was 0035. Barely five and a half hours to go. We'd have to break this man Fazluddin in the next two hours or less. As the soldier led him down I stopped Ismail. 'Why don't we separate the men whom we'll interrogate now?' I told him. 'The police can take the rest of them out to wherever they like. Less trouble for us.'

'No,' he said, 'we should keep the lot here. We break some of them, and if they break but don't know, we find out from them who knows and then break that man.'

I arranged another platoon to guard the prisoners— more SOF presence mostly to overwhelm them—and proceeded to the cellar where Venky, Chauhan and Ismail were already getting to work on Fazluddin, now tied securely up in a chair.

0040 now. Barely five and a quarter hours to the deadline.

Part of the training in the SOF curriculum is the resistance of torture, and following that, for officers, basic interrogation techniques. While the word torture is never mentioned, it gets quite obvious that interrogation is quite painful for the interrogatee. In the next hour or so, in that cold and stuffy cellar, aided by electricity, lengths of plastic flex and tube, buckets of water to revive the man when he flagged, some knowledge of nerve endings, and a sharp knife, we broke Fazluddin. We broke him completely, Ismail and Venky and I, and in the process felt ourselves broken and diminished in some ghastly fashion.

Ismail, his normal air of aristocratic diffidence gone, hounded the man. 'What did you plan to do if we missed the deadline?' he asked right at the beginning.

No answer. Ismail brought out his combat knife and cut a gash in Fazluddin's cheek. 'I will carve you up into tiny pieces and feed you to the pigs,' he said. 'Tell me.' And so on, with threats and violence in between for an hour, until eventually Fazluddin's head sagged forward. With the next application of electricity, he screamed, a thin stream of blood trickling out of the side of his mouth. 'Enough!' he gasped. 'Enough. In God's name, enough!'

'Tell us what we want to know and you will have a doctor,' Ismail said. 'You will have treatment, and rest. Water if you want, as much of it as you want. But you have to speak first.'

He raised reddened eyes, half closed in relief, breathing in short gasps. 'I'll tell you,' he said, his words slurring from fatigue and the treatment. 'I'll tell you everything I know. A little water first. Please.'

Ismail gestured to Venky to fetch some water, but I held him back. 'After he speaks,' I said. 'We haven't the time to waste. Give him water and he might hold out some more.'

'Hotel,' said Fazluddin. 'Hotel. In Bombay. President. Trade conference. Half a kilo of gas in a small cylinder. In the air-conditioning. Water.'

'That's not enough,' I said, 'there's more. There has to be more. You're not telling us everything. No water until you tell us everything. Every little bit you know.'

'I don't know any more,' Fazluddin slurred. 'You promised me water if I told you. I've told you what I know and now you say you won't give me water, you bastard!'

'Tell me what else there is, and you get the water,' I told him. 'You gave us two deadlines, one in a few hours and another tomorrow. Tell me everything you planned to do after those deadlines and I'll think of water for you. Then we'll wait for our friends the police to verify what you say.'

349

Chauhan and Venky, standing by, had already left for the police communications truck parked in the garden.

They returned minutes later. They'd told Kelkar and the police about the gas in the air-conditioning system. The CBI were already moving in on the hotel, Chauhan said, and we'd know in twenty minutes whether Fazluddin was telling the truth. 'In the meanwhile we'll keep going with our friend here for the next action,' said Venky, leering at the captive. He'd practiced his leer until he got it just right. In his eyes was that mixture of lust and wildness, and in his smile a hidden menace. Venky's one theatrical achievement.

The terrorist's will gave way. 'I don't know,' he said, his voice faint now, 'I don't know anything. But . . . but I heard the others talk. They didn't tell me anything. They said they have someone on your side. They said he's helping . . .'

The blasts took us entirely by surprise. Fazluddin never completed his sentence, because the roof came down on us, and after a split second the walls. I leapt away towards the corner of the room and saw out of the corner of my eye another section of the wall descend on Venky, and then I knew no more.

chapter seventeen

In its death throes the krait thrashed about but the mongoose was safe. The mongoose leapt at the krait and caught its flailing body in its teeth, and shook it a few times.

They let me out of hospital the next day, my left arm in a sling to keep it from dislocating again, and chest strapped tightly in sticking plaster, every step sending shooting pains through my body, to face the debriefing and disgrace.

I learnt the details of what followed the blasts in the office. A canister of gas had burst and spread its contents over the farmhouse. The fire engines had taken over immediately, the birds nearby collapsed. Of the seventeen terrorists in the poison-gas operation, three were killed in the assault. Two more had died in the blasts, and another two had been cut down when the follow-up team waiting in the grounds had climbed the walls and streamed into the premises of the farm immediately after the explosion,

Fazluddin was dead, his body bruised and neck broken by the first blast. Tied to the chair he'd not had a chance.

Eight commandos died. One in the firefight in the farmhouse, three in a rocket blast when one of the terrorists managed to get away and shoot the rocket launcher at a wall as the follow-up team were climbing in, and four more in the initial blasts. Among the dead was Venky. Eleven more were in hospital with injuries.

And another fourteen were being treated for gas poisoning.

The toll mounted rapidly. The FKF struck at two other places that we didn't know about, restaurants in hotels in Delhi. In one of them they had put in a cylinder of sarin disguised as a cooking-gas cylinder. The top had blown off early in the morning, and thankfully the chef, suspecting a gas leak, had cleared the area before thinking of sarin and calling the police. Two more people who had been affected in the theatre died. Hari, in spite of the poor prognosis, hung on to life.

Ismail, who had dragged me out of the cellar and directed the follow-up team as they came in, said that the first blast had taken everyone by surprise. Sappers coming in behind the follow-up teams found a radio-control device, a receiver to set the bombs off when it got a signal. They found traces of explosive in the walls . . . Someone had actually buried detonators and lumps of plastic in the walls of the farmhouse, hollowing out cavities by removing a brick here and there, filling it in with Semtex.

Someone among the terrorists could have set it off. Or it could have been someone from outside: the radio was powerful enough. The strange thing was that we didn't find the transmitter that had sent the signal. We didn't know who had set it off. Was it one among us?

Half the farmhouse itself had been destroyed in the explosions. The first floor had collapsed entirely, burying the cellar under tons of rubble, and most of the roof had disappeared. Two terrorists had been buried inside, and were rescued hours later by SOF men with a company of engineers. More bombs had gone off in the compound but had done little damage.

In the grounds, which the engineers had begun to dig up the moment they found someone had planted bombs within the walls, had been found one Stinger launcher with six missiles, several grenade launchers, one rocket launcher and no less than eighteen rockets and eight kilos more of plastic explosive, besides the rifles and ammunition. Also found were bits of sophisticated communication equipment, much like what we had found in Madras and Bangalore, all destroyed by the second blast. They had all been stored in the south-west corner, and we were lucky nothing had gone off in sympathetic detonation.

In Bombay, the police, acting with amazing speed and thoroughness, had found suspicious containers in the air-conditioning vents of three major hotels. The hotels had been evacuated in record time, sleepy guests woken and told to move without waiting to pack or anything.

No one knew where else the FKF had planted sources of gas. The public in the big cities began to panic. Trains and buses going out of the cities were crammed with fleeing citizens, the highways choked with cars.

More worrying was the horrifying aftermath outside. A large and visible police presence in the area had prevented mass violence in the vicinity of the theatre but elsewhere Hindus had attacked the Muslims in sweeping force. Mosques had been torn down, men hacked to death, women raped, children dismembered and killed. The Delhi government had for once acted with commendable speed, bringing out all its reserves and getting more from the Centre. Elsewhere in the country, in Hyderabad, in Lucknow, in Bhopal, the violence continued.

The debriefing degenerated into an interrogation and then a witch hunt. The investigators, now out in their plenty, questioned the basis of the interrogation in the farmhouse. Sitting across the table from them in the conference room, looking out of the window at the lawn, I tried as best I could to answer their repeated and attacking questions and often failed. Why had I insisted on continuing in the farmhouse when I'd known there might be large caches of explosive in the storerooms? Why had I not stopped the interrogation when at first the terrorist gave way? Why had I not kept a team on full alert outside, just in case something happened? Why had I not let the police conduct the interrogation? Why had I not told the political decision-makers about the risks involved?

They listened with apparent neutrality to my answers, when I spoke of leaks and the Krait, of the impossibility of detecting explosives actually implanted in brick walls, of someone outside having set off the bombs in the cellar. Why, they asked when I'd finished, had I not brought up the possibility of leaks before going in? Had I, in my desperation to get the mission sanctioned, understated the risks involved?

In between sessions I sat in my room, staring out of the window at the sunny lawn below, fighting off the depression which came pounding back during those long, empty minutes, and in the evenings I returned to the flat because I didn't want to face my noncommittal colleagues at the mess. Families of colleagues crossed the road to avoid seeing me. Strangely enough, the men came when they could. While the officers hung back, the men came in from time to time to ask when I'd be back on duty. Soon, I told them, there were a few details to be tied up.

The bodies of the dead soldiers were sent back to the units from which they'd come. I attended one funeral that evening in Delhi, in civvies, unnoticed.

Venky's father arrived for his funeral, and avoided me.

The ghosts of the dead hung heavy on my conscience.

Kelkar, who was as much under a cloud as I was, stayed away. I never got to see him once during the debriefing. He must have been going through it himself, at a much higher level.

I avoided reading the newspapers, which had pilloried me, accusing me of ignorance and arrogance, quoting

Munshi, the man from the home ministry who had objected to the interrogation in the farmhouse, forgetting conveniently that he had opposed the two successful missions as well. Sadanand, the Madras newspaperman with whom I'd had that confrontation, had been particularly vicious: I'd violated all the norms of interrogation.

I wondered how they'd known so quickly—about my session in the cellar with the terrorists.

I thought through the day of calling Sandhya, holding back because at the back of my mind lurked a growing dread of what she would say, hoping against hope that she would call.

Before they wound up, at the end of the day, the men from Intelligence called me aside. This was a sensitive matter, they said, but on the evidence they had they could only conclude that I had gone in with insufficient intelligence, with more enthusiasm than judgement. Did I have anything else to say?

Of course, I said, the FKF had set a second deadline and therefore planned another action.

None of my business, they said, and when I persisted said that in view of the numbers of terrorists killed or taken in the farmhouse it was unlikely they would mount another poison-gas operation in the near future. And did I have anything else to say?

Yes, I said, if the radio transmitter that set off the bomb was outside the premises that we'd attacked, that pointed at collusion, at someone positioned outside the farmhouse. Had they investigated that?

None of my business, they repeated.

There'd been no real choice, I told them, we couldn't have given in to the FKF. Given that, we'd had to attack to find out what they planned to do, and I'd done the best I could. They shook their heads and left it at that, and departed vaguely unsatisfied. I was on medical leave, they said, for a couple of weeks, after which I would face a review board and probably be shifted out to another battalion, probably the Mahar unit from which I'd come to the SOF.

At the end of the debriefing that evening, a Thursday, I went home to a chill flat. I had to report to the hospital every day, to change dressings and so on, but the rest of the time I was free. Ajit called, saying he was sure it would work out in time, reminding me of his offer of work with his bank.

And Sandhya didn't call.

After a sketchy and tasteless dinner that Thursday night, at about nine, unable to bear the isolation any longer, I called her. 'Hi there,' she said, her voice floating down the wire, bringing almost unbearable relief. 'What happened to you? I read you'd been injured, and the people at your office refused anything on your whereabouts.'

'The usual debriefing security,' I said. 'I'm okay. Mobile now but some bits hurt now and again.'

'Cut out that hero crap,' she said, her voice returning quickly to normal, 'and tell me clearly what's wrong.'

'A dislocated left shoulder, which they fixed on the spot. A couple of cracked but healing ribs. Torn ligaments in my right knee and ankle. Bruises all over. Six stitches in the left arm. All from being too close to a bomb when it went off.'

She was silent for a long time. 'Have you eaten?' she asked finally.

'After a fashion,' I replied.

'If you're mobile you could come over now,' she said slowly. 'If you want to talk. Eat. Stretch out. Whatever.'

'Tomorrow,' I replied, 'as early as you can bear it.'

'Come for breakfast then. Spend the day with us. Kiran misses you badly.'

'Do you?' I asked.

'Ummm . . . Yes,' she said. 'Come by nine.'

'I'll be there,' I promised, and hung up.

I got to her house still faintly apprehensive, uncomfortable in the glare of the heightening summer morning, still shaky from the blast. When she opened the door her smile disappeared, to be replaced by a look of horror. 'You . . . you didn't tell me all of it,' she said. 'You should be in a hospital.'

'Glad to be out on my feet,' I said.

'You're going to lie down now,' she said, moving over to the couch and arranging the pillows so I could lie comfortably. 'You're a madman.'

I was dizzy from the warm winter sun. 'That sounds good,' I said. 'Give me fifteen minutes to get over the sun. Where's the youngster?'

'Out with the other kids. He's on holiday.'

'Aren't you going out of town for his holidays?' I asked, hoping she wasn't.

'In a week. We're going to Calcutta in the middle of next week. What about you?'

'I'm on medical leave for a couple of weeks. I'll probably be transferred out of here after that.'

'Where will you go?' she asked, laying out the table for breakfast.

'Back to my old unit. To Sagar, probably, or Simla. But I might quit the Army altogether if they transfer me.'

'I thought it was pretty bad,' she said. 'The papers said you were taken completely by surprise at the explosions in the farmhouse. They said you were torturing one of the terrorists in the farmhouse . . . Did you? Torture someone in there, I mean?'

'I don't know if I can talk about it,' I said.

'I need to know,' she said. 'Yes or no.'

'Yes,' I said, looking into her stunned eyes. 'Believe me, there was no choice.'

She looked blindly down, shaking her head in distress. 'How could you?' she said at last, her voice husky. 'I thought it was all lies . . . I hoped it was all lies.'

'It wasn't,' I replied. 'Listen, if I'd got my hands on Psycho and I wanted something out of him I'd have done the same to him, too.'

She looked up at last. 'I don't know,' she said, 'when you put it like that I can sort of understand but I just don't know. I need to think about it.'

'Do,' I said. 'I'm not proud I did it, and I didn't like doing it, but it had to be done and I happened to be there.'

'And how's the Army treating you?' she asked.

'I've been sort of excommunicated. It's not pleasant. I might just leave.'

'You should get out of here for a while, then. It's more than a bit of the sun troubling you if you're thinking of leaving the Army. You'd be a fish out of water anywhere else.'

'I guess so,' I said, 'but there are the ghosts of those hundreds of people who say I should be out.' The table was laid. I got off the couch and joined her.

'What happened?'

'Something went wrong just when I was beginning to think we had made it. It all blew up in our faces.'

'What thing?'

'The farmhouse. We got in there, we took them by surprise, we got control of the farmhouse, and we were actually inside and withdrawing when the bombs went off. It was a massacre. The follow-up team broke their way in and dragged us out. I was lucky to get away as lightly as this.'

'Listen, you can't blame yourself for all this. You win some, lose some. You have to grow up, Raja, you have to learn to take a loss.'

'Sure,' I said slowly, a new thought emerging slowly from the memories of the operation. 'I think we were set up. Those bombs went off just when they'd do us maximum damage. Whoever blew the place up got it right down to the nearest second.'

'So what?' she asked. 'It could have been coincidence. The papers all said one of your men set off a tripwire.'

'We found bits of a radio there, in the farmhouse, with one of the bombs that failed to go off. The kind of thing you explode bombs with from a distance. The device we got would have had a radius of something over a kilometre. The thing we found was a receiver, but we never found the transmitter end of it, and the range of the thing would depend on the transmitter.'

'Couldn't one of the terrorists have set it off?' she asked. 'He could have set it off and maybe it was destroyed by the blasts so you missed it.'

'In the first place we searched those guys. We'd have found the radio control. Besides, the forensic team went over the grounds with a fine-tooth comb. They'd have found the bits and pieces if it had been any where in there.'

'So who do you think set it off?'

'Someone outside, who knew when we were going in . . .'

'Who could it have been?' she asked. 'If it were someone close to you . . . That's scary.'

'Yes,' I said, 'and if that is the case, transferring me out of this unit is the last thing they should do. I should stick around until we find the man. The Krait.'

'I don't like that name,' she said, and shuddered. 'Didn't you tell the investigators all this?'

'I did, but they didn't listen . . . There's a cover-up on.'

'So what are you going to do about it?'

'Nothing . . .' I said slowly, 'I don't know. I have a feeling this is going to be the beginning of a different kind of terrorism. This is the third time running he's tried to attack and lost his entire team, and he should know when to cut his losses. He'll come up again, but in a different context, with a different kind of crime . . .'

'What kind of crime?' she asked.

'I don't know,' I said. 'He's into drug smuggling and gunrunning already. There's this new explosive called red mercury . . . They say it might not exist but the point is that if it does he can get it quite easily, and if he has enough of it he can make a briefcase-size bomb powerful enough to kill everyone within half a kilometre of it. My guess is that he'll organize car bombings, assassinations . . .'

'You have to find him before he does that,' she said, 'nip him in the bud.'

'There's no such thing,' I told her. 'Unless I'm mistaken, Pakistan's ISI are behind this. They have the money and the rest of it. If we get the Krait now all we're doing really is setting them back a year or two. They'll have someone else in place before long, and then this whole thing will start all over again.'

'You mean . . . it will never end?' she said, shuddering again.

'It won't,' I said, 'we just have to keep plodding on, hoping the other fellow never gets too much of an advantage. If you can hold your own, that's enough.'

'There'll always be people like you, then.'

'Yes. Unless people change dramatically, and that's not possible. Crowd too many people in too little space and sure as little apples are green you'll have fights.'

'You're a pessimist. You see only the bad side of people.'

'There's as much good in them as there's bad,' I said, 'both show up when the pressure's on. It's just that we tend to remember the bad. Which do you tend to notice, a news item on a messy divorce or one on a golden wedding anniversary?'

'I never thought of it like that,' she said slowly.

'I've had to. Part of the job. People driven by the need to fight.'

She shivered again. 'Leave it be,' she said, 'I don't like talking of violence. Talk of something else.'

'Talk cricket, then,' I said, 'it's in the air.'

'If there's one game I detest more than polo it's cricket,' she said.

'I'll go home soon, then,' I said, not wanting to miss the day's match, a league match between Sri Lanka and India, the winner to meet Pakistan in the next day's semi-final. Besides, I hadn't expected Sandhya to react as she had to my session with the terrorist in the cellar . . . I wasn't sure she wanted me around any longer. 'How's Ismail treating you?' she asked, changing the topic. 'And General Kelkar?'

'Ismail's been in touch. He's the only one of the lot who's been decent to me but he's on his way out. He got his brigade a couple of weeks earlier, and he was supposed to hand over charge to me the day after we left. He was there purely as an observer . . . The General is in as much trouble as I am. He keeps his distance.'

'What did the investigators say?'

'It looked like I'll be the scapegoat.'

'But . . . but there must have been others involved in the decision. It couldn't have been all yours.'

'Yes. Like I said, the General's in trouble, too. But they say I sold him the operation. Played down the risks, distorted things . . . And there was a man from the home ministry who said it wasn't going to work out. We had some trouble with him before, when I said I wasn't giving him our operational plans. He said nasty things before the Madras operation, and the Bangalore one, but nobody cares about that. Now he's got what he wanted and he'll get his own back. With that newspaperman, Sadanand. Have you been reading his articles?'

'Yes,' she replied without looking up, avoiding my eyes. 'His paper's condemned you without a trial. Going by what they say you're incompetent, arrogant, insensitive . . . But there's nothing really libellous in what he says . . . I wanted to ask you if you intend to take him to court for his articles. I know a few good lawyers, they'd waive their fees for you.'

'That's not worthwhile,' I said, 'it'll take too long, and at the end of it there'll still be a question mark over what I've done . . . The damage is already done.'

'Let me know if you change your mind.'

'I will,' I replied, a faint lump in my throat. 'Thanks . . . Thanks for standing by . . . it makes all the difference.'

'Least I could do,' she said as she shut the door.

Back at home I tried to get in touch with Chauhan and got the brush-off. He spoke briefly to me, said he was in a meeting, promised to call back, and never did.

Ismail called to ask how I was getting along. I told him I'd get out of the Army if they forced a transfer on me. Was there anything he could do to help, he asked, offering to speak to Kelkar or other seniors to see if the transfer could be avoided or even postponed. Forget it, I said, I'd get by.

Jayanti wrote to say she'd get married as soon as the divorce came through. She'd read about the Mehrauli incident in the newspapers and she was sure it was nothing serious but if it was I'd probably asked for it anyway. Uncle wrote to say that I had already done enough damage to the family name with my divorce and did I have to go and cause the biggest massacre after Jallianwala besides, and get caught torturing someone afterwards. I was never to visit him again; as far as he was concerned, I was dead, and he was going through the mourning rituals to announce it to everyone he knew. I tossed the letters in the dustbin and thought instead of the Krait.

In Madras we'd had to tell the committee some of our plans. The men from the ICF would have been able to figure out our plans in any case, from the trial runs. The Krait's contact could have been anyone on the committee, anyone from ICF, anyone from the Tamil Nadu police.

In Bangalore we'd managed much tighter security. The committee had been told in the beginning that we'd planned a ground attack, and the FKF had been prepared for just that. We hadn't told the committee about the plan to attack from the air: only the Army and the Air Force had known about that. Not even the airline staff who had flown the diversion had known about our plan, or the Air Force men who had dropped us over the farmhouse. No, none of them was involved. That more or less cleared everyone in the services.

In Mehrauli we'd gone in as soon as I'd told Kelkar the plan. The committee had got to know, but just minutes before the attack, and they hadn't stirred from their places after that. Not enough time, I'd say, for anyone to have slipped out and made a quick telephone call, then get back . . . I'd asked around and been told that the men in the room had all stayed where they were except for one, who took a quick trip to the toilet . . . But if it weren't someone from the Army it must have been someone on the committee. Whoever had passed information over had to have been in the know about the Madras plan, in the dark about the Bangalore plan, and very precisely informed about the Mehrauli plan. It could have been anyone, even Chauhan . . . He'd got along well with the FKF. Was that why? Was he deliberately turning the investigation around so nothing would show up? He was ideally placed for it.

But why would he do such a thing? There was money, of course. People had done it before and would certainly do it again. But if the traitor were Chauhan, who was the Krait? Chauhan hadn't been free long enough to set up the networks, and didn't have the military experience to set up these operations. So who was the brain behind all this?

Something about it irked me. I was missing something, somewhere. On the edge of my consciousness lurked a fact that I couldn't dredge up. I couldn't put my finger on it. God, how could I have missed it for so long?

I turned instead to cricket on television. Turned on the TV set to see Sri Lanka in the field, playing India, the winners to meet Pakistan the next day at Eden Gardens in Calcutta. The Sri Lankans were batting first, and Sanath Jayasuriya, their hero against Pakistan in Sharjah, was beating the daylights out of India's pace attack of Salil Ankola and Javagal Srinath. But it couldn't last, I knew, and just four overs into the match Jayasuriya fell, yorked by Srinath for twenty-eight runs, collected off sixteen deliveries.

On impulse, I called Ismail. Told him there was something about the Krait floating in the back of my mind that I couldn't recall.

Good, he said, my hunches were quite accurate. I was to continue to turn it over while he checked it out. He'd also follow up with Chauhan.

Don't, I said, what if Chauhan himself was passing information across?

That's worrying, he said, but he'd get in touch with Chauhan anyway to see if the investigation had made any progress. But I wasn't to get in touch with Chauhan until he, Ismail, did some more digging. He could find out about Chauhan's opportunities to get in touch with the FKF during the operations.

Use your other contacts, I said, forget Chauhan.

No, he said, he'd try Chauhan. Even if Chauhan was on the Krait's payroll, he would lull the man's suspicions.

All right, I said reluctantly, when would he get back to me.

Tomorrow, he said, and in the meanwhile how was my girlfriend.

What girlfriend, I asked.

The one on the train, he said, the one I sneaked off to meet so often. The one in Gulmohar Park.

Wishful thinking, I said, nothing like the reality.

Keep working on her, he advised me, persistence paid.

Not if I was out of a job, I said, I didn't want to do anything on that front now.

Ismail laughed. This was a once-in-a-lifetime thing, he said, I'd be a fool to give it up so easily. I was to use my free time—the free time forced on me—as best I could, and the best thing to do was to chase her. It would keep the depression at bay, besides.

I'd think about it, I said, and hung up.

There was little I could hide from Ismail. We'd been colleagues for many wearing years, during my stints with 9 Para and the SOF, and friends for many of those. He had learnt in those years to sniff out my thoughts with almost unfailing accuracy. I could, of course, do the same, but with him there was an inner core of reserve that I'd never been able to penetrate. But he was committed and sharp, and never made a promise he didn't keep. I turned away from the telephone a great deal more cheerful than I'd been when I picked it up.

Sandhya rang up minutes later. She was sorry she had been cold to me in the morning, she said, and had been thinking things over and when would I visit again. With a lighter heart I told her I needed to be alone for a day or so but would call her the next day. We lingered on the telephone despite knowing we would meet in a couple of days. What news, she asked, was I getting anywhere with my digging.

Not yet, I told her, but Ismail promised to help.

That's a strange man sometimes, she said, he'd called a couple of times to find out how Kiran was, and how I'd been when I visited her, but she still didn't like him.

Ismail playing matchmaker was something for the books, I thought, and told her about his advice on my free time. I was going to follow it, I warned her, if the Army wouldn't let me continue with the SOF.

She laughed, said it wouldn't come to that. Said goodbye, and hung up.

At Eden Gardens the Sri Lankans had settled in. The pitch had been well prepared and the ball was coming on to the bat. The Indians would have done well on a pitch like that. The afternoon sun in Calcutta was hot, and it would have been terribly humid out on the field.

On the TV screen a plump, miniature Arjuna Ranatunga slashed at the last ball of Venkatesh Prasad's sixth over, well outside his off stump. There was a solid click, and behind the wicket Nayan Mongia leapt to his right to hold an easy catch about the level of his chin. Three down, twenty-three overs bowled, a hundred and two runs on the board, last man out for forty-one.

In the stands a less-than-capacity crowd of sixty thousand watched desultorily as the new man came out to face Rajesh Chauhan bowling from the other end. This was Doordarshan, unfortunately, and they didn't update the scores quickly, or have the quality of commentary that Gavaskar and Tony Greig managed on Prime Sports.

Between overs the camera took a long look around the audience in the stadium, all sixty-thousand people in there. In the floodlights at the corners the stadium looked like a bowl, empty at the centre. A giant bowl.

A bowl would hold things in. Including gases, if they were heavy enough.

If someone let off gas in the stadium it would sink downwards, staying inside the stadium. Upto a hundred thousand people in that giant bowl. The humidity in the air would degrade the gas but that would take time. Wouldn't it? The floodlights, wouldn't they cause the gas to degrade?

Tweedledum would know. I reached for the telephone, dialled the number of the labs where I knew he would be at this time.

No, he said in answer to my questions, hydrolysis on a large scale would take hours regardless of the humidity, and floodlights let off only negligible ultraviolet light. What was I thinking of?

Clearing up some doubts, I said, that's all.

Welcome, he said, he had read the newspapers and he was on my side, regardless of what the fools in the plush offices said. A bit of torture wouldn't affect the terrorists in the least but it had saved the lives of people at the hotels in Bombay, and I was to call him for any technical help, at home if I thought necessary.

I thanked him, hung up and wondered whether the Krait would strike at Eden Gardens. The bowl would hold the gas, and after sundown there would be no sunlight to break it down. I remembered reading somewhere that inflicting substantial fatalities over an area of a square mile would take roughly a ton of sarin. How much would a stadiumful take? It was less than 160 metres each way, I thought, less than a tenth of a mile. Square area of a hundredth of a mile, which meant eight to ten kilos of sarin.

Much less, actually, since most of the crowd would be along the periphery of the stadium, not in the centre, and they would move instinctively out of the stadium, not towards the centre . . . he could easily manage ten briefcases out of which the gas was to be released, near the exits . . . He could make do with less than eight kilos. How much less? I didn't know. Diluted to one part in three that meant twenty-five to thirty kilos of solvent . . .

The stadium held a clear hundred thousand people. Even if we could evacuate people at the rate of a hundred a second—far more than was really possible, I thought— it would take a thousand seconds—well over sixteen minutes—to clear the stadium. Of course, it was ideal. But it would be worthwhile only when the stadium was full . . . When?

The India–Pakistan match! The stadium would be full to capacity if India played Pakistan here, as it was likely to. I reached for the phone to call Ismail.

'This is Raja,' I said when he picked up the phone, 'I know where they'll hit.'

'Where?'

'Cricket match. India–Pakistan. Eden Gardens.'

'Explain.'

'The stadium's like a bowl. It'll keep the gas from spreading out. A hundred thousand people watching. Two or three kilos of gas is all they need. Probably set off by remote control for timing: they can watch the match on TV and decide when to let it off.'

'That's good thinking, Raja. Brilliant. But why?'

'It's obvious. A hundred thousand people in there, no sunlight, few exits, confusion . . . It fits.'

'Indeed it does,' he agreed. 'Who else have you told?'

'No one. I don't want to risk a leak. I don't want our friend with the FKF spreading the word. I thought I'd check with you first.'

'You did just right. I'll get through to some of my friends. Where are you calling from?'

'Home.'

'Stay right there. Don't tell anyone. We have time. I can call the defence minister and have that match cancelled if need be. Just stay where you are, and see me in the evening. I'll try to get General Kelkar to come along.'

'Where?'

He told me. Somewhere in Panchsheel, not far from Sandhya's house, at seven.

I left early to meet Ismail that evening, at a quarter-after-six, in the gathering twilight, desperate by then for a

372

dose of Sandhya's lightness. Outside the apartment block I climbed on to my bike and started on my way to Gulmohar Park, cruising through the traffic that was now beginning to lighten, letting the impatient ones roll past, taking my time at the lights.

Somewhere near the IIT gate, a souped-up white Gypsy buzzed me, flashing by inches from the bike's crash guard. I swerved away, slowed down and let him pass. In the heavy traffic on a two-wheeler, though, I made faster progress than the Gypsy, and a kilometre or so ahead found it behind me once again. In the wash of light from the passing headlamps and the orange sodium street lamps I could make out the faces of the two young men in it, one with spectacles, the other bearded, both lean and smiling. Rich kids making like Ayrton Senna, I thought. I wouldn't go anywhere near them, and if they tried to pass I'd give them all the room I could.

Three minutes later, turning left on to the road to Panchsheel, past the Asian Games Village, with the traffic much lighter, I looked in the rear-view mirror and found a pair of headlamps closing up fast. The white Gypsy again. I wasn't going too slowly myself, and as I lost the headlamps going around the curve I eased off on the throttle and moved over to the side, giving the small vehicle about three times the room it needed to pass. It came up quickly, levelled off with me, and then, without warning, turned sharply left into my path. I swerved and braked hard, still going at about thirty kilometres an hour, climbed with a thump on to the pavement and then the front wheel went into an open manhole. The impact lifted the rear into the air and I cartwheeled aslant over the handlebar, landing soggily some three metres away on my right side, thankfully on soft ground. I rolled over, got to my feet, my chest on fire, turned to see where the Gypsy was, and felt an almighty blow to the kidneys. Went down on my knees, head bowed, awash in a sea of pain, retching, my middle now afire, feeling the salt taste of regret in my mouth. The second blow, on the back of my head, knocked me down on my side, and a kick in the ribs from behind threw me around on my back as the merciful blackness descended.

chapter eighteen

The mongoose withdrew in victory, tossing the corpse of the snake in its mouth. But in its burrow the krait had laid a clutch of eight leathery white eggs that would hatch in midsummer. Of the three six-inch young that would hatch, two would die. But the third would survive to adulthood to threaten the mongoose that had killed its parent.

I surfaced slowly, painfully, well into the day, on a cold, hard floor, back arched uncomfortably, something hard holding my head down. Twice I opened my eyes and closed them again, hoping the nightmare would go away, dimly remembering falling off the bike and being hit afterwards. The third time I knew it wasn't a nightmare. Heard the sound of water pouring softly on to plastic, on to the floor, looked up and waited for a pale, white patch of light on a white door in front of me to swim into focus. Felt some difficulty breathing, found my mouth stuffed with something soft and fibrous, my lips covered with something sticky. Tried to get it out of my mouth, found I couldn't move my hands, stuck behind my back. Tried to straighten up, and felt something cold and hard above. Tried to use my legs to drag myself out of there, found my ankles, too, were tied. The pain in my ribs intensified as I crouched there, trying to get my bearings.

My eyes took their time adjusting to the light. I was in a small bathroom somewhere, sitting on the floor, legs straight out in front, wrists tied behind my back near the floor to a pipe. To the left was a toilet seat, and to my right, a little above eye level, a tap from which poured a thin stream of water into a bucket underneath. White tiles three feet high, almost yellow in the bright sunlight pouring in, and above them white walls. On the wall opposite was a towel rack, empty now, with the door to the left, facing the toilet seat. I was under the sink, tied securely to the waste pipe.

The bucket under the tap was full, and water had overflowed on to the floor. The drain must have been blocked, for the pool on the floor was growing. That was what had woken me up. My trousers were sopping wet, and freezing.

I ached abominably. My kidneys still hurt, in a grinding ache. So did my head. In that unbearable cold I shivered like an old man with malaria. My chest was on fire, the pain raging through with each breath. Those ribs are gone again, I thought inconsequentially, Luthra's not going to be happy.

I couldn't for the life of me figure out why I was here. Then it began to fall into place. The FKF. Sarin. The cricket match. Ismail.

Ismail! I had told him about the Krait's plans and he'd had me trapped. I'd told no one else about my meeting with him, or that I thought the Krait would strike at Eden Gardens . . . Oh my God! I couldn't believe it. Ismail had put the FKF on to me. Ismail, my teacher. Ismail, my boss. Ismail, my best friend . . . Ismail, the Krait!

What was he up to? Why?

The answers could wait. First I had to get out of here. I had to stop that match. I had to stop Ismail, the Krait.

How? God, it was cold! I slid my tied hands up the waste pipe. Couldn't move them more than twelve inches or so; after that the strain on my back and ribs became too much. I tucked my legs underneath me, raised my bottom a little, and slid and rumbled over on the slippery, wet floor, the rope on my wrists—it felt like thin, nylon washing line—tightened, cutting unbearably into my wrists. I scrambled back into my original position, and the pressure eased.

I tugged at the ropes. They were tied too firmly to permit me to wriggle my hands out. The more I struggled the tighter the knots would get, the harder to get out of. I tried my ankles, with identical results. Waves of pain pounded their way up from my ribs. I moaned, waited for the pain to subside, gritted my teeth through the cotton stuffed into my mouth.

377

If there were a rough patch on the pipe I could rub the rope against it, fray the thing through. For that I'd have to feel the pipe all the way up. No way to do it.

The slippery soles of my shoes would slip on the wet floor. I couldn't get any leverage out of my feet. The shoes were formal lace-ups, no way to get them off with my hands tied.

I tugged again at the pipe, hoping for some play, hoping to find a weak spot, hoping to break the pipe or at least bend it. Nothing. It didn't budge. It was formidably substantial. Probably plastic; water would have corroded and weakened it if it were metal.

With growing despair I tugged again, with the same result. The bottom would have been stuffed right down into the tiles on the floor. Maybe it was looser at the underside of the sink. But there was no way I could get my hands that high.

Unless I jackknifed my legs underneath and got my knees under me with my feet against the wall.

Damn that man Ismail. He'd beaten me on every count.

A wave of blinding rage sliced through my belly. The rage woke me up and after a while reason returned. The seconds passed and slowly the rage turned into shame. I'd been taken, mercilessly. The rage was at my credulity, not at his betrayal.

Why had he left me tied up here like this? To pick my brains. He knew I wouldn't give in normally. He knew about Sandhya. He was a kidnapper, used to taking hostages and holding them to ransom. After massacring the crowd at Eden Gardens he might take Sandhya hostage, the price of her release being the information I had.

I couldn't let that happen.

The anger came surging back. I tugged again at the pipe. Felt it shift a fraction of an inch. Or was it my imagination? I tugged again, as hard as I could, and slid backwards on the wet floor. The pipe gave a fraction, very little but unmistakable.

I slid my hands down all the way to the bottom and tugged again, ignoring the rope biting into my wrists. Slid my hands back up and tried again. This time the pipe gave away. It was loose at the top.

I was out of breath already. I waited a while, waited for the pain to subside then managed to bend my legs at the knee and tuck my feet under my bottom. I forced my torso forward and pushed backwards until my feet were firmly against the wall, my face only inches from the floor. The pain in my chest came back, daunting in its intensity.

I rested like that for a moment, the ropes now cutting hard into my wrists. My hands were numb. If the ropes cut off the circulation in my hands . . . No time to think of that. Now I could get some leverage, with my feet against the wall.

Faint memories of semi-consciousness returned. I remembered vaguely the phrase, 'Kill him after the match. Let off a fire extinguisher here.'

I tucked the memories away and with all the strength I could muster, heaved desperately against the pipe, the rope cutting savagely into my wrists. Nothing happened. The

379

pipe moved a millimetre, and stopped there. I stopped, gasping now, knees shaky on the slippery floor. Heaved again. Almost gave up.

Thought of Sandhya. If Ismail's attack worked I'd never have the nerve to approach her again. I couldn't permit that. Heaved again. Rested again. Thought of the eager crowd of cricket fanatics. Felt the pain flare up again in my ribs.

I was past caring. I had to get out of that bathroom. Over the minutes I fell into a rhythm. Heave once, then again. Stop for a while, count five breaths, try again.

Count the heaves as well. Anything to keep the mind occupied against the pain that now racked my chest. My wrists were numb. Breathe. Heave. Heave again. Breathe.

On the tenth heave the pipe seemed to give a little more. With renewed energy I gave it one last, mighty heave.

With a crash the sink came right off the wall and I tumbled into the wall opposite. The sink fell on my back, fell off, shattered on the floor, the plastic pipe bending easily under my weight. There was still an unbroken chunk of the sink on the top of the pipe. Lying on my side, I gripped the pipe behind me in my hands, felt it's weight, hammered it against the floor, and felt it break with a crunch. Then I tugged again, and my wrists came free of the pipe.

I lay there for minutes, slack with relief, stretched out on the floor, letting the resurgent aches and pains subside. Wished I had one of Luthra's dusty pills to take the pain away and let me sleep for ever and ever.

He'd led us by our noses all along, and we'd followed, like buffaloes. I'd followed. I'd almost loved the man.

I got on to my knees, and bending with creaking ribs, slid my hands past my bottom to the backs of my knees, thankful I was trim enough to get them there. Eased my wrists past my ankles, got my hands in front of me.

My wrists were bleeding where the rope had chafed and bitten, and my hands were swollen and numb. I wanted to bite that rope off my wrists but the gag in my mouth prevented that.

I got groggily to my feet, leaning against the wall for support. Hopped to the door, tried the handle. Couldn't feel it with frozen hands. The handle turned with a squeak but the door refused to open. It was bolted from the outside.

The toilet seat was close to the door. I lowered the cover, sat on it. I was getting to be like an old man now, having to rest every few minutes. I sat on the toilet seat with my back against the cistern, and tried to stretch my legs out. There wasn't enough room. The door was in the way. I braced my back against the cistern, put my feet against the door, pushed outwards as hard as I could. The door, bolted at the top, gave maybe a quarter of an inch. If I could try lower down on the door it might give some more. I lowered my legs as far as I could and tried again. It gave a little more but stayed firmly shut.

In anger I raised my legs high and thumped the door as hard as I could. The bolt at the top gave way and the door slammed open. I slid off the toilet seat and landed on the floor on my back, my head cracking on the edge of the seat. I waited for my vision to clear, and painfully, achingly, stood up, holding on to the wall. Found the light switch, just inside the door, turned it on. The bathroom was in a shambles and so in the mirror was I, but at least I was free. Or half free.

I had to cut those ropes off. I found my way to the kitchen, bumping into a chair due to unsteady knees, the thought of approaching freedom making me hurry. The kitchen was about twenty-five feet away, down a hall and then left, its door wide open, the light switch again just inside the door to the left. I located the sink and found beside it a long, sharp saw-toothed knife with a greasy blade. Ideal for the job. Picked it up with trembling fingers, then put it down. Had to free my month first. I tried to peel the plaster slowly off my mouth with my fingers. Couldn't feel a thing with them. I picked up the knife and tried to lever its point in between my skin and the plaster. It hurt, but by and by a strip came off. Enough to grip, even with numb fingers. I ripped it off with one pull, leaving my lips raw. My hands tied, I struggled to pull out the cloth they'd stuffed in my month. My jaws ached with relief. Breathed freely for a while.

Picked up the knife again, stuck the handle in my mouth, gripped it in my teeth, and sawed away at the nylon rope. Blue rope, I noticed. The teeth on the knife bit quickly through the fibre and then my hands were free. I waited a bit, caught the fierce burning agony of returning circulation as the blood pounded back into my hands, each pulse a sledgehammer on my fingers. My body sagged with the pain, and my eyes watered. I waited long minutes for my hands to get back to normal, then cut my ankles free.

In the cool afternoon I limped unsteadily out of the kitchen, wondering what to do next. Instinct said, head for the office, for Kelkar. Reason said, wait for the guys who locked me up, they should be back soon. Use the telephone to get in touch with the minister. I looked in my pockets for my wallet, for money, and found none. They'd emptied out my pockets. No time now to look for it.

I was too tired. My knees buckled. I knelt, waiting, praying for strength to return to overworked muscles.

I nearly waited too long. As I reached the telephone, I heard voices and footsteps on the staircase outside. The men who had brought me here, returning from their excursion.

I ducked back into the kitchen, hoping they wouldn't have noticed the movement from outside. Looked for a handy weapon, found none. Saw a gas cylinder on the floor, hefted it. It was empty, light enough to throw at them as they came in the front door. Went out to the living room carrying it in my hands, ducked behind a corner.

There were two of them. I heard them talk outside as one of them unlocked the door. He came straight in leaving the door open for his comrade and walked past me to the kitchen. As he passed the corner, I lifted the cylinder high and hit him on the head with it. Dropped the cylinder, sure that the blow would have knocked him cold, and charged out from behind the corner, straight into his comrade, who was already reaching for his gun. I caught him off balance, punched him in the solar plexus, pushed him out backwards with sheer momentum, through the door and over the railing. He fell backwards, landing on concrete two floors below.

Ismail would wait until after the Eden Gardens job before returning here, if at all he did. I had to stop that match.

I looked around, trying to get my bearings. Outside, through the window, I could see across the street a bank. Central Bank of India, Vasant Vihar, said the sign above. I knew where we were. A DDA-built housing colony. I'd been here before. The DDA were notorious for the shoddiness of the houses they built. Thank God for the DDA, I thought inconsequentially, if an honest builder had built that block of flats I'd never have been able to take that bathroom apart as I had to get out of it.

I could hear voices in the corridor outside. The neighbours had found the man. The bell rang, and outside stood a large, red-faced man with a drinker's nose, others behind him. I pointed the gun at him. 'Find a telephone,' I told him, 'call the police. Quickly.'

He looked at the gun and took a step back, then asked, 'Who are you?'

'Colonel Menon. The men here were terrorists. Please call the police as fast as you can. I'm not going anywhere.'

I don't know why but he believed me. He turned to go into his own flat and I stopped him. 'Call D.S. Chauhan, deputy director of the CBI, as well. He'll confirm my identity.'

He stopped, led me into his house, waved expansively at the telephone in a corner. I dialled General Kelkar's office first. He was in a meeting, I was told, would I leave a message?

It was urgent, I said, about the gas attack, topmost priority, and I was chief of the SOF.

Hold on, said the voice.

I turned on the TV set in the corner, changed channels to Prime Sports. The Pakistanis had batted first, and scored 263 for nine wickets in fifty overs. A huge score, requiring an average of nearly 5.3 runs an over. The lunch break was over and the players walked back into the lazy warmth of the stadium, the Pakistanis taking up fielding positions against the Indian openers.

Kelkar came on the line. 'What's the emergency?' he asked.

'I know where the FKF are going to strike,' I told him. 'At Calcutta. The cricket match. Towards the end of the match, at the tensest moments.'

'How do you know?' he asked.

'I told the Krait,' I told him, 'and he grabbed me. Locked me up in a flat. I just broke out.'

'I heard something about you falling off a motorcycle yesterday evening,' he said. 'Chauhan got in touch, asking where you were. There was a little bit of a panic when you disappeared. But then we thought, if the FKF had taken you they'd get to us, and otherwise you're a grown boy, old enough to take care of yourself.' He paused. 'But who's the Krait?' he asked, his voice suddenly soft.

'Ismail,' I said. 'He had us fooled all along.'

I heard him sigh, almost grieving. 'I just met someone,' he said, 'who told me he saw Ismail in Agra when that lad was kidnapped. It must be true . . . Where are you?'

'In a flat, used by the FKF as a safe house. I've just got rid of two of them who came back here. They're outside, one perhaps dead. I've left them to the neighbours. I don't know the address here but I'll give you the telephone number.' I read it off the dial to him.

'Stay right there,' he said, 'I'll be there. And the CBI. I'll get the Calcutta police started on this straight away.'

'Do,' I said, 'but tell them to go easy.'

'What do you mean?' he asked.

'You can't just barge in there and stop the match,' I told him. 'If you just stop the match Ismail's men in the stadium will set off the gas in any case. You have to set up systems for the crowd to get out before you stop the match. You have to assume the gas will be let off in any case and have fire engines ready. The local police will have to do all that stuff.'

'I hadn't thought of that,' he said.

'Yes,' I said. 'And bring Luthra, sir.'

'Anything serious?' he asked.

'No. But I need help all right.'

They all arrived fifteen minutes later, two minutes behind the police from the station the neighbours had called. The terrorist on the floor had been taken away by the first lot of policemen and Chauhan loudly demanded him back. I'd found my identity card before the local police arrived, but they were beginning to get rough when the others arrived and threw them out. Even as we talked, Luthra had my shirt off to strap up my chest once again. He bandaged my bleeding hands, told me to lie down.

At Eden Gardens, the Indians had made an unsteady start. Ten runs off four overs, and two missed chances already from Sachin Tendulkar.

Barely three hours left of the match. 'The first thing is to stop that match,' said Kelkar.

'How do you think they're going to release the gas?' asked Chauhan.

'I don't know.' The camera at that moment focussed on the stands. Way back, behind the uppermost row of people, stood a rack of fire extinguishers, an exit almost directly below the rack. Fire extinguishers! The phrases I'd heard vaguely returned, still vague, but their meaning sharp and clear. 'Get the administrators of the grounds to check if they got new fire extinguishers in the recent past. In the last week or so.'

On the TV screen Wasim Akram ended his fifth over. The first ball of the over had been a no-ball that almost broke Sachin Tendulkar's guard. Tendulkar had blocked the next five balls on the front foot. The last ball of the over, straying off Tendulkar's leg, had gone to the fine-leg boundary. Nine overs gone, thirty for no loss.

The police finished their preliminary search of the flat while Luthra checked me out and strapped my ribs once again. 'Do try and stay out of trouble for the next couple of weeks, sir,' he said as he stuck the last bit of plaster on my wounds.

'We'll move now to SOF headquarters,' said Kelkar. 'It'll be easier to coordinate from there.' One SOF man and three policemen stayed behind at the flat to grab any FKF man who returned.

'Lucky that stadium is in the Calcutta maidan,' said General Kelkar. 'It's in the open. We'll have ladders set up on the outside, fire engines standing by, and have the police take down all barricades. Evacuate the VIPs first, right away. Then, when everything's in place, we'll have the police move in and direct the spectators out.'

The telephone rang. The Calcutta police, told of the impending gas attack, had traced the superintendent of the stadium. Three men had turned up the previous day with a letter from the chairman of the cricket board, ordering the installation of a new set of fire extinguishers to handle the fire risk caused by enthusiastic fans setting off firecrackers in the stands. The superintendent had been far too busy, and had tried to fob the man off, saying he couldn't pay. The man from the fire extinguisher suppliers hadn't turned a hair. All right, he'd said, he'd leave the extinguishers and come back for the money after the tournament. The superintendent had tried to call the chairman but failed, and had accepted the fire extinguishers, which the man and his two assistants placed at various points in the stands.

Someone brought a TV set into the office. Tweedledum arrived, to stand silently by in case the Calcutta police needed help.

Eleven more overs gone by. Tendulkar, opening with Jadeja, had got his eyes properly in since I last saw the match. Jadeja had left in the tenth over for twenty-two, and Sidhu had taken his place. Sidhu played his workmanlike style, no flourishes, the runs coming steadily, but at the other end Tendulkar had for three overs thrown caution to the winds and stepped out to face the best of the Pakistani fast bowlers. In those three overs he had put twenty-one runs on the board. An absolute riot.

Twenty overs gone now, with the score at seventy-two. Remarkably fast by Indian standards, mostly thanks to Tendulkar's quick-fire forty runs. One hundred and ninety two runs to win, in thirty overs, at an average of just under six and a half runs an over. It wasn't impossible but victory was slowly slipping out of reach.

Aaqib Javed, the youngest of Pakistan's pacemen, bowled the twenty-first over to Navjot Singh Sidhu, the steadiest of India's batsmen.

'How is the gas set off?' asked Kelkar.

'Three ways,' I said. 'First, he can have hooked them to timers so they go off at a fixed time. This is unlikely. The best time for the gas to go off is close to the end of the game and that could happen very soon if the Indian batting collapses.

'Second, he has a man in the stadium watching the match, waiting to set the cylinders off at the right moment. This, too, is risky for the one who is going to set off the gas. Getting out of that stadium will be harder than getting out of a theatre.

389

'Last, he'll have someone watching on TV, somewhere close by, not more than a couple of kilometres away. I think that's most likely. He himself will be watching the match, and he can ring up his man in Calcutta to tell him when to let the gas loose. I overheard something to that effect but I was half knocked out so I can't be sure.'

Ismail must have planned everything, knowing the opposition as well as anyone could.

Ismail, who'd taught me everything about soldiering that I knew. He'd betrayed me. The enormity of his betrayal took a while to sink in. I was tired beyond words, beyond anything I'd ever felt before. I didn't have the strength any more to fight.

On the screen, Sidhu had begun to attack Javed. The first ball he played back to the bowler. The second, straying a little outside the off stump, he square cut to the boundary for his first four of the innings. The crowd, bored with Sidhu's defensive play so far, cheered. And the next ball, a bouncer, Sidhu pulled almost contemptuously over the square-leg boundary, into the stands, for a huge six.

The crowd went wild. Firecrackers burst in the audience, and a couple of youngsters clambered across the fence and ran on to the field, running in to shake hands with the cricketers. White-uniformed Calcutta policemen chased after them. The minutes ticked past, and eventually the police got the fans off the pitch. The delay helped. Every minute helped now.

Chauhan got to the commissioner of Calcutta's police. They were to block off traffic in the area of the Maidan.

They were to evacuate the Maidan now, have the fire engines in place, talk to the match referee, Clive Lloyd . . . It would take time. They had barely three hours left.

'I don't understand how it's been happening,' said Kelkar.

'Ismail was the man behind it all,' I told them. 'The Krait, the planner. And the traitor. He was ideally placed for it.'

'I hope you know what you're saying, Raja,' warned Kelkar. 'If we find you've got it wrong you're in deep trouble.'

'I know what happened, sir,' I told him. 'I know why the farmhouse operation failed. I know who set off those bombs. Ismail did it. That's why he asked to come along as an observer, knowing I wouldn't ever refuse him something like that, especially when he was still officially in command. He came in behind us, and set off the bombs at just the right time to cause maximum damage.'

'If he were on their side he wouldn't have wanted to kill his own people,' said Kelkar.

'He'd given up,' I said, the weariness now beating down. All I wanted to do now was lie down and go to sleep. After so many years I actually felt like going to sleep. I raised my head and continued slowly, 'He knew we were going in. He'd planned on us giving in, because he thought that handling the poison gas threat was beyond us. He didn't bank on us finding the doctor and that computer service centre so quickly. He couldn't do anything about it because we were with him all the time. Then he decided to participate in the interrogation and when his man was on the verge of breaking he set off the bombs.'

'What about Madras?' he asked.

'In Madras he had warned the FKF to watch out for the diversion, the helicopter. He must have told them also that we would attack in the wee hours. When the rain came down I decided on the spur of the moment to go in straight away, and we took them completely by surprise. No wonder I found Psycho napping. They were preparing for the fight they thought would come at three: the thunderstorm screwed things up from their side. And once we'd decided he didn't have a chance to get the news across . . .

'Remember, sir, he wasn't very happy about going for the heads of the lookouts? He wanted the snipers to go for chest shots. That would have sabotaged us. They were wearing body armour and if we'd gone for chest shots they'd have been warned and then the hostages would've been massacred on the way in.

'And remember, he killed Psycho. I tried to get him alive but Ismail thought Psycho would lead us to him, so he climbed in and killed the man.'

'All this is purely circumstantial, Raja,' said Kelkar. 'Is there any more?'

'Yes,' I said. 'In Bangalore he must have warned them of the ground attack. He was stuck in hospital when he got hurt during that dummy run. He wouldn't have been able to warn them that we'd come in from above. They'd expected us along the ground, so they'd had a reception committee waiting in the car park, which was why Yadav died. They had four men waiting in there, instead of the two we expected.'

'Why did Ismail put you here?' asked Kelkar.

'I don't know for sure,' I told him. 'I spoke to him yesterday, told him I thought the Krait would attack at Eden Gardens. He asked me why, and I told him. I told him I thought it was our friend Chauhan here . . .' Chauhan looked at me in surprise, and I continued, ignoring him. 'He must have decided then that I should be taken out of circulation, so he told me not to tell anyone else, to meet him at Panchsheel yesterday evening. He must have decided to go on the offensive, to take me in and pick my brains.'

Ten more overs down. I dragged my mind to the cricket. Sidhu was gone, bowled by Javed in his fifth over for thirty-three. Azharuddin, the captain, had come in and left almost immediately without scoring. In his place now was Vinod Kambli. Left-handed and athletic, Kambli was inconsistent, but in this series he'd found his form. Twenty overs to go, a hundred and thirty-one runs to get.

The telephone rang again. The news came in bits and pieces. The fire engines were in place. The VIPs were out of the stadium. They had included the Central minister for environment. Ladders were beginning to go up on the outside of the stadium, so people could climb out. The barricades at the exits were down. Nothing unusual visible on TV.

It was then that I thought of it. Go for the centre. Get those deadly extinguishers out of the stadium. 'Remove the source,' I told General Kelkar, 'remove those extinguishers while the cameras are focussed elsewhere. It'll be easier than getting a hundred thousand people out of there.'

He caught on immediately, reaching for the phone even before I stopped.

I turned back to the match. Six overs to go. Half an hour, at an average of five minutes an over. Akram had had his team mates bowl their earlier overs fast and saved time to think towards the end. Wily man, and a brilliant bowler.

The gas could go off any time now. Please, I thought, hold it a little while more.

Forty-three runs to make, at slightly over seven runs an over. Next to impossible against the fiery pace of Wasim Akram and Waqar Younis. Younis sprinted through his run-up, arm flashing overhead as he brought the ball down two-thirds of the way down the pitch in a screaming bouncer. Vinod Kambli, superbly fit, spun on his toes and hooked the ball over square leg for an effortless four.

Kambli played the next three balls out of the book. The fifth ball of the over was a yorker, and Kambli, moving before Younis let go the ball, took three long steps down the pitch to convert the yorker to a full toss. The ball flew into the stands past midwicket for a six. The next ball yielded a single. Kambli would keep strike, facing Wasim Akram. Thirty-two runs to go.

Wasim Akram got Kambli's leg stump on the next ball. Kambli, the last of the specialist batsmen, had kept the score moving. Now there were only Mongia, the non-striker, and Javagal Srinath who could be expected to score any runs at all.

Srinath signalled to the umpire that he wanted middle stump covered. Hours earlier, he had been hit all over the stadium by none other than Wasim Akram and now he sought revenge. Akram greeted Srinath with a yorker but Srinath, like Kambli in the previous over, took three steps forward and drove the ball squarely over the bowler's head. One bounce to the boundary, four more runs on the board, and the crowd erupted in cheers. Twenty-eight runs more.

On the telephone we were getting a regular commentary on the work backstage. Everything was in position for the evacuation, but they would try to get the extinguishers out. Clive Lloyd, the former West Indian cricket captain who was the match referee, had been told, and had taken it in his stride. So had the cameramen, and the men with the TV networks. No views of the stands until the police told them.

Akram's next ball swung out. Srinath misjudged, and the ball struck his pad. Akram turned to face the umpire, hands high, screaming 'Howzzat!?'

The umpire stood still, then called his colleague from square leg. While the batsmen chatted in the centre of the pitch the two umpires conferred at square leg. Thirty seconds later, the umpire raised his arms in a signal that he wanted the third umpire to decide the appeal.

While the cameras focussed on the players standing around, in midfield, and then switched to advertisements, the extinguishers were taken out. Soldiers from Fort William moved into the stadium. The positions of the new fire extinguishers had been pointed out to them, and with the cameras on the audience they covered the extinguishers with tarpaulins and carried them towards the exit, taking them to refrigerated trucks with airtight bodies, to be driven away under police escort. As the last extinguisher was taken away the evacuation began.

It was over. We had foiled the Krait. There was nothing he could do now.

Not out, signalled the third umpire, and play resumed. Srinath played the remaining four balls of the over in magnificent style, scoring a total of nine runs, two boundaries and a single off the last ball to keep strike.

Nineteen runs to go, and three overs.

Waqar Younis came in on the other end. His first two balls screamed past Srinath, beating him completely, but the third got an edge, bounced just out of reach of third man, and sped to the boundary. The fourth ball, a leg break, was turned to square leg for two. The fifth Srinath played out of the book. And the sixth, an attempted yorker, he stepped down the crease and hit over midwicket for four.

Nine more runs, but he had lost the strike. Mongia the wicketkeeper faced Wasim Akram in full, fearsome cry. Akram nearly yorked Mongia but the ball missed the off stump by a fraction. The second ball Mongia managed to get his bat to, steering it towards midoff, and scampered for a single. Srinath responded, long legs windmilling as he covered the distance between the wickets like an Olympic sprinter, but Mongia failed to make his crease by a foot. He left without waiting for the umpire to declare him out.

Anil Kumble, tall, bespectacled, scholarly, a formidable spinner, walked grimly down to the crease and took up his stance. In the glare of the floodlights he swung wildly at the inswinger with which Younis welcomed him, got an edge, and the ball went to the boundary, placed more or less by accident between fielders. Five runs to go. The rest of Younis's over passed without a run, Kumble playing each ball carefully, not attempting a stroke.

As Wasim Akram took up the ball for the last over, the stands exploded. Five runs for India to get, off six balls. Akram, always a bowler who depended as much on his brains as on the scorching pace he generated, put down a slower one to Srinath, who was in an attacking mood. Caught off balance, Srinath managed to steer the ball towards midwicket, thought he saw two runs in the stroke, and called Kumble for a run. Too late he saw the fielder run in, cutting off the second run. Four more runs to go, off five balls, but the man facing Akram was Kumble, an indifferent bat at best.

There was a collective sigh from the crowd but Kumble ignored it. His intention was to take a single off the first ball he faced, returning strike to Srinath, but Akram had anticipated that, and the field closed in. Kumble played the next four balls Akram sent down but every shot was fielded by a close-in fielder, with no chance to take a single.

Last ball, four runs to go, and the field opened out. Akram sprinted up and as the ball left his hand Kumble for once took his courage in his hands and stepped out, picked the ball up on the rise, driving it high over the bowler's head, over the sight screen at the ropes, behind the bowler, knowing as his bat connected that it was a six!

India had scraped through to the finals.

By now Ismail would know that his plans hadn't worked. The gas should have been out by now. He might do something crazy, I thought, in his frustration. He'd flee, I thought, and someone else could chase him. I was too tired to care any more.

A cold hand gripped my heart. He'd want revenge. He'd go for Sandhya. He didn't know I was loose and it would please him enormously to kill Sandhya first and then me. I leapt out of my chair for the parking lot, grabbed a jeep, headed for Gulmohar Park.

I ran up the stairs to Sandhya's first-floor flat, saw the line of yellow light outside, heard faint voices from inside. Sagged with relief for a moment, then rang the doorbell. Heard hurrying footsteps, saw the door open, and she stood there in the dim light of a table lamp placed in the far corner of the living room, tearing worry in her eyes, speechless with relief.

'Are you all right?' I asked hoarsely, unable to find anything else to say.

'Of course,' she said, looking closer as she saw my bandaged wrists and drawn face, her eyes widening in distress. She took a step back into the room with me following. She stopped, and pointed at the corner by the lamp. She said, in a sort of whisper, 'He's looking after me. He came ten minutes ago.'

398

And there, in the shadows thrown by the lampshade, rising to lunge at me was Ismail, his eyes now full of maddened rage, his lips drawn back in a rictus of anger, exactly what Sandhya had sketched months ago. He saw the silenced pistol in my hand and drew back, his face returning to its normal, aristocratic calm. 'You should have killed me when you could,' I said heavily.

He smiled, relaxed. 'You deserved better, Raja,' he said. 'I wanted Chauhan and the rest to think you were the Krait. I'd have killed you there this evening, leaving behind evidence that you'd been turned by ISI.'

'Why would they turn me?' I asked.

'Money,' he said, 'what else?'

Sandhya stood at my side. She touched my arm. 'Is Ismail the Krait?' she asked, her voice dangerously soft.

'Yes,' I replied without taking my eyes off Ismail. 'He had us fooled all this while.'

'Was he . . . Did he have my son tied up?' she asked.

'Yes,' I said. 'He was behind it all.' There was a pause. 'Why, Ismail?' I asked. 'Did you do it for the money?'

'Of course,' he replied.

'I thought you had enough,' I said.

'You wouldn't know, would you?' he replied, his voice rising. 'My people were rulers, princes. My grandfather stayed here through the Partition. He helped keep this country quiet. And at the end of it they changed the law and took away his land, took away his money, his privileges. Practically all of his land, because he wasn't smart enough

399

to parcel it away, divide it among his brothers and nephews and so on. Because they all went to Pakistan.

'They took it all away from us, Raja. One day we were fine. We owned whole villages, districts. Everyone looked up to us. They bowed to us. And the next day there was nothing. They spat in our faces. Told us that the feudal days were over. They told us they'd run the country. Stupid peasants, how could they do these things to us?

'It killed my grandmother, you know, and later my grandfather. It shamed my father . . .' His voice trailed off.

'And when did you turn?' I asked.

'Early. I kept quiet until the SOF practically dropped in my lap. And I asked for you, Raja, because I know you. I know how you think . . . I thought I'd always be able to outthink you. And but for falling into that well in Bangalore I would have.'

The power went off without warning, leaving us in the dark. In the split second that I stood stock still he charged, tugging the lamp off the table, throwing it where he remembered my head to be. I heard it crash into the wall and break, and then he came for me in the darkness. Instinctively, knowing that in my weakened state I had no chance against him, I bundled Sandhya out of the door and slammed it shut behind her, leaping sideways on to a low table, knowing Ismail would come in low.

His eyes were better than mine. He would have had a knife but it was useless in the dark, and he came swarming at me. He was bigger than I was, though not as fit, but I'd been through the wringer and my body now hurt

400

unrelentingly. He found me in the dark and pulled me off the table without effort, punching mercilessly at my chest, hitting at ribs he knew were healing, his punches working through my weakened arms. I kicked at his groin but he turned away in time. I scratched at his face and he pulled back for a moment, only to return to the fray with redoubled vigour. He let loose a flurry of blows that had me stumbling backwards in no time, and then I tripped on a chair and fell backwards on the carpet.

Dimly I saw the lights come back on, and then I was on the carpet, Ismail practically kneeling on my chest, on my broken ribs, his hands around my neck, pounding my head on the floor, not letting me breathe. Out of the corner of my eye I saw Sandhya run for the TV set in the corner. She tugged at it but the electrical cord held fast in the socket. She reached down, ripped out the plug, raised the TV set high in the air, brought it screen down on his head as hard as she could.

The screen imploded on impact, and the set came down over his head, covering his eyes, the sharp edges of the shattered screen cutting viciously into his face. He screamed, raising his hands to his face, bending, then rising a little in reaction.

The pressure on my neck eased and I rolled, wrestling him off me. Staggered to my feet, paused for a moment to draw in a long, delicious lungful of air, ignoring the pain that flared up in my chest. And then, screaming in agony, Ismail ripped the TV set off his head, his face a mask of blood, and came at me again.

Blinded as he was by his own blood in his eyes, he weaved, giving me time to recover. I leapt aside, picked up a chair and whipped it across on to his head and shoulders. He went down on his knees, and I kicked him weakly in the solar plexus, then brought the chair down once again on his head. It broke, and he subsided, eyes closed, breathing hard, turning over on to his side as he fell.

I couldn't leave him loose. 'Get some rope to tie him up with,' I told Sandhya, who still stood frozen, hands on her cheeks, contemplating in shocked horror the effects of her blow.

She jerked out of her shock, ran for the bathroom. While my attention was on her, Ismail, incredibly, turned, whipping himself off the floor, found the knife he'd dropped, and came at me yet again. His injuries were slowing him down, and when he swung the blade at me I caught his wrist and twisted it up and around his back until I heard the ligaments crack. Then I turned to put all my force behind him and ran him into the wall. He hit it with a thump, bounced off it with his head at an odd angle, and collapsed with his head at the same strange angle.

No, I thought, I want him alive. To sing me a song.

I bent down, felt his pulse. There was none. His head lolled when I touched it. I pushed him over on his back, looked at the face, masked in drying blood, at the sightless eyes, and was nearly overwhelmed with regret.

Heard quick footsteps behind, and turned to see Sandhya. 'What happened?' she asked. 'I heard someone scream. I thought it was you.'

I shook my head. 'We won't need that rope after all,' I said. 'He won't be going any place now.' I pushed the broken TV set on the floor to a side of the room, crunching over the broken glass of the cathode ray tube, straightened up, staggered to the couch, sank down on it. I shut my eyes, relaxed. Then I looked for Sandhya, didn't find her, and in those few moments missed her.

She returned to the living room, sombre faced. She sat beside me, held my hand again. 'Where did you go?' I asked.

'To check if Kiran's all right,' she replied. 'He's still asleep.'

I reached for the telephone to call Chauhan. I dialled his number from memory, caught him still awake at midnight. 'I've got the Krait,' I told him. 'At Gulmohar Park. Come and get him.'

'Keep him safe,' he said, 'I want to talk to him.'

'You can't,' I told him. 'He's dead.'

'You killed him,' he said, flatly, accusingly.

'I did. It was him or me.'

'You should have been careful.'

'Like I said, it was him or me. If you don't like it, fuck off.' I hung up.

A moment later the phone rang. It was Chauhan. 'What do you want now?' I asked.

I heard him draw a deep breath. 'Where the hell are you?' he asked. 'They told me at your office that you just disappeared. They said you just got up and ran out, grabbed a jeep, and went away.'

'I'm in Sandhya's flat,' I told him. 'I thought Ismail would go after Sandhya, especially as he didn't know I'd broken out. I caught him here.'

'I'll be there in fifteen minutes,' he replied.

I called Kelkar. 'Did you find him?' he asked.

'Yes,' I said, 'in Sandhya Upadhyaya's flat. Do you remember, the lady on the train?'

'Yes,' he said. 'Give me her address, I'll come as soon as possible. And what about Ismail?'

'We fought. He's dead.'

There was relief in his voice. 'The best way, perhaps.'

He didn't want the boat rocked. 'I'll be there soon. And I'll call Luthra.'

I hung up, turned to look for Sandhya. Found her still beside me, still silent. Felt her hand in mine, gripping hard. I looked at her, managed a smile. We were both in no shape to speak, so we sat there quietly waiting for Chauhan, hoping Ismail wouldn't wake up.

Chauhan got there as promised, his arrival heralded by wailing sirens and screeching tyres, and then the sound of heavy men running up the stairs outside. Behind him were two colleagues and several large, rough Delhi policemen led by an inspector. Seconds behind the policemen, trailing his SOF bodyguard, running lightly up the stairs came Kelkar. The policemen came stomping noisily and self-importantly into the flat, picked up Ismail's inert body, and carried him away.

Until that day I'd never believed all the stories I'd heard about how insensitive the police could be. They threw the furniture around, tramped through the house throwing things around, invading where they had come to help. General Kelkar produced an identity card, told them roughly to shut up. They looked at his card, looked at his bodyguard, formidable in his black combat uniform, and subsided, a new politeness in their voices. Their toughness was any use only against women and the unprotected.

Luthra arrived, and ruthlessly rebandaged me, leaving me breathless and a little dizzy. More white pills. He looked around with interest at the chaos in the house, drew back from the policemen, and left as soon as he could.

The policemen put the scattered chairs back in place, cleaned up the glass on the floor, and left, while Chauhan and Kelkar sat down facing Sandhya and me. One of Chauhan's henchmen settled down in a chair beside us, ready to take notes.

'What the hell was he doing here?' Chauhan demanded.

'He came to take Sandhya hostage,' I said bleakly, 'to get me talking easily. He must have been waiting for a call from the men who caught me. He didn't know I'd escaped.'

'He was waiting for a call,' Sandhya said, shivering. 'He came in here at about ten minutes ahead of Raja. I had no idea anything was wrong. I had tried to call Raja but no one responded at his number. Then I heard he'd disappeared, about his bike being found, and I was on the verge of panicking. Then Ismail came, and said that he, too, had been looking for Raja, that he'd asked some of his friends to search for him, and to call him here.' She shivered again, her eyes still shocked. 'He was so solicitous, I was glad to have him here. And when Raja turned up he just turned off the light and attacked . . .'

'What happened then?' asked Chauhan.

'Raja pushed me out of the door, and then he attacked Raja,' she said blankly, still coming to grips with her own violence. 'And then I came back in here and turned on the light and found them on the carpet and hit Ismail with the TV set . . .' Her voice trailed off.

When eventually the police and the rest of the uniforms left—one SOF man stayed behind, on guard against more kidnap attempts—she continued to sit in her chair, elbows on her knees, hands on her face. I knelt by her side. 'Do you want me to call you a doctor?' I asked, taking her hands. 'Help you get back to sleep?'

'No,' she said, 'I'll manage.'

'I'll leave now. You'll be safe. There's a man on guard.'

'I wish you'd stay.'

For a moment surprise kept me quiet. 'I thought you didn't want me to,' I said.

'When Ismail sat on you and began to beat you up,' she said, 'I thought for a moment that he was going to kill you. And then I found it didn't matter, the violence . . . I wanted to get back at him for what he did to my little boy . . . I know you better now. You do what you have to do . . . So stay.'

I did.

406